Witl
Preju

Andrew Rosenheim was born in Chicago in 1955 and grew up there and in Michigan. A graduate of Yale University, he came to England in 1977 as a Rhodes Scholar and has lived near Oxford ever since. He is the author of *Stillriver* and *Keeping Secrets*. He is married and has twin daughters.

Without Prejudice

ANDREW ROSENHEIM

arrow books

Published by Arrow Books 2009

2 4 6 8 10 9 7 5 3 1

First published in Great Britain in 2008 by Hutchinson
Random House, 20 Vauxhall Bridge Road, London SW1V 2SA

www.rbooks.co.uk

Addresses for companies within The Random House Group Limited can be found at:
www.randomhouse.co.uk/offices.htm

The Random House Group Limited Reg. No. 954009

A CIP catalogue record for this book
is available from the British Library

ISBN 9780099510093

The Random House Group Limited supports The Forest Stewardship
Council (FSC), the leading international forest certification organisation. All our
titles that are printed on Greenpeace approved FSC certified paper carry the FSC logo.
Our paper procurement policy can be found at www.rbooks.co.uk/environment

Typeset in Sabon by
Palimpsest Book Production Limited, Grangemouth, Stirlingshire
Printed and bound in Great Britain by
CPI Bookmarque Ltd, Croydon CR0 4TD

For my brother Dan
(who was there)

I

1

'BOBBY, YOU THERE?'

The week before the phone had twice rung in the middle of the night. Each time a husky drunken voice had asked, 'Wilma around?' So now he'd let the answering machine answer.

Yet this voice was familiar. Why? No one had called him Bobby for over thirty years. He scanned a mental list of possibles. Nothing clicked.

'Bobby, pick up. It's me.' The voice was slightly muffled by background noise, as if a party were going on.

What time was it? Outside the street was silent. The windows were open to catch any breeze in the sweet mug air, and from Sheridan Road he thought he heard the hushed slide of passing cars, or was it the lake breaking against the shore? He could not detect the faintest hint of morning light. Lifting his head he saw why: the luminescent clock on the walnut dresser across the room read *12:47*.

Who was it? As he reached for the phone and Anna stirred next to him, he felt an unsuppressible anxiety stick in his chest like a stone. 'Hello,' he said, trying to sound calm.

'Is that you, Bobby?'

'Who is this?'

'Can't you tell?' It sounded like the voice of a black man, but Robert wasn't sure; he had been away too long to make the distinction automatically. Whoever it was, the man sounded subdued, almost dismayed that Robert didn't recognise him.

'No, I can't.'

'You used to be able to,' the man said, and this time the hurt was undisguised.

'Who are you?' Robert asked impatiently.

'Duval.'

Robert took a deep breath. 'How did you know where I was?'

'Lily. She gave me your number.'

Silence hung between them in the sponge-like air. At last Robert said, 'Do you want me to call you back?'

'Why do you want to do that?'

'I thought maybe you weren't allowed to make calls.' He looked again at the luminescent numbers across the room. 'At least not this late.'

'I guess you don't know then.'

Know what?

The voice sounded more relaxed now. 'I'm out, Bobby.'

Robert didn't say a word.

'You still there?'

'I'm here, Duval.' He paused momentarily. 'Congratulations.'

Duval said, 'I know it's late, but I wanted you to know.'

'Wait a minute.' Robert sat up in the bed. 'Don't go, Duval.'

'Somebody's waiting to use the phone,' he said. 'I'll be in touch. Don't worry – you'll hear from me again.' And the line went dead.

The tape machine whirred inconsequentially, then stopped. Next to him his wife stirred again. 'Who was that?' she asked with a voice full of sleep.

'Nothing important. Go back to sleep.'

2

When Anna didn't reply he realised she had. He lay there, fully awake himself, the sheet drawn down, listening. He heard nothing but Duval's voice in his head. *I'm out.*

He wondered if he would call again, and hoped he wouldn't. He tried to picture Duval from the last time he'd seen him, over twenty years before, in that cramped courtroom downtown. He'd sat looking dazed, seated at the table next to the public defender. A row behind him Vanetta had sat hunched over, her hands clasped together in a twisted prayer.

But Robert couldn't visualise the face. All he could see now in his mind's eye was the little boy he had known so long ago – the high cheekbones and long jaw, the cheap thick-lensed glasses, the shy expression when they had played together.

Suddenly he shivered slightly and pulled the sheet up. But he wasn't cold – he realised it was a sudden stab of fear he'd felt. Why am I scared? he asked himself. And old as he was, he wished Vanetta were still alive.

2

'What exactly did he do?'

They were sitting the next morning at the white marble table in the breakfast room that adjoined the kitchen. They had so much space in this house: Anna had taken one look at the kitchen during their first visit with the realtor and laughed out loud. 'Every housewife's dream,' she'd said lightly, and he'd laughed then at the incongruity. Anna's satisfactions had always been professional ones; it was surprising to see her enjoyment from a household cause for bliss. He supposed it was the equivalent of his own love for baseball.

He himself missed their old kitchen in London, so small that when company sat at its table you couldn't walk around it. The room there had held a semi-functional Rayburn, a porcelain sink and warped draining board, and a dresser with drawers that stuck. In the corner by the back door there had been one oversized willow basket stuffed with umbrellas and wellingtons and trainers. Here in Evanston, just blocks from the lake, they ate breakfast in front of a bay window that overlooked the back yard – 'the garden' as his wife called it, half an acre of lawn with two large beech trees, a mock-orange, two scraggy lilac bushes, and not a single flower bed.

His daughter Sophie had eaten breakfast, and she was out back somewhere, crushing the cat with love before going to school. Spring was almost over, but the sultry sweaty heat of a Chicago summer had yet to arrive.

Robert returned his wife's enquiring gaze, noticing how her aquamarine eyes were, in this morning's bright daylight, paler than usual. She was confirming the old saw that bone structure came true in the end – well, not end, since Anna was only rising forty. Her features – striking eyes, a short, sharp nose, and high cheekbones – seemed like the product of carefully considered design, until you took in the mouth, which was generous, slightly full in the lips for an Englishwoman, at odds with the convention of her looks.

He said now, 'He attacked a nurse at the university hospital. He was working on the security desk there.'

'He did twenty-four years for that?'

'She almost died. She was raped too.'

'And he was guilty?'

'The judge and jury thought so.'

'Did you?' she asked, raising an eyebrow.

'No. At least not at first.' He shrugged. 'It didn't matter what I thought.'

4

She stood up and took her cup and plate to the sink. She was dressed for work, in a fawn-coloured linen skirt and matching jacket, bought on sale at Saks. Anna liked to tell him that clothes cost only half as much here as in London, and he'd decided not to spoil things by pointing out that this didn't help much if you bought twice as many.

'Why did he call so late?'

'He apologised – he said he didn't realise the time. I suppose it takes some getting used to.'

'What does?' She turned from the sink, and pushed her chestnut hair back against her ears.

'He's had over twenty years of a routine he didn't set. The last thing he wants to do now is watch the clock.'

'Will you see him?'

'I don't know.' He looked tensely at his watch, a handsome Swiss make with a Roman numeral face and a caramel leather strap. Quite smart for him – Anna had bought it as his wedding present.

'Is it safe to see him?' she said, in a cool voice she used to mask emotion.

'You mean physically safe?' She nodded and he looked at her face, surprised by her concern. 'I knew Duval when we were little. When I was nine years old, we were like this.' He held up two fingers and put them together. 'He wasn't a violent kid,' he added firmly.

'You've never mentioned him.' She came and picked up her briefcase from a chair.

'He's been in prison so many years that I guess I started to think he'd never get out.'

'Or you forgot about him,' she said sharply. That was what had always upset her most about her clients back in London – once they'd been convicted, however unjustly, no one wanted to know. 'What do you think he wants?'

'Beats me.' He looked closely at his wife, unable to tell what she was feeling. She didn't like surprises, which must have made the fact that they had got married almost by accident unsettling.

The back door slammed, feet slapped on the vinyl tiles, and the accident burst in. 'Hello, spider monkey,' he said, still allowed to use nicknames at home, though never within a hundred yards of teachers or school friends.

'Hi, Dad,' Sophie said. After nine months her voice had gone entirely American. She was wearing khaki shorts with big pockets, a pink T-shirt, and trainers on her feet. Already she was concerned about looking cool, which made him miss the uniform she'd had to wear in London.

He contemplated his daughter with a sense of wonder he did his best to disguise. In summer her hair was strawberry blonde, in winter almost downright red, explicable by a great-grandmother on Robert's mother's side. Watching Sophie watching him, he realised yet again that she was stunningly, yet still unknowingly, beautiful. This was not parental fatuousness, but the simple truth: the first time he and Anna had been asked to let their daughter model, Robert had laughed in unanxious amusement; the fifth time they'd been asked he had grown alarmed.

Now she flicked her hair back in a smaller replication of her mother's tic, and asked sarcastically, 'What is the Important Man going to read today at the office?'

'A History of Impertinent Daughters,' he said, batting it back. She was quick for her age, her tongue precociously sharp. If he'd been half as lippy with his own father he would have paid a price, but even when piqued he was wary of crushing her – he couldn't bear the prospect of her fearing him. Her emotional development seemed in any case strictly normal for nine years

6

old – a withering remark she made could be followed within seconds by the tantrum and tears of a toddler.

'We'd better get going,' Anna said to the girl. Ordinarily they would have all left together, since Anna's job at the consulate was only a few minutes' walk from his own office off north Michigan Avenue. But today she was going out near the state line for a meeting with some Wisconsin businessmen, and she would drop off Sophie on her way north.

'Good luck with the presentation. Will Philip be there?' His voice was teasing, but held the hint of an edge.

'Of course. Why?' She gave him a *don't start that* look.

'Just wondered. Anyone else?'

'Maggie Trumbull.'

Maggie was a lawyer, too, but American-trained. 'Well, at least you won't get sued. I'm sure you'll be fine,' he added in a gentler voice, since he knew she hated public speaking.

Anna leaned down and kissed Robert goodbye lightly on the lips. 'Cheese makers don't sue. Now you take care with this Duval chap.'

'He may not call.'

'I bet he will. Why else bother you in the first place? Especially after all these years.'

But Duval didn't call that day, or the day after. Robert's new job, which had brought him back to Chicago after years away, was still novel enough to preoccupy him utterly during the day – and, as Anna and Sophie sometimes complained, occasionally at weekends as well. So by the end of the week, thoughts of Duval had receded, if not quite disappeared altogether.

He came out of the Friday staff meeting in a good

mood. Dorothy Taylor, his publishing director, who was stroppy and combative and seemed to have trouble accepting him as her new boss, was away on holiday, so it had been relaxed. He found Vicky, his assistant, waiting for him outside his office. 'Your lunch appointment rang to ask if you could meet him at twelve thirty,' she said.

'Anything else?'

She followed him into his office, a high-ceilinged corner room with a view of a small playground, which filled up in the afternoon with mothers, nannies and their upper-middle class charges. Robert liked hearing the children's shouts and make-believe screams, since the only other external noise audible above the hum of the office air conditioning was an occasional horn blast from a driver on Lake Shore Drive.

'You've got Andy Stephens here at three.'

The accountant from the university, to review the quarterly results. They'd been good so that would be easy enough.

'And that's it?' he asked. He'd learned to check: Vicky was a young graduate from Michigan, an English major who wanted to be an editor and didn't seem to think the secretarial parts of her job were going to help get her there. She wore the international uniform of publishing youth: black trousers, black top, black sneakers – it was a wonder to Robert that she hadn't dyed her big mop of golden hair black as well. She had a slight overbite that made her seem even younger to Robert, though men her age seemed to find her very attractive – Hari, the Indian graduate student who doubled as mailroom boy and receptionist, would find any excuse to hover around her desk. Robert shared her with Dorothy Taylor, who had plumped for Vicky's CV out of the enormous pile of applicants.

'Oh,' she said, happy to have remembered, 'some-body else called. A man.'

'Did he manage to say who he was?'

She shook her head; obviously it had been too much to ask. 'He wouldn't leave a name or a number. Said he'd call back.'

'What did he sound like?'

She looked at him with mild disbelief. 'He was just some guy. *Sorry,*' she added tartly. 'But he did say he'd call again.'

'Was he old or young? Caucasian or a person of colour?' He didn't know why he was pressing her – actually, he did. This might be Duval.

Vicky pursed her lips. 'You mean African-American?' He felt embarrassed and she looked cross.

The press was part of a university, and Robert had lunch downtown with one of its trustees, a banker near retire-ment age named Everton. He seemed more interested in talking about his own visits to London than discussing Robert's publishing plans. Each time Robert tried to discuss ways to raise the profile of the press, Everton would deflect the conversation onto the wonders of the British Museum and the lunch he'd once been given in the Athenaeum.

Afterwards, Robert walked back along Michigan Avenue, stopping at the river to look down at its small greased coils as it passed under the bridge. The river ran famously backward, long ago reversed to send water from the lake down its thin channel. It was the least impressive river of any city of Robert's acquaintance – he thought fleetingly of London and Paris. Yet it had enjoyed a curious revival thanks to the boats conducting architectural tours of the city's downtown; even in London, prospective visitors to Chicago were told to 'take the river boat tour', which corresponded to the stereotype of the place. A city of man-made heights, preoccupied throughout the last century with sky-scrapers, as if vertical lift could somehow make its mark against the drear spread of so much zero-elevation soil. There was no natural drama to the habitat here, only the blankness of the prairies edged onto a lake with an unvarying shore.

He moved on, the avenue sloping straight and profes-sionally downhill as it spread north towards its newest congregation of expensive stores – Saks, Neiman Marcus, Lord & Taylor – which had displaced the old shopping centre of the city in the Loop. The shoppers here were overwhelmingly white, unspoken reason for the emigration northwards.

Here too the city opened up, with lower buildings, and plazas and small parks, though further down the avenue the Hancock Tower loomed like a charcoal monolith, a hundred tapering steel storeys of offices and apartments. There was a bar on the ninety-fifth floor; Robert remembered going there as a teenager one night with his brother Mike, a week before his brother's marriage. Robert had sat facing south, drinking in the view, the city's hatch lines of streets stretched out before him on a grid that was dazzlingly illuminated by streetlights against the dark underlying plains. How he longed for his youthful ease with heights; merely the memory of having been so close to the clouds started a thin line of anxiety trickling across his chest like a barium tracer.

His office was on a side street off Michigan Avenue, in a low-slung building of cream stone, with modernist windows lying flat as a map against the line of its outer skin. The press was on the third of five storeys. The university's main campus was in the near north suburbs, not far from Robert's new home, but its famous medical school was based here in the city, and the press had been tucked in as well. This suited Robert; he could think of nothing more dreary than to be located 'on campus'. Occasionally, noises emanated from his university overseers that it might be useful to have him closer, on tap. He ignored them, determined to preserve a distance he intuitively associated with independence.

On the third floor he walked down the corridor, flinching reflexively as he passed Dorothy's empty office, until he saw Vicky at her desk. She was on the phone and waved at him frantically. She cupped the receiver with one hand and said, 'I've got David Balthazar on the line.'

'Really?' He was surprised. 'Okay, tell him I'll be right there.'

Balthazar was a New York literary agent Robert had first known during his own time in Manhattan when he worked at Knopf. Once in London, Robert had not lost touch – perhaps every other year, they had a drink together during the city's book fair. Still, Robert was surprised to find him phoning. He could not conceive of what business they might now do together, unless Balthazar was trying to foist off a client he could no longer sell to more commercial houses.

'Hello, Robert, so how's the Second City treating you?' asked the agent.

'I'm okay, David,' he said, ignoring the traditional New York jab at Chicago. Balthazar thought of himself as a smooth operator; Brooklyn born and bred, he had worked scrupulously to eradicate any trace of the borough. He dressed with natty fastidiousness: a silk paisley handkerchief jutting out like a gigolo's badge from his Paul Stuart blazer, gold cufflinks with the punch of an ancestral family on the cuffs of his bespoke soft shirt. Although Balthazar was tactless, even obnoxious, he was someone Robert found impossible to dislike – you had to admire the sheer industry of his social climb.

'Enjoying the new job? It's a good little press.'

'It's *pretty* good. I'm trying to make it really good.'

'Ah,' said Balthazar. 'You know, some people wondered why you wanted the job. I mean, going from a big one to, um . . .'

'Such a small one?'

'Something like that,' he said, acknowledging his tactlessness. 'I mean, it's not as if the job's a *sinecure*. Or that you got in any trouble in London.' He made both statements with such certainty that they were obviously questions.

'If I had screwed up over there, David, I'm sure you'd know about it.' Balthazar had the decency to laugh. 'But no, I wanted to come back to America, and Anna wanted a change.' This was more or less the truth, though it was also true that he had been spinning his wheels in his old job, thanks to a cloud over his reputation which he had been powerless to dispel.

'It must be nice to be back in your hometown.'

'I suppose so.' Robert looked out the window towards the lake, the city's one natural advantage – a blue sea-sized body of water rimmed by yellow sand. In the distance he could just make out a lone tanker. An ore boat, cruising to Duluth for another load? He had never understood the complicated commerce of the Great Lakes. 'Though it's not like I know the place. I left here when I was thirteen – they shipped me to boarding school out east.'

'A preppy, eh?'

'Can't you tell?' They both laughed.

He found himself thinking of Duval. Had he been phoning that night from Chicago? His mother had

12

moved years before to St Louis – Aurelia, that was her name. Would she still be alive? Given her history back then, Robert thought it unlikely.

'Does your wife like it here?' asked Balthazar, snapping him out of his reverie.

He spoke with energy to cover his abstractedness. 'Very much. I was worried she might find it all a bit too alien, but she's taken to the place.' She had indeed, to his intense surprise.

'She can't practise here, can she?'

'No, but she's got a job at the British consulate. She gives legal advice to companies that do business in the UK.'

A pause followed, and Robert sensed small talk was over. Balthazar said at last, 'I had an interesting meeting yesterday with a colleague of yours.'

'Really?' Mentally, Robert surveyed the list of candidates. Dorothy seemed the only possibility, but what would Balthazar be doing talking with her? Did he want to take her off his hands? A happy thought.

'Well, maybe not a colleague. It was Bud Carlson.'

'Our football coach?' It seemed preposterous, the socially ambitious New York agent breaking bread with a man who ran gladiators – that was how Robert viewed American football, with its padded behemoths knocking each other around. His mind whirred as he considered new possibilities. 'Where was this?' he said, trying to sound casual.

'Here in my office,' said Balthazar. Robert could picture the agent in his midtown room, leaning back in his padded leather chair, his handmade shoes propped on his desk, looking out at his splendid view of the Chrysler Building.

'What was he doing in New York?'

'He's almost finished his memoirs.'

'Good. We can schedule them then. You must know they're contracted to us.' It was the one big trade book they had in the forward list.

Balthazar said nothing, and Robert emitted a small groan. 'Don't tell me. He wants you to represent him – and renegotiate his contract.'

Balthazar coughed politely. Robert supposed there was no point being an agent if you embarrassed easily.

'Well . . .' said Balthazar.

'Spare me the palaver. How much?'

Balthazar hesitated, as if pained by Robert's bluntness. 'I'm not sure money is the problem.'

Any uncertainty about this call was gone. Suddenly irritated, Robert said, 'You're telling me he doesn't want to renegotiate? What does he want then? Another publisher?'

There, it was out in the open now; he had done Balthazar's work for him.

'Look, Robert, nothing's set in stone. Why don't we set a time now to talk in a couple of weeks? Then I'll know how Carlson wants to proceed. I don't want you to think I went looking for this.'

No, thought Robert, but you didn't send him away either. Not that he could really blame Balthazar. As he waited while Balthazar consulted his busy diary, Robert thought wryly, Some sinecure.

He was disconcerted by the call. Balthazar was precisely the prosperous face of the trade publishing Robert no longer had a role in – indeed he'd been delighted to escape. But he didn't like being patronised by a big shot from New York and he bristled in time-honoured fashion at the designation of Chicago as the Second City. He had thought that New York's own sense of self-importance had diminished; not in the book business, it seemed.

14

Robert had only met Carlson once, at a reception given in the president of the university's house. A tall, loose-limbed man with a floppy kind of handshake. Affable, perhaps a little shy, quite unlike the stereotypical crew-cut bully, half drill-sergeant, half Nazi, who paraded through American popular culture with a policeman's whistle around his neck. They'd talked briefly and innocuously, and then President Crullowitch, a former ambassador to Mexico, had intervened to move the coach onto a rich alumnus. There had seemed no point following up this brief encounter, since Dorothy Taylor had secured the book to begin with and said she knew the coach well. Hands off, had been her unspoken message, so Robert had gladly left her to it. Maybe he shouldn't have.

For here was Balthazar the Beast, as he was known in his press profiles, poaching the one big trade book he had – about of all things an American football coach. Robert had known baseball books could do well, but then it was in Robert's view a subtler, more graceful game, which appealed as much to intellectuals and statisticians as it did to jocks. Football seemed leaden by comparison. Yet books about it were now in vogue – *Publishers Weekly,* the American book industry's bible, had recently run a spread on the genre. No wonder the press's rep force spoke with unbridled enthusiasm about the prospects for Carlson's book, happy to be selling in a popular title for a change, one that didn't require explanation or excuse, unlike the rest of the press's obscurantist titles. The rights person had said a big book club deal was a possibility; the publicist had talked unprecedentedly about television appearances for the author. Even the university's president and trustees (Everton excepted) seemed positively excited.

Admittedly Carlson was an unusual football coach, as interesting as he was successful (three times Rose Bowl champion, countless winner of the Big Ten). Even for the football non-enthusiast like Robert, there was something admirable in Carlson's recruitment of countless black players from the Deep South, and in his insistence that all of them – even those turning pro – complete their educations. Carlson was the respectable amateur face of a college sport infamous for its professionalism, but he was also that rarest of things – a white hero to the black community. Robert couldn't think of many others.

There was a knock on the door and Vicky came in. 'Andy Stephens is waiting,' and he could see the man standing by Vicky's desk. One of the university's cadre of accountants, he wore a cotton suit that was the colour of martini olives, a uniform of summer poised uneasily between comfort and convention.

Vicky handed him a pink message slip. 'While you were on the phone,' she said tersely, apparently still annoyed by his tetchiness before lunch.

He looked at the message. *Duval called.*

'He said he could meet you at Nelson's Coffee Shop on Wacker Drive at three fifteen.'

He looked at his watch: he had ten minutes. 'Did you get his cell number?'

She shook her head sharply. 'He said he was calling from a pay phone.'

Damn. He could stand up Duval or postpone Andy. A need to get it over with (though he couldn't have said exactly what 'it' was) and some other unarticulated sense of obligation meant he felt there wasn't any choice.

He went out into the corridor. 'Andy, I'm really sorry, but I've got a kind of emergency. I've got to see somebody; I shouldn't be gone more than an hour.'

16

Stephens looked at him with irritated, unaccepting eyes. 'I suppose you want me to stick around?'

'Could you? I apologise, but it's family.' Was this a lie? Well, Duval had almost been family once, or at least his grandmother Vanetta had.

II

IT WAS SEPTEMBER 1965, and the ambulance was a converted station wagon with two back fins. It came around the corner by the maple tree, then slid slowly to a stop on the gravel driveway in front of the old Michigan house. Two attendants emerged, wearing starched white uniforms. One wore yellow chukka boots on his feet and as he followed the other into the house he stopped to admire the rusting pump, verdigris with age, that sat unused in the back yard.

They wheeled his mother out in a large steel-framed bed, and his father locked the back door behind him – their own car was packed and ready to go. She was sitting up, propped against two pillows, wearing a fresh nightgown and a terrycloth robe draped around her shoulders. Her hair was freshly brushed, the auburn traces of its brown ends catching the glint of the midday sun. Bobby thought she looked like a beautiful queen. They let him come up to the bed to say goodbye, and even took down the side rail, but he still couldn't reach her face to kiss her. She stroked his cheek instead and told him to be a help to his father.

He had thought before the men arrived that she was just going for a ride, and wondered if this meant she was getting better – after all, she had been in bed for days now. But his father had explained she was going all the way down to Chicago, as were they – 'You're already a week late for school as it is,' his father explained. Bobby felt a twinge of jealousy as the ambulance departed, since his mother got to ride in it while he was stuck in the Chevy, sandwiched in the back between the twins. They were five years older than him, so he always had to sit in the middle over the hump. His father was driving, talking to Uncle Larry in the front passenger seat.

He often felt sick on the long drive and today was no exception. Worse, his father had forgotten the Dramamine and they only stopped once – usually his mother insisted on a picnic lunch, at one of the state parks down near the Indiana border. Today they just barrelled ahead, pausing only to fill up with gas, after which Uncle Larry did the driving. They moved from the hilly fruit country, with its occasional glimpse of Lake Michigan, down through the endless flatlands of the southern belly of the state into the big snow pocket in the lower corner. You could just make out the dunes in the distance west of them, where so many Chicago people went on weekends. His father scoffed at the idea, as if proud of the effort they had to make to get to their own house, three hours' drive farther north.

Why did they have to go back to Chicago anyway? He didn't like the city. His mind's images of it were always dark: the brown brick of their own building, the black gaunt trees, the tawny shit of the neighbourhood dogs. Even the snow would darken within hours, speckled with soot.

Near Benton Harbor Uncle Larry reached 100 mph on the speedometer and in the back seat they all squealed, but as they moved into the Indiana steel basin the car was quiet. Usually his father would start to sing, or maybe turn on the radio at this point, and young as he was Bobby would sense he was trying to lift his spirits, since he didn't want to go back to Chicago either. But today his father didn't even pretend, and when Bobby spied the enormous brewing vats of the Blatz beer company and tried to sing the jingle – 'I'm from

19

Milwaukee and I ought to know' – his brother Mike elbowed him sharply to keep quiet.

On the Sky Bridge he held his breath as he always did, scared they would slide over the side into Calumet Harbor, and then they swooped down onto Stony Island Avenue and his father said 'Bip your bips' and everybody locked their car door – it was dangerous here, though he didn't know why. 'They don't give a damn about *your* civil rights,' Uncle Larry said bitterly, pointing to some men holding cans of beer in their hands on a corner.

And then they were on Blackstone Avenue, leafy and hot, the wet asphalt of a new patch in the middle of the street actually steaming, and he got out and took deep breaths until the nausea went away. There was no sign of the ambulance.

Upstairs Lily opened the door to the apartment while his father and uncle and Mike unloaded the bags from the back of the station wagon, and Bobby raced down the long dark hallway, almost slipping on the torn bit of carpet his mother always wanted to replace, and the bedroom door was closed, which seemed right since they'd told him over and over again that his mother wasn't feeling well. He stopped long enough to knock very lightly on the door, and ignoring whatever Lily was calling to him from the hall he slowly twisted the copper-coloured door knob. The door budged grudgingly then suddenly cracked open. He started to put a big smile on his face until he saw his mother's bed was neatly made up – and unoccupied.

'I told you, she's not here,' Lily said, and went towards the kitchen without further explanation. Puzzled, he left the apartment and went downstairs, where he tried to help unload the car. But everything was too heavy and he had to make do with carrying his baseball glove upstairs to the apartment.

When they finally finished unloading, his father and Uncle Larry sat down in the kitchen, each with a cold beer from the icebox, not saying much and paying no attention to him – not deliberately, but almost dreamily; he realised for the first time that grown-ups could get tired, too. He went back to the bedroom he now shared with his brother, having been displaced the year before from his own room by his sister's sudden demand for privacy, which to his fury his parents had encouraged, not just acceded to.

Mike was reading on his bed. He looked up from his book. 'You wanna wrestle?'

'Where's Lily?' His sister got upset if they wrestled in front of her, and then their father would get mad.

Mike gestured, like he was shooing a fly. 'She's in the sun porch. Shut the door.' He came down off his bed and got on all fours. 'Ready when you are.'

It was a standard ritual. Bobby ran and jumped onto his back and they were away. Within minutes, just as Mike was about to pin him for the second time, Bobby squirmed in desperation and bit his older brother on the shoulder. Mike howled, then hit Bobby right below the eye. His crying ended the fight. This was standard, too.

His father came in, drawn by Bobby's wailing, but for once he wasn't angry. He didn't shout at Mike and he was too old to be spanked; he didn't comfort Bobby; he just stood in the doorway with a pained expression on his face. 'Come on, you guys,' he said. His voice sounded unexpectedly sad. 'Not today, okay?'

They had an early supper, which his father did his best to put together – pork chops, and some lettuce, and a scoop of Boston baked beans, which Bobby liked for their molasses. Then his grandparents appeared, and he played fish with his grandfather, a dapper man who

21

combed his sleek greying hair straight back, and wore a tie pinned to his crisp ironed shirt with a gold clip. They sat at the dining-room table, until Gramps said it was time for bed and began to play gin rummy with Lily and Mike, which Bobby wasn't old enough to play, or so his grandfather said.

He had a shower and since his mother wasn't there his father came and rubbed his hair dry with one end of the towel until Bobby thought his skull would bleed. Then he got into bed and his grandmother came in to read to him. It was a long story he found very boring, despite Gram's efforts to use different voices for the different characters, and he stopped trying to follow it, since he had other things on his mind. He was about to ask when his mother would come in to say good-night when suddenly it was light outside again and Gram had gone and he realised it was the morning and that he had fallen asleep unawares.

He sat up and yawned twice then waited, since normally his mother would be there by now – she would wake him up in the mornings, saying 'Hello, sleepy-head' – and as soon as he had shaken the sleep out of his eyes she would choose his clothes and help him get dressed for nursery school. She was always cheerful and energetic; Bobby would struggle happily just to keep up with her.

But now she wasn't there, so he simply waited – a long, long time it seemed, and his mother didn't appear. Then Lily came in, saying impatiently, 'Come on, let's get your clothes on.'

'Where's Mommy?' he asked.

'In the hospital, silly. You know that already.'

'Oh,' he said, and even to himself his voice seemed flat.

In the kitchen he found his father, standing at the

stove where his mother usually cooked breakfast. His brother was sitting reading the sports section at the rickety pine table, which had a leaf that had once collapsed during lunch. Bobby sat down, feeling uncertain, and his father passed him a glass of orange juice. It was warm and frothy, made out of frozen concentrate in the blender – the water from the tap was never cold. Then his father gave him a plate with a fried egg on it that was sliding in grease and speckled by black bits from the pan. He looked at it dubiously – he was never hungry at breakfast. His mother could always cajole him into appetite with a piece of fruit (apple in winter; berries when the weather was warm), or a thin slice of toast with cherry jam – bits and pieces to tempt him until with the aid of a glass of milk they somehow added up to breakfast.

He must have made a face because his father said sternly, 'Eat what's on the plate, Bobby.' So he did, slowly slurping up the egg white, and then when a piece of half-toasted bread appeared from his father's hand dabbing up the yoke with the soft centre of the slice hoping his father would ignore the crusts he left on the outer edge of the plate. He did.

His father walked him to school, which at least was unbewildering, and he was happy to play with a large plastic tractor on his own, since every now and then Miss Partridge would come by and see how he was. She had soft eyes, and blonde hair the colour of bleached straw, and she wore a scent that gave off a faint whiff of peach which he liked to smell when she hugged him – which was often, if not as often as he liked.

Today she spent more time than usual with him, then when nursery was over he found his father standing at one end of the room. He had come from work, wearing a jacket and tie, and in his hand he held a brown fedora, which Bobby was told not to play with each time he tried to bring it out from the front hall closet.

They walked home along 57th Street, past one block of low shop fronts, then a series of four-storey apartment buildings. Ahead of them he could see Sarnat's on the corner across from their own apartment, the drugstore where his brother and sister would take him to buy candy or in summer months Popsicles, lifted out of a freezer compartment like Ice Age statuettes. 'Where's Mom?' he asked his father, trying to sound hopeful.

'She's in Billings,' his father said. 'The hospital.' Bobby could tell he was trying to be patient. 'She's going to be there for a while.'

'So are you going to look after me?' he asked doubtfully, for if this were the case, why was his father wearing a tie?

'Gladys is home today,' his father said, and Bobby's heart sank. Gladys usually came once a week to clean the apartment. She was immensely fat – when Bobby hugged her his arms went nowhere near around her waist – and not much fun at all. If his father was taking him home, why did Gladys have to be there, too?

When they got to the apartment Gladys was in the kitchen, frying something at the stove. 'Here we are,' his father said, with a cheery note Bobby could tell was forced.

'I'm making the supper, Mr Danziger,' she said. She wore an enormous apron that accentuated her girth, and held an oversized fork in her hand, poised over the sizzling skillet. 'You just leave the boy here with me. He'll be fine. Go on, you get on back to work.'

Bobby's face froze – what was she thinking of, telling his father to go away? He grabbed his father's hand and looked up at his face, where his father's dark eyes were watching him anxiously. 'You'll be okay,' his father said. 'Lily and Mike will be home in a while.'

He gripped his father's hand more tightly, clinging to it for dear life. He figured as long as he didn't let go, his father couldn't leave him behind.

'I bet Gladys will let you help her do the cooking.'

This seemed unlikely to Bobby: the fat woman didn't even look at him when his father said this. He didn't want to help Gladys with the cooking anyway, which looked hot, sweaty kind of work.

'You'd like that, wouldn't you, Bobby?' his father went on, and there was a tone to his voice which he sensed meant his father was trying to reassure himself, and that he wanted Bobby's help. So he nodded and smiled weakly.

'Atta boy,' said his father, and then he was gone.

He did not know what to do with himself, so he sat at the kitchen table while Gladys stayed standing at the stove. 'You want something to eat?' she said without kindness in her voice, and he just shook his head. She turned, fork in hand, and looked at him. 'What you starin' at, boy? Why don't you go and play?'

He shook his head again, because awkward as he felt here in the kitchen, with no toys to play with and no sense that Gladys wanted him around, he knew that he didn't want to leave the room – not with no one else in the apartment. Who knows what could happen to him back in the bedroom with no one within calling distance? This scary fat woman was paying no attention to anything but the sizzling going on in the skillet right beneath her eyes.

He knew about choice now – between, say, chocolate and butterscotch top cones at the Dairy Queen in Michigan – but had never faced a situation where the choices seemed equally bad. The strain was too much and he began to cry, and he hoped this would somehow resolve the situation. And normally it would have – someone would have comforted him. Even Mike was nice to him when he cried – unless it was Mike who had made him cry.

But Gladys ignored him, and concentrated on the pork chops she was lifting now, one by one, onto a platter lined with paper towel. 'Don't that smell good?' she said out loud, which made Bobby only cry harder. She put down her fork and turned off the gas burner on the white enamel stove top, then began to untie her apron. Bobby moved towards her, still wailing, and she stood stockstill – which encouraged him to think she had time for him now, and he held his arms out, unambiguously asking to be hugged.

She reached out and patted him on top of his head, but ignored his outstretched arms. 'Child, you stop your crying now.'

But he couldn't, and as the tears kept running down his face he saw through his watery eyes a look of exasperation start to spread on Gladys's face. Suddenly, she reached down and grabbed his wrist, then waddling towards the door began to lead him out of the room. He resisted at first, but she tightened her grip and kept moving her bulky frame until he was forced to go with her or risk being dragged across the floor.

She took him all the way to the back of the apartment, down the dark hall, then along the short passageway to the back bedroom.

'Go on and play with them,' she said, pointing at the pool of marbles he'd left on the thin carpet between the twin beds. He looked at them dumbly, wondering why his mother wasn't there and why in the world he had been left alone with this fat mean woman. And then she left, too.

He sat on the floor with his legs crossed Indian-style, staring at the marbles almost without recognition, so focused was he on his own misery. He cried again, and kept crying, unselfconsciously, although a little part of him hoped that by crying louder – he did this at one point – it would somehow draw someone back to comfort him.

In desperation, he twice went up to the kitchen: the first time Gladys said nothing at all but simply clutched him again by the wrist and led him back to the back bedroom. The second time she wasn't in the kitchen, and he started to panic, since somehow being left alone was worse even than being left with this Gladys creature, and he ran out into the dining room and into the sun porch and through the living room, his fears growing into uncontrolled agitation, until he found her in the front hall dusting the big chest of drawers.

His relief was so great that he could not understand why Gladys did not share it, for she gave an exasperated sigh and this time when she deposited him again in the bedroom in front of the untouched array of marbles, she closed the door solidly behind her as she left.

He waited as he heard her slow heavy steps go along the hallway towards the front of the apartment, then he quickly went to the door. But he couldn't open it: the brass handle would start to turn in his small hand then slip back. He tried using both hands but it didn't work.

This time his crying was solely for himself – he had given up on the idea that it would bring comfort from Gladys, or even her presence. He cried for so long that he wondered if there could be tears left inside him to come out. He thought with desperation about his mother. Normally she would collect him from school, his face lighting up as he saw her, tall in a cotton dress in the kindergarten doorway, her hair a mass of blonde curls. They'd bustle along the street towards home, while she chattered away, and then she would give him a snack in the kitchen and plan the rest of their afternoon – he could watch *Captain Kangaroo* and *Mickey Mouse*, then sit in the kitchen with a pad of paper and a fistful of pens while she started supper and sang along with the radio.

But he found the images of her kept being replaced by an entirely imagined one of her lying in a hospital bed, which did not comfort him at all. He lay down himself, on his back on the floor, and stared without interest at the cracks that ran like routes on a road map across the ceiling.

He was still lying there when the door suddenly opened and Gladys stood there, breathing heavily. 'Y'all come eat now,' she said, and at first he looked at her with incomprehension.

'Food,' she said, and at first he thought she'd said 'fool', which would not surprise him, since recently it had been Lily's favourite putdown for him, but then Gladys added, 'Come get your supper now, child.'

He followed her reluctantly back to the kitchen and he sat at the rickety table as she put his plate down. It was heaving: an immense fried pork chop with a long protective rib of fat, a mound of mashed potato and a heap of yellow corn kernels, a biscuit, and a large cup of milk. She eyed him carefully as he took his fork, unsure whether he was meant to use the knife as well – his mother always cut his meat for him – but then blessedly the phone rang, which distracted Gladys.

From the way she answered and talked he realised she was speaking with his father. 'Yes, sir, we be just fine. I'm giving him fried food for his supper and I bet

28

he eats it all. Now don't worry, and I'll see you later at the end of the day.'

She paused and he could hear his father's voice – rich and deep – on the line. Gladys said, 'Yes, he cried after you left, Mr Danziger. That boy cried his share, and then some. But he done crying now.'

Which was true. His tears had stopped the very moment futility had taken over.

After this, Gladys was there every day. He didn't know if he hated her more than he feared her, just that he felt both emotions. He tried to tell Lily this, but she scolded him in that prim way of hers that made him realise it had been a mistake to tell her how he felt. 'She's a Negro,' Lily said. 'That's why you don't like her.'

'What?' he'd tried to protest, astonished by her accusation. What was a Negro anyway? It couldn't be anything good if Gladys was one.

At first, he asked for his mother each morning at breakfast, and daily his father replied evenly that she was still in hospital. One morning inspiration seized him and he asked if he could go and see her. No, his father explained, little kids were not allowed there, and Bobby wondered what he could do that might make his mother even worse.

His father always took him to school in the morning, and sometimes his father would tell the funny stories he had always told – about the polar bear field, which is what he called the empty lot on Dorchester, and the exotic animals that lived there whom only he and his father could see. But now he was often preoccupied and in a rush to get to his own grown-up kind of school, and even at home he would hole up in his study, typing and smoking, leaving Bobby to Gladys.

Miss Partridge was his sole ray of light. 'Your teacher

is a bird,' Mike said at breakfast one day, and Bobby said, 'But a nice bird' so seriously that his father's laugh got cut short when he saw Bobby's expression. And then one day at school she wasn't there, and Mrs Jacobs, who was perfectly all right but not a woman he had any real liking for, told him in the sickly sweet voice he was learning to associate with bad news that Miss Partridge had got married and wouldn't be teaching there any more. And he was baffled at first, then stunned by yet another betrayal.

Within two weeks his father didn't even reply to his daily question about his mother's whereabouts, only shrugging slowly as he stood like a poor man's Gladys over the morning's skillet of bacon and eggs. So Bobby stopped asking. He brought it up with Mike once, but Mike said tersely, 'She's real sick, Bobby. I think Dad's scared she's going to die.' Which explained the evening when right before bed he heard his father speaking on the phone to Gramps, saying, 'It's kind of tough, Dad,' and then suddenly his father's voice seemed to choke and Bobby realised he wasn't saying anything because sobs had replaced words in his throat. That scared him more than almost anything, because he had never seen his father cry – he had been a captain in the army way back in a war, so how could he cry? Did this mean his mother was really going to die?

He felt he was in a dark tunnel, like the lightless hallway in the apartment that ended in the back bedroom. He could not understand why this had happened to him – he had no previous awareness of misfortune. Sometimes his parents had talked about an 'accident', and he knew that people sometimes died, which meant they went away for good. Like his mother? Not according to Mike and Lily, though he detected uncertainty there too, and they grew angry with him now when he asked when their mother would come back. Yet truth was, if his mother wasn't dead, then why wasn't she at home? She might as well be dead, he thought in an inchoate way, since four weeks seemed a year at least to a little boy his age.

He was too little to understand anything about memory or time, but he knew enough to conclude that life was something to be endured, and that in this respect he had a long, long way to go before it was over. He felt he had been propelled out of a happy existence into a misery which bore only the most superficial relationship to what he'd had before. He still had a brother and sister, there were still meals to be eaten; he still slept in a bed – but the switch to happiness was now turned off.

Then one day his father picked him up from nursery, and as they left the big brick house on Kimbark Avenue he said enigmatically, 'I've got a little surprise for you.'

'Where?' said Bobby, rather than what, since 'where' remained his focus – especially where his mother was.

'At home. It's not Mom,' he added quickly, but Bobby had not allowed himself to think it was.

His heart sank nonetheless, and he muttered, 'Gladys,' thinking his father thought the prospect of helping her roll out biscuits was a treat.

'No,' said his dad. 'Not Gladys. You'll see.'

When they got back to the apartment, his father whistled when he opened the door, and called out, 'Hey ho, we're here.' He sounded better than he had for ages. Bobby went with him through the corridor to the kitchen, where Gladys was standing at the stove. Only it wasn't Gladys: this woman was as black as Gladys, but much younger. She wasn't fat at all, he thought to himself, though she had a large bosom beneath her grey sweater. Her skirt was short, and he could see her legs

– Gladys had always hid hers in long white cotton shifts and the ubiquitous apron the size of a tent. This woman had youthful pretty features, and she looked directly at him before his father had said a word.

'This is Bobby,' his father said hopefully.

She nodded. Then she slapped her cheeks with both hands. 'Why, ain't you the cutest little boy I ever done seen,' she exclaimed.

His grandmother had called him cute once, and his brother Mike had never let him forget it. But right now he didn't care what Mike would think, and he smiled shyly at this woman. She smiled back and her white teeth gleamed, though looking up at her mouth Bobby could see the gold glitter of several fillings.

She turned to his father and said, 'Maybe you need to find something in your study, Mr Danziger.' For a moment, his father looked puzzled. Then he took the hint and left the room.

The woman smiled again at Bobby and said, 'Come here, honey, and let me take a look at you.'

He took a small step towards the stove and she leaned down until her face was almost level with his. Suddenly he wanted to run to her, but he hesitated. When he tried to hug Gladys she usually shooed him away. 'Child, don't be bothering me,' was her automatic response.

But this woman was holding her arms wide open in an unmistakable signal. He waited just the same. For he was old enough, perhaps experienced enough even in his young years, to sense that he simply could not bear being let down again.

Then she said, 'Come here, baby,' and the next thing he knew he was in her arms. They were warm and comforting, but he began to cry anyway. The tears he shed may have been for his mother – yes, almost certainly – but they were also for the despairing days he had been through since his mother had gone away. And tears from sheer relief at this embrace, the first sign that maybe life didn't need to seem endless after all.

'That's all right,' she was saying into his ear, and he felt his tears streaked along her cheek. 'You just cry as much as you need to. I ain't going nowhere. Vanetta and you are going to have us a good time together. Just you wait and see.'

III

THE COFFEE SHOP was a vast tiled room on the ground floor of the Marchese Building, an early brick-fronted skyscraper of twenty-odd floors that sat on Wacker Drive, a stone's throw across the Chicago River from the pearl-veined stone of the Wrigley Building. This late in the afternoon the place was almost empty, and the waitress told him to take his pick of tables. He scanned the room for Duval, but saw only an elderly couple nursing cups of coffee, a family of tourists having Cokes, and an old black man with a beard reading in the far corner. Robert breathed a sigh of relief, glad to be there first.

He didn't know what to expect, didn't even have a good sense of what Duval looked like. The skinny awkward kid Robert had known must have filled out. Didn't all convicts lift weights, grow muscle-bound? Presumably for protection – Robert knew prison life was violent, scarily so; even the most unrealistic television dramas showed a life of brute force and fear. He had to assume Duval would be toughened unrecognisably by years spent in the company of murderers, perpetrators of violent assaults, extreme degenerates. Then he remembered what Duval himself was supposed to have done.

He looked out the windows at the construction hole where the Sun Times building had stood – a modern aluminium shell, it had lasted only forty years, and he could almost feel the Marchese crow at the demise of its upstart neighbour.

'Just coffee, please,' he said to the waitress as she held out a menu. She filled his cup while he wondered what Duval might want to talk about. They hadn't seen each other in over twenty years, had not been friends for over thirty. There had to be some agenda, something Duval wanted. He realised his curiosity had been overtaken by apprehension. He wanted to leave, but this seemed cowardly – besides, Duval would probably just call him again.

He looked around, noticing how the couple was sitting mute. Was this the silence of complete familiarity, or recognition that after so many years they had exhausted all possibilities for conversation? Probably both. Thank God he hadn't reached that point with Anna. Whatever the ups and downs they had between them, there was always conversation – sometimes funny (she often made him laugh), sometimes heated, sometimes calm. But always talk.

Behind the elderly couple the black man was studying his book intently. He wore old-fashioned wire-framed reading glasses, and when he looked up the frames glinted in the light. His eyes caught Robert's and he nodded shyly, then suddenly his face broke into a toothy smile. And Robert thought, Oh, my God, it's him.

'Duval?' The man nodded. Robert stood up and moved over to the man's table, where he put down his cup. They shook hands; Duval's was dry, and roughly calloused. He had taken his glasses off and his dark brown eyes looked intently at Robert, in a slow assessment that made Robert uneasy, as if he were being compared to some long-stored image.

They both sat down, Robert with his back now to the river. Duval wore a dark suit, brown-and-silver tie, and a white shirt with an oversized collar that bobbed around his throat. His face was long and oval-shaped, and his wiry hair was cropped short. A thin line of beard ran along each side of his jaw until it widened like a protective cup around his chin. Duval sat upright, like a man of the cloth ill at ease in restaurants.

'I could tell you didn't recognise me. Bet you thought, That old black guy can't be Duval.'

This was so true that Robert felt enveloped by awkwardness. 'Maybe something like that,' he conceded.

Duval smiled. 'And here I was thinking, That old white guy can't be Bobby.'

Robert laughed with relief. 'It's good to see you, Duval.'

Duval nodded but didn't say anything.

'You look well.' He hesitated, feeling ill at ease again. 'Nice suit,' he added, and felt stupid for the remark.

Duval pinched the lapel with his long fingers. 'Thirty years old and still going strong. Of course it didn't get a lot of wear for twenty-four of them.'

There didn't seem a suitable response, so Robert decided to stick to the present. 'Where are you living?'

'I'm staying with my cousin Jermaine. He's got a spare room. Real nice.' The voice was soft, a touch above middle range of pitch.

'What happened to Vanetta's house?'

'She left it to my mama. Aurelia needed the money, so she sold it right away.' He said this without emotion.

'How is Aurelia?'

'She passed away a year after Vanetta did.' He was silent momentarily, then seemed to gather himself. 'You know,' he said, an almost imperceptible tremor to his voice, 'I didn't just want to see you to say hello. I also wanted to thank you.'

'Thank me?' Robert was nonplussed.

'Yes,' said Duval. 'For all that you and your family did for Vanetta while I was away.'

Away? Duval said this as if he'd been gone on an extended business trip, seconded to some faraway city – Mexico City, say, or Rio – by his parent company.

'I don't know if we did anything all that special, Duval.' He'd sent Vanetta a present every year, usually a hundred-dollar bill folded in a Christmas card. His father would have wanted to do the right thing but no more – a Christmas card, a phone call once or twice a year to say hello. And Robert couldn't believe his stepmother had indulged in any display of largesse. Not that tight old stick.

'Well, Vanetta said you did. Not long before she died. She came regular to see me.'

'I know.' She'd faithfully made the long drive as often as the rules allowed. Once a month? Something like that.

'Why else would she tell me to come see you when I was free again?'

She had? Suddenly, for all his discomfort, Robert was content to see Duval again. I'm paying a debt to Vanetta, he told himself; it seemed the least he could do for her.

The waitress appeared, holding a Pyrex jug half-full of coffee. 'Fill you gents up?' she said.

They both shook their heads. 'You want something to eat, Duval?' asked Robert out of politeness, then saw the man hesitate. 'Go on. I had a big lunch or I'd join you. Have a hamburger – my treat. It's good to see you again.'

'Actually,' said Duval, and he looked shyly at the waitress, 'what I'd really like is a piece of pie.'

The waitress recited. 'Blueberry, cherry, chocolate cream, or lemon meringue.'

'Blueberry.'

'A la mode?'

Duval looked puzzled.

'You want ice cream on top?' asked Robert, and Duval nodded.

The waitress went away and Duval smiled with a

37

little embarrassment. 'I forgot that expression. We never got it that way.'

'You sure that's all you want to eat?'

He nodded. 'I got me a sweet tooth but it's easily satisfied.' He laughed, then put one hand to his mouth as if he was trying to stop a cough. He put his hand down on the table and spread it; he had lengthy fingers and carefully tended nails.

Robert asked, 'What's Jermaine up to these days?'

'He's still working for R.R. Donnelley's. He wants to retire in a couple of years.' This was said wistfully, but then it must seem peculiar to find someone retiring when you were effectively starting out.

Mention of Jermaine eased something in Duval, like a blocked drain inexplicably cleared, for he started talking, hesitantly at first, then without self-consciousness, describing the present state of Vanetta's vast extended family. He told Robert about Daphne, who'd just had a bypass, then Marvin ('he passed last year') and Rodney, who'd totalled his van on I-94 two years before but had emerged miraculously unscathed.

'You remember Shonelle, don't you?' Duval asked at one point, and Robert smiled with false knowingness.

For the truth was he didn't remember any of these people. It had all been so long ago, and he had never known most of them to begin with – they were just names mentioned by Vanetta. As Duval talked about a new generation of grandchildren and great-grandchildren – Lemar and Dennis and Kaleen and Lynette – Robert merely nodded and kept his head down, staring at Duval's clasped hands on the table in front of him.

Suddenly noticing his gaze, Duval held up his ring finger, where he wore a slim gold band. 'This was left me by Vanetta. It used to be Alvin's.'

Vanetta's younger brother; that Robert did know.

He'd died while Robert was at boarding school, almost breaking Vanetta's heart – the worst thing that ever happened to her, she'd told Robert. But that was before Duval's arrest.

Then Duval asked, 'How about your family? Is your daddy still alive?'

'Just my stepmother. Dad died three years ago.'

'I'm sorry.'

'He was old, Duval, and in a lot of pain. The last few years were hard. I don't think he wanted to go on.'

'But Merrill's all right?'

'Yes,' said Robert, amazed Duval remembered her name. 'Lily looks after her.'

'Where's Mike?'

'He's up in Washington State, near Spokane. He was an army officer; retired last year. He's fine, taking it easy.' He deserved it; he'd fought in both Gulf Wars, real fighting too.

'Vanetta said you got married and had yourself a family. Boys or girls?'

'One girl.'

'Really now. That's what I call intelligent planning.' He chuckled, but again his hand went to his mouth.

'Well, actually, I've been divorced once – the first time didn't work out. But I had a son – he's grown now and lives in England.'

'What's he do for a living?'

'He's studying.'

Duval nodded earnestly. Robert thought of his boy, still technically an undergraduate, but just hanging in there by the skin of his backside if his tutor's report was anything to go by.

'I bet he's doing good.'

'I'm not sure he'd share your confidence. My boy's a bit wild.'

'Wild?' Duval looked concerned for the first time. 'You want to nip *that* in the bud.'

Robert shrugged. 'He's an adult now, Duval. Legally at least. He tends to listen to his mother more anyway. We didn't have the friendliest divorce in the world, and he sided with his momma.'

Duval was sobered by this. Then his face brightened and he asked, 'But you married again then?'

'That's right. She's English, but she's here too. And we got a little girl, Sophie.' *We got,* and a moment before *momma* – he heard his voice slipping into the half-black patois he'd used as a boy with Vanetta. Stop it, he told himself. Duval might think he was making fun of him.

'A little girl – ain't that sweet?' Duval seemed to muse happily on this. The waitress delivered his pie, and his eyes shifted to his plate. 'Say,' he said, as he lifted his fork, 'I meant to tell you, I went out to Hyde Park after I was released, had a good look around. It has changed, hasn't it? You see that new building behind your place on Blackstone?'

'I haven't, actually. I haven't been out there since we moved back.'

Duval looked disappointed. 'You haven't been out there at all? You should, you know. Sarnat's is gone.'

'Yes,' said Robert measuredly. It had been gone for twenty years, turned into a restaurant.

'And the Christian Science church got turned into a mosque for the brothers of Islam.'

'That was a while back.' Way, way back, he wanted to say.

'Well, it ain't no mosque no more. Place was all closed up, and the back entrance had barbed wire and a padlock big as my head. You know what I was doing there, don't you?'

Should he? 'What was that, Duval?'

'Oh, come on, you must know,' he said. Then perhaps sensing he'd only be disappointed again, he went on. 'I was going to see the Secret Garden. All these years I could imagine it, and then when I get there it was all locked up.'

Christ, thought Robert, he must have known it wasn't real. Of course they'd just been kids, when you could believe almost anything, but by now Duval had to know it had just been a fantasy.

Duval said, 'I was going to go through the alley by the apartment and have a look that way, but they got a big gate up there too. I didn't know really how I could explain myself if they asked what I was doing there.'

I can see that, thought Robert. It was not that there was anything physically threatening about Duval: he remained a beanpole; there was no evidence of weight-lifting, no bulk there. But there was something disconcerting about his deep gaze, and how he stifled any laugh. The way his conversation veered around topics, moreover, suggested that the internal verbal mechanism of social discourse was slipping in and out of gear, like a car jerkily driven by a learner.

Duval reached inside his jacket and drew out a thin billfold of faded leather. 'I got something to show you,' he said with a sly smile, and handed over a small snapshot – it was framed by a tiny margin that had gone brown with age.

Robert peered at it, then held the photo up to the light. In the middle of the tiny square he could make out Vanetta, standing in a kitchen, facing the camera in a white skirt and a dark blouse. She had her arms around a boy on either side, and he could see that it was the young Duval, dressed in a white shirt and dark trousers, as if for church. He wouldn't have been more

41

than eight or nine, and his front teeth stuck out as he smiled for the camera.

On Vanetta's other side the boy was white, shorter than Duval, with dark hair and dark eyes. Robert realised it was a picture of himself.

'That's us,' he exclaimed. Why was he so surprised?

'You remember when it was taken? It was Vanetta's birthday. She had just moved to the house on Morgan.'

'You got a good memory, Duval.'

'I've had a lot of time for remembering,' Duval said quietly. He reached out and took back the little snap-shot. 'I can't be losing this now. It survived my whole time inside.'

You could get a copy made, Robert thought, but something held him back from saying so. Duval had kept this photo with him during all those years in prison, like a lucky charm. To think that Robert hadn't had Duval in his head for years.

'Are you working, Duval?'

'Not yet. They trained me, but only as a TV repairman.'

'Are you getting by?'

'I'm trying my best, and Jermaine ain't asking much rent. I get benefit. It's okay,' he said. His voice was increasingly familiar to Robert, but he realised there was no mystery to this – it was simply an older version of the voice he'd known almost forty years before. And he still spoke in the tone of passive acceptance which Robert now remembered. When they were boys Robert would say, 'Want to play whiffle ball?' *Okay.* Or, 'Want to go to Sarnat's?' *Okay.*

'Could you use a loan, Duval?' He had been expecting to say this, he realised, and part of him wanted to give Duval money so he wouldn't have to see him again. How much should he offer – a couple of hundred dollars? That wouldn't last long. But more would be too much – and suggest some debt was being repaid.

To his surprise, Duval shook his head emphatically. 'No, sir. I don't need a loan.' He paused, then said, 'I'm pretty good with my hands – and I like carpentry. Fixing things, that's what I like to do. But I can't get into the union.'

'I see,' said Robert, wondering what opportunities had been afforded by the state facilities in Joliet or Dixon. If the showers leaked, did they call in an inmate? If the governor's desk wobbled, would the likes of Duval put a wood chock under its creaky leg?

'So if you know anybody who was to need a handyman, that would be something I could do.'

'Gosh,' said Robert, using an Americanism no longer natural to him, 'let me think.' He was trying to buy time. He said, sounding lame even to himself, 'If I hear of anything I'll let you know. Have you got a number where I can reach you?'

'You could call me at Jermaine's,' said Duval. He had demolished his pie; only a teardrop of ice cream remained on the plate.

'No cell phone?'

'Not yet.' He smiled weakly. 'They kind of expensive.'

'Right.' Robert looked down at his cup, trying to look thoughtful, then made a show of looking at his watch. 'Duval, I'm going to have to get back to work now.' He wanted to say. 'You know how it is,' but doubted that Duval would. Robert felt surrounded by a minefield of language he didn't feel he should use.

Duval nodded a little sadly. 'Of course,' he said. He started to reach into his jacket and Robert realised he was going for his wallet.

'No, this is on me. Next time you can pick up the tab.'

'Okay.' Duval's pride seemed salved.

Robert got up, leaving six bucks on the table, and together they left the coffee shop. In the building's foyer Robert stopped and pointed down a side corridor. 'I'm going that way.' He held out his hand. 'Let's keep in touch,' he said.

'Absolutely.'

Robert walked away quickly. He felt relieved. It had gone well – or at least not badly. He was glad that he'd done the decent thing, but he felt it wasn't likely he would see Duval again – which was a relief.

Then he heard Duval call out behind him. 'Bobby,' he said, and for a moment Robert wondered if he'd left something behind.

Duval was standing in the corridor, one arm extended with his finger pointing at Robert, almost accusingly. There was a strained look on his face that hadn't been there before. 'There's something I want you to know.'

Robert felt his earlier apprehension return. 'What's that, Duval?' he asked.

'I didn't do it.'

At least that's what it sounded like. 'What did you say?' Robert demanded.

Duval shook his head. He seemed suddenly possessed by an angry righteousness; there was nothing passive about him now. He stood, still pointing his finger at Robert. 'I *said*, I didn't do it.' Then he brought his hand down and walked away.

Astonished, Robert stared at the retreating figure, trying to take this in. The matter-of-factness: *I didn't do it.*

Said so many years ago about something else. The same denial. And now, after twenty-four years in a man-made hellhole, he was saying the same thing again. *I didn't do it.*

IV

HE HAD KEPT the light off and the door half-closed, thinking this would hide his presence in the pantry. Then a voice came from outside the door, light and laughing.

'I hear me a little rat in there. Well, the little rat better understand that I'm going back to the linen closet and when I come back here the little rat better be out of there or it's going to find its tail in a trap.'

He heard Vanetta move down the hall and he came out with three cherries in his hand, pilfered from a plastic carton in the freezer. He popped them quickly into his mouth.

They were so cold they burned the insides of his cheeks. Slowly warming in his mouth, through the ache they brought to his jaw, he tasted their dense and icy sweetness. He had just finished them when Vanetta reappeared. The ironing board was up next to the stove, with a stack of laundry waiting for her. She spread out one of his father's shirts, hooking the collar over the board's narrowed nose, and picked up the iron, saying softly, 'I hope you left some in the carton, Bobby.' She was only half-smiling. 'Your daddy's got people for dinner on Saturday and Merrill wants to serve those with some ice cream.'

'There're lots left, Vanetta,' he said, avoiding the issue of whether he had taken any, though they both knew he had.

It was January and they were in the kitchen, Bobby at the rickety table with his homework. Outside the wind was blowing new snow into the back alleyway. Mike D'Amico had come up the outside stairs in back with the vegetable delivery, and when Vanetta held the door open for him cold air had overwhelmed even the warmth from the stove.

His father had taken a freezer locker in Fennville, where he'd stored the cut-up half-steer he'd bought on the advice of his friend, the county agent, along with several lugs of fruit. Cherries, of course – it was cherry country – but also sliced strawberries, raspberries, and sliced peaches and plums frozen in syrup. On a weekend trip north that autumn they had collected fruit, put it in plastic cartons, and brought it down in a cool box to deposit it here, in the South Side freezer.

Fruit meant summer, fruit meant warmth, fruit was a talisman of another place than this large, dark apartment on the South Side, where Bobby didn't want to be. He sensed Vanetta didn't want to be there either. So he would prod her into talking about her own childhood, deep in the Mississippi delta, on her father's small farm. 'What did you grow on the farm, Vanetta?'

He knew the answers, but the shared imagining of her telling took them both out of the dark cold winter of Chicago. She said, 'Oh, most everything we wanted to eat. There weren't no store near us – it took two hours to get to town. That was on a horse – we didn't have no car.

'We grew every kind of vegetable. Beans, and peas, and corn – nice corn – and tomatoes so fat and soft they made your mouth pucker just looking at them. Potatoes too each spring, and sweet potatoes.' The latter were Vanetta's favourites.

'And fruit?' He was never very interested in vegetables.

'We had all sorts of fruit. Strawberries, just bursting with juice, and raspberries too. Not so many cherries – we had one tree but it's awful hot for them in

Mississippi. But come summer there'd be peaches as big as baseballs – there's nothing better than a good peach pie, especially with home-made ice cream. You had to work so hard making ice cream back then it made it taste extra good.'

She was chopping cabbage for coleslaw, made with oil and so much vinegar his eyes popped eating it. He loved its sourness.

'Please sit down with me, Vanetta.'

'Let me just finish this, baby.' When she had she went to the fridge and took out a bottle of Pepsi and a snow-ball – two coconut-coated balls of rubbery fluff surrounding chocolate cake with a cream centre. She cut one of them in half and put it on a plate before him, then opened the Pepsi and poured a couple of ounces out for him into a plastic cup. Then she sat down at the table, too. Biting into the other half of the snowball, she nodded appreciatively and closed her eyes, dreamlike.

'Hard to believe spring is ever going to show up – but it always does. Only I can't remember a winter as cold as this. Seems like the snow's forgot to stop.' She picked up a deck of playing cards she'd had on the table and started laying out her own, semi-impossible game of solitaire. Bobby hated it because you almost never won. But he liked to watch her play, liked staring at her hands, their rich deep brown with pinkish half-moons around the cuticles. The brown skin meant she was a Negro. He understood that now, and he had laughed like someone in the know when she'd told him about the little boy in another household who'd complained that her skin was always dirty.

Now he asked, 'Was there ever snow in Mississippi?'

'Almost never,' she said. 'Cotton don't like snow, so snow's not allowed there.'

He laughed at the ridiculous logic of this and Vanetta laughed too.

She picked up a card off the table, held it thoughtfully against her mouth for a moment, then put it down at the end of the longest row. 'You is distracting me, Bobby, so I'm going to lose.'

'Sorry,' he said.

She laughed again; she was always laughing. 'Don't worry, I was going to lose anyway.' She collected the cards in a pile and sorted them, then put the pack down on the table. Finishing her Pepsi, she stood up. 'I got supper to make now. You want to help, or you want to go watch TV?'

'What's for supper?'

'Baked chicken. And rice, and slaw.'

Of course, it was Friday – his least favourite day because it meant the advent of the weekend when there was no Vanetta. She cooked by an invariable schedule: Monday was pot roast (yuck), Tuesday was ribs with barbecue sauce, Wednesday soy-soaked hamburgers, and Thursday – well, Thursday was pot luck according to his father, which could mean anything, Chinese takeaway if they were lucky, his father's adored lamb kidneys if they weren't, which made Bobby want a dog even more than usual, since then he could have slipped the offal to the dog.

Recently Thursday was even dodgier than the food, because every other week Merrill had taken to coming to supper, and Vanetta would stay late. Then they ate in the dining room, rather than around the kitchen table, and he and Mike had to comb their hair and change their shirts. Merrill wore a dress and usually had a necklace on, which Lily seemed happy to imitate. Merrill would insist on proper conversation, which only his father and Lily seemed to enjoy. They discussed issues

48

with a capital 'I' – the worsening situation in Vietnam, Richard Nixon, sometimes (with lowered voices and an eye on the swing door to the kitchen) the growing unrest among the Negro population. The discussion was as formal as school to Bobby, and as dull. Once when Mike made a silly face, Bobby laughed uncontrollably, and his father sent him to his bedroom, where he cried until Vanetta came to say goodnight and slipped him a bacon sandwich in a napkin.

Now he watched as Vanetta took jointed chicken pieces on a plate and put them two at a time in a paper bag which already held salt-and-peppered flour. She shook them hard in the bag, then dipped each one in a bowl of beaten egg, before laying them carefully in a roasting tin which she then put in the oven. She was wearing a sleeveless sweater and a black skirt; unlike Gladys, she didn't like to wear an apron, and she refused to wear a uniform.

When Lily came home (Mike had basketball practice and came home later), Bobby would go back to the bedroom to watch TV or play with his marbles, or use his father's old putter, stroking a golf ball across the bare brown carpet into a speckled plastic cup that served as the hole. He didn't mind being alone there, even before Lily got home, as long as he knew Vanetta was in the apartment.

When he went to the back of the apartment, the door to his father's bedroom was always open. He kept it that way, ever since Bobby's mother had died two years before. Even at night his father didn't close it, so he could hear his children if they needed him. Bobby didn't want it closed again – it would mean someone else had taken his mother's place.

He wondered why Lily acted as if she liked this woman Merrill, unless it was because she really did. Mike loathed

49

her, though in front of their father his antipathy was only evident because he never talked about the woman at all. Oh, Merrill was polite enough and pleasant looking and, according to Vanetta, she dressed nicely, but she made you feel you had to be on your best behaviour, and you couldn't ever be yourself. His mother had been pretty, girlish and had liked to dance; Merrill was handsome and acted lady-like. She called his father Jonathan, for example, when everybody knew his name was Johnny, and he was different when he was with her – there were not so many jokes. His dad had always been naturally funny, but there was nothing natural to Merrill, and her increasing presence worried Bobby.

She also tried to tell Vanetta what to do, which wasn't right at all. Vanetta took it in her stride, he supposed, but he couldn't believe she liked it. And Lily didn't help – she was arguing with Vanetta these days, being downright rude, about when she would go out and when she'd see her friends and how much time she could spend on the phone even though she hadn't done her homework.

'She's just being a teenager,' Vanetta had explained to his father, when Lily was giving him a hard time too, but Bobby was apprehensive nonetheless and didn't like the arguments.

When Vanetta asked her to do something, Lily would say, 'Don't boss me.'

'Child, I'm not asking you anything your father don't want you to do. If you wants to make a fuss, make it with him.'

And Lily would roll her eyes and sigh.

He figured as long as Merrill didn't actually live there he was safe. He wished instead that Vanetta could live with them. Or at the very least be there more of the time – especially weekends, when there were just the four

Danzigers stuck in this dark apartment, especially during winter. They seemed never to go out; the only expedition was on Saturday morning when his father took him (Mike and Lily always turning down the privilege) along for the weekly shop. He said he needed help, but Bobby knew he needed company.

Yet how could his father be lonely? There didn't seem any need for his father to see Merrill. He had his children, didn't he? – and his friends, and Uncle Larry and Aunt ZZ. And Vanetta as the lynchpin for life in this apartment. Yet there was his father finding company with Merrill, some lady who lived in the Cloisters, a vast armoury-shaped apartment building, which Bobby passed each morning with his father on the way to school.

His father, bizarrely, seemed concerned that Bobby was lonely too. One day Bobby heard him and Vanetta talking in the kitchen while he stood in the doorway to the long hall; they must have thought he was back watching *Superman* on TV.

'How's our little guy doing, V?'

'He's okay, Mr Danziger. Time helps, you know.'

'It will be four years next fall.'

'Yes, sir, though he's still got to be missing his mother.'

'I know.'

Vanetta said, 'He be doin' okay. But that's one deep boy, Mr D.'

His father laughed but there was a melancholy strain to it.

'I tell you one thing,' Vanetta offered. 'He could do with some company his own age.'

'I know, but he's got Lily and Mike. They're nice to him, aren't they?'

'They're okay. But they're so much older that they won't play with him, except when I ask them to.' Vanetta said 'ask' like the word 'axe'; Bobby had corrected her once, and she had said thank you. But she continued to say 'axe'.

His father must have been frowning, for Vanetta added, 'It's only natural, Mr D. Kids like to play with kids their own age.'

Had anyone but Vanetta said this, Bobby would have felt betrayed. What she didn't understand was that he was happy with the way things were. He knew his mother was gone for good, he did his best quite faithfully to remember her, staring at the photograph his father kept on top of his roll-top desk, trying to match the picture with some image in his head, and he knew too that something hard, and awful, and enduring had happened to them all.

But the terrible thing he couldn't admit even to himself was that he didn't actually miss his mother much; he had trouble enough just remembering her. And with this secret came another one he kept to himself. As far as Bobby was concerned, Vanetta was his mother.

There was actually plenty of company in the apartment, even if it wasn't of his own age. Like Mike D'Amico with his grocery deliveries twice a week; he'd sit down sometimes and have a cup of coffee, especially if Vanetta needed time to go around the kitchen and sort out what they needed – the potatoes were in the pantry, but the fruit was on a shelf near the icebox, and the veg was in the icebox itself.

Or Mr Tipps, a white Southerner who at Merrill's instigation (according to Mike) repainted the entire apartment, and would take a break in the kitchen in the late afternoon, where he would explain to Vanetta and Bobby how man had descended from the coconut. 'Just look at one,' he'd say, tugging on a strap of his painter's overalls. 'Two eyes and hair just like a man's.'

On the ground floor, below their apartment, lived the Edeveks – Eddie, the janitor, and his wife. You had to be careful about jumping around in the living room or dining room, since they were directly below. But in the back bedroom there was no problem, since it was just the cavernous basement beneath. Once when Mike had broken a window in the back yard their father had paid Eddie to replace it, singing, 'I write a cheque/ for Eddie Edevek', which Bobby had thought absolutely hilarious but was forbidden to sing himself. A couple of times a year his father would do more than nod hello to Eddie, stopping in the vestibule to talk about their army days. Eddie never said much, but Bobby's father described him as an amiable Polack, and said he had more common sense than all the academics of the neighbourhood put together. His father liked to tell how once, after a big storm, Eddie had pointed out at the street where snow lay unploughed and uncollected for the fifth day running in the sub-zero sun, and declared, 'What this ward needs is a crooked alderman.'

He was big enough now to walk part of the way home from school, and he'd go up the leafy block of Kenwood, until he reached the news-stand at Steinways. Then Abe, the old man who owned the news-stand, would take him by the hand, flag down the cars, and walk him across the street. It seemed unnecessary and humiliating to Bobby, and he hated the way Abe would envelop his little hand in his own sweaty one, his thumb black from newsprint. But his father insisted, and once a month would press a five-dollar bill on Abe to pay for the dubious service. Once across, Bobby would run the first few yards, keen to wipe away all trace of the old man, then skip down 57th Street until

53

he'd catch sight of Vanetta waiting for him at the corner of Dorchester, her arms folded and a smile on her face. He'd sprint and jump up into her arms and she'd twirl him around before putting him down all dizzy, and then they'd walk the fifty yards past the empty lot to the back yard, along the thin alley next to the Christian Science church, up the stairs and home.

From the kitchen's lair – cosy in winter, airy with just the screen door during summer – they would sometimes set out on what Vanetta called 'expeditions'. Lily and Mike were occupied with extra-curricular activities, which as far as Bobby could tell meant organised sports for his brother and bossing people on the student council for Lily, and his father was always busy now. So Vanetta took over many parental errands. She took Bobby to buy new shoes at Kiddie Kicks on 53rd Street – he noticed how she whistled in wonder at the price on the box of school shoes the man helped him pick out, saying, 'Seems mighty high to me,' and she took him once a week to swimming lessons at the Hyde Park 'Y', where she waited on her own amidst a crowd of middle-class mothers. She even took him down to Jeffrey and 72nd Street when he needed a tetanus shot from Dr Rosenfeld.

And if Vanetta needed to run an errand, she brought him with her now, since most afternoons he was the only child in the family she had to watch over. He'd even seen where Vanetta lived, when she'd forgotten to leave a note for the gas man, explaining something about the meter in the basement. They'd driven over on Garfield, past the Wonder Bread Company where her brother Alvin worked. This was definitely 'Bip your bips' country, since the street corners seemed inhabited by black men standing around with nothing to do, a beer can or a port bottle in their hand. When they stopped at one light a man waved at Vanetta, and seeing Bobby next to her, his head barely visible above the dashboard, he shouted out something – Bobby could tell it wasn't nice. The man began walking towards them, and to Bobby's astonishment Vanetta drove forward, even though the light was still red. Bobby looked at her with his eyes as big as moons, but she just laughed, shaking her head. 'I ain't waiting for that fool to bother us, Bobby.'

Indiana ran north–south and was lined by brick and grey stone apartment buildings. Vanetta parked on the side of the street. 'Now when I get out you get out on the kerb side and you come quick. We don't want to be hanging around outside, okay?'

Her apartment was on the third floor where the only light on the landing came from a dim candle-shaped bulb. There were a lot of locks on her door; it took Vanetta three keys to open up. Inside was a little hallway, smaller than at Blackstone Avenue, and a living room with a TV in one corner. There was a low yellow sofa and a big stuffed armchair, which had plastic sheets draped over them. No books, Bobby noticed; his daddy had books on almost every wall. But he liked the room, and Vanetta had put some marigolds in a copper vase on the coffee table in front of the sofa.

He followed her into the kitchen. Another spick-and-span room, with a small Formica table and three kitchen chairs with metal legs. Vanetta went to the sink and made Kool-Aid in a plastic jug, getting ice from the fridge's freezer top. 'You drink this, Bobby,' she said, handing him a cup. 'You must be thirsty. We won't stay long. I'll write a note for the gas man and then we can leave.'

While she did this he sat and looked around. There was a cabinet on one wall with a glass front; inside it he could see plates stacked and some glasses. Above the sink on two shelves sat saucepans, and hanging from the wall on big iron hooks was a series of cast-iron skillets.

'I like those,' said Bobby, pointing at the wall. 'They look like giant fish hooks.'

'Ain't they neat? Alvin put them up for me.' She sounded proud of her brother.

He finished his drink and wiped his wet lips with his arm when Vanetta wasn't looking. 'Can I see your bedroom, Vanetta?'

'I don't see why not.' He stood up and she walked with him down a dark hallway – like his own apartment's, but shorter – and stopped at an open door.

It was a nice-sized room with two tall windows facing the back, though the view was blocked by another apartment building. The bed was mahogany, and made up neatly, with an old-fashioned quilted spread and two big pillows stacked up against the headboard. On the bedside table lay an illustrated bible, next to a small lamp. A small chest of drawers sat across from the foot of the bed; on top of it a brass picture frame held a photograph of a handsome man. He was dressed up in a fancy frock coat and a high-collared shirt. His head tilted slightly, almost rakishly, and a dazzling smile was bursting across his face.

'Is that Mr Simms?' Bobby asked. He knew Simms was Vanetta's last name.

'No. I don't keep no pictures of that rat.' This time 'rat' was not meant nicely.

'Was *he* a rat?' Bobby asked, pointing at the picture.

'Earl? No.' Her voice softened in recollection. 'He was my first husband. My first boyfriend too. Handsomest man I ever saw. And a gentle man.'

'He sure looks young.'

'Too young for me, you mean?' Vanetta laughed. 'He must have been thirty-five years old when he had the picture took, but I wasn't more than sixteen or so. I was only fourteen when we got married.'

'Fourteen?' Bobby was nonplussed. 'Where is he now, Vanetta?'

'In heaven, baby. Leastways he deserves to be.'

'Did he get sick?' He knew about that after all.

Vanetta hesitated. 'No. He got killed in an argument on a river boat.'

He thought at first she'd said 'accident' – that seemed to kill people too. But no, she hadn't said that. 'An argument? What was he arguing about?'

'It was about cards. It happened in a card game.'

'A game?' asked Bobby, bewildered.

'Yes, but it wasn't no game really. That's how Earl made a living. Playing cards.' She shook her head and looked sorrowfully at the photograph. 'He was good to me, Bobby.' She made it sound a rare occurrence in her life.

What had made Vanetta, he often wondered in an un-articulated way. Was it Mississippi and a childhood that sounded magical? Certainly most of her stories were set there, including a few he made her repeat over and over. The black widow spider that bit her in the outhouse when she was about Bobby's age – she wouldn't say where it had bit her, laughing each time Bobby pressed the point. He winced as he imagined it crawling up from the privy pit below. She'd got so sick, she said, that she almost died.

And the rascal preacher (he was a rat too, Bobby figured) with an eye for the girls in the congregation. Once when Vanetta had been twelve years old, she had shaken his hand in the line after service and the minister had tickled her palm with his forefinger. When she'd told her daddy, he'd threatened to shoot the minister if he did it again.

They made other expeditions on the South Side, deep into the ghetto where Bobby's father would never have taken him. Bobby felt safe with Vanetta, and she never communicated any apprehension to him. Once on 63rd Street, they stopped at a barbecue takeaway, and while they waited for their order of batter-coated shrimp ('srimps' said Vanetta, and he had learned by then that it wasn't his business to tell her how to talk), a younger woman with straightened hair and a scab on her face shouted at Vanetta, 'What you doin' wit that white boy in here? He ain't yours, now is he?'

Bobby had been astonished; it never occurred to him his presence might be unwanted. Vanetta stared long and hard at the woman before she spoke. 'If you say one more word about some little boy, standin' in line, waiting his turn for his srimps, polite and quiet like everybody else, I will put your scrawny ass in that hot fryer there.'

A big man at the front of the line laughed out loud at this, and the younger woman did not reply. What struck Bobby was the sheer intensity of Vanetta's anger – he had never seen that before.

That night Bobby told his father what had happened, certain he would share his pride in how Vanetta had protected him. But his father looked unhappy, and after that Bobby noticed Vanetta didn't take him to 63rd Street any more.

'Life is about change,' Mike had taken to declaring, and Bobby felt old enough to feel his brother didn't know what he was talking about. Bobby would have said life was about *avoiding* change if you could, at least when you were happy with the way things were. And he was, if waking up each morning looking forward to the day was the evidence. In his case, he looked forward to seeing Vanetta.

Early in spring, as he left school one day, he was still wearing his winter coat, a heavy quilted jacket his father had bought for him in Michigan at a dry goods store's sale. It was too big for him, and the way the weather was warming he decided to ask Vanetta if he could wear his nylon baseball jacket the following day. Funny how he was thinking about Vanetta as he approached the corner of Steinways, for he saw Vanetta standing next to Abe, waiting for him.

'Why did you come all the way down, Vanetta?'

'We got some company today. I want you to meet someone.'

Bobby waited with as much suspicion as curiosity. Slowly from behind Vanetta emerged a tall, bony, bespectacled boy. His cheeks were high mounds the colour of mocha, and when he opened his mouth – though right now he didn't say a word – two front teeth protruded, rabbit-like. He was a little goofy-looking, awkward, with elbows that stuck out like chicken wings. His eyes, magnified by his thick lenses, seemed unnaturally round, as if the world were a source of continuous astonishment. Bobby was in no mood to feel charitable. Why was this boy here? He knew Vanetta had family – even children of her own. But they were *grown* children, no threat to Bobby, who was entirely happy to be just a little boy, if that meant he had Vanetta to himself.

The three of them walked home along 57th Street, with Bobby in a sulk. Vanetta ignored this, and talked animatedly to this boy Duval. Bobby thought he didn't look very tough, this ungainly boy, taller than Bobby but weak-looking. Bobby was confident he could out-wrestle him – even Mike admitted Bobby was strong for his age.

When they got to the apartment Duval came in with them, and Bobby hoped he wouldn't stay for long. But Vanetta said, 'Why don't you two go play outside in the back?'

'I want to stay in the kitchen,' he said, noticing that Duval hadn't said a word.

Vanetta looked at him sternly. 'You got company, Bobby. You can't just sit here.'

'Why not?' he asked.

'Come here a minute, baby,' said Vanetta, but instead of holding out her arms, she took his hand, and led him out into the hallway. There she said, 'We need to have a talk.'

'Okay,' he said, but not brightly.

'Duval's mother ain't well. You know what that's like.' He nodded dumbly. 'She's my daughter and he's my grandson. So I got to help, now don't I?' He nodded again; he could see the logic of this. 'That means some days I got to look after Duval. But I got work to do. There's laundry, and supper to fix, and the house to clean. I can't do all that and look after another little boy, now can I?'

He could see the problem all right, though he didn't know what he was supposed to do about it. He looked up at Vanetta, puzzled. She said, 'So this means I need some help. Some days you need help; I try to give it to you. You're a big boy now, so if there's some days it's *me* needing the help, well then, I'm asking you to provide it. That make sense?'

'What do you want me to do, Vanetta?' he asked, feeling he was being led down a road where he could not reverse.

'I want you to be good to Duval. Show him your toys – you got wonderful toys. Play your marbles games with

60

him. Go in the back when it's nice out – the sun's shining today – and play ball in the yard.'

Where was Vanetta in all of this? She seemed to read his mind. 'I'll be here,' she assured him, 'and Duval ain't going to be around every day. But when he is, be his friend.' She put an arm gently on his shoulder. 'You growin' up, Bobby, or I wouldn't be asking. So will you do this for me?'

He didn't answer directly, but she must have understood his assent, for he was already on his way back to the kitchen.

V

1

WITH THE SUN sunk and only the faintest moonlight shining on the tall beech in their front yard, Anna and Robert sat side by side on the deep soft sofa in the living room, each with a glass of red wine from the bottle they'd opened at dinner. Even after sundown, the air was moist and warm, and Anna wore shorts and Robert the blue jeans Sophie always teased him about – *Dad, you're too old for jeans*. Upstairs the little girl lay asleep at last, after two visits by Robert, each precipitating a hurried click of her bedside lamp switch to disguise her furtive reading.

Constrained by Sophie's presence at dinner, he had given Anna only a short account of his meeting with Duval. Now she asked, 'So what was he like?'

'I think we were both nervous. To tell you the truth, I was a little apprehensive about meeting him again.'

'Was he anything like you remembered him?'

'Yes, that was the strangest thing about it. I expected someone *harder* – after so many years in prison. But there was the same innocence I remember.'

'Innocence?'

'I'm not sure how to explain it. He seemed like a little child – a kid – who's got lost and doesn't know where to go. It reminded me of Dr Wembley.'

'Who?'

'He was my father's closest friend in Michigan. He was very commanding: we were all a little in awe of him. In a small Midwestern town the GP is next to God

– even when I was grown up I still called him Dr Wembley.

'Once when I was little, he visited Chicago – there was a medical conference at the Palmer House. My dad said Wembley hated cities, so I don't know why he went. He was going to spend a night with us in Hyde Park, and I went along with my father to pick him up. We drove down to the Loop. I remember seeing him standing in front of the Palmer House hotel, almost right under the El tracks. He was holding an old pigskin bag and looking around for us, and suddenly I realised that instead of the formidable figure I knew, he looked incredibly *anxious*. Like he'd entered a time warp and come out into a nightmare.

'Then my dad honked and Wembley saw us and came over. And by the time he got into the car all his usual authority was back. I said, "Hi, Dr Wembley," dutifully, just as I always would. But for a minute I'd seen a completely different man, one who looked utterly lost. And it was that expression I saw on Duval.'

Anna sighed. 'It can't be easy after so many years in prison. Doesn't he have a parole officer?'

'I assume so, but the guy's probably more concerned that Duval stays out of trouble than with actually helping him.'

'I don't understand why he wanted to see you.'

'He said Vanetta asked him to, to thank me for all my family had done for her.'

'Like what?'

'Not a lot. I sent her money sometimes – not very much. And I flew back for her funeral. Big deal.'

'Did he want anything else from you?'

He shook his head. 'I offered him a loan, but he wouldn't take it. He did say he was looking for work. They trained him as a TV repairman, but how many

63

TVs get repaired these days? He said he's good at carpentry, but he can't get a union job and can't seem to get a start with word-of-mouth jobs.'

'Is he broke?'

'Not yet. I figure he will be soon enough. Benefit isn't enough to live on.'

'Can't you help him?'

'He wouldn't take any money from me. He was adamant.'

'I don't mean that. There must be some job you could send his way.'

He was interested that she seemed so concerned, but then, she had always had the ability to empathise, even with those clients of hers that were manifestly undeserving.

'Not really. We've got maintenance people in the building. If there's ever a carpentry job, they just call down somebody from the main campus. That's all unionised too.'

'Did he talk about his life in prison?'

'He made only the slightest reference to it – you'd never have thought he'd spent practically his entire adult life there. He made it sound like some brief hiatus.'

'How peculiar,' said Anna. She looked pensive, as if torn in two minds.

'It was. But there was nothing unpleasant about him. It was just,' he hesitated, trying to convey the sense he'd had of slight dislocation, 'a little *spooky*.'

'Will you see him again?'

'I'm not planning to. But I have the feeling he'll want to see me. He kept talking about the past – all his relatives I can't even remember, and about Hyde Park and the apartment building. He was disappointed I hadn't been back.'

'You should, you know. Sophie keeps saying she wants to see where you grew up.'

64

'Yeah, well,' he said neutrally. It was a small point of contention; when he and Anna had first become involved she had told him all about her life, while he had baulked at her requests to hear about his past. *I'm too old even to start*, he'd said. *If we start going backwards we'll never have a future.*

Moving to Chicago had brought up this same point again. Anna had expected him to embrace his old haunts, show them to her and Sophie, expose his past at last to her curious eyes. He had come to realise she had expected him to show the way. But to Anna's annoyance, he had acted as if the city were as new to him as to her – which was how he felt, and how he liked it.

As he got up to find the bottle of wine, he realised he hadn't told her the most important thing. 'Oh, Duval also said he didn't do it.'

'*What?*' Anna demanded. He realised his announcement must have sounded bizarre, but he hadn't been able to think of any better, undramatic way to say it.

'I know. I couldn't believe it at first.' He went and got the bottle from the kitchen, and as he poured them each a refill said, 'I wish he hadn't.'

'What, said it?' Anna was sitting up now, no longer relaxed.

He nodded. 'Yes. What's the point? No one can give him all those years back.'

'Maybe he didn't do it. What do you think?'

'At the time it seemed inconceivable to me. He was a sweet kid. Now I just don't know. Part of me hopes he was guilty.' He ignored her look of astonishment. 'Otherwise I don't see how he could cope – locked up all those years *wrongly*. Not that he stood much of a chance anyway. Black kid, white girl – rape, assault. That made for a done deal in a Chicago courtroom back then. I think the jury were out for less than an hour.'

65

'How racist.' This was her one bugbear about Chicago. London wasn't exactly a multi-racial utopia, but she insisted Chicago was much worse. He wasn't sure, though he certainly found himself more conscious of race than he had been in all his years in England. But he assumed that was inevitable in a city that probably contained more black people than the whole of the UK.

'I'm not being racist,' he said now. 'Just honest. The judge was white, the prosecutor was white, the defence attorney was white; as I remember, the jury was mainly white, too. That's not racist; that's the facts.'

'I didn't mean you,' she said quietly. He tried to calm down, since when he got worked up, Anna's tactic was to take no notice anyway.

She added, 'Though you do sound rather cynical.'

'You're saying *I'm* cynical?' It was *her* politics that always imputed bad faith to any kind of authority.

She ignored this. 'What was the evidence against him?'

'Mainly the testimony of the nurse. She said her assailant had been wearing a blazer with a badge on it. Duval worked as a security guard at the same hospital, and that's the uniform they wore. She IDed him from a bunch of photographs they showed her. When she was well enough to attend a line-up at the police station, she picked him out right away. And there was blood, too.'

'Whose blood?'

'His. It was found on the girl. This was pre-DNA, but it matched his blood group.'

'Why would *he* have been bleeding?'

'I don't know. It's so long ago I can't remember. Maybe she scratched him.'

'Or it was somebody else's blood.' She put a finger to her lips, musing. 'So it hinged mainly on her identification. I don't like those cases – people so often get it wrong. I'm surprised the jury could be so certain.'

'You might not say that if you'd heard the girl testify. It was horrifying. You felt her life had been destroyed. Correction: you *knew* her life had been destroyed. By the time she got off the stand, you wanted to see the guy who'd done that to her put away for ever. And that's what happened. I'd call twenty-four years near enough to for ever.'

Before they went upstairs he rang his sister Lily on the West Coast – she was usually home by six. He could picture her in the large, spick-and-span kitchen of her ranch house in Palo Alto, with running shoes on, just back from a 10K run around the local meandering hills.

She was the most successful of the three Danziger children – at least in financial terms. She had gone west to Stanford after high school, and never moved back, building a career as a senior executive in a succession of Silicon Valley firms. During the Dot Com boom she had managed to cash in her options in a start-up company that had briefly enjoyed a paper value of two billion dollars.

Lily had persuaded their father and stepmother to move to neighbouring Cupertino five years before, when the cold Chicago winters were proving increasingly isolating for their father in particular. Although he had died two years later, Robert's father's final days had been happy ones – he'd rejoiced in the company of male residents who, like him, were veterans of World War II. Mike had said it was like living with a hundred Eddie Edeveks, and their father's last months weren't spent talking about the literature he'd taught for all his working life, but swapping stories about Basic Training.

Lily had looked after him very well (no one could question her diligence) and still saw their stepmother almost every day. Robert supposed this caring attention gave Lily the closest thing she had to family life, for she had never married, and if she had wanted children she had never said so. There had been a line of live-in boyfriends, but each time Robert learned to ask after Lance or Edward or Fred, someone new would turn out to be installed. Robert had last been to California three years before for his father's funeral. His own relationship with Lily, never close, seemed epitomised by the fact that he had stayed in a motel.

He said, 'I saw Duval today. I gather he rang you.'

'Frankly, at first I didn't even remember him.'

'How could you forget Duval?'

'His last name isn't the same as Vanetta's.'

'I suppose so.' Vanetta had never meant as much to Lily anyway. 'You might have warned me.'

'Why? Don't worry: I didn't give him your address. He just wanted your number. I thought you'd want me to give that to him. You were pals once.'

'All right. Did he have much to say?'

'Not really,' said Lily. 'But I didn't have time to talk. What could we talk about anyway? "How have you been keeping, Duval? Did you enjoy your time in Joliet?"' Her voice was dripping in sarcasm. 'I always thought he was a weirdo anyway.'

'Really?'

'Remember my panties?'

Not as well as Duval, he wanted to say, but restrained himself. You did not win an argument with Lily. She was intolerant of any conduct that she construed as falling short of her own high standards. Lily thought that if X did Y or X did not do Y, then X was a shit and a crook and a 'bad person', and *bang* – the case was closed. In Robert's view, she would have made a terrible lawyer, but thrived as a hanging judge.

He moved on. 'Anyway, how are things with you?'

'I'm fine, thank you,' she said crisply, as if she felt he didn't really care. Did he? Sometimes, he supposed.

'Have you heard from Mike?' he asked.

'Yes. His old battalion's in Iraq, so he's happy to be playing pinochle all day. Better bored than dead, he said.'

There was a pause while Robert wondered what to ask next. Small talk was never easy with Lily.

She said, 'Aren't you going to ask about Merrill?'

'I was saving the best for last. How is the old clothes horse?' He could picture his stepmother, with her hair swept back in a leonine mane, dressed like a wealthy Parisian housewife. She could not be more different from Robert's dim memory of his own mother – simple cotton frocks, bare legs and tennis shoes.

'Not at all well.' And Lily started on a long recital of Merrill's medical travails. They involved an array of internists, consultants, specialists, and even – Merrill had returned to the faith of her youth – an Episcopal minister who came each day with oleander blossoms from his garden. Only half-listening, Robert wondered how someone as healthy as his sister could find another person's maladies so interesting. Easy, he supposed; the contrast in fortunes reinforced her sense of the justice of her own.

The litany slowed at last, but before Robert could speak, Lily said, 'Hey, I found something the other day. I was finally going through all those cartons I've been storing for Merrill.'

He remembered; her garage was full of the overflow from the Chicago apartment. Books and pictures and table lamps, which would never have fitted in the smaller Cupertino rooms, but which his father had been loath to throw out. Not his father, Robert thought, correcting himself. It had been Merrill, convinced that she would one day again be living in spacious quarters.

'What's that?'

'A box of stuff that must have belonged to Vanetta. God knows why it's here. It must have been in the basement back in Chicago, and got shipped with everything else.'

'What's in it?'

'A bible, of course,' Lily said with a derisory laugh. She had always mocked Vanetta's Mississippi-born religion.

'Anything else?'

Lily sighed. 'Some knick-knacks. And a few clothes. Nothing fascinating. What should I do with this stuff? Throw it out?'

'No,' he said. 'Send it to me. I'll find out if any of her family wants it.'

'God,' she said dramatically. 'It's a big box – it'll cost a fortune to mail. Can't I just send you the bible?'

'No. Send it all. Send it Fed Ex. I'll pay.'

Maybe Duval would want Vanetta's stuff. Robert figured he owed him that much.

2

They left for the dunes Saturday morning, their wedding anniversary, driving as usual, going along Lake Shore Drive and its shoreside string of parks, then skirting Hyde Park, his old neighbourhood, driving through Jackson Park and the Museum of Science and Industry – where each time they went by, Anna would point to its immense front façade and say, 'You must take Sophie there.' He'd nod and say, 'Of course,' and this time he did wonder why he'd been avoiding his old neighbourhood since his return.

He felt a slight build-up of tension as they joined the

Skyway, an ageing highway link between the southernmost tip of Chicago and the decayed industrial hinterland of northern Indiana. As they approached the Skyway Bridge he gripped the steering wheel tightly. He stayed in the middle lane, away from the edge, trying to focus on the grey ribbon of road that rolled like a treadmill under his front wheels.

'Thanks for the flowers, by the way,' said Anna. 'They're lovely.'

He was about to ask what flowers when Sophie shouted, 'Look!' and he jerked involuntarily.

'Shhh,' said Anna next to him. 'Daddy has to concentrate.'

'I just wanted you guys to see the view.'

'That's precisely what your father doesn't want to see,' said Anna.

He could imagine the prospect on this clear sunny day: Calumet Harbor hundreds of feet below, with its stale landscape of ageing jetties full of cranes and towers and derricks, stretching out towards the vast fresh blue lake. Behind them, fifteen miles north, the skyline of the city downtown, the Sears Tower jutting up like an upended domino, in picture-postcard clarity. But he didn't dare look.

He had first been afflicted in New York. He had kept it to himself as best he could, though during those years in Manhattan colleagues must have noticed his unease, seeing him sweating and shaky in some meeting on the thirty-seventh floor; they couldn't have failed to notice how at its conclusion he'd rush for the elevator, wordless and tense until safe inside and descending.

So what a relief London had proved, where for twelve years he had rarely to venture above the tenth floor of any building. This was well below his fear line – which got triggered around the twentieth floor. From that height (and above) the view of the world below lost any sense of immediate dimension; the result was tremulous panic.

'Why don't you like heights, Dad?' Sophie asked.

Anna answered. 'Daddy gets dizzy up high, darling. Lots of people do. It's called vertigo.'

Vertigo? No, it was a mental dizziness of plain fear, which now subsided – they were on the downwards slant of the bridge and he was breathing easier. In just two or three seconds, even if the whole thing collapsed, he would fall on dry land, an irrational but critical mollifier of his terror.

They travelled, insulated by toll road, past small bungalows with tar-paper roofs, and litter-strewn parks and slime-infested little lakes. Even the gold-leaf dome on the Gary courthouse looked shabby and decrepit.

'Gary Indiana, Indiana,' sang Sophie, who had loved *The Music Man* DVD he had brought home. Then she stopped and leaned forward, her face right behind the back of his driver's seat. 'What's wrong with Indiana, Daddy?'

'What do you mean?'

'Mom says you have a . . . what do you call it?'

'Prejudice,' said Anna firmly.

'Prejudice. Against Indiana.'

He shrugged, unable to explain a lifelong bias, probably fostered by the drives like this he'd endured as a child on the way to Michigan – his father had called Indiana the New Jersey of the Middle West. Nor could he explain the odd American fixation with states, how it shaped a sense of identity only second to belonging to the country as a whole.

To Robert, Indiana meant not only the ineffably drear landscape he was progressing through now, but also a southern expanse of rattlesnake-infested flatlands, which

72

were probably no different from those of Illinois but were, well, in a different state.

The concrete jungle gradually gave way to suburb, then farmland fields of young corn as they moved east towards the Michigan border. He glanced at Anna, whose sunglasses perched on her forehead like a headband. She was wearing a summery outfit of white jeans and flowery cotton shirt, and she turned her head to the window as they passed a Victorian farmhouse, a graceful rectangle of slim white pine boards topped by a high-pitched gable. Then he remembered. 'What flowers?' he asked.

'Huh?' she said, glancing back. 'Oh, you know, the flowers I got at the office yesterday. A day early, but very nice.'

'Was there a card with them?'

'No, but I wasn't going to tell you. The florist must have screwed up.' She stretched an arm out and kneaded his shoulder. Increasingly, he found he got stiff while driving – his back, his shoulder, his knees. Not yet fifty, he feared his father's arthritis, and the prospect of twenty, maybe thirty years of pain.

He exhaled, trying to keep his voice calm. 'I didn't send you flowers.'

'Really?'

'I guess you've got a secret admirer.' Robert knew he could be hypersensitive, but figured who wouldn't be, with an ex-wife who had already run off with a man twelve years her junior?

Anna took her hand away. 'Well, it wasn't Philip, if that's what you're thinking,' she said sharply.

'I didn't say it was, honey. I just know it wasn't me. Anyway, how do you know who it was or wasn't?'

'Because I rang the florist's, to see if they'd left the card out by mistake. They couldn't find any trace of the order. They said the flowers must have been bought and delivered by the customer himself. Philip's in Washington, visiting the embassy, and why would he be sending me flowers anyway? He's my *boss*. I assumed it was you.'

'No,' he said, and glancing at Anna could see she was mystified. Leave it, he told himself, happy to know it wasn't Philip.

The Schwaggers had been meat-packer magnates in Chicago's heyday as the cattle capital of America, and had built an immense mansion in the extravagant style of a French chateau on the shores of the lake, five miles from the Indiana border with Michigan. This had burned down in the 1920s, and been replaced by two large houses, one for each Schwagger heir, large squat shingle-style houses that sat on the dunes above the sandy beach. An original coach house remained on the property, and it was this small but elegant building that Robert and Anna had taken on a long-term rental from the Poindexters, owners of one of the two houses and descendants of the original Schwaggers.

The coach house was nestled in a curve of the drive. It had no view of the lake, but was only 250 yards or so from the water. A handsome, blue cedar-shingled structure with dormer windows upstairs, it had been converted to a residence fifteen years before, and done in some style – you entered into a large kitchen, then walked past a staircase along a book-lined corridor into a two-storey living room with a railed gallery running around three sides. Upstairs there were three bedrooms; they had already promised Sophie that some weekend she could bring a friend to stay. 'If she gets one,' Anna had said six months before, though now her worries about Sophie's move to an American school had long

74

subsided. Their daughter's small private school was full of foreigners, or foreign blood – Guatemalan and Chinese adoptees, Indian children from the near North Side, a pair of French twins.

Gradually, if a little grudgingly, Robert had grown to like this weekend place, particularly the beach, which was never crowded and was layered by bottomless soft sand. Outside the coach house they had a small garden, but the illusion of a large one – there was only lawn and trees between them and the two big houses at the end of the drive. There was a garage, useful during winter, which had a spartan bedroom above it, with a tiny kitchen and bathroom.

'We can put my mother there,' said Anna, since she was threatening an autumn visit. Anna didn't like her, once describing her mother as a suburban housewife with the soul of a shopkeeper – tight-fisted, pessimistic, critical of her daughter. For someone with such *Poujadiste* views, Anna's mother had been curiously unambitious for her daughter. Robert got along well enough with her, but he could sympathise with Anna's resentment. Her father had been the supportive one, pushing her to do well at a comprehensive school where it was the norm to give up, encouraging her to go to university (Goldsmith's in London) where she had read politics and, Robert learned from a chance meeting with a former tutor, been one of the best students of her year. Robert had never met Anna's father, who had died soon after retiring. Anna claimed the prospect of spending days with his wife had literally been too much to bear.

When they arrived it had turned overcast and even Sophie didn't want to swim. They spent the afternoon puttering – Anna planting irises in a new bed by the garage, while Robert read manuscripts, with half an eye on a TV baseball game, and Sophie spent her allowed weekly two hours on his laptop playing games. For dinner he grilled chicken on the barbecue Anna and Sophie had given him for his birthday, managing not to burn it. He liked to cook at the weekends; during the week he made supper if he got home first, but then it was a chore.

They went early to bed, keeping a hall light on for Sophie, whose bedroom was at the far end of the corridor. Anna was reading a spy thriller while he scanned through the detailed accounts Andy Stephens had given him. This was the dull but worthy side of the job – he was much more interested in the actual books the press published – and by the time he had finished he was tired. In a moment Anna put down her book and turned off the light.

'How's it going then?' she asked, her voice floating through the dark.

'How do you mean?'

'Those are your results, aren't they?'

'Yep. They're pretty good.'

'You don't usually have accounts to read these days. Not like London.' This was true. He got to spend much more time actually reading what they planned to publish. 'You like that, don't you?'

'Sure,' he said laconically.

'I mean, it's better than just looking at numbers all the time.'

What was she getting at? Was she asking if he was happy they had moved to Chicago? His relief that she was so obviously satisfied with the move had masked, even to himself, his own ambivalence.

But he didn't want a heavy conversation now, so he took her literally, saying, 'Some of the books are pretty dull – like the local history stuff. A history of Lake Superior isn't going to compete with Nick Hornby for publishing excitement. But a lot of it is actually pretty good. And I guess it helps that I'm a Midwesterner when it comes to all *The Role of Michigan in the Spanish-American War* stuff.'

'And you've always got Coach Carlson,' she said, then giggled. Anna found it as comical as Robert that the memoirs of a football coach were the press's most commercial prospect.

They had taken Sophie to one football game back in November, on a cold crunch of a day, when the wind from the lake shivered the bones and kept the three of them huddled together in their mediocre seats behind one end zone. Sophie had cheered indiscriminately each time anyone had scored – usually the university, who had trounced a weak Wisconsin team, 47–10 – while Anna consumed the lion's share of the cherry brandy he'd brought in a hip flask. Once home, both Anna and Sophie said that though they had had a swell time, they would be happy to wait a few years before going again.

'Actually, I'm not sure we do,' he said. He described his phone call with Balthazar, and the agent's clear suggestion that he would move the book.

'He can't do that.' She sounded indignant on his behalf, a loyalty he admired but which wasn't always helpful: it was hard enough keeping his own feelings in check without having to moderate hers.

'I was surprised, I have to admit. After all, Carlson initially came to us; it's not as if he was wooed. Dorothy Taylor signed him up and she's never let me within a mile of him.'

'Well, she got it wrong. The witch.' She had met the woman once, at a party at the president's house, given to welcome Robert to the new job. Anna hadn't liked her at all. He remembered the two of them, eyeing each other with equal coolness. 'Can you undo the damage?'

'I'll have to try. But I think it's too late. Balthazar wouldn't have brought it up if he weren't determined to move Carlson to a New York house.'

'Maybe he just wants more money.'

'No, he said money wasn't the issue.' He had always thought publishing was more about experience than IQ, but the way Anna inevitably got the point right away sometimes made him wonder. But then she was unusually incisive. With Anna he always felt he was half a step behind; she was that quick, which even his vanity wouldn't let him deny.

'Then I doubt there's much you *can* do. Except take the blame.'

'Yep.'

'So let the witch sort it out. She made the mess. Let her unmake it.'

He thought about this as she reached out and draped an arm over his chest, which was how she usually signalled she wanted to make love before they went to sleep. But then she said in a voice that was daylight clear, 'I thought I'd have a look at the transcript of Duval's trial.'

'Why do you want to do that?' he asked. He didn't like the idea at all. Once started on something, Anna never let go.

'Your account of the trial bothered me.'

'Why?'

'You said it was a "done deal".'

He turned sideways and struggled to see her face turned towards him in the dark, but he could not make out her expression. Outside the night wind had picked up. He felt a slight chill that normally would have led him to snuggle up to her. But he kept his distance. 'And?'

'I asked Maggie Trumbull how to do it. Maggie never practised, but her husband does, so she knows the ropes.

78

She told me to call the Cook County Courts at 26th and California – that's where the archives are.'

'And what did you discover?' he asked, keeping his voice neutral, wishing she'd saved this news for the next day, when it would not disturb the intimacy of their time beneath the covers.

'There isn't a transcript. There wasn't an appeal; I guess the lawyer must have felt there weren't any grounds for one.'

He wondered why he felt so relieved. 'End of that story then.'

Anna sighed and stretched, turning onto her back. He could see her profile clearly now, and wished she would turn back towards him. 'Not quite. I've had the file pulled. I'm going down Monday morning to see what's in it.' She paused. 'I just want to have a look.'

He turned over, his back to her now. 'That's what Pandora said. Happy anniversary.'

3

It was warm by breakfast time – already in the low 70s – and he thought Sophie and he should have their ritual Sunday morning time early, before the sun got hot and high enough to burn them. He decided not to swim, and waited with a beach towel while Sophie put on her suit and hunted for her flip-flops. Anna said she'd stay behind and make lunch, tacit recognition that this was his time with his daughter.

The tarmac drive curved towards the Poindexter house and they cut across it for the beach. A banked ridge of dune on the landward side was stable enough to support a few trees – mainly aspens and poplars – but once they reached the crest there were only clumps of marram grass between them and the thin flat beach. The sun slanted in from behind, and a steady breeze gave a light running chop to the waves, which surged and broke in the brightening light.

He stopped for a minute to catch his breath, and Sophie waited impatiently.

'I bet you're sad school's out,' he said.

'*Dad*,' she said in her complaining voice.

'Anything special you want to do over the summer? I mean, other than day camp and maths.'

'Math,' she said like a little Midwesterner and he laughed. 'Can we go to another baseball game?'

'We'll see,' he said. He'd taken her once that spring, on opening day, sending a note to her school saying she had a dentist's appointment. They'd gone to Wrigley Field on the north side to see the Cubs in their old-fashioned ivy-lined stadium, rather than his own boyhood team, the White Sox, who played in a hideous, modern concrete shell just off the Ryan Expressway in an especially rough part of town. Sophie had loved it – the lush green of the playing field, the caramel corn and oversized cups of Coke, the way the crowd went wild when Aramis Ramirez had hit a home run. But as they boarded a bus to go home, they'd been spotted by Miss Every, Sophie's math teacher, who spent the rest of the term sourly asking Sophie how her teeth were.

Sophie skipped down the dune and he watched the little pink figure head towards the waves, resisting the temptation to call her back until he had come down, too. She was a good swimmer, thanks to her mother's insistence on weekly lessons, and he knew he was over-protective, with a tendency to restrain rather than release. If he let himself, he saw cause for alarm in any opportunity Sophie had for pleasure.

They had the immediate beach to themselves. Further

down he could see the Poindexters lugging a Sailfish into the water, and to the right a tall man was walking a labrador, moving away from them. Robert squatted on the sand and watched as Sophie waded to the first sandbank, then lowered herself into the water with a squeal. It was early enough in the season for the lake to be cold.

When she came out she was shivering, and he handed her the towel.

'Can we go to the boathouse?' Sophie asked.

He looked at his watch. 'If we're quick.'

They moved double-time down the beach, with Sophie racing ahead as he sang *Run Sophie Sophie Sophie, Run Sophie Sophie Sophie* in an adaptation of his own father's chant when he was a little boy in Michigan. They came to the dilapidated boathouse about half a mile down the shore, nestled far back from the shore in the lee of the dunes. It must once have been impressive, wide enough and deep enough by Robert's reckoning to hold a trio of speedboats, yet it was now little more than a shell, its pine timbers rotting or missing altogether.

They went through a missing door into the one large cavernous room. A rusting frame of a boat cradle and a work bench in one corner were all that was left of the structure's former maritime glory. The concrete floor was fractured and crumbling, the rear window frames covered with silky cobwebs the colour of spun sugar, like a tinselled Christmas tree.

'Can I play for a while, Daddy?'

He looked around uncertainly. The sun was too high now to cast much light into the room. Stop it, he told himself; let her play. 'Okay, but just for a little while. We should get back for lunch.'

He went out the doorway to the beach and heard her game begin, some concoction of imagined characters

81

and different voices. Her propensity for imaginary play stayed strong, but perhaps that was because she was an only child. Two years earlier she would have wanted him to stay and play with her; now when he came into her room in Evanston and found her on her bed surrounded by animals, she would stop her game, and ask if he could please go away so she could be 'private'. He remembered how even as a young teenager, miserable at boarding school, he had liked nothing better on returning home than to play with his marbles.

A jet ski shot along parallel to the shore, its rider in a black wetsuit. Robert watched it for a minute, wondering where the appeal of these aquatic equivalents of snowmobiles lay. They gave pleasure to a single rider, while making life a misery for anyone within earshot. The jet ski turned in a sharp arc, slowing down until the nose swung round and pointed out towards deep water again. Then the engine revved and the rider hunched forward, arms extended, his hands gripping the drumstick handles, his backside perched in the air.

'Sophie.' He turned and called towards the boathouse. She didn't call back. Patiently, he called again, but still she didn't answer. He walked to the boathouse and peered inside, saying, 'Come on, monkey, time to go.'

Sophie wasn't there.

He felt his heart beat faster, an ominous growing thump that rose up into his throat and ears. Anxiety coated him like sweat. He tried to still his racing thoughts and took a last penetrating look inside – there was simply no place to hide in the vast empty space. Then he ran out, looking around him like a camera on a dolly. He realised she couldn't possibly have come this way without his seeing her – her and the abductor he was starting to fear.

He could see what had happened: they'd been

followed, unknowing as they blithely made their way along the beach, all the while watched by someone with the patience of a hunter. His ten minutes staring goon-like at some stupid jet-ski rider would have given plenty of time to move.

His panic rose, but the logic seemed clear enough, so he went around to the rear of the boathouse. A path led up through the dune and he looked at the seemingly endless moguls of sand. As if footprints would be visible. He began to run up the dune, his feet sliding with each step in the baseless bleached grains. Reaching the small summit, he could see a large ranch-style house in the distance, several acres of lawn and hardwood trees around it. A perimeter fence at the foot of the hill screened off the property, and the fence ran on either side for several hundred yards.

He shouted out, 'Sophie, Sophie,' but could hear only his wheezy breathing.

He sensed time was critical – isn't that what the police always said? He turned and retraced his steps down the dune, accelerating downhill until he almost fell when he hit the flatness of the beach. He circled to the front of the boathouse and then out onto the beach. Scanning the stretch of sand on either side, he could just make out the Poindexter sailboat moving briskly away from shore. There was no sign of the labrador man.

'Sophie, where are you?' he cried. He found it hard to think clearly; it seemed unreal.

He started back to the boathouse, atavistically returning to the initial point of panic. He peered inside, his eyes adjusting to the light, baffled and terrified at the same time. He wondered where to look next – should he run back to the coach house and call the police? Or climb the fence over the dune and run to that house for help?

Then he made out a faint noise. A tinkling sound, gurgling like running water. He looked to his left, in the dust-enshrouded corner of the boathouse, just as he realised the noise was that of laughter – a child's laugh. Sophie stood there, with one hand over her mouth, her shoulders shaking in her deep amusement.

'Jesus,' he said in astonishment as she came scurrying out of the corner.

'I fooled you,' she said, and he felt a monumental anger replace his relief. Before he could even stop to think, he had grabbed her by the arm, and in one quick motion slapped her tiny rump. The smack echoed in the room.

Sophie clutched her bottom with both hands, a look of outrage on her face. Her mouth, gaping in astonishment, suddenly fell into the turned-down wobble of a crying jag, and she wailed in pain before running out of the boathouse.

He followed her, furious that she had let his fear grow into panic. He hadn't expected her to come out right away – inevitably her games needed some terminating flourish beyond his time limit – but she had crossed a line she had never crossed before.

They walked like this all the way home, Sophie striding angrily ahead, the hurt transferring from her bottom to her pride, Robert grimly following, ashamed of himself for smacking her, but still angry that she had played this trick on him. Fifty yards short of the coach house she sprinted down the tarmac, and by the time he came into the kitchen she had her face flush in Anna's stomach, arms around her waist, shaking with sobs.

Anna looked at him with bewilderment. 'There,' she said, as the crying slightly subsided. 'Go upstairs now and change. Lunch is ready.'

Sophie released her hold and pushed past Robert,

unwilling to look at him. When she'd gone upstairs and out of earshot, he said, 'I was scared.'

'So you had to spank her? You haven't done that in years.'

He sighed, and went to the refrigerator, where he found the last of the white wine they'd had the night before. He poured himself half a tumbler, and drank it off in one big hit. He was still shaken by the terror he'd felt. Anna continued to look at him for an explanation. He put the glass down and said, 'I couldn't find her anywhere. And there wasn't any place to hide.'

'So did you think she'd run away? Why would she do a thing like that – for goodness' sake, she's only nine. Did you have a row or something?'

He shook his head, moving around the kitchen, aware of Anna's reproving gaze. He fingered the coffee maker, then gathered up a pair of dirty spoons and put them in the sink. He barely noticed what he was doing, saying, 'I assumed the worst.' He shrugged, fatalistically, to acknowledge the weakness of his own fears. 'I'm sorry. She's getting older and more independent, and I guess I'm just not adjusting to that very well. I still think of her as four years old. And I still worry that somebody's going to snatch her.'

Anna sighed. 'That's every parent's fear. And she's not four years old any more.'

Robert felt like a faltering athlete given a pep talk by a coach. 'But she's still so little – and so pretty.'

Anna considered this; Robert supposed she had a mix of different impulses – maternal pride, a theoretical belief that looks didn't matter (easy for her to say, he thought, looking at his attractive wife), possibly even some of the same defensive anxiety he felt. He waited for her to speak, gradually gaining confidence to look her in the eye.

'Yes, she is. And most parents would be proud of that. You make it sound like it's something terrible.'

Yes, he wanted to say, I do. And that evening, driving back to Chicago – Sophie asleep in the back, her sulk having been removed by the game of gin rummy he taught her that afternoon – he realised he saw her beauty as an impediment. If she were weak or insecure, she might let herself be exploited by the men who wanted her – and since she was beautiful they would be virtually limitless in number, careening towards her like bowling balls intent on scoring. If she rejected them, they would hate her because they couldn't have her. Women would envy her: he'd seen and heard it, how they'd talk about better-looking girls – 'What has she got to worry about? If I looked like her you wouldn't catch me moaning.'

But this was years in the future, blessedly. What nagged at him now had nothing to do with the courting of his daughter in ten years' time. He'd been scared of losing her altogether.

It was dark as they came over the Skyway, and he was too tired, emotionally at least, for nerves. Anna pointed at the metropolis lying ahead of them like a lit-up checkerboard. 'This city's just so big.'

'Not as big as London.'

'I suppose, but there are so many parts to Chicago I've never seen.' When he didn't reply, she went on, 'I went to see a client the other day in the Sears Tower, and looking out I realised whole parts of Chicago are virgin territory to me.'

'We've been up along the shore. Winnetka, Lake Forest.'

'Those are suburbs. I meant the city.'

'Lots of the city just isn't that safe. And it's about as exciting as Archway.'

'We didn't stay away from Archway because it wasn't safe.'

'I don't remember any late-night walks in Brixton, darling.'

'That's different,' she protested. 'That's just one neighbourhood. If I listen to you, three-quarters of this city's off limits.'

'So? Chicago just happens to have lots of Brixtons.'

'The only place I see lots of black people is in the Loop; otherwise I'd have no idea this city is, what? Half black? Forty per cent?'

'You'd prefer a smaller percentage?' he asked, trying to make her laugh.

But she just shook her head. 'You know what I mean. It's not right they're so invisible.'

'No. It's just Chicago.'

They were on Stony Island now, about to enter Jackson Park, touching directly on Hyde Park. If he changed one lane he would probably be able to see his father and stepmother's apartment building, a thirties brick block, squat and solidly constructed. The light turned green, and as he drove forward he pointed westwards, towards the full weight of his childhood. 'With Sophie out of school, maybe we should come down here,' he said impulsively. 'I could show her where I grew up.'

4

Dorothy Taylor was back, but all morning made no effort to say hello. Robert had a lunch on Printers Row in the south Loop, then met for coffee near the Public Library with an academic keen to edit a series on consciousness. Caught by a brief cloudburst on his way back to the office, his linen jacket was spotted like an ink-stained blotter when he stopped by Dorothy's office.

She was gazing intently at a terminal full of sales figures and gave him the barest nod. She possessed what Robert thought of as classic Wasp features, despite her manifest blackness: a short sharp nose, equally angular jaw, high-boned cheeks, and a tight thin-lipped mouth. Pert, handsome rather than pretty, with nothing soft about the eyes. She dressed smartly but not showily, carrying herself with a reserve that suggested considerable professional pride. Never raising her voice, Dorothy was formally polite with everyone except Robert, and very rarely smiled – she was not, as Robert once overheard the production controller complain, 'exactly a barrel of laughs'.

'Hi,' he said cheerily. 'Welcome back. Can we have a word when you have a minute, please?'

She didn't look directly at him but did a half-turn, gesturing with a flat palm for him to sit down in the visitor's chair in front of her desk. He ignored this, saying, 'Come down in a few minutes if you can.' And walking off whistled a little to show that yet again, she hadn't got to him. He had fired enough people in his time to know that if push came to shove Dorothy could go, too.

He didn't know very much about her, and as the organisation's head didn't feel he could ask around, in the standard way one learns about a colleague. Her CV was clear but uninformative: she'd attended a public high school on the West Side, then studied communications at the local college UIC for her bachelor's degree. After five years' work for a technical publisher, she'd joined the press as a marketing assistant, then managed a nimble move to take over rights, before becoming a commissioning editor. For the last three years she had been the publishing director, and it was clear to Robert from the start that she'd wanted his job as the press's overall head. And expected it.

He often wondered why she hadn't got it. She was intelligent, thorough, reliable, and by now quite experienced. More important, a cynic might say, she was a woman and she was black – strong cards these days with a university as keen on equal opportunities as their employer. She was thoroughly respected, though not liked; if there had been an internal ballot for new director, Robert imagined she would have received very few votes. Yet popularity didn't seem to count for much these days in the choice of management; sometimes it could be a positive liability. He could only imagine that the search committee had wanted a more senior figure to spearhead the press and its anticipated move – into what exactly? They hadn't said, and not for the first time the absence of a brief made him uneasy. Sadly, Coach Carlson's memoirs seemed to be the only title most of the trustees were interested in.

'Good vacation?' he asked as she came in and sat down.

She nodded, never happy when he was familiar. 'I see last quarter was good,' she said.

Have it your way, he thought. 'We've got a bit of a problem,' he said, and detected the smallest sign of a smile – Dorothy must have thought it was strictly his problem. 'Bud Carlson wants to shift house.'

She reacted at once. 'When did he tell you that?'

'He didn't.' He described his conversation with Balthazar. Her face turned stony.

'So, what do you think we should do?' he asked.

'I'll call Coach Carlson and go see him,' she said shortly. 'I can't believe he wants to move. Somebody's got to him.'

89

'You mean Balthazar?' He found it unlikely the agent would have done the soliciting. He had plenty of fish to fry who came to his net of their own accord.

'Who else? These New York agents.' She made a prim moue with her mouth.

'Maybe *I* should go see Carlson.'

'No.' He was taken aback by her sharpness, and watched as she tried to regain her composure. 'I mean, you don't even know the man,' she said.

They stared at each other, until her eyes moved and targeted his desk instead.

He said, 'I've met him. But you're right – I don't really know him.' He made a show of thinking about it, but he had already decided. 'Okay. You signed him. You keep him. Let me know when you've had your talk.'

And he turned in his swivel chair and looked out his window, not rudely, but as a clear sign their conversation was over. He could tell she was angry, though he didn't really understand why. It was her baby and he was letting her handle things. What more did she want?

She stood up to go while he looked out at the playground, deserted in the rain. No, almost deserted; there was a lone man sitting on a bench under a sycamore tree in one corner. It seemed odd: adults were not allowed in the playground unless accompanied by a child – a neat reversal of the usual formula.

He realised Dorothy was still in his office, standing in the doorway. 'I saw an old friend of yours. He asked me to say hello.'

'Who was that?'

'Simon Hilton.'

'You were in London?' he asked, feeling somehow that his guard was down.

'On my way back.'

90

'How did you happen to meet him?' he asked. Hilton had been a colleague rather than a friend.

'I went to a launch party.' She still stood there, and he wondered what more she wanted to say. 'I met somebody else who used to work with you.'

'Oh, yes,' he said carefully. He turned round and looked at Dorothy. She was trying to suppress a smile, and looked unaccountably triumphant. Then he learned why. 'Latanya Darling said to say hi,' she declared.

He blushed, and was powerless to stop it. He forced himself to look Dorothy in the eye. She was watching his reaction carefully. Christ, he thought, and tried to keep his voice steady, though he knew it was wavering as he said, 'Thanks, Dorothy. Say hi back if you get a chance.'

She couldn't suppress a smirk before she went out the door.

His heart sank. 'Say hi' – Latanya Darling would have had a lot of things to say to him, but 'hi' wasn't one of them. So Dorothy would have had the story; doubtless it would be around the building by lunchtime the following day. To think that he had believed he could start with a clean slate, leave the knowing looks and the unspoken intimations four thousand miles behind him. He was fleeing rumours rather than reality, scuttlebutt rather than fact. How could you leave behind a mistake you hadn't even made?

In the playground, the man on the bench stood up, and seemed to look around him – the rain made it difficult to tell. Then Robert realised it was Duval.

He quickly went down the hall to the elevator. Passing Dorothy's office, he was conscious she might think he was running away, stunned by her unpleasant interjection of a previous world. He reached ground level and went outside into the rain, but despite the clear view he had all the way to Michigan Avenue there was no sign of anyone. What was Duval doing, hanging around here? It couldn't be a coincidence.

Then he saw him, across the street from the playground, sheltering from the rain under the ivy-green canopy of an apartment building. Avoiding a speeding yellow cab, he crossed the street at a run until he was alongside Duval, who was standing completely still, looking in the direction of Michigan Avenue. He wore green work pants and a faded long-sleeved shirt.

'Duval,' he said quietly.

At first he saw only bewilderment on his friend's face, then he seemed to come to and recognised Robert.

'Hey, man.'

'What are you doing here?' The answer would be crucial – if Duval said he was just passing by Robert knew he wouldn't believe him. And thereafter would be sceptical of everything his old friend said.

'Right now, I'm just trying to get out of the rain.' He gave a weak smile and Robert noticed for the first time that one of his front teeth was cracked. 'Actually, I was hoping to see you,' he explained, to Robert's relief.

The doorman in the foyer of the building was peering out anxiously. Robert signalled with a half-wave that they would be moving. 'Come on, Duval. Let's go.'

'Man, it's raining hard. I don't want to get wet.'

'Duval, there're people living in this building. We can't stay here.'

'That's what you think,' said Duval. It seemed a reflexive defiance, which was a change from the Duval he had known. Doubtless the product of too many years being told what to do.

Robert sighed; he didn't want an argument with the doorman. He could imagine its escalation, the arrival of the police. 'Come on over to the office and dry your-self out.'

He was going to take Duval's arm but thought better of it, gesturing instead for him to follow. He started to cross the street, feeling the rain on his neck as he waited to let a passing cab go by. Then he ran, dodging puddles, and he could tell Duval was behind him – he heard him laugh like a kid as he dodged the puddles, too.

Upstairs Vicky was reading Donna Tartt. He didn't introduce Duval, but led him into his office and motioned him to take the same chair Dorothy Taylor had vacated ten minutes before. He took off his own wet jacket and hung it around the back of his swivel seat.

'Bet you could use some coffee.'

Duval nodded gratefully, and Robert went out and filled two mugs from the machine next to Vicky's desk. There was sugar but no milk. 'You should go home now,' he told Vicky. It was not a suggestion.

In the office he handed the mug to Duval. 'I hope black's okay,' he said, and handed him a sugar packet and a plastic stirrer. Sitting down, he blew on his own mug and took a cautious sip. It was scalding.

'You should have told me you were in the neighbour-hood,' he said, having to work hard to sound friendly. He was disconcerted to have seen Duval, sitting on his own in a children's playground. Didn't Duval understand he shouldn't have been there? He must be on a sex offenders register – he'd been convicted of rape, after all.

'I was going to call but I left the phone number at Jermaine's. I didn't want just to show up, without an appointment, I mean.'

They sat in silence for a moment, sipping their coffee. 'It was good to see you in the coffee shop,' Duval said.

'It was good to see you, too,' Robert said, but curtly. Go on, he thought, spit it out and tell me what you want. He wondered how much cash he had in his wallet. 'Is there something you wanted to talk to me about?'

Duval didn't say anything at first. He was leaning forward now, holding his coffee, eyes on the floor. And then to Robert's horror this tall middle-aged man put his head in his hands and started to cry. Sobbing quietly, his shoulders shuddering. Robert's impatience evaporated, and he felt awful at how brusque he'd been. He wished he could comfort him. He wasn't used to seeing a grown man cry – not like this anyway, inexplicably, in his office at the end of a working day.

Duval's shoulders stopped moving, and then he lifted his head and rubbed his eyes with his hands. 'I'm sorry.'

'What's the matter, Duval? Are things tough right now?'

He shook his head and looked away. He seemed embarrassed. Then he said in barely more than a whisper, 'I'm just so lonely.'

'You must have had friends where you were,' Robert said cautiously. 'It would make sense if you missed them.'

'No,' he said, shaking his head with insistence. 'In Stateville a man ain't got no friends – not real ones. Anybody tell you the opposite is lying.'

'How about Jermaine, and his family?'

'They're good to me; I can't complain. Wasn't for Jermaine I'd be living in some halfway house or shelter. I don't know,' he said wearily, as if facing a predicament he couldn't fathom. He looked at Robert, then at his own hand, as if it could help him find the right words. 'The thing is, Vanetta was the one who visited me. Jermaine would only come every other year or so. My momma would come sometimes, but she never won her battle with junk. It was Vanetta who stuck by me all those years. And I always thought when I got out I'd be living with her. I can't tell you how long I planned that.' His voice went flat and his eyes turned dull. 'Then she passed.'

For a moment, Robert thought Duval might break down again. 'Listen,' he said gently, 'everything's going to be okay. It's just going to take a while. You're making a hell of a big adjustment. You need to find a job to keep you occupied and make some money.'

'I had me a job for a while. Three days,' Duval added with a small derisory snort. 'Fixing up the attic for some old lady lives down the block from Jermaine. Then she says all of a sudden, "Sorry, I can't be using you no more." I said, "Is something wrong with my work?" No, that wasn't the problem. So I asked her what *was* the problem. At first she wouldn't tell me. Then finally she says that her daughter was coming to stay, and she didn't think it would be a good idea if I was to be in the house with her. She said I might be tempted. I asked her, "tempted to what?" She just shook her head. She tried to pay me for an extra day but I wouldn't take her money.

'Then I got work at the launderette, fixing the machines – that kinda thing. There's a Vietnamese lady to do the laundry for people who just drop it off, and when it's busy I helped her out loading the clothes and switching them to the dryer. Then some girl in the neighbourhood starts whispering to the Vietnamese lady and next thing I know I'm out the door. Shit – I ain't done nothing wrong.'

Robert wanted to sound encouraging. 'Look at it this way – you've found some work. I know it hasn't lasted, but one of these jobs will stick.'

'Maybe,' said Duval, though he sounded sceptical. He seemed to have pulled himself together; he was sitting more upright now, and you couldn't tell that he'd been crying. 'I'm sorry that I got upset. And I shouldn't have bothered you here.'

'Not a problem,' said Robert.

'I got no one to talk to. Jermaine, he's busy, and if things go wrong he don't really want to know. He just wants me to get enough money to move into my own place. I can tell – they don't really make me feel at home.'

Robert thought for a moment, suddenly aware that he was treating this as if he had an unhappy member of staff before him, not an ex-con with beat prospects he happened to have known almost forty years before. 'Look, if you think talking to somebody would help, you can always call me.'

'I don't want no money.'

'I know that. I'm just offering you my ear. You can pay for the coffee.' He smiled to make it clear this was a joke.

'You've known me since I was little, Bobby. Why, I told somebody once you was the only white friend I ever had.'

Poor bastard, thought Robert. Duval was calmer now. He said, 'Though it seems like you always be helping me. I ain't never done much for you.'

'I don't know about that. Anyway, isn't that what friends are for?'

'Sure is. Say, you remember those three kids in the back yard at Blackstone?'

'Yeah.' He didn't want to, but he did.

'You saved my ass that time. You was brave. They were going to hurt me bad if you hadn't been there. That dark nigger, he was mean.'

He was slightly stunned that Duval had said 'nigger'. 'I didn't do that much.' He paused, finding himself drawn in by memories, none of them nice. 'Did I ever tell you they came back?'

'No.' Duval seemed startled. 'When?'

'About a year later. I wasn't so brave that time.'

'They hurt you?'

'They did their best.' He smiled insincerely, and Duval laughed.

He realised someone was at the door – it was Dorothy. She must have been listening, though she made a show of knocking on the open door to announce herself. 'Sorry to interrupt,' she said, and looked over at Duval.

He felt he had to introduce them. 'Dorothy, this is Duval Morgan.'

'Pleased to meet you,' Dorothy said crisply. Duval didn't stand up, though he managed a thin smile. Robert watched, intrigued, as they gave each other long appraising looks, some kind of weighing-up going on that he didn't understand. He felt effaced by this exchange, like a referee in a boxing ring after he's made the fighters tap gloves before the opening bell rings, then moves away, suddenly invisible.

At last Dorothy turned to Robert. 'I spoke with the coach. I'm seeing him next week.'

'Oh, good,' he said, though the memoirs of Bud Carlson seemed less urgent right now. 'Let me know how it goes.' She nodded, taking a final look at Duval as she left the room.

Duval asked in a semi-whisper, 'She work here?'

'She does.'

'You a lucky man,' Duval said, in a richly lecherous voice. And Robert was so struck to think someone actually fancied the woman he considered such a pain in the ass that he found himself joining Duval in raucous laughter, which must have travelled down the hall to Dorothy's office.

Two days later Robert's phone rang as he was getting ready to go home early for the weekend. It was raining hard, heavy drops smeared the windows of his office, and would no doubt snarl up the Friday-night traffic on the Drive. He planned to leave early to beat the rush.

'Hey, man, it's Duval.'

'You okay?' he asked, trying to keep impatience out of his voice.

'I'm all right. Might have me a job.'

'Glad to hear it. Doing what?'

'I'll tell you if it comes through. Don't want to jinx my chances.'

Robert was about to suggest meeting the following week – anything so he could get away – when Duval said, his voice turning husky, 'Bobby, you remember what I said when we were leaving the coffee shop?'

'I do.' The last thing he wanted to get into.

'Well, you see, I'm going to need a lawyer if I'm going to get anywhere with this. Do you think you could find me one?'

'I don't know, Duval. I've only been back—'

'You must know some lawyers.' No note of pleading to the voice, just a flat statement of fact.

'The thing is, Duval, I'm not sure how much a lawyer can do. I'm worried you'll just be disappointed.'

There was a long pause. 'Let me take that chance.'

'I'll see what I can do.' It seemed impossible to say no.

'I could find him a lawyer,' said Anna. They were in bed that night, the lights off, lying half-wrapped in each other – it had been weeks since they had last made love. The rain had stopped, replaced by a warm muggy front, and they had pushed the blankets down, leaving only a sheet for cover. Through the screened open window a mild breeze off the lake cooled the room like a low fan.

'I don't want to encourage Duval – he'd just be wasting time and money.'

'If he's not working much, time isn't a problem, is it?'

'He needs to get on with his life. Not go backwards. What difference would it make now?'

She put her head on his arm, her soft hair splayed out over one side of his chest. 'I had a look at the file, you know.'

He sighed. 'What was in it?'

'Not a lot. The names of witnesses, and lawyers, and the name of the judge. Arthur Bronstein. He's dead – I found an obituary in the *Tribune* archive.'

'You went to the archive?' He knew he sounded irritated, but he was.

'No, I Googled him. And I didn't have to go to 26th and California for the file. They were willing to fax me the contents.'

'Anyone else listed?'

'The witnesses. Mainly cops – I suppose the ones who first found the girl and then the ones who interviewed her when she IDed Duval.' Her voice hesitated, skipping a beat. 'And I found the name of the girl.'

He remembered her appearance on the stand. She'd had long, straight auburn hair, a pale complexion with girlish freckles on both cheeks. Her appearance had seemed neither sexy, the unwarranted male expectation in rape cases, nor virginal. Just drab, a limp sadness to her face that her physical carriage – she walked awkwardly, one shoulder sloping slightly down – did nothing to dispel.

'What was it?'

'Peggy Mohan.'

'I wonder what happened to her.'

'Google wasn't much help, unless she won the 400-metre relay at Boise High School last year.'

So Anna had been looking. He couldn't understand why she was getting so involved. Hadn't she plenty to do already, between her job and looking after Sophie and, hopefully, him?

'There was also a Peggy Mohan in Paris who teaches English for foreign learners. Do you think that's the equivalent of those cards in the windows of London newsagents, offering "French lessons"?'

He gave a small grunting laugh and stretched his hand down and laid it, half-cupped, half-taut on the soft surface of Anna's belly. He could not dislodge the image of the Peggy Mohan he had seen. She had sat rigid in the witness box, her voice monotonic at first, as subdued as her clothes. Yet within minutes Robert had been perched on the edge of his seat, oblivious to everything except the horrifying words of her story.

He said, 'After what happened, I can't blame her for hiding.'

6

On Saturday morning he let Anna lie in while he cooked pancakes with lemon and sugar for Sophie. They'd established that Anna would stay at home, waiting for Mr Pica, the plumber – since as she said, 'I want to be present at an unprecedented event – a plumber coming out on a Saturday.'

He hurried Sophie through breakfast, since he wanted to beat the inevitable crowds at their first stop in Hyde

Park, the Museum of Science and Industry. She was already dressed, but wasn't wearing her usual day camp gear of khaki shorts, T-shirt, and baseball cap. 'Those are smart,' he said of her white trousers.

'Mom bought them for me.' He noticed she wore a blouse with a collar, and then the penny dropped. She wanted to look grown up for this expedition.

They drove along the Outer Drive with the lake crystal blue and the air windless and clear. After they passed the vast soulless convention centre of McCormick Place, the lake front turned into a series of green parks, strung together like a links course along the shore.

'Nobody's there,' said Sophie, pointing at them.

It was still early, not even nine o'clock. Glancing to his left, Robert could only see a few men walking their dogs. 'It'll start to get busy later on. People come out in their cars and have barbecues – see the grills they can use? And they play touch football and frisbee. When we come back later you'll see what I mean.'

'Could we have a barbecue there?'

'Well, maybe not right here, but we can have a barbecue at the dunes.'

'Can't we come here?'

He shrugged. How much did you say, how much did you ignore? 'It's not that safe over there for you and me.'

'Why?' she asked, with her mother's tenacity. He admired the trait, though it made him feel that nothing he said was taken at face value.

'It just isn't,' he said shortly. He didn't want to say it was because they were white and the parks there were strictly African-American. He thought of his conversation with Anna, her complaint that so much of the city seemed off limits. It was depressing after so many years to find this kind of de facto apartheid surviving, but it would be reckless to act as if it did not exist.

The museum was the one surviving building from the 1893 World's Fair. It was a Chicago Parthenon, with Corinthian columns and an enormous gabled roof. Long crumbling inside and out, the museum had recently been entirely renovated. Robert parked the Passat in a new underground lot that could have belonged to one of the swanky condominium towers on the North Side.

In his youth the museum had held state-of-the-art exhibits that were part toy, part puzzle, part learning tool: a captured German U-boat, a coal mine deep in the building's bowels, a massive train set running at a child's eye level, even an early computer that never lost at tic-tac-toe. Robert was pleased in a nostalgic way to find those exhibits still there; he'd forgotten the incubator of chicken eggs, which Sophie promptly fell in love with, insisting on watching one slowly crack bit by tiny bit, until a small beak poked through an opening and the shell wall imploded, exposing a new-born chick, which emerged hungry, curious, and cross.

After almost two hours, half of him hoped Sophie would want to call it a day. But she said firmly, 'Now I want to see where you grew up.' So they retrieved the car and driving up into full sunshine went west.

He drove under the Illinois Central tracks and along the north side of the Midway, a mile-long expanse of grass, divided into three by avenues for cars, with an excavated middle stretch that was flooded each winter to form a skating rink. He pointed out his old school to Sophie, and further along his own father's office in the ornamented Gothic stone of the university's original buildings. He was hoping he might get away with a sighting-by-car tour, but no, Sophie said she wanted to go to his old haunts on foot. So he turned around and came back to Blackstone Avenue, the leafy tree-lined street of his boyhood, where so many members of the

English Department had lived that it was known as the English Channel. At 58th he turned and turned again until he found a solitary parking place a stone's throw from the Cloisters.

They were in the posher part of Hyde Park, famous as the site of the University of Chicago, and as an integrated oasis in a fiercely segregated city. Despite the conservatives associated with the university (like the Chicago economists whom Pinochet had found so helpful) the neighbourhood was a hotbed of liberalism, and fabled as the city's one integrated neighbourhood. In Robert's youth, it was viewed with suspicion by the rest of a deeply conservative city, for Hyde Park residents were thought to have long hair and smoke marijuana; its streets held too many bookstores and coffee houses. It was a kind of Berkeley of the Middle West.

His father Johnny had done his best to ensure his children grew up untouched by this, for he had been a conservative, not in a political sense (he had little interest in politics) but in his deep-rooted aversion to change. Johnny Danziger believed in the university he worked for, the small town in Michigan where he had a summer house, and in the US Army, where he claimed to have learned more than in college or graduate school. It was the army that had made him suspicious of intellectuals (though he was a card-carrying one himself), political radicals, and the counterculture Hyde Park embraced. Robert could think of no one else in Hyde Park with a son (Mike) who had made the military a career, nor imagine any resident who would have been so proud of the choice. No wonder Johnny and Mike had been so close.

'That's where Papa and Merrill lived,' he said as they got out, pointing to the heavy-set thirties building.

He was astonished to find Jackson, the doorman, on

103

duty in front of the building, looking as if it had been ten minutes instead of fifteen years since Robert had last seen him. He stood ramrod tall in the building's entrance, wearing a blue suit with gold chevrons on its shoulders. A wide-brimmed grey dress hat was tipped back slightly on his head. The only sign of ageing was Jackson's moustache, now the colour of snow.

Merrill had adored him; he would sweep open the door for her like a royal flunky, and let her park for hours in the strictly drop-off zone in front. In return, each Christmas Eve she gave Jackson a wad of bills in an envelope. Robert remembered seeing him one year, thanking Merrill effusively, then counting his stash like a bookie in the privacy of the doorman's cubicle.

With Robert and Mike, Jackson had dropped the obsequious façade, and the banter that took its place contained an ill-concealed hostility bubbling just below the surface.

Robert called out now, trying to sound cheerful, 'Hello, Mr Jackson.'

The doorman looked at him sceptically. Why did I think he'd remember me? thought Robert. 'I'm Johnny Danziger's son. I wanted to show my daughter the fountain. Would that be okay?'

'Be my guest,' said Jackson unenthusiastically.

The building's four tiers of apartments were ringed around a small, open courtyard that contained a water garden lined by low box hedges, through which two tiled channels carried flowing water from a small stone fountain at the far end. The space had seemed almost magical to Robert when he and his father moved here, an improbable sanctuary of greenery during the gloomy winter months, and about the only thing he liked in this vast brick tomb of an apartment block.

Yet now it seemed pathetically small; he could tell

Sophie was unimpressed. 'Come on, Dad,' she said, as if the real show were somewhere else.

'Thanks,' he said to Jackson as they left the building.

'This your little girl?' asked the doorman.

'That's right. Sophie, say hello to Mr Jackson,' he said, sounding like his own father, a stickler for manners.

She obeyed dutifully, smiling shyly.

'She *is* a pretty little thing. You sure he's your daddy?' He laughed, pointing at Robert. Sophie looked confused.

'Yeah, she's sure,' said Robert.

'You must have got yourself a beautiful wife then.'

'I do, Mr Jackson. I do.'

Jackson crooked his finger at Sophie. 'Because this girl ain't got nothing of your ugly mug at all.' He cackled at his own joke.

'Thank you, Mr Jackson. Nice to see you too.'

They walked along 58th Street and he could see that the old cinder track of his school had been modernised, the softball fields replaced by new tennis courts. They passed Robie House, one of the classic Frank Lloyd Wright prairie houses. His father said that living so close to it was like having a Monet next door. For Robert its beauty had had nothing to do with its low-slung roof, prairie-emulating in its sweep, or the Japanese influence on the building's vertical windows. He'd loved it because it was a *house* – his dream. Anything but an apartment.

They were coming into his father's heartland now, approaching the main quadrangle of the university. His father had spent seventy years in this strange place – undergraduate, Ph.D candidate, lecturer, professor. From podgy sophomore to lean ex-GI, mature family man, then ancient emeritus; the constant in his life had been the institution, and sometimes Robert had thought his father loved the university more than his family. Johnny had often boasted that there were more winners of the Nobel

Prize at his cherished University of Chicago than at any other university in the world. Yet for all this intellectual snobbery (how his father had sniffed at the Evanston counterpart where Robert now worked), the place was chippy about its subordinate status to the more famous confreres on either coast – Harvard and Yale in the east, Stanford out in California. Insecurity was a Midwestern disease.

'Did Papa grow up here?'

'No. It just seemed that way.'

'But he was from Chicago. Mom said so.' Puzzlement spread like concern across her face. She was young enough to think that mysteries were unfair.

'He grew up in Winnetka.' Then a small town, now a suburb of great affluence.

In bright sunshine, the buildings of the campus looked beautiful in a way Robert always found preposterous, for they seemed so out of place. Their medieval Gothic stone belonged in Oxford or Cambridge, not here in this brash, rugged city on the edge of the plains. He took Sophie around the many small courtyards and grass swards, with the nooks and crannies that he'd loved as a boy. He showed her Botany Pond, where Robert had once seen a snake swallow a frog, and he told her the story of how corn had grown for many years on the main quadrangle's lawn, the result of an undergraduate prank that, almost unbelievably, had literally taken hold. Then they peeked inside Bond Chapel, small and tucked away, almost Calvinist in its grey stone austerity.

'Papa was married here.'

'To Merrill?'

'Well, yes,' he said, startled. 'But also to my own mother.'

'I didn't used to understand your real mummy died.' She was shifting back to little-girl speak, which was when her Anglicisms – 'mummy' – re-emerged. 'How old were you?'

'Oh, five or so. Almost six.'

'Old enough to remember her?'

He gave a grunt. 'Old enough to think I did.'

'And Vanetta? You remember her okay?'

'Of course. Haven't I told you all those stories about her?'

Sophie giggled. '"Child,"' she said, imitating him imitating Vanetta. '"You best be good. You little rat you."' Her eyes screwed up in her own effort to remember. 'Was she "fried foods"?'

'No, that was Gladys.' Who had barely used the oven, happiest in front of a skillet of sizzling lard.

'The witch?'

'If a witch can weigh 300 pounds.'

'Was Vanetta fat?'

'No,' he said, almost offended. 'Vanetta was buxom. You know what that means.' He put both hands in front of his chest and Sophie giggled. 'She wasn't skinny, but she wasn't fat.'

'You know, Daddy, when I was little I used to think Vanetta was your mother.'

'She couldn't have been my mother, darling. Vanetta was black.'

'Why does that matter? Wendy Chang's Chinese, but her mother's not.'

'Okay.' It was certainly true that he had wanted Vanetta as his mother, though he had kept the desire a secret, for fear of being laughed at, especially by Lily. His father would not have liked to hear it, either, at least not once Merrill appeared on the scene – for his father must have hoped Merrill would take a mother's place in Bobby's heart. Fat chance.

He remembered trying to explain to his ex-wife, Cathy,

107

how important Vanetta had been to him. 'Don't tell me,' she'd replied, then adopted a mocking tone. '"She was like a member of the family, and like a mother to me. And she loved me just as much as I loved her."' Her voice grew scathing. 'Neatly ignoring the fact that she was paid to be nice to you. Which small detail never seems to enter into your head.'

Sophie now grasped his hand, a rarity – he had to force himself to keep from clutching hers when they crossed streets, or she complained he was treating her like a baby. 'Dad, when you met Mom did she have a boyfriend?'

One or two, he was going to say, though initially it had seemed a dozen of the creeps were hanging around. He said, 'No. That's why I became her boyfriend.'

'What about you?'

'You know I was married before.'

She nodded seriously. 'Why did you get . . . not married?'

He suppressed a sigh. She was too young to tell, though there would never be good reason to give his take on the busted flush of his former alliance. Justice had nothing to do with being a good father; through the angry mist of his own sense of grievance, he retained enough sense to see that. 'Sometimes people drift apart,' he said deliberately. 'That's what happened to us.'

Glancing sideways he could see she was unhappy. 'What's the matter?' he asked. 'Come on. Tell me what's wrong.'

She shrugged, then spoke with an obvious effort at nonchalance. 'Couldn't that happen to you and Mom?'

So that was it. He tried to sound equally casual. 'Nah, I'm too old to drift.'

He saw the question forming in her young head – But is Mom? – and watched as she decided not to pose it.

How would he have answered it anyway?

Theirs had been an accidental marriage, but it seemed to work. They had met when he was at a low ebb – still angry about his wife's desertion, ducking the obsessive attentions of Latanya Darling. He'd been angry, depressed, impulsive – a mess. Yet what had stabilised him in such a brief time after meeting Anna was the need to stabilise *her*. Her mad life – relentless hours helping asylum seekers, with one heartbreaking story after another; her personal life a chaos of exploitative men. She'd hung onto Robert like a shipwreck victim clasping to a buoy, and then one day he realised he was in love with the victim.

He and Sophie had a pizza at the Medici, once a sad coffee house with bohemian pretensions located further down the street. Now it was lively and full of affluent students. Sophie was quiet, unusual for her since she was young enough to find restaurants exciting. He asked about her day camp, and she said it was okay. He asked if she liked Mrs Peterson, the cleaner who looked after Sophie when Anna worked a full day, and again, she said she was okay. Would she like it if they went to the dunes house the following weekend? *Okay.* As he waved to the waiter for the bill, he wondered what was on her mind.

Sophie finished her Sprite with a final gurgle, then took the straw out of her mouth. 'Who's Philip?' she asked, and wouldn't look Robert in the eye.

'Philip? I know a couple of them. Maybe Mummy's boss? Why?'

'Just wondered.' The waiter brought the bill and Robert pretended to study it as he watched Sophie out of the corner of her eye. She had her eyes fixed on her empty glass and was swinging her legs under the table. He waited until she said, 'I heard Mom talking on the phone.'

'To someone named Philip?' he asked, taking his wallet out of his jacket.

'Yes. I heard her say, "Oh, hello Philip."' Sophie did a very good imitation of her mother's English tones.

'Yeah, well, he's her boss. He's allowed to phone.'

Sophie paid no attention. 'And then I heard Mom say, "I'm flattered."'

Flattered? Why flattered? He didn't want to hear any more, but he knew Sophie needed to tell him. I mustn't react, he thought, though he felt anxiety and dread, as if a hoodlum had joined them at the table. 'He was probably praising Mom for her work. She's very good at her job.'

'Mom said, "I'm flattered but you know my situation." Then she saw me and she said, "I've got to go," and she hung up real fast.'

'Well,' he said slowly, as images he didn't want to have raced through his head, 'I think Philip would like Mom to spend more time at the office than she does.'

Sophie looked unconvinced. 'He called her on a Saturday.'

Why did she have to be so quick? 'I wouldn't worry about it, you know,' he said, and gave her a reassuring tap on the forearm. He didn't think he could sit there calmly any longer, so he left money on the little plastic tray – far too much money, the waitress would think he was crazy or in love with her. He stood up and said, 'Come on.'

He was intent now on distracting Sophie, worried that on their walk back to the car she would want to ask more questions about 'Philip', or worse, provide more revelations. He tried to tell himself he was being stupid. Could Anna really be interested in this man? Would she contemplate an affair – as in new city, new job, so new lover too? He didn't want to think so,

110

though it was clear her boss was keen on Anna. Why not? he thought, briefly cruising a wave of self-pity, I'm just an old has-been with a cloud over my head.

Relief came with anger. He thought, If that prick calls her again on a Saturday I hope I get to answer the phone. He laughed as he remembered his brother Mike's reaction when a fellow officer had made a pass at Mike's wife: 'I hit him so hard he didn't get up.' A simple enough solution, and Mike had spent enough hours teaching him how to fight. But if he did do something stupid, what satisfaction it would give Latanya Darling. 'See,' she'd say jubilantly, 'I told you so.'

At the corner the news-stand had been replaced by a coin-operated machine full of copies of the *New York Times*. He pointed down Kenwood Avenue and its big houses and tall, shady trees towards his old school. 'This is the way I walked home from school.'

'You walked home by yourself?'

'Not when I was little. Vanetta used to wait for me right here. Sometimes Duval would be with her.'

'Who's Duval? Mom mentioned him on the phone, too.'

'To Philip?' he asked in alarm.

'No. I don't know who she was talking to. Maybe you.'

He shook his head.

Sophie said, 'Can I see where you lived back then?'

'There's not much to see. And it's a bit of a walk.'

'It can't be that far if you walked home when you were little.'

'You should be a lawyer, too,' he said, starting down 57th Street.

Sophie seemed happier now, taking his hand again for a bit, then skipping with excitement, as they got closer to his old apartment block. They came to it from

111

behind, where he tried the back gate, but it was locked. Frustrated he gave it a rattling shake, then heard footsteps on the other side. The gate swung suddenly open.

'Can I help you?' The voice was aggressive and belonged to a young woman, crisp-faced with short straight brown hair, wearing jeans and a man's shirt. She seemed keyed up.

'I'm so sorry. I grew up here. I was just going to show my daughter.' He waved vaguely towards the yard on the other side of the gate.

She shook her head uncomprehendingly. 'Did someone famous live here once? I mean, like Barack Obama?'

Robert laughed. 'Don't think so. There was a senator named Paul Douglas – he had his mailing address here, but I never saw him.'

She was looking at Sophie. 'You might as well come in,' she said. They walked along the paving stones until he was in the back yard again, trying to understand what had changed. Something had.

The black iron fire escape that ran like snakes and ladders up the back of the building had been painted a dark green that did nothing to diminish its skeletal starkness. The charcoal-coloured brick needed repointing, and in the yard itself the lawn was high and unmarked as virgin pasture – no kids must play here these days. Along its edge, a shallow flower bed ran the length of the adjacent wall of the old Christian Science church, studded with grisly marigolds.

The woman hovered behind them, as he pointed out to Sophie the windows of the bedroom he and Mike shared. There was something sad about the place. He had expected the site of so many memories to turn out to be smaller, though not so drab, almost grim. Yet that wasn't the difference he sensed.

'There's been this other guy around,' said the woman.

'I don't think he lived here though.' Behind the sharpness to her voice, Robert detected unease, even fear.

'What did he look like?'

'Tall. About your age.' She hesitated. 'He was African-American. If I see him again, I'm going to call the police.'

'Don't do that. I'm pretty sure I know who it is. He used to play here when he was a kid. With me,' he added, hoping this would reassure the woman. She looked doubtful. 'Honest, he's harmless.' He turned towards her, ready to do more persuading.

She said, 'He keeps going on about some tree that used to be here. It doesn't make any sense.'

And then Robert understood what had really changed. He looked at the back corner of the yard, near the high wall; here the grass hadn't taken. 'When did they cut it down?'

The woman looked at Robert, clearly wondering if he were crazy, too. 'Cut what down?' she demanded.

VI

HE WISHED IT would stop raining. Spring seemed to be coming at last, yet now he couldn't go outside. The winter had been long and lethal, a succession of snowstorms and freezing cold. After the first big drop of snow in January, he and Duval had rushed outside and made an enormous snowman, with stones for eyes and a carrot for his nose. It was speckled with grime in two days, and the snow on the ground soon turned crusty and hard, losing all its moisture – no matter how hard you tried to make snowballs, they collapsed into dusty powder. The severe cold made it impossible to stay outside for long – when he and Duval came in, their fingers could barely unsnap the buckles on their rubber boots.

During the previous spring, he'd groaned each afternoon when he saw Duval standing across from Steinways, waiting with Vanetta. He remembered his promise to Vanetta, but he didn't like it. Yet even on the days when Duval was there, Vanetta had the knack of making Bobby feel special. She still called him 'my baby', and though he was growing fast, she'd hug him and squeeze his shoulders, until he'd laugh and back away. 'You too big for a hug?' she'd say mock-wistfully, and he'd shake his head, then lay it on her breast just like he did when he was little.

Slowly he got used to Duval, and he understood that something else was going on that explained Duval's presence. He had overheard his father talking to Vanetta, when they must have thought he couldn't hear. 'I'm glad it's working out okay – it's good for them both to have

114

someone their own age to play with. I just hope your girl can make a go of it.'

'She's clean right now, Mr Danziger. She has been for eight months now.'

'Glad to hear it,' his father said, and then they talked about the vacuum cleaner and whether they needed a new one right now.

But in the autumn something had changed.

'Baby,' said Vanetta to Duval one afternoon, 'you're coming home with me tonight.'

'Yes, Vanetta,' is all he said, without asking any questions.

Later, back in the bedroom as they were setting up soldiers, Bobby asked, 'Why are you going to Vanetta's? Is your mom sick?'

'I don't know what she is,' said Duval.

'Why not? She's your mom.'

'Sometimes she is and sometimes she's not. With her it ain't a regular thing.'

Right now watching the April drizzle, Bobby yearned to be outside. Life in the apartment was cramped. It had eight rooms, but there were only two he was always allowed in – the bedroom in the back he shared with Mike, and the kitchen, where Vanetta was ensconced from four o'clock until she left for the night with Duval.

Duval was friendly, cheerful and he didn't seem to have a temper – which Bobby knew was not the case with himself. Most important, he seemed happy to do whatever Bobby wanted – 'Okay,' he'd say to almost any suggestion. That was the problem – sometimes Bobby didn't really want to do anything but curl up with a book. But Duval didn't like to read – 'I gets too much of that in school,' he said. If Bobby lay on his bed with a book, Duval would watch the old black-and-white TV, then after a while Vanetta would come back and switch it off. 'You watched enough now,' she'd say to her grandson. Which would leave Duval with absolutely nothing to do. If he went up to the kitchen Vanetta would send him back – 'to play'. And Bobby would sigh then, put his book down and try to think of something they could do.

There were only so many games they could play. Board games grew boring, and make-believe wore thin. They'd take a blanket and fold it up, then one of them would tuck three dozen plastic soldiers in its fold, defending a mountain pass, like the Germans fighting in Italy in the history book Bobby had read. The resulting game could easily take until it was time for Duval to go home with Vanetta. But if you played it every day, it got dull.

Though now at least there was music.

Theirs was not a musical family. There was a piano in the living room which Lily played dutifully in preparation for her weekly lesson; no one else touched it. His father had the radio on when he made breakfast – WMAQ, where show tunes and crooners from what seemed to Bobby a Neolithic era alternated with the traffic reports and weather forecast. And Vanetta listened to the radio too – WVON, the Voice of the Negro – as she ironed in the kitchen, humming to the songs. Once when her heroine Aretha Franklin got played, she burst into song herself, singing along to 'Do Right Woman', then laughing when she saw Bobby staring at her in amazement.

Then Mike got a new record player for Christmas. He had been a Beach Boys fan, once attending a concert at McCormick Place; for the first time their father let him take the car. Lately, he had been buying harder-sounding stuff, the Rolling Stones in particular; he played 'Sympathy for the Devil' over and over, until Bobby begged him to stop.

But Duval inspected Mike's collection of LPs with disbelief. 'Where are the 45s?' he asked.

'Mike doesn't buy those. He says they're a waste of money.'

'Yeah, but where's the real stuff, man?' He had started lately to call Bobby 'man', which to Bobby seemed grown-up and cool.

'What real stuff?'

'You know, the Temptations, Marvin Gaye, the Four Tops. I don't see none of that here.'

And the next time he came to play he brought a dozen 45s in his school bag, a green book bag Bobby had been glad to give him now that his father had bought him a satchel case. He put a record on and the room filled with a slow deep beat. Duval turned up the sound. Fortunately only Vanetta was home.

It was 'What Becomes of the Broken Hearted', familiar-sounding from the radio. But the actual record sounded different, almost as if the singer was in the room with them. It was beautiful.

He saw that Duval was singing along, and then to his astonishment he realised that the pure voice he'd been marvelling at was Duval's. His friend was simply amazing: he had a rich melodic voice that didn't seem to belong to his little boy's body. When the scratchy needle dug into the vinyl grooves, the slightly buck-toothed geeky guy was transformed, as he shed all his inhibitions and lost himself in the music.

When the record ended Duval smiled shyly. 'That's Jimmy Ruffin. Good, ain't it?'

He had to say something. 'You can really sing, Duval. You're great.'

Duval shook his head modestly. 'You should hear my cousin Jermaine. Now *that* is singing.'

* * *

117

One Wednesday when they met across from Steinways as usual, they didn't head for the apartment but instead got in Vanetta's car. 'Are we going to your place?' asked Bobby as they drove west out of the neighbourhood, through Washington Park and along Garfield Avenue.

'Nope,' said Vanetta. 'It's a surprise.' And for a moment Bobby fantasised that he and Duval were being kidnapped, taken by Vanetta away ... to where? Mississippi, of course, and he wondered what it would really be like, since he was of an age now to know intuitively that dreams did not always correspond to fact. Maybe the farm wouldn't have all that Vanetta said it did, yet he was sure there would be the small pond where Vanetta said they'd swum as kids, and the watermelon patch and a peach tree, too. And even though he knew deep down that a grandmother couldn't really be kidnapping her grandson, he continued to fantasise that they were on the way to Mississippi until Vanetta pulled up sharply in front of a vast old building of brown stone with a sharp pitched roof and a wooden bell tower that needed painting.

'This is our church,' Vanetta explained as they got out of the car and went inside. She led them into an enormous room which looked like a dilapidated assembly hall in a school. Rows of chairs sat in lines on the hardwood floor instead of pews, and although the windows were tall and thin, none of them held stained glass. There was an altar of sorts, tucked at the back of a large, projecting stage, where people were now congregating. A few were as young as Duval, but most were teenagers or young adults, with a handful of older people. Gradually they assembled into two outward-facing semicircles, one male and one female, and the lone figure of the choir leader stood facing them, his back to the audience.

'Go on, boy,' Vanetta said to Duval now. 'Get on up there. We late enough as it is.'

When the rehearsal began Bobby and Vanetta sat down on two of the chairs. The singing began with several old Negro spirituals, including a solo by a pretty girl with bad teeth who hit the highest note spot on. Vanetta leaned over and whispered, 'She sang with Mahalia Jackson last year downtown.'

'Oh,' he said, trying to sound impressed, though he didn't know who Mahalia Jackson was. After the spirituals came hymns, of the staider sort he'd heard before on the rare occasions he went to church – usually Rockefeller Chapel at the university, when his father roped them all in for service on Christmas Eve and Easter morning. The rhythms seemed looser here, the range of the voices greater. When a skinny boy stepped forward to sing a solo, Vanetta nudged Bobby. 'That's Jermaine, Duval's cousin. Listen to him now.'

And he had a sweet alto voice that projected well. Bobby wondered if Duval would have a solo, too, and was disappointed when he remained in the chorus. It wasn't fair, thought Bobby, since he knew how well his friend could sing. Didn't people understand? It didn't seem right. He told Vanetta they should let Duval sing, and she squeezed his shoulder. 'He's good, but lots of them can sing real good too. You just prejudiced on account he's your friend.'

The choir stopped then for a while, as the choir leader talked them through their performance. Vanetta got up and led them to a back corner of the room where two trestle tables had been set up, with paper tablecloths. Six or seven older ladies were putting platters and bowls of food out, and there were paper plates and plastic cutlery. An enormous tin coffee receptacle sat at one end, four stacks of foam cups next to it.

The women all greeted Vanetta warmly – 'Hey, V!' and 'How's it going, baby?'. Feeling shy, he tried to hide behind her.

'Come on out here, Bobby, and show yo' face.' Vanetta sounded different here, her voice more thickly Southern, and black. He let her take his arm and lead him out. 'This here's Bobby,' she declared. 'Ain't my baby cute?'

'*Your* baby?' one of the woman said, snorting. 'I ain't seen any white boys in your family before. There some secrets you been keeping from me, sister?'

Someone else snickered, and Vanetta turned towards her. Her teeth were clenched, and her soft jaw jutted angrily. For a moment, Bobby thought she was going to lose her temper, just as she had on 63rd Street, but she managed to control herself, and her features grew more composed. 'Ain't no secrets, Wanda, as you well know. Let's be nice now, we're in church.'

And for the first time Bobby felt self-conscious, wondering now if people were looking at him because he was white, and if they were wondering why he was there. He hated feeling like this, because he had been having such a good time. He liked the church, and these laughing, joking women, and the trestle tables loaded with wonderful food – they had corn on the cob, and fried chicken, and green bean salad and coleslaw, and soft dinner rolls with butter sticks piled up and jelly in a little dish, and pies and cake for dessert – and the singing had been riveting. He found himself wishing he could blend in unnoticed. It would be nice to be black, he thought, if only for the afternoon.

He had some friends at school, though not many, since he was quiet there in a way that would have been unthinkable at home. He was happiest now, anyway, with Duval, since his friendship took place under the loving eye of Vanetta, the closest thing to a mother he had. When he was invited to a sleepover by his classmate Ernie Dreisbach, he told his father he didn't want to go.

'You sure?'

'Not unless he invites Duval.'

'But Ernie doesn't even know Duval.'

'Then I don't want to go.'

A few minutes later he found his father in his study, in the short hall off the kitchen. 'Dad, could Duval sleep over here sometime?'

'Don't you see enough of Duval during the week? Besides, we haven't really got room. I can't make Mike sleep on the sofa in the living room so you two little monkeys can raise Cain all night.'

What was Cain? 'Then maybe I could go sleep over at Duval's.'

'That's not a good idea,' his father said.

This usually signalled the end of any discussion, but this time Bobby didn't give up. 'Why isn't it a good idea, Dad?'

His father sighed. 'There aren't any white people where Duval lives.'

'But there aren't any black people here.'

His father's silence told him he had won the argument; it also told him it was not a victory he was going to get to enjoy.

Merrill was an increasing presence in the household. Bobby knew by now that she was a widow, and that her husband had been a surgeon at the university hospital. Like her husband, Merrill was from New England, which she never let the Midwestern riffraff she was now surrounded by forget.

Bobby was sure she disapproved of Duval spending so

121

many afternoons there. Sensing this, Bobby was at pains to keep a low profile for his friend, but sometimes he forgot himself. One dinner time he announced, 'Duval says Negroes are better at music than white people.'

Merrill raised an eyebrow at his father.

Lily clucked derisively. 'Name a famous Negro concert pianist.'

'I'm not sure he could name a white one,' his father said mildly.

Mike stifled a laugh as Bobby frowned. His grandmother had taken him to a concert in Orchestra Hall the spring before. He said tentatively, 'Daniel Barenberg?'

'Barenboim,' corrected Lily, but Bobby could tell she was surprised.

'Well done,' said his father.

At dessert they were talking about Vietnam again, Lily saying it was an evil war, while his father stiffened. Bobby knew his father didn't like the war either, but he seemed to hate the draft dodgers even more. He said the protests were unpatriotic; when he saw demonstrators on the television news it put him in a bad mood. But tonight seemed okay; Merrill's presence always kept all of them on their best behaviour.

Eventually Bobby thought he should make a contribution to the conversation. 'Duval says—' he began.

'Duval says, Duval says,' his father thundered. 'If I hear one more time what a little coloured boy thinks about world events ...' He paused, and Merrill interrupted, speaking in her soothing, syrupy voice.

'Don't you have any other friends, Bobby?'

After this, he knew not to talk about Duval at the dinner table.

That first spring, Duval had said he didn't like baseball, which Bobby could understand since he saw at once that Duval was no good at it. He claimed he *was* good at basketball – *B-ball be my game*, he said – but when Bobby took him down the block to visit his friend Eric, whose father had put up a basketball hoop in their back alley, Duval turned out to be absolutely hopeless. He was fumbling, and near-sighted, and without any hand-to-eye coordination. Eric ran Duval ragged, dribbling around him almost contemptuously, laying the ball up for an easy two points again and again.

After that they stayed home and played baseball. At first, Duval couldn't hit the ball, so the score was lopsided. It wasn't much fun – the opposite of playing with Mike, who won every single time, which made Bobby understand now why Mike didn't often want to play with him. Then he had a small inspiration, and pitched underhand to Duval, softball style, and Duval could hit the ball, sometimes anyway.

The game was constrained by the strange geography of the yard, with right field bordered by the windowless wall of the Christian Science church. Next to it stood the one tree of the yard, a mature maple with thick branches and dense leaves. If you climbed up high enough, you could look down over the wall at a little square of yard behind the church. Very rarely the ball would be hit there, and whoever hit it there lost the game, since the ball was irretrievable – the only entrance to the back of the church was barred by a locked gate in front on Blackstone Avenue.

More often the ball would get stuck in the dense growth of the maple. No big deal, provided Bobby went and got it. The first time he suggested Duval retrieve the ball – he'd hit it there after all – the boy had hesitated, approached the tree, tried to pull himself up on its big low branch and promptly fallen down.

'You got to heave yourself up, Duval,' explained

Bobby. 'Here, watch me.' He climbed up quickly to the high branch where the ball nestled, retrieved it, and hopped down.

Duval couldn't do it. With Bobby's help he managed to get up on the lowest limb, but his legs were wobbly, his stance uncertain. When he tried to move up, he lost his grip and fell, sliding hard down the trunk, banging his arm against the big branch. He landed on his back, the wind knocked out of him.

Catching his breath, Duval sat up slowly. There was a look of such dazed hurt on his face that Bobby felt terrible.

'I'm sorry, Duval,' he said. 'You don't have to get the ball. I'll get it from now on.'

He did, and though he didn't really mind doing it, he was keenly aware that Duval couldn't climb the tree. One day, perched high up on a branch, reaching out for the whiffle ball, ensnared in the thick maple-leaf clusters just beyond his reach, he happened to gaze down at the tiny walled-in yard of the Christian Science church. How dull it looked – a rectangular patch of grass against the back wall, two rows of badly laid paving between that and the back wall of the church itself. Something stirred in him, and looking down at Duval, waiting anxiously, he said, 'You'll never believe what I can see. It's amazing,' he said.

'What is?' asked Duval.

He pointed, knowing Duval couldn't see over the wall. 'Down there, behind the church.' He thought of the most interesting way to describe it, then remembered the story his grandmother liked to read to him. 'There's a garden there, a kind of secret garden.'

'You makin' it up.'

'No, I'm not. It's unbelievable.' He put drama into his voice. 'It's got a fountain in the middle, with a tiny

124

stream running up to it. The water comes out in a big kind of spray and the water's blue as the sky. It's *beautiful*.'

'What else is there?'

'Flowers. I've never seen them like this. Every colour of the rainbow, and some are really big – there's a yellow one bigger than your head. Hey, wait a minute.' He pantomimed a ship's lookout, peering out over the waves. 'There's a bush in the corner, big and green, and it's got fruit on it. Beautiful fruit.'

'What kind of fruit? Apples?'

'Nope. They look like oranges, only smaller. And wow! There's another bush, only this one's got plums. You know those big red plums we had that time –' they'd had a picnic, if you could call eating in the sun porch a picnic – 'well, there's a little tree with some on it.' He started to climb down.

'Wait,' Duval said, with a pleading note to his voice. 'Is there anything else?'

Bobby jumped from the lowest branch. 'Nope,' he said. 'That's it for now. I'll take another look the next time the ball gets stuck up there. My turn to bat.'

Later when they went in, Duval said to him in the alleyway, 'You sure you're not making it up about that Secret Garden?'

Their game had been surprisingly close, so he had forgotten all about his fantasy.

'Of course not,' he said indignantly.

But he felt bad about fooling his friend, especially when Duval went on, 'You know, if it was anybody but you, I wouldn't believe them.'

Bobby told himself the lie was harmless, but couldn't help but think about the look on Vanetta's face if she learned he'd tricked Duval. 'Listen,' he told Duval, 'we should keep it to ourselves. You know Vanetta doesn't like the place.' Which was true – there was something about the Christian Scientists that Vanetta distrusted.

'Good idea,' said Duval with an eagerness that only made Bobby feel worse.

As time passed, he felt stuck with the secret, and might eventually have confessed had not Duval so enjoyed Bobby's accounts of life over the wall. 'Is the yellow flowers there?' he'd ask, and laugh gleefully if Bobby suggested a purple one had moved in and was hogging the sun. 'That water still flowing?' and Bobby would say yes, as if it were a matter of course and Duval shouldn't be so stupid as to ask.

The rain stopped at last. He fetched two bats from the closet and a baseball-sized whiffle ball. 'Come on, Duval. It's ball time.'

In the kitchen Vanetta was chopping onions. She looked up. 'You two going to be warm enough? It ain't hardly spring out there, you know.'

'We're okay,' said Bobby.

In the back yard they flipped a coin and Bobby won, so he batted first, picking up one of the white ash bats stained with its natural grain. It was his favourite bat – short, only 29 inches long, but signed at the thick end *Floyd Robinson*, his favourite player. He'd got it free at a White Sox Bat Day.

For once Duval threw a strike, and Bobby swung and missed. When he turned and flipped back the ball, Duval wasn't looking and it fell onto the grass. Duval's eyes were on three black boys who had silently entered the yard.

They must have been twelve or thirteen years old, though one of them was as short as Bobby – a runt, thought Bobby. He was very dark, with skin the colour of cooking chocolate and a hard, mean face. Behind him stood a tall lanky kid in a Bears T-shirt, and next to him was a mulatto boy, wide-shouldered, with pigmentation stains on his face.

Bobby saw at once that the runt must be the leader, for his two friends waited while he went up to Duval. 'Got a dime?' he asked.

The standard opening gambit with the black ghetto kids who came over from the other side of the Midway. It had never happened to Bobby, but his brother Mike said it happened to him all the time. You could give the dime and not have to fight, though Mike said only a pussy would do that. But if you said no, then you might have to fight. Mike never gave them money, and he'd had lots of fights. But Mike was tough; Bobby wished he was here.

Duval shook his head now, keeping his eyes on the runt, who pointed at Bobby. 'Check him out, Mule,' he said, and the mulatto boy came over to Bobby.

'You got a dime?' he asked.

'No,' Bobby said truthfully, for he didn't have any money at all. He always emptied his pockets before playing in the back. Change and his pocket comb just got in the way.

Mule looked back at the runt, who said now to Duval, 'What you doin' here, man, playing with this ofay? What's the matter wit you?'

'Yeah,' said the skinny kid, joining in, 'you some kinda Uncle Tom?'

Duval said nothing, and Bobby realised he was scared of these boys. And though the mulatto's attention had switched back to the runt, Bobby was scared too. Yet Bobby felt he had to say something. 'You're not supposed to be here.' He was holding the baseball bat still in one hand.

'Shut the fuck up,' said the runt and turned back to Duval. 'I asked you a question. What you doin' here?'

127

'Just playing,' said Duval softly.

'Don't give me that jive. When I asks somebody a question I want an answer.' He spoke with a slight lisp, but there was nothing funny about it – it made him even more menacing. He held his arms down by his waist, like a cowboy getting ready to draw. Duval was standing frozen; Bobby could see his eyes blinking furiously behind his glasses.

Out of nowhere the runt's right hand landed against Duval's left ear. Astonished and hurt by the blow, Duval put a hand up to the side of his head, and accidentally knocked his own glasses off.

Bobby moved to pick them up before they got stepped on. But the boy called Mule blocked his way, then shoved him backwards, hard enough for Bobby to stumble and almost drop the bat. He gripped it tightly, worried these boys would try and steal it.

Mule took a step forward and clenched his fist. Bobby wanted to run but Mule's bulk blocked his way. As the mulatto boy's fist moved in a roundhouse arc through the air, Bobby instinctively raised his right arm, which was holding the bat.

The bat shuddered in his hand. '*Shee-it!*' Mule screamed. He began walking in small circles, clutching his right hand, blowing on its fingers in a desperate effort to ease his pain. '*Goddamn!*' he shouted. His friends stared wonderingly at him, and Bobby realised that Mule had punched the bat instead of him.

As the pain began to subside, Mule stopped walking. He glared at Bobby. 'I'm gonna get you, motherfucker,' he said, his teeth clenched. He took a threatening step towards him; again out of instinct, Bobby raised the bat in the air and Mule stopped in his tracks. Bobby realised now that the bat was a weapon, not just baseball equipment, and emboldened by this discovery he

128

took a step towards Mule, raising the bat high in the air.

Mule moved away, stepping backward so quickly that he bumped into the skinny kid in the Bears T-shirt, who was himself so frightened that he pushed at Mule, desperate to keep him between himself and the baseball bat.

'Be cool, man,' the runt said. Mule retreated to the back fence. The skinny boy had his hands up and looked absolutely petrified.

'Just go,' said Bobby, trying to sound forceful. There must have been a faltering note to his voice which the runt heard, because he didn't back up. For a moment Bobby thought he might actually come forward – he seemed fearless.

But the runt stepped sideways instead, landing his foot quite purposely on Duval's glasses. 'Come on,' he shouted, and all three of them ran out of the yard, Mule still holding his wrist.

Bobby went and picked up the glasses – one lens was shattered like crushed ice, and the frames were badly bent. He handed them gingerly to Duval. 'I'm sorry, Duval.'

Duval didn't say anything, but folded them and put them in his shirt pocket. He looked dazed.

Upstairs Vanetta was still ironing in the kitchen, and as they came in she took in at once that something was wrong. 'What's happened?' she said, sitting the iron on the board.

'Some boys came into the yard and wanted money,' said Duval. He added quickly, 'They didn't get none.'

Either out of relief or shock, Bobby started to cry.

'They hurt you?' Vanetta said to Bobby. He shook his head, and started to wipe his eyes, embarrassed that he was crying and Duval wasn't.

'He hurt *them*, Vanetta,' Duval crowed.

'What happened?' she asked and pointed at Duval's glasses. 'They break your glasses?'

Duval nodded.

She unplugged the iron, setting it upright on the board, then untied her apron. 'Shit,' she said, which was very rare. Bobby had only heard her swear like that when he'd scared her once, jumping out of the linen closet down the hall, shouting *boo*. Now she grabbed a broom and started towards the door, her jaw set in determination. 'They still out there?'

'They're gone, Vanetta,' said Bobby. 'They ran away.'

She put the broom against the wall. 'You sure they didn't hurt you?'

'One of them slapped me up side the head,' said Duval. 'But I'm all right. They was gonna hurt Bobby, but he hit one of them with the bat.' He pointed to *Floyd Robinson*, lying on the kitchen table. 'Bobby was brave. He stuck up for me.'

Bobby didn't say a word. He knew he had been brave by accident.

That evening when Vanetta said goodnight, she hugged Bobby fiercely. 'That's for being brave,' she said. 'You two just like Damon and Pythias.'

'Who?' he asked, certain it must be people from the Bible. It almost always was.

'Friends who helped each other when they needed it.'

Duval appeared with his coat on. 'Come on, baby,' she said affectionately, and turned to Bobby. 'And goodnight, my other baby. Though you two is getting too big to call you babies any more. You be fine young men quicker than I can spit.'

After this Bobby felt even closer to Duval, though he remained embarrassed that his friend thought he had

130

been heroic. They still played whiffle ball in the back, though Bobby was nervous the first few times, and kept a bat within reach, even when it was his turn to pitch. The safety of their play had been lost, and now when he climbed the maple to fetch the ball, he was reluctant to describe the Secret Garden. When Duval insisted, he would give only the most perfunctory account – 'No new flowers, the fountain's not got much pressure today.' Somehow the fantasy had lost all its allure, especially since Duval seemed so unalterably gullible.

Though in other respects, Duval was more worldly than Bobby. Once a month or so Vanetta's older sister Trudy would come to the apartment, usually when Vanetta had fallen too far behind in the ironing to get through it all without help. She was as grumpy as Vanetta was cheerful, but Bobby liked her just the same. If you talked baseball her mood would lighten, and when he mentioned Hoyt Wilhelm, the ancient relief pitcher who seemed old enough to be Bobby's grandfather, the sour expression on her face would change to a grin, and she'd give a snorting laugh. 'That ol' Wilhoun,' she'd say, 'ain't he something?'

But Trudy wasn't as nice to Duval. 'Why's she always mad at you?' Bobby asked him one day.

'She mad at the world,' said Duval, with unexpected sageness. 'She black as coal and ugly with it. There ain't no man in her life.'

'There ain't no man in Vanetta's either.'

Duval looked at him a little scornfully. 'Vanetta been married twice. Vanetta can have a man quicker than you can whistle. Look at her – she got big titties, and a pretty face. That's all it takes, man.'

When it came to the facts of life, Duval for all his gawkiness knew more than he did. Bobby's own knowledge was theoretical and skewed; his father had taken

131

him aside and told him a long story about trout, and eggs, and sperm, which meant for a long time he imagined sexual intercourse to be two adults swimming oddly together. Sex was something that lay across a big divide for Bobby, the way Michigan was on the other side of the lake or England across the ocean. For Duval it seemed closer to home.

'You ever seen your sister nekked?' Duval asked one day.

'What?'

'You know. *Naked*.' He exaggerated the long 'a', mimicking the way Bobby would have said it.

Bobby was confounded by the question. No, he guessed he hadn't – at least, not for several years. Lily was punctilious that way. She dressed with her door firmly closed, made it clear that the bathroom was a strictly no-go zone while she was in the bath – everyone else took showers. But his sister's anatomy was not a topic he wanted to discuss.

Duval took no notice. 'Bet she got nice titties.'

'Come on,' Bobby said, disturbed rather than annoyed. He wished Duval would shut up, though he couldn't have said why. It wasn't as if he felt obliged to protect his sister's honour.

Yet Duval seemed fascinated with Lily, to Bobby's bafflement – it was as if Lily's indifference was a challenge to Duval. Bobby couldn't see any other way to explain his friend's interest in someone who wasn't remotely interested in him.

Then one afternoon Lily came into the back bedroom, where he and Duval were setting up the blanket for a game of soldiers. 'Have you been going through my drawers?' she demanded of Bobby.

'No,' said Bobby, bewildered. Why would he bother doing that?

'Are you sure?' she said insistently, in what Mike called her Little Madam voice.

'Yes, why?'

'Well, somebody has, because my . . . my clothes are all messed up.'

When she left, trouncing along the hallway to her room, he looked at Duval and shrugged, as if to say his sister was nuts. But Duval was smiling, as if he had some information he was keeping to himself.

'What is it?' Bobby asked. Duval didn't usually act like this; Duval was normally an open book. 'Go on, tell me.'

But he wouldn't, and it was only the next morning when Bobby opened his drawer to take out new underwear that he saw what Duval had done. Underneath the pile of socks on the right side something white protruded; when Bobby tugged at it and pulled it out he found himself holding three pairs of his sister's panties. Duval must have taken them out of her drawer. But why? It wasn't funny, it just seemed weird. That afternoon when Lily was still at school Bobby returned them, taking pains to leave the other contents of the drawer undisturbed.

Lily must have not complained to his father or Merrill, because there was no comeback. But a week later she came back to his room again, fuming. 'Did you put this in my bed?' And she threw a magazine at him.

He looked at it with amazement. It was an old copy of *Playboy*, dog-eared and beat-up. He'd never seen a copy up close – when he peeked furtively at the men's magazines in Sarnat's, Mr Odess would always cough loudly until Bobby stopped looking.

This time Lily must have talked, for that evening his father came back to his bedroom after supper, while he lay on his bed watching television. 'What is this about *Playboy* magazine?' his father asked, switching off the set.

He shrugged, avoiding his father's eye. It was a crucial moment; for years he would have told his father what had happened immediately, without hesitation and truthfully. But life had changed since the arrival of Merrill. He knew he still had his father's love, but he no longer felt he had his attention. There was no one else to explain the situation to: Lily would hang Duval out to dry without a second's thought; Mike would have listened, even been sympathetic, but there was nothing he could do to help. And Vanetta, usually the one emotional certainty, was the person he most wanted to protect from the truth.

'It was just a joke.'

'Your joke, or Duval's?'

'Just me. Duval had nothing to do with it.'

'Where did you get the magazine?'

'I found it at school. In the playground.'

His father eyed him suspiciously, but Bobby looked him directly in the eye – his father always claimed liars didn't do that. 'Well,' said his father at last, 'it wasn't a very funny joke. I want you to apologise to your sister, and not do it again.' His voice softened. 'Girls get a certain age, Bobby, and well, you know, lots is going on with them, and they get very private about things.' He was sounding resoundingly inarticulate, which meant his father really didn't know what to say. And at least he hadn't blamed Duval.

He felt almost sorry for his father, he had been so easy to fool – or that is what Bobby thought at first, though he was perturbed to hear Merrill talking about it with his father in the living room. Merrill sounded 'concerned' – almost her favourite word, which Bobby was learning meant she was on the warpath. He heard his father say, 'I'll speak to Vanetta.'

The next week Duval only came on one afternoon to the apartment. When he asked Vanetta where Duval was, she didn't give him an answer – 'He's busy today,' she said on both days he asked. When he did come, Vanetta shooed them both outside right away, and when they came in later he heard her tell Duval to stay in the back bedroom with Bobby. 'Don't you be goin'' where you don't belong,' she said fiercely.

So his father must have said something to Vanetta, which meant he had seen through Bobby's lie. Bobby felt mortified on his friend's behalf – what was such a big deal about a pair of panties and a magazine? He wanted to talk to his father about it, but didn't want to be confronted by his earlier lie. While he tried to get up the courage to approach Johnny, events overtook his plans.

'Baby,' said Vanetta the following Monday as, Duval-less, she met him across from Steinways. 'I got some bad news.'

He felt panicked. 'You're not leaving, are you?' he asked. Maybe Merrill had persuaded his father to let Vanetta go.

'No, Bobby, I ain't goin' nowhere. Don't you worry about that. But Duval's not coming to see us any more.'

'Because of Lily?' He started to feel outrage.

'It's nothing to do with Lily. It's Aurelia; she's moved to St Louis, and Duval's gone with her.' She shook her head unhappily.

'He didn't even say goodbye,' Bobby said as the news sunk in. Then he burst into tears.

When Vanetta hugged him Bobby realised she was crying too. 'He said to tell you goodbye, baby. He says y'all to look after the Secret Garden while he's away.'

She stood back, wiping her own eyes. 'He'll be back to visit. He got to come see his grandmother, now don't he? You'll see him, don't worry.'

Later that day, just before supper, Vanetta told his father the news.

He said, 'I hope she can kick this thing, V,' and Bobby knew they were talking about Aurelia.

'I just don't know,' said Vanetta, and she did not sound optimistic. 'I'm worried about Duval, but I didn't think I could try and take a boy from his mother.'

'Of course not,' said his father. Why not? wondered Bobby. Aurelia didn't seem like much of a mother.

For the first six weeks Bobby was bereft at the departure of his friend. He knew Vanetta felt the same, but by mutual pact they didn't talk about Duval. Life intervened with other things to worry about: Vanetta's brother Alvin got real sick, and she was anxious, and on edge – Bobby had never seen her so snappy before. When summer arrived they went to Michigan for a month, where Duval was never part of his life anyhow, and when the school year started Bobby found himself going down the block to see Eric again, and discovering he liked basketball almost as much as baseball.

As Vanetta had promised, Duval came back to visit, and in the following year Bobby saw him three times. But these visits were awkward, as if they each sensed a split between them greater than mere geography. On Duval's first visit, they played a desultory game of whiffle ball, seizing the excuse of a drizzle that would never have stopped them before to go inside. The next time they didn't even pretend to play ball, but watched TV together instead. On the last visit they stayed in the kitchen, talking more to Vanetta than to each other.

After that he had only indirect news of his old friend,

136

though once it proved memorable. One day he came home – unaccompanied, since his father said he no longer needed a chaperone – and found Vanetta very excited. She told him there had been a fire in an apartment next to Duval's church in St Louis. Duval had saved a woman's baby, braving flames and getting badly burned. She proudly showed Bobby a clipping from the St Louis paper, which had a picture of Duval receiving an award from the Chief of the St Louis Fire Department. Bobby noticed how tall Duval looked, a good head higher than the white fire chief, but the face was the same: the shy smile and the slightly protruding teeth, the ugly glasses and the dark eyes. He was a real hero, thought Bobby.

Lily made appreciative noises when Vanetta showed her the picture, but with Bobby she was contemptuous. 'I don't care what he's done. He's still a creep in my book.'

Sometimes Bobby still played in the back yard, but now it was by himself, in the shallow alleyway by the fire escape. He was throwing a tennis ball against the wall one day when he became aware that he had company.

This time there were just two of them, the runt and Mule. The runt went to the end of the alleyway leading to the apartment, while Mule blocked the way out through the gate.

'What do you want?' asked Bobby, trying to sound nonchalant, but he knew his voice was shaky. He threw the tennis ball high against the wall. As he moved forward to catch it two arms reached out and grabbed the ball. Mule laughed, holding the ball high above his head.

'Give it back,' said Bobby. The big boy held one arm out, holding the ball, but when Bobby reached for it

Mule flipped it underhand to the runt, who had re-appeared. He let the ball fall to the pavement, where it dribbled slowly onto the grass. Then he turned menacingly towards Bobby.

'What do you want?' repeated Bobby. 'If Mr Edevek catches you back here you'll be in big trouble, man.'

'"*When Mr Edgevick catches you . . .*"' The runt was imitating him, in a higher-pitched white man's voice, prissily enunciating each word. 'Fuck Mr Edgevick.' His voice lowered an octave as he spat out the words.

Mule suddenly grabbed Bobby by the shirt. 'You not so brave now, are you, white boy? You ain't got no bat today.' He held up his other hand, its fat fist clenched. 'Look what you done to me.'

Bobby stared at the fist, which looked like one of the ham hocks sold at the A&P. The fingers were mottled and one was bent so the knuckle stuck out. That must have been where he hit the bat, thought Bobby.

The runt came closer now, and Bobby watched his eyes carefully. 'You thought you scared us away, boy,' said the runt. Before Bobby could answer he stepped forward and punched him in the stomach.

Whoof. The air was knocked out of him, and he felt suddenly sick to his stomach; he would have fallen to his knees but Mule was grabbing him tightly by his collar. Tears came to his eyes; he wanted to yell but he was too busy trying to catch his breath. He thought for a moment the runt was going to hit him again, but the runt stepped back. 'Come on, Mule,' he said. 'Let's get out of here.'

Bobby's relief was short-lived. Suddenly Mule shook him hard by the collar of his shirt, and before he could wriggle out of his grasp, hit him with a clenched fist on the chin. Bobby felt a lower tooth crack as it hit his upper teeth. He fell back, and his head hit the iron railing of the fire escape so hard that its steps shuddered. He collapsed, falling onto a concrete plinth by the fire escape, cutting his leg on its sharp edge. He felt sick, as if trapped on a roller-coaster that wouldn't stop. The plinth felt cool against his hand and he moved his head onto its surface as the dizziness increased and the world outside started to go quiet and dark.

Just before he lost consciousness he heard a man's voice, and knew dimly it was Eddie Edevek, announcing – was someone else there? – 'Those goddamn niggers.'

He spent two nights in Billings with a suspected fractured skull he didn't have, and a hairline fracture in his jaw which he did.

Released, his injuries healed well enough, but his life had changed. He was scared now, in a way previously inconceivable. He didn't want to play in the back yard any more, which Vanetta noticed, but didn't press him on. And for the very first time, he was conscious of the colour of people on the streets; when a gang of boys was white he was unworried; when they were black he tensed and moved away. He went straight to school and came straight home. He even stopped playing with Eric, for he didn't like walking in the neighbourhood unless he was with Mike, who seemed both oblivious and fearless, or with his father.

Perhaps it was fear, or the departure of Duval, but his relationship with Vanetta was changing, too. He loved her as much as ever, but there was a distance he had never felt before. Some of that may have happened anyway – he was a white middle-class boy, after all, who went to a smart-ass superior private school. There he learned all sorts of abstract things which a woman who had grown up on what was effectively a plantation wouldn't know, a woman who – though naturally

139

very bright indeed – had left school at the age of twelve and could write down phone messages only with difficulty. But it was more complicated than that; the true gulf had nothing to do with formal education. Bobby had secrets – he hadn't been brave; the Secret Garden didn't exist; and after the runt and Mule, he feared the male members of her race – he could not confide in her.

There was no one else to turn to. Mike these days was nice to him, but abstracted – the age gap between them seemed especially great. Even when they wrestled now, Mike didn't lose his temper, though admittedly Bobby no longer tried to bite. Lily was out of the question; she hadn't ever understood his friendship with Duval, so she certainly wouldn't understand his new feelings of fear.

His father had been distant for some time, moreover, a detachment magnified when he announced, three days after Lily and Mike had their acceptance letters from college (Mike was going to the University of Minnesota, Lily to Stanford), that he was getting married again. The twins beamed and made congratulatory noises, to Bobby's surprise – he knew Mike loathed the woman. Then he recognised this as a sign of their own detachment: the marriage would hardly affect them, now that they were leaving home. For the first time Bobby could see that his mother's death six years before had taken the usual sibling bonds – sometimes tense, sometimes tender – and placed them into cold storage. It was not that they didn't know each other – they did – but that the death had forced them to make individual accommodations, and independent lives.

Not only was his father getting married, but he announced that after the wedding he and Bobby would move to the Cloisters – a swanky apartment building two blocks away. They moved three months later, after a marriage ceremony in the university's Bond Chapel and a stilted reception at the faculty club. After the move, Bobby found that his memories of the old Blackstone apartment faded rapidly, perhaps because the causes of his happier recollections – his mother, his time with Duval – were no longer part of his life. Vanetta remained, but she was preoccupied by Alvin's cancer, and she did not get on with Merrill, who kept pressing, if not quite ordering, Vanetta to wear a maid's uniform. Merrill also liked to set a week's worth of menus in advance, full of French foods Vanetta didn't like to cook. They didn't have ribs any more, or fried chicken – instead it was 'Coke o' ven', as Vanetta called it when she inspected the week's roster of expected meals, wrinkling her nose.

The new, stiff life with Merrill in the fancier apartment wasn't much fun, and his father's simple joy in his new marriage was almost too much to bear. It reached absurdist heights when Bobby overheard Merrill declare over coffee at one of her dinner parties, 'They're like my own children to me. And I believe they think of me as mother.'

Who are you kidding? Bobby thought with anger that turned to incomprehension when his father added, 'That's right.'

Bobby found himself calling his brother Mike as often as he could at his college dorm, until a mammoth phone bill was waved under his nose by his irate father. After that he found he stayed in his room, reading. At least there he could count on being left alone, save for the odd enquiry from his father ('You okay, son?') which he found easy enough to deflect. He wasn't happy at school as he became a teenager, since he was now essentially anti-social, and frightened by drugs – half his schoolmates talked about marijuana in hushed thrilled

141

tones, and the other half seemed to be smoking it. He didn't know why it scared him, but it did, and he felt himself isolated from his peers and unable to meet anyone else – there were no introductions forthcoming from Merrill.

If he'd thought about it, he might have realised he missed having as close a friend as Duval, but he was becoming so immersed in his own flat unhappiness to remember a livelier, happier time. Merrill was not strict with him, but then she did not have to be – he had no energy for misbehaviour, just the lassitude of the unrecognised depressed.

How long this would have gone on he never knew because one evening Merrill started talking at supper about her family out east, and some school that all the male members of her Yankee clan attended, and what a nice place it was, just outside of Boston, which was of course, Merrill acknowledged graciously, a smaller city than Chicago but (and you could tell she thought this) perhaps more cultured. As she went on about this school he started daydreaming – or dinner-dreaming, since he often did it while he sat at supper, sole child with his father and his second bride.

But this evening his father suddenly said, 'What do you think?'

And he replied instinctively, 'Think about what?'

His father sighed and said with an overt display of patience Bobby knew he didn't feel, 'How do you feel about what Merrill said? Would you like to go to boarding school in Boston?'

And he didn't even think about the momentousness of this, or of how he might miss his home (only where was home now, the Cloisters?), or of how much he might miss Vanetta and whether he would really like being 850 miles away in a place where he knew not one living soul. Because all he knew was that life had become endless again, just as it had in those awful months when his mother went away and he lived like a prisoner under Gladys's eye. Suddenly now some impetus for change or escape took hold, and he said, 'Okay.' And the deed was done. On the day he left, he noticed Vanetta had at last given in to Merrill and was wearing a uniform.

VII

1

'HOW DO YOU happen to know Charlie Gehringer?' said the man named Rycroft, unbuttoning his suit jacket as he sat down in a padded chair.

'Who's Charlie Gehringer?' Robert replied, looking out the wall-to-ceiling windows.

The view from the apartment's living room took in the lake, a vast black pond this late at night, and an angled perspective of the Golden Mile of Michigan Avenue, where the Hancock Tower's antenna glowed like a towering luminescent bulb. They were on the thirty-fourth floor of this modern apartment building on Lake Shore Drive, but Robert's usual anxiety on this score had been dulled by two large whiskeys downed in the first half-hour after his and Anna's arrival.

Drinks before dinner had separated the boys from the girls. Maggie Trumbull's husband David had been a friendly and talkative host, but he was the kind of Midwestern fraternity guy who Robert had always avoided. He and Rycroft had talked shop before dinner while Robert stood, listening politely and wondering when they would eat. To include him they had switched the conversation to sports, which would have been fine – he had found his boyhood enthusiasm for baseball had come back, he even sometimes watched games on television now. But Rycroft had only talked football: he had been an offensive lineman at Grinnell, and looked as if he had only recently run to fat.

It was now after dinner, and the Trumbulls had laid

on hospitality with more bounty than finesse. They'd sat down at a polished mahogany table to a four-course meal, with a different wine for every course. Robert had risen from the table feeling bloated and tipsy enough to turn down his host's offer of a liqueur.

His slight fear that Anna's boss, Philip Masters, would be present had not materialised. Looking across the room, he saw Anna. God, she looks good, he thought. Anna wore a simple sleeveless black dress that showed off her dunes-acquired tan, and scarlet slingback heels. Her hair was tied back in a tight bun, which made her look even younger; her face seemed strikingly unaged. He found himself desiring her with the forlorn pang of a schoolboy out of his league; she seemed as unavailable as she was desirable. Why? he thought. I'm married to her.

She was gossiping with Maggie Trumbull, and he was glad to see her enjoying herself in the company of all these lawyers, even if most of them were of the fat cat rather than committed sort. He missed having equals he could talk to at work; even the friendliest conversation he had was tinged by his status as boss.

'Sorry,' Rycroft said without embarrassment. 'Your wife said you were from Chicago so I figured you knew Charlie before she did.'

'Never had the pleasure,' said Robert, trying to sound friendly.

'Interesting guy. He's a public defender, has been for over thirty years. Talk about lasting the course.'

'Is there a lot of turnover in that job?'

'You betcha.' Rycroft gave a lazy unconscious scratch across the wide front of his belly, his shirt quivering beneath his fingertips. 'I lasted four years, and that was longer than most.'

'It's not very well paid, I suppose.'

'Hopeless.' He took a large sip of his cognac. 'And

depressing. The people you're defending are not what you'd call an appealing bunch.'

Robert said dryly, 'Your clients are mainly black and poor then?'

Rycroft gave an unruffled grin. 'Yeah, but that wasn't the problem. I *wanted* my clients to be black and poor – it made me feel I was doing the right thing. Your average public defender starts out as an idealist; I did, believe it or not. What I started to realise after all of three weeks in the job, though, is that not only were my clients black and poor, they were all guilty too. Scumbags, without exception. And that's what eventually got to me; hell, that's what gets to everybody. Except for Charlie Gehringer. The rest of us do our stint – like I say, I made four years – and then we move on to cleaner pastures.'

'Cleaner? Or just more corporate?' Robert found himself saying. Christ, I sound like Anna on her high horse, he thought.

'Touché,' said Rycroft and gave a rich belly laugh. 'I can see you think I'm just defending a higher class of crook.'

Robert found himself laughing, too. There was too much self-knowledge in this man for Robert to dislike him; he found it impossible to judge people who had already judged themselves.

'But actually,' said Rycroft, 'some of my current clients haven't done what they're accused of. And even when they have, it's not the same – not in my book anyway. I wouldn't claim it was always victimless crime – pilfering a pension fund is pretty horrendous if it's your pension that gets lifted. But the people I defend nowadays don't shoot anybody, they don't stab anybody, and they don't sodomise little girls for kicks.' There was nothing humorous in his voice now. 'How Charlie Gehringer stands it after all these years is beyond me. The man's a saint, I guess, or a lunatic. Probably he's a bit of both.'

Half an hour later Robert and Anna said goodnight to the doorman, a square-shouldered Irishman with gold braid on his coat that spelled *Barry*, then walked along Lake Shore Drive. Through the lollipop line of sparse poplars, a faint breeze rustled, barely audible above the rush of late-night cars heading downtown on the Drive.

'Jesus, they're rich,' said Anna. He couldn't tell if this was said admiringly or scathingly. Perhaps it was a bit of both.

'Well, he's a senior corporate lawyer, so he must make a lot of money.'

'Still,' she said with a wondering shake of her head.

They turned at the corner, then turned again onto Astor Place where he had managed to find a parking place earlier that evening. Quieter here, the street was lined with mainly Victorian townhouses, the trees old and tall and leafy. As they walked north he pointed to a modernist building of three storeys across the street.

'That was one of the first Bauhaus houses built in Chicago. Hard to believe.'

'I'll say. It looks brand new to me.'

'1936.'

'How on earth do you know that?'

'Years of secret study.' He laughed. 'Actually, it was designed by my great-uncle. He was an architect – at least in theory. I think this was the only house he designed that ever got built.'

'Is it listed?'

Robert scoffed. 'Come on. This city hasn't got a heritage, just a history that sounds like a cartoon. Mrs O'Leary's Cow and the 1871 fire. The Water Tower, only building to survive the fire. The Black Sox scandal of 1919. Al Capone, Mayor Daley, that's it. Captions for tourists.'

'That's awfully superficial,' she declared.

'Like Chicago,' he said. He realised he was the one sounding like a European, snooty about an upstart's short history.

Ahead of them he saw in the glow of a streetlamp a man approaching them. He was tall, black, and striding forward aggressively. Was the man talking to himself? It looked that way. Drunk? Robert tensed almost imperceptibly, and took Anna's arm protectively. Then he relaxed when he saw the man was wearing a familiar long wool coat, with gold braid visible on its front collar that said *Daniel*. Barry the doorman's shift must be over.

'Did you think he was going to rob us or something?' asked Anna when he'd passed.

'Old habits die hard,' he said. 'I can see the headline now. "Activist lawyer and husband mugged on Astor Place."' But that wasn't it at all. For a split second he had thought it was Duval walking towards them.

'Don't be ridiculous. No one would ever try and mug you.'

'Why not? I'm not a big guy.'

'No, but your face on the street looks like ice.'

'Fear, masquerading as *machismo*.'

They reached the car and as he squeezed his key and heard the metallic snap of the power locks, he asked, 'Who is Charlie Gehringer?'

Anna stood still by the passenger door. 'He's a public defender.'

'I know. That man Rycroft said Gehringer's been there thirty years, defending scumbags. Rycroft's word, not mine.'

'Hard to believe Rycroft once did that job. I thought he was positively revolting. Maggie says he bills out at twelve hundred dollars an hour.'

He was startled by her vehemence, at odds with her

148

demeanour during the evening. It was interesting to see her former fiery principles flare up again; he'd been starting to wonder if they'd been extinguished in their fat American life. 'So what about Gehringer?' he asked.

Anna sighed and he studied her face in the amber cast of the streetlight. She'd had some wine, and her cheeks were flushed, a few stray strands of hair escaping from her bun. She spoke across the top of the car. 'He was Duval's lawyer – his name was in the file.'

And he remembered him from the one day he'd gone to court during Duval's trial. A tall sandy-haired fellow then, not that much older than Robert. They'd talked during one of the recesses. They'd been meant to talk again, but never had. He wondered if Gehringer would remember that.

They drove north in silence, cutting across the edge of Lincoln Park onto the Drive. They crossed the city line, then stopped for a light on Sheridan Road and a sports car pulled up next to them with a bunch of teenage boys stuffed into its toy-like seats. They grinned at Anna, and one of them leaned forward and beeped the horn. When the light turned the sports car rocketed ahead of them. As the noise of their exhaust receded, Robert said, 'Are you going to talk with Gehringer?'

'I don't know.'

'What's holding you back?' he asked.

'Part of me thinks I'm being silly – I'm not used to having time on my hands so maybe I'm just looking for something to do. But another part says it's important.'

'Important to whom?' He tried to keep his tone easy.

'To Duval, of course.'

'But you barely know him.'

'I didn't know half the asylum seekers I used to help, either.' She sounded resentful, and she reached down and opened her window an inch.

'Duval has done his time and that's the one thing he'd like back. But nothing can ever give him that.'

'Maybe not, but he can be given other things – money, for one thing. From what you say Duval could use some. It's incredibly hard for an ex-con to find a decent job. He'd get 180,000 dollars right away – if he sues, he could get a lot more.'

'You seem to have been doing a lot of research.'

She ignored him, saying, 'And think of the stigma. What woman would want to go out with him if she knew what he was supposed to have done? But it's more than that: just because he's not behind bars, Duval isn't free; I bet you haven't any idea how much he's restricted by the conditions of his parole. He has to get approval of where he's going to live, and who he's going to live with. He can't travel without permission; he can't take a job unless it's given the once-over by his parole officer. As a sex offender he wouldn't automatically have access even to his own children.'

'If he had any.'

She groaned in exasperation. 'Why are you so cynical? I thought you were never convinced he was guilty.'

'I wasn't – he was such a sweet guy, and he'd been a hero. I couldn't believe he'd done it.'

'What changed your mind?'

'I've never said I have.'

'Did something happen back then?'

'No,' he snapped. He thought of his return to Chicago for the trial, the anxious days that followed, then his conversation with Vanetta. 'But I wasn't a lawyer. Or a cop. Or a private investigator.'

'So you stayed out of it.'

He was sure there was contempt in her voice. 'There was nothing I could do.' Vanetta herself had told him that.

They had turned into their street, and he could see the maple in their front yard, looming like a ragged umbrella in the dark. She said quietly, 'You don't have to justify yourself to me.'

'That's big of you,' he said crossly, then waited for her to react.

Instead Anna pointed at their house, where he could see the light in their living room – the new babysitter would be watching television. 'Look upstairs,' she said, and he saw there was a light on in Sophie's room as well.

Sophie had played her old trick on this new sitter. She would have claimed she was scared of the dark, and the sitter, a nice-acting girl the neighbours had recommended, would have let her keep her light on. Sophie, who wasn't scared of the dark at all, would have stayed up reading happily for God knows how long after her bedtime.

He laughed, and Anna joined him, all crossness gone, but his own thoughts lingered on what she'd been saying. *You don't have to justify yourself.* Didn't he though, if only to himself? The problem was that when he had returned to New York even before the verdict came, it was not because it had been the 'right thing to do'. He'd gone, leaving Duval to his fate, because he had been told to.

2

Vicky was out with flu, which he suspected meant a day at the beach, and Sylvia Nowell from publicity was doing her best to help. One of the trustees had complained out of the blue about production standards, and Robert felt obliged to rebut him, harnessing facts from the production controller to show this wasn't true

151

– all their books were now acid-free, the glued perfect bindings they used were as durable as the sewn ones of the past, all the rarefied palaver designed to appease a self-proclaimed lover of 'quality books'.

He was also expecting the accountant, Andy Stephens, after lunch, so when Dorothy Taylor popped her head through his open door, he felt exposed, his desk a mess of accounts and unanswered post – for the head of a university press, he had a surprising number of non-email correspondents. Dorothy, by contrast, had a single file folder under her arm and looked confident.

'Yes?' he asked, lifting his head. He didn't motion her in.

'I saw Coach Carlson for breakfast.'

'Go okay?'

She nodded, looking pleased with herself.

'So what's the story then?'

'He said people say a lot of things, and we should pay no attention to Balthazar.'

Robert considered this. Balthazar could bullshit with the best of them, but Robert had never known him to tell an outright lie. And in this case to what purpose? Might Coach Carlson be the one playing games? Perhaps he'd feigned agreement with the agent just to get him off his case – God knows, Balthazar could be annoyingly persistent.

He said finally, 'Let's hope you're right.'

'I am. He said he's just putting some finishing touches on the script and then it will be ours.'

'Well, I'm glad it's been a false alarm.'

He wondered whether to compliment her; not that it seemed to help their relationship when he did – since Dorothy treated praise as if it were simply her due. Yet he knew it was important to commend even unlikeable employees, so he added dutifully, 'That's great. Well

152

done.' Goodbye, he wanted to say, looking at the piles of papers on his desk.

Yet she remained in the doorway. 'That man in your office the other day – do I know him, Danziger?'

'I wouldn't think so,' he said. *Danziger*. How he disliked this habit of calling him by his surname, yet he saw no easy way to change it. He'd offered first names at the beginning, but she wouldn't bite. To insist on a 'Mr' would be absurd. He noted that she couldn't bring herself to ask straight out who Duval was.

She persisted. 'I felt I'd seen him before.'

Not unless you've been a visitor to Stateville Correctional Center in Joliet, he longed to say. 'I doubt it. We grew up together.'

Her face betrayed surprise, or was it disbelief?

'It was a million years ago,' he said to lighten things.

'He didn't look that old,' she said accusingly.

'You mean he didn't look as old as I do?' he teased, and for the first time since he'd joined the press Dorothy blushed.

'Where did you grow up together?' she said, recovering.

'On the South Side. Hyde Park.' Dorothy must have known he was from Chicago.

'Oh, Hyde Park,' she said, with a satirical lilt to her voice. It was clear that in Dorothy's book Hyde Park was la-di-da. 'Is that where your friend grew up, too?' There was a challenge in her voice.

'Not far from there.' They both knew what this meant – Duval had lived in the ghetto.

'You have quite a past,' she said without admiration, and he noted the animus in her eyes.

'I'll let you know when I write my memoirs.'

'From what I hear, you'd sell a lot of copies in London.'

VIII

IT HAD FOR a long time seemed cut and dried. Latanya Darling was an exotic figure, half-black (her father had been Jamaican) at a time when London publishing saw no need to diversify the composition of its racial make-up. She was quick-witted and ambitious, moving at a young age from publicity into sales, where she prospered, rapidly running the rep force for one of the divisions at Robert's old employer in London.

She was an obvious rising talent in a business that left many people stuck for good in the same job, and she was also fun – friendly, sassy and without airs. She partied hard, hung out with the hipper, younger end of the trade book editors, and doubtless snorted her share of coke from the lid of a Groucho Club loo. On the tall side of average height, she wore heels that made her look taller, and her hair was a mass of gold that ran in a rich shower down to the tops of her shoulders. She was striking rather than beautiful, with *café au lait* colouring and blue eyes from her Swedish mother, but there was an energy about her that was absolutely galvanising. Robert remembered a group sales review when all the men had been so bowled over by the contributions of this girl-woman that they had found themselves tongue-tied.

Yet for all her jazzy easy ways, there was something detached about Latanya, and she made it crystal clear that as far as romantic relationships were concerned, she would not find hers among her work colleagues. You couldn't blame her: most of the men around her were either married or gay, or both, but it intrigued

154

people nonetheless. Any eligible candidates seemed to lack the basic *utz*, as Robert's older brother Mike would have called it, that element of testosterone, either literal or professional, that would be a match for her.

Why she fastened on Robert was a mystery to him. He was eligible, he supposed, since his marriage had fallen apart, and like any of the building's eligible men he had been well aware of her. But not in a month of Sundays would he have figured himself a catch for the glamorous likes of Latanya Darling.

He felt battered by his wife's betrayal, mystified by his resentful son, and old suddenly beyond his years. At work he managed to project a forthright, decisive self in the meetings he conducted, but he felt his authority put on, and had no inner convictions about anything at all. Since publishing was not an easy way to get rich, Robert had always impressed upon his staff that it was essential to have fun while doing it, but it was not an edict he was now following himself. The humour he was known for, which sometimes strayed too close to the anarchic for his own professional good, seemed to have deserted him – like a pair of too-tight trousers, put in the back of a closet with only the dimmest hope that a diet might allow them once again to fit.

It had come to a head at a sales conference, after the closing banquet. They'd had a good year and the CEO had splurged and sent half the company to Italy, where they convened in a luxurious villa hotel on the outskirts of Rome. The resort was a mix of old estate villa and modern hotel block, and Robert had a spacious double room on the ground floor of the villa. Before the finale dinner he'd rung London to speak with his son, only ten and still taking the separation of his parents hard. But Cathy had claimed the boy was asleep, while Robert could hear his marital successor in the background, talking loudly and clinking his glass.

After the dinner Robert had come back to his room as soon as he civilly could, since at his age he found he could no longer sustain the late-night foolishness of his youth, tipping drunk into bed at four in the morning. He changed into a polo shirt and swimming trunks, read a proposal for a book one of his editors wanted to spend £150K acquiring, and was feeling unusually sorry for himself when someone knocked. He thought of ignoring it, but went and opened the door, annoyed at the intrusion.

Latanya Darling was standing there, wearing mauve heels and a raincoat, belted tight at the waist. She held a bottle of champagne with a red ribbon wrapped around its neck. 'One of the authors said he doesn't drink,' she said, waving the bottle.

'Don't keep shaking it, for Christ's sakes,' he said, and she took this as an invitation, walking past him into the room. Five minutes later she undid the belt to her raincoat to reveal bare legs and a silk nightgown, and two minutes after that they were in bed.

The upshot was – well, he hadn't wanted an upshot. He could not deny the slightly fantastic element to the time they were together that night, or the fact that he felt like a small boy who'd fallen into an ice-cream sundae. They had made love, then finished the champagne at two in the morning before falling asleep, only to wake and make love again.

When morning came and she left for her room, he didn't feel any remorse; he felt replete. It seemed an unreal episode, entirely enjoyable, and would be spoiled only if they tried to repeat it.

But Latanya must have felt differently. When they'd landed at Heathrow she'd come up to him in the baggage reclaim area. 'You can't avoid me now,' she said with a nervous giggle, and put her hand on his shoulder, then let it slide down to his ass.

He had ducked her the next day at work, though there had been a flurry of emails – over a dozen, alternating between accounts of her day and plaintive requests for an answer. He wrote only one back: *Absolutely buried right now xr.*

The weekend came and he was out of his flat all day Saturday, returning only in the evening with the bachelor comfort of an M&S ready meal. He was living in Camden Town, while his wife stayed encamped in south London, not far from the house they'd recently sold in Wandsworth. Then at ten o'clock, as he started to think of bed, the doorbell rang and he found Latanya on his doorstep, wearing a skirt five inches above the knee and a smile that said she'd already been to a party. When he let her in she sashayed through his flat like an established girlfriend; he could only think it lucky that she hadn't brought a suitcase full of clothes. He had tried to protest but she kissed him quiet, and spent the night.

In retrospect he realised this was an even bigger mistake than their original assignation. For it gave Latanya the false sense that he was as interested in being with her as she was with him. And in bed she had insisted on talking shop into the wee hours – about her ambitions (considerable), her career plans (complex, but well thought out), and most alarming to him, her conviction that together he and she could form a partnership that would result in ... what? Promotion within the company hierarchy, large bonuses, unrivalled influence and power – she sketched out a virtual dynasty they would forge between them. 'No one would ever fuck with us,' she said triumphantly as the small clock on the mantelpiece struck five, and he started to feel there was something slightly hysterical about Latanya, something unstable.

How do I get out of this? he wondered as he made them coffee Sunday morning. He tried as she left that morning to play things down, suggesting he would be busy for the rest of the weekend, indeed the week ahead as well. But he soon realised that as far as Latanya was concerned they were a couple, and the onslaught of emails in the office continued, written in a tone that suggested he and she were now a workplace alliance as well as 'an item'. At the end of the day she had appeared in his doorway and he'd pointed to the papers on his desk with a groan, saying he wouldn't be free for hours. He'd tried the same on Tuesday but when he went home found Latanya on the doorstep in Camden Town.

'Why are you avoiding me?' she'd said as he let her in.

There was no point dissembling; he'd already been dishonest enough. So he told her directly, 'I'm just not ready for a relationship; I'm still leaving the last one.'

She seemed to accept this, but then she asked, 'Is there somebody else?'

'No.' Which was true. He'd met an interesting woman the night before at supper with friends – a radical lawyer, attractive, funny, clever in an unaffected way – but she hadn't seemed very interested in him.

'So what's the problem?'

You are, he'd wanted to say, but instead repeated that it was all too much too soon; he wasn't ready for anything serious. Blunt but true, so he had been taken aback when she continued to argue with him for what seemed hours. Fruitlessly, since each time it came back to what could not be overturned – he didn't want to be with her. She seemed increasingly agitated, then startled him by demanding in transparent desperation, 'Is it because I'm dark?'

'What do you mean?'

'You know what I mean. I'm not *Caucasian*.' The anger in that word; ostensible indifference peeled back like a raw onion to show a deep, festering rage.

'Jesus, no, Latanya. What I'm saying is there isn't an *us*. I'm sorry – if it sounds patronising to say I'm not right for you, then okay, you're not right for me.'

'Why? You were as big as a house with me.'

Is that what it came down to – his undeniable physical attraction to her? He shook his head wearily, but she had come over to the sofa and was all over him, kissing him, stroking him, trying to take his shirt off.

'Stop it,' he said.

He stood up and moved towards her, ducking his head back when she tried to slap him, then grabbing her arm. A siren wailed, or at least he thought it was a siren until he realised the sound had come from Latanya. She had screamed, and he dropped her arm in astonishment. The two of them were barely eighteen inches apart but her unfocused eyes were on the ceiling. He looked at her throat, thinking randomly how beautiful it was, as she tilted her head back and started to scream again.

Soon lights would go on in the neighbourhood, phone calls would be made, and eventually the police would arrive, tired and vexed by yet another 'domestic'. Latanya had gone past any acceptable boundary of anger; Robert didn't need a psychiatric handbook to recognise she was hysterical. When she started to scream again he slapped her hard across the face.

He regretted it right away – until he saw that it had worked. Shocked, she lowered her head and her eyes met his at last and her mouth shut like a clamp. And then she burst into tears, falling forward into his arms, limp as a doll until he made her sit on the sofa, then sat down himself and held her sobbing, cradled in his arms.

She stayed there almost until morning, alternately weeping and dozing, such was the emotional exhaustion she seemed to feel. And what he felt during this bizarre vigil was a tenderness that had nothing to do with the desire, part sexual, part child-like, that had motivated him. How could I have done this? he thought to himself, repelled as much by his own complicity as by her deranged intensity.

Daylight broke at last, and this time when she stirred she sat up. There were no tears. 'Coffee?' he asked gently, but she shook her head.

'I'll be going,' she said.

It was necessarily awkward for a while after this, though he found that he could usually avoid encountering her alone at work. Sometimes they were in the same meeting, when he found himself unusually reticent, but whole days could go by without a glimpse of her. He was in any case involved with Anna, the lawyer he'd met, a new relationship that soon took him over far more than he'd anticipated, as he uncovered the sheer chaos of her personal life. When, seven months later, news was announced of Latanya's departure for Australia – she would be sales and marketing director there for a rival firm – almost all of his anxiety about their brief embroilment had gone away, and he simply thought, Good for her.

He didn't know how many people in the company knew of their brief liaison, and he didn't care – his life had moved on so resolutely to Anna that it seemed irrelevant. And when Anna got pregnant, intentionally or not, he had more on his plate than a two-night fling with a colleague.

Only Frank Prothero, an American friend who worked for HarperCollins, said anything, over drinks in a bar around the corner from the Savoy. They usually met three or four times a year, in a friendship that was strictly unprofessional and based on their mutual yearning for baseball. Prothero was a finance guy at Harper, and very senior – it was said even assorted Murdochs listened keenly to what he had to say. He was an unlikely-looking accountant, preferring shaggy tweed jackets to suits, with dark bags under his eyes that reminded Robert of a hound dog.

When Robert mentioned Latanya's departure for Oz, Prothero was unusually blunt. 'No bad thing either, from your point of view.'

'What do you mean?' Robert demanded suspiciously.

'I don't know what happened between you two, and I don't want to know.' Prothero raised both hands to reinforce his detachment. 'But that woman bears you no goodwill, that I can say.'

Robert tried to shrug it off. 'It's all in the past. No big deal. I wish her well.'

'Not likewise, pal. Like I say, it's a good thing she'll be far away. You don't want her going on about you the way she has been.'

'What way is that?' He was curious despite himself.

'You don't want to know,' said Prothero, and would not be further drawn.

She came back to London seven years later, to a bigger job with a different publishing company. Robert saw news of it in the *Bookseller*, but without any sense of alarm – he was too caught up with his job, increasingly tense as their corporate parent demanded unreasonable returns, and his home life, where he and Anna, now long married, were so busy raising their little girl. There didn't seem any reason to worry about his misguided fling so many years before.

But then there were flickers, intimations of something he sensed but could not describe. There had been a particularly riotous agents' party he'd given a miss, going home to look after Sophie while Anna had a late-night conference with a bunch of forlorn Ethiopians, arrested in Clacton, of all places, and now awaiting deportation. The next morning he was outside the conference room, reviewing the agenda before the acquisitions meeting, when he heard two young women editors, already in the room, discussing the party.

'Did you see Latanya Darling?' one asked the other.

'She was putting it back,' said the other appreciatively.

'And awfully indiscreet about you-know-who.'

When he entered the room just then, the two young women looked embarrassed, but also disapproving, as if there were stains on his trousers. Why? They were too young to have been at the company when Latanya had worked there. He couldn't believe a two-night stand almost a decade before would constitute current gossip value. A proverbial light bulb was flickering that he didn't like.

Then he had an argument with another division head, an experienced woman he'd always got on with well enough. But the argument had been a bad one – she'd accused him of poaching an author who had actually begged to shift divisions to his – and he had almost lost his temper. She'd looked at him coldly. 'I see what they mean about you,' she'd snapped, then stalked out of the room.

So it seemed perversely logical to hear an explanation

of what was going on from Prothero again, this many years later. 'You know Latanya Darling's back?' Prothero said as they sat in the very same watering hole off the Strand.

'I know,' he said heavily. All he'd wanted was to have a drink after work, share the usual moan about their respective employers, talk a little baseball, and then go home to his family.

'I'd like to say the girl was carrying a torch for you, Robert, but it's more like a flamethrower.'

'It was years ago,' he said wearily. 'Look, it's not like we even had a relationship. We spent the night together twice. Okay?' He looked at Prothero's face, which was unexpectedly earnest. 'Jesus, Frank, I need Latanya Darling in my life like I need a hole in the head.'

Frank clawed at the bowl of peanuts between them, then chomped on a handful. 'The thing is, she's saying some pretty rough things.'

'About me?'

Prothero nodded. 'I didn't think you'd exactly *want* to know, but I thought you needed to.'

What was she saying? What was the worst a spurned woman could say? That you were bad in bed? Unanswerable, unless you provided a large erection for public display. Or was it something else? That he was kinky – wore a leather jacket underneath the sheets? Liked pain? Or that he was gay? Or that he was a drunk? – though that would be rich coming from Latanya Darling.

'All right. I'm ready. What's she saying?'

'She says you used to hit her.' Prothero was looking at his fingers.

'Oh, for fuck's sake.'

Flabbergasted, he looked wildly around the room. When he looked back at Prothero his friend seemed no less tense for unburdening himself.

163

'Don't tell me you believe that, Frank.'

'Of course not. But you were pretty hot-tempered back then.'

'What do you mean, back then?' he demanded. He was going to get hot-tempered very soon if Prothero didn't explain.

'When you and Cathy were splitting up.'

'That was eight years ago. I was fine as soon as I met Anna.'

'I know that. But people have long memories – and you were pretty tough in the office. That's what I was told, anyway. So when this woman starts claiming . . . things, people think, "Ah, that makes sense." You know, for most people a little smoke makes a big bonfire.'

Did it? He had never conflated gossip with fact. 'Cheer up,' said Prothero suddenly, signalling early for another round. 'Sometimes bonfires go out of their own accord.'

This one didn't. It smouldered but never burst into flame, which meant Robert didn't get the opportunity to fight the fire. He tried not to become paranoid, ignored the meaningful glances at the occasional party where he and Latanya were in the same room – when interestingly, Latanya always ignored him completely. But he felt that some force was gathering against him.

In his own company, the CEO left, but where once Robert would have been in the running to replace him, it was made discreetly clear to him that now he wouldn't be. So when a job running a much smaller publisher came up, one which five years before he would have disdained, he applied – to the gleeful surprise of the headhunter, who clearly considered Robert to be a catch for the position.

The interviews went well, and he was confident he'd get an offer – not out of arrogance, but because, as the headhunter said himself, this was one he ought to walk.

Only he didn't, and the headhunter was embarrassed. After Robert's insistent probing he told him there had been 'some personality issues'.

'But they don't even know me,' Robert protested.

'I know. It's weird. It's as if somebody's told them something about you.'

He realised that he was in a trap, one he wouldn't be able to escape, for he was being done down by a rumour no one would put to his face. If he had been accused of breaking some law – or even the rules of his company – he could have confronted the charges head on, been cleared or convicted. Instead he suffered from an insidious campaign that damned him *sub rosa*. His professional life, once a seeming succession of new opportunities, was becoming hemmed in. He felt he was operating in a room with shrinking walls, and sooner or later the lack of space would begin to pinch. He didn't know what to do.

It had been Anna who proposed a solution. He had never told her about Latanya – in the past there hadn't seemed any point, as he didn't want the sheer sourness of his fling to infect his new relationship; later, it simply seemed pointless bringing it up. Yet she knew he wasn't happy, even if she didn't know quite why.

'I think we need a change,' she'd declared one night, when she came home late, exhausted from another futile case. 'I barely see my daughter; you aren't enjoying work – don't deny it. We're getting stale here.'

'We could move to the country,' he said, though he dreaded commuting.

'No. That's not what I had in mind. I meant a real change – like a different country kind of change.'

It was as simple as that. He'd put out feelers immediately for any job in any place that was far away. It had seemed unfortunate that the first significant opportunity had come from his native city, but when he flew out for an interview he found almost no reminders of a past he would rather forget.

There was a lot that could be done in the new job – he saw considerable potential that was going unrealised – and this without the grinding demands and ferocious politics of a large corporation. The trustees had not only been welcoming, they had seemed actively to want him. The press's offices were modern, spacious, and located on the North Side; Hyde Park could have been in a different city altogether. Houses seemed incredibly inexpensive, moreover, which meant the sale of their small London home could buy a large Midwestern one in a pleasant suburb like Evanston – next door to the city and its culture, yet leafy, green and safe, and with a good school for Sophie. Anna had positively glowed during their three days in Chicago, and had leads already in place for work at the British Consulate.

In short, there was nothing stopping them from moving, and plenty of reasons to prod them westward ho. When the 747 had lifted off the ground, he had vowed to leave all thoughts of Latanya Darling behind him. He was making a fresh start.

IX

1

DUVAL ORDERED APPLE pie this time, with ice cream again, after eating a double cheeseburger with fries – all at Robert's urging as they sat again in the coffee shop of the Marchese building. He had the sense that Duval didn't take many meals with his cousin Jermaine and his family, and that he wasn't particularly welcome there, a lodger foisted on them through a family tie they couldn't quite bring themselves to sever.

Duval was dressed in black trousers with cuffs and a light blue, short-sleeved shirt that was at least one size too big for him – it made his arms look thin as sticks. Again, there was an anachronistic air about him, and as they sat under a large ceiling fan – ornamental rather than functional since the coffee shop was air-conditioned – Robert felt they could have been in a 1950s movie.

Although quiet at first, Duval seemed in good spirits, which was more than Robert could say about his view of his old friend's prospects. His own efforts at finding work for Duval had come to nothing – Flynn, the maintenance head in the building, had shaken his head unambiguously when Robert sounded him out about prospects of work for Duval. 'Union's got it all tied up,' he said. 'I even tried to get my nephew a few hours helping me paint the ground floor. Nothing doing. Sorry.'

When Robert related the bad news Duval looked unaffected, though not because he'd found anything much off his own bat – the job prospect he'd mentioned on the phone had not materialised. There had been some other bits and pieces – a few days offloading delivery trucks for a warehouse on the West Side, a cleaning job in an office block on the fringes of the Loop when the regular cleaner had been out with the flu. And that was it.

Robert asked how he was spending his time. Duval didn't give a very full explanation – sometimes he went to the library, he said, but otherwise he was vague about his routine. There didn't seem to be one, and though he mentioned his parole officer, Robert couldn't tell how often Duval was required to see the man. He did say he liked riding the bus, and Robert envisaged Duval on a series of aimless travels around the city, content just to have the freedom to move wherever the bus took him.

Duval grew more talkative as he ate, but he talked mainly about the distant past, as if he chose simply to ignore his adult years in prison – unlike an archaeologist, he didn't sift through the layers on his journey backwards to childhood. Robert found himself colluding with this excavating leap. Perhaps it was the trip to Hyde Park with Sophie, but he was not only intrigued to watch his old friend root around, he was also happy to do this himself.

'Do you go to church these days?' he asked as the waitress refilled his coffee cup for the second time and delivered Duval his pie. He didn't remember the boy Duval as especially religious; church then seemed to mean choir, and the feeding of the singers afterwards. But Duval had been reading the Bible when they'd first met here in the coffee shop.

'I go, though not always to the same one.'

'How about singing?'

Duval shook his head. 'I done lost my voice. Not that

168

there was much opportunity for singing where I been.' He paused. 'Squealing, yes. Singing, no.'

Squealing? Robert didn't know what to say. On Duval's face a strange smile was creeping into the corners of his mouth. Then he looked down at his pie, and the two men were silent while Duval ate his dessert.

Finished, Duval put down his fork and wiped his mouth carefully with his napkin. He said, 'Do you remember how you used to sing in the back bedroom?'

Robert laughed. 'If you could call it that. You were the singer.'

And Duval suddenly sang, quietly but loud enough for a couple near them to stare, *For once in my life I have people who need me, people I've needed so long.*'

The words weren't quite right, but the voice remained pitch perfect and clear. Robert laughed, and it looked as if Duval were going to sing some more, when a female voice said, 'You must be Duval.' Robert looked up, half-expecting the waitress, but it was Anna.

'I was done early,' she said, addressing Robert. 'I thought I'd come by and save you the trip.'

The trip was all of two blocks. He frowned, then remembered his manners. 'This is my wife Anna.' Both he and Duval stood up awkwardly.

'I don't want to interrupt you gentlemen.' She looked at Robert, her expression absolutely neutral. 'I can do some shopping and meet you later at the office.'

'No,' said Duval. 'Join us. I'm glad to be meeting Bobby's wife.' At the name 'Bobby' she looked surprised, then amused. Duval got a chair from a nearby table and Anna sat down between them.

'So how's it going?' she said pleasantly to Duval. She wore a cheerful summer dress, a print frock of small cherries on a white cotton background – but looked tired.

'Just fine,' said Duval. He had gone back into shy mode, sitting with his hands together like a pious student. 'We was just talking about old times. We used to sing together when we was little.'

'You did?' Anna was laughing. 'You must have been the lead then. Robert's got a tin ear as far as I can tell.'

'Thanks,' Robert said, watching her.

She looked around at the coffee shop. 'So is this your new hangout?'

'Yes, ma'am,' said Duval, sensing a joke.

'It's where the best folks come to eat the big dinner,' said Robert. 'You want some coffee?'

Anna shook her head. 'No, thanks.' She laid a tanned arm lightly on the table. 'Well, Duval,' she said, then paused. Robert watched her lips press together as she weighed up her words. He was pretty sure he knew what was coming. *Robert's told me about your case and I think maybe I can help*. But he was wrong. She said, 'Robert tells me you're having trouble finding work.'

'It's tough,' Duval conceded. He snuck a look at Anna. 'It's not that I'm fussy, it's just no one seems to want to know. If they do hire me, it doesn't usually last long. I work hard, but if they hear about my record—'

He left the sentence unfinished, but Robert noted that Duval was openly acknowledging the problem to Anna. She had a remarkable facility to get people to tell the truth about themselves.

'What kind of work are you looking for?'

'Like I said to Bobby, I like working with my hands – carpentry, decorating, that kind of thing.'

'Do you mind being outside?' She ignored Robert's stony look.

Duval gestured towards the windows on Wacker Drive. 'Not when the weather's like this.'

170

Anna laughed, and Robert watched her warily. What was she up to?

She said, 'I couldn't guarantee the weather, but we have got a few jobs at home that need doing. I don't seem to have time to get round to them. And Robert,' she pointed an accusing finger at him, 'is absolutely hopeless at that kind of thing.'

He looked at her frostily. He wasn't cross about the aspersion on his DIY ability; he was angry about the invitation.

Anna was speaking briskly. 'There's a fence needs painting – the neighbours have done their side, and keep waiting for us to do ours. And I know there'll be other little jobs once you show up.'

Duval laughed, with that same curious motion of his hand covering his mouth. 'That sounds Eye-deal.' Robert saw that he was already at ease with Anna.

'Could you come out on Saturday? Sometimes we go to the Indiana Dunes, but not this weekend.'

'I'd like to,' said Duval.

'We can't pay union rates,' said Anna, 'but we'll pay you in cash. 15 dollars an hour. That sound okay?'

'Yes, ma'am.'

'Call me Anna,' she said, with a smile to reinforce it. 'Can you get to Evanston all right?'

'Sure, I was telling Bobby here I know half the bus routes by heart.'

'Let me give you the address,' said Anna, reaching down for her briefcase and a pen.

'I know where you live,' said Duval.

'How did you know that?' Robert asked sharply.

Duval looked at him calmly, his faint theological air back in place. 'I called you, remember? You're in the phone book, Bobby.'

*   *   *

He was so angry that as they walked down Michigan and turned towards the parking lot he didn't trust himself to speak. From Anna's own silence, he knew she was just waiting for his explosion, and once they reached the quieter pavement of the side street, he let rip. 'Are you crazy? That man's been in prison twenty-four years and you want him to come to our house?'

'He says he didn't do it. You told me so yourself. And he's done his time. It's thinking like yours that keeps him from getting a job.' She must have been expecting his reaction, so composed were her arguments.

'Do you know what prison's like over here?' His voice was rising. 'Do you realise how violent it is – how horrible? People get raped all the time and beaten up and murdered. It's not like the UK. The racial thing is horrendous – the blacks are in gangs and hate the Hispanics, who have their own gangs, and both hate the whites, who in self-defence all join the Aryan Brotherhood.'

They passed an old lady with a mink-collared coat who looked as if she had been listening to them argue.

'But the thing is—'

'No, you listen to me,' and when he looked he saw the old lady stop and look away, frightened by the harshness of his voice. 'If Duval had robbed a piggy bank, I still wouldn't want him around – not after twenty-four years in prison. But he didn't, did he? He was convicted of rape and aggravated assault – the girl was lucky not to die.'

'You told me that.'

'I'm telling you again. And you want to bring him into our house? You want him near our little girl? What the hell are you thinking of?'

'If you'd just stop shouting for a minute, I've got something to tell you.'

172

'I bet you do,' he said angrily. She didn't respond to this. 'Go ahead,' he said, waving a hand dismissively.

She said with an elaborate show of patience, 'I spoke with Charlie Gehringer this morning.'

'Don't tell me: he remembers Duval. Or at least he says he does.'

'He remembers him all right. He said he's always been haunted by him.'

'Haunted?' Someone was being melodramatic. He couldn't tell if it were Gehringer or Anna. 'Why?' he demanded.

Anna was looking at him coldly; he disliked the certainty she wore like a coat. And she spoke now with an even greater show of calm. 'Because Gehringer thinks Duval was innocent. That's why.'

'All right,' he said, shaken by the rage he'd felt. 'Tell me what you've found out. It better be good.'

2

She had first telephoned Charlie Gehringer, several times, but had not had a reply. She wasn't surprised; he would have literally dozens of calls each day, most of which went unanswered, or he would never get the job done.

So she'd taken the bull by the horns and gone down to 26th and California. The place was a zoo: there were lawyers and cops and people who looked like defendants, all milling around the hallways, which had a bewildering number of rooms leading off them behind closed doors – offices and of course the courts themselves.

Eventually she'd stopped a lawyer, who told her what floor the public defenders' offices were on, but she'd found her way there barred by a security guard. She'd told him she had an appointment with Gehringer, and though she wasn't listed on the duty sheet, he had let her through – she was dressed like a lawyer, after all, not like some former client with a grudge.

'That was sneaky,' said Robert, leaning back against the sofa in the living room while Anna commandeered the rocker near the window. Sophie was upstairs, watching a DVD of *Anne of Green Gables*.

Anna gave him a *come off it* look and continued the story. She'd found Gehringer in his office, an enclosed cubicle at one end of a large open plan. He was seated at his desk, talking to a middle-aged black woman, perhaps the mother of a client. He was a trim man, and looked more like an insurance salesman than the defender of lost causes she was expecting. He had light, sandy-coloured hair, carefully combed, and was neatly dressed in a suit and tie – 'Not perhaps a suit our friend Mr Rycroft would choose to wear, but presentable.' She could see his office was neat as a pin, with a bank of filing cabinets against one wall, and a clean desktop.

She'd found a spare chair and waited, completely ignored in the hustle and bustle of the room – phones kept ringing, people laughed and shouted; it was a scene out of one of those hard-edged TV shows – *Homicide* or *Law and Order*. At last the black woman left Gehringer's cubicle, and then Anna stood up and tapped on his door, just as he started to pick up the phone.

She'd been nervous as she began to speak, unsettled by the man's clear-eyed gaze. As she'd told him why she was there, her words sounded terribly lame even to herself – explaining that a former client of his was a friend of her husband's, that he'd recently been released from prison (she didn't want to say how many years he'd been there, it just made the whole thing sound even more bizarre), and that he was still protesting his innocence. As she'd stumbled her way through this small speech, Gehringer didn't say a word, but his expression became increasingly sceptical, especially when she said that she had offered to look into the case, just to see if there was any way of reopening it.

She added that she was a lawyer, though an English one, as if he couldn't have told from her accent. And for the first time he perked up a bit, giving her half a smile, and explained he'd spent an entertaining afternoon at the Old Bailey, watching an English trial. She could tell he had thought it was quaint, m'lud and wigs and all.

But she still expected to be thrown out on her ear at any moment, and from the way he looked over her shoulder she knew there were others now waiting for his attention, in the same way she had waited. And then he'd asked her the name of this old client of his. She'd hesitated, certain Gehringer would not remember Duval's name – how could he when he'd had so many cases of similar crimes and what must seem similar clients now behind him? Perhaps a thousand of them. Or more.

But when she'd said Duval Morgan he had reacted at once. 'I remember him,' he'd said, looking as surprised as she was. 'You say he's out now?' he asked, almost disbelieving.

And when she'd said yes, absolutely, she had even met the man herself, Gehringer had got up and gone to his door, where she could hear him explaining to whoever was waiting that he would be a little while, sorry, but something had come up. When he'd sat down, he'd leaned back in his chair, hands crossed on his lap, and a wistful expression on his face.

He said at last, 'I'm glad he made it. I didn't think he would. He wasn't the kind of guy who would find it easy to survive in the joint.' *Joint* – she was startled by the word, it was the first time she felt the hard reality of what this businesslike man did for a living.

'I was worried you wouldn't remember him. You must have so many cases.'

'You always remember your failures.'

Not of course that there was much besides failure in a job like his, he explained, since very few of the people he defended got off – the best he could do in ninety-eight per cent of the cases was to cop a plea that reduced their sentence. Yes, he did his best to help them all, and yes, he believed that they deserved both the best defence he could give and a fair trial. But he wasn't stupid, and it went without saying that almost all of the people he represented had done the crime.

But Gehringer hadn't been sure about Duval – he had been different from the start, with an air of innocence about him that seemed entirely genuine. Gehringer wasn't naïve: he'd had plenty of innocent-looking clients even by that time, early in his career – there'd been one young woman in particular, sweet-faced and soft-spoken, who'd still managed to strangle her nephew. But with Duval he'd been convinced that it hadn't been an act: he seemed too bewildered by his situation. He'd been a hero, too, said Gehringer. Duval had saved someone in a fire, and been badly burned himself.

But facts were facts, and the case against Duval seemed open and shut. The victim had said she was attacked by a security guard, which was Duval's job at the hospital, and he had just gone off shift when the attack took place. There was a match of blood types as well, not that it meant very much – Gehringer recalled that it was 'O', which many, many people had. The real clincher for any jury was the victim's instantaneous, unwavering identification of Duval in a line-up.

176

But then something peculiar had happened: Gehringer had received a tip-off. This was not unknown – sometimes there'd be scuttlebutt about a case that helped him, usually when some cop went overboard with a suspect. Not wanting to be disloyal yet troubled, another cop would tell him about it on the understanding that the information stay unattributed. This time, however, the tip came in the form of an unsigned typewritten note. 'It shows how long ago this was,' said Gehringer now to Anna, 'because I could tell it was from an IBM Selectric.'

And the note said that when Peggy Mohan had first been interviewed, under guard in a Billings Hospital room (the same hospital where she had been attacked) she had not identified Duval Morgan as her assailant.

'*What?*' asked Robert, sitting up suddenly on the sofa, drawn in against his will.

Anna gave a small, cynical smile. 'That's what the note said.'

'But she identified him when she was on the witness stand.'

'Yes. And she also did at a line-up in the police station on 63rd Street.'

'Oh,' he said, his growing excitement faltering. 'What does that mean then?'

She shrugged. 'The inference was clear, according to Gehringer. The police had it in for Duval. It had nothing to do with racism, since they already knew from the victim that the assailant was African-American. But Duval was the obvious suspect. Gehringer said there would have been a reductionist logic at work that made the police reluctant to clear Duval.'

'I'm confused.'

'Are you? Gehringer made it clear as day; it must be me who's complicating things. What he meant was that the police were sure it was Duval, and if the Mohan woman hadn't identified him initially, they would have worked on her. Informally, of course. By the time she was well enough to attend an identity parade, she would have seen Duval's photo so many times she would have picked him out if there had been five hundred black men standing in the line-up.'

'What did Gehringer do about the note?'

'He talked informally with the police, especially the one who first interviewed Mohan in hospital and showed her mug shots. But this cop, who was called Ferraro, told him an entirely different story, saying Mohan had picked out Duval right away. When it came to court, Ferraro said exactly the same thing. Gehringer did his best to shake him, but he couldn't – after a while, Judge Bronstein got impatient and told him to move on.

'So they lost the case, which didn't surprise Gehringer, though even he was taken aback by the severity of the sentence – Bronstein had given Duval fifty years. He'd had nothing to work with in the trial except testimonials to Duval's unblemished character – the fire chief in St Louis sent a letter about his bravery that Gehringer had read in court. Though even then, one of the character witnesses had pulled out at the last minute.'

Robert wondered who that could have been. 'And that was it as far as Gehringer was concerned?'

'No. He wanted to appeal, but there weren't any grounds for it – Bronstein might have been a monster, he said, but he did things by the book. He didn't put a foot wrong during the trial, and his instructions to the jury were unimpeachable. Gehringer said there simply weren't any grounds.

'But he said the case gnawed at him; he couldn't forget it. It was a long shot, but he went to see Ferraro. He still denied that Mohan hadn't fingered Duval at once, but Gehringer thought there was some uncertainty in the policeman, maybe even guilt. But when he saw him again, he actually went out to Ferraro's home on the West Side – this time Ferraro wouldn't talk to him. Ferraro must have asked his boss to call Gehringer's boss, because back at the office Gehringer was told to leave Ferraro alone or he'd be suspended. After that, Gehringer's hands were tied.'

Robert said, 'He would have been scared he'd lose his job if he persisted.'

'Gehringer wouldn't give a toss about that,' she said, and she looked at Robert as if he didn't understand. 'This is a man who's truly committed to helping people. But if he got fired, he wouldn't be in a position to do that any more. *That's* what kept him from pursuing Ferraro.'

She stood up and went to the window, where the lowering sun cast a long carrot of light across the front lawn. Robert found himself dreading that she planned now to confront Ferraro herself, and he tried to pre-empt this. 'Maybe there wasn't anything to it. You said yourself Gehringer admitted it might have been some twisted attempt at revenge. Or a nasty rumour – bar talk. Doesn't mean it was true.'

'Yes, well, we're never going to know for sure.'

He was puzzled by this apparent abdication. 'Why?'

'Ferraro retired twelve years ago. He moved to Meyer's Beach on the Gulf side. I spoke to his wife on the phone this afternoon. She was a nice-sounding woman.'

'Yes, but what did Ferraro say?' How typical of a woman to start talking about how nice another woman sounded on the phone.

'He didn't. It turned out I was speaking to his widow.' She paused, her voice suddenly dull with disappointment.

'Ferraro died three years ago. When I asked her about Duval's case, she said she didn't know what I was talking about.'

'Oh, shit,' he said, but it wasn't because he was sharing Anna's sense of let-down. It was because he could guess what she was going to do next.

3

The weather got warmer still, hitting 90 by noon the next day. The mothers and kids in the playground formed a vivid tableau of skin and scanty clothes, and a hydrant burst down the street, shooting an angled stream of water into the steaming air. That morning the radio had announced the water temperature in Lake Michigan would hit 75, which meant even Anna would find it warm enough to swim. They could spend all Saturday in the water at the dunes, he decided, with a picnic on the beach. Then he remembered the Saturday appointment in Evanston with Duval.

Just before lunch, he had a phone call from David Balthazar. Their conversation was short and to the point, and when Robert put down the phone he called out to Vicky. She came in, carrying the copy of Nicole Krauss she was reading. 'Could you please ask Dorothy to come see me right away?'

She looked meaningfully at the phone on his desk. Why did she look younger when she was acting out? He said nothing and she left with a sniff, but was back in a minute. 'Dorothy's going to lunch. She said she'll come in after that.'

He suppressed his irritation – no, it was more than that, he felt a growing fury. 'Go catch her now before she leaves. I need to see her immediately.'

'But she said she's meeting someone and she's late already.'

He looked at Vicky, trying to stay calm. 'If you'd like to work for the National Dispute Resolution Committee, I'll see what I can do. If you'd like to work for me, then do what I ask.'

This time there was no sniff, and within a minute Dorothy came in the door, with her leather handbag slung over a shoulder. 'I'm not used to being summoned like some flunky.'

'Close the door, please, and sit down.'

She hesitated, and for a moment he thought she was going to walk out. But she closed the door, quietly, and sat down in a sulk, putting her bag in her lap.

'I've had a call from David Balthazar. He tells me that last week he received an email with the full script of *Fourth and One: The Memoirs of Jay "Bud" Carlson*.'

'I told you he was almost finished.' She spoke confidently, but he could see uncertainty in her face.

'Balthazar, unsurprisingly, says it's very good. So good, in fact, that he is sending it tomorrow to the following houses.' He looked at his notes of the phone conversation. 'Morrow, Random House, Houghton Mifflin, HarperCollins, and Doubleday.'

'What about us?' Her voice was quieter now.

'We can buy a copy when it's published.' He swung around in his chair and looked out at the playground. A little boy had fallen off a swing, and his mother was comforting him. Robert swung back to face Dorothy. 'Naturally, they'll return the advance. What was it, 25K?'

She gave a reluctant nod. 'At least that will help the balance sheet.'

Was she serious? He'd sent her on a finance course six months before and wished he hadn't. He said, 'The university doesn't care about the balance sheet. Cash flow, yes – though it's not as if we spend a lot of money on advances. P and L, yes. But not the balance sheet.' He looked at her with disbelief. 'Jesus, Dorothy, you said it was all okay. What happened?'

'Carlson told me he had lots of agents sucking up to him. He acted like Balthazar wasn't any different.'

'But did he say explicitly he would stay with us?'

For the first time she hesitated. 'It didn't really come up. It was just a given.'

He sighed, and she said angrily, 'Anyway, why should we believe Balthazar?'

'What reason would he have to lie?'

'Because maybe he's still trying to talk the coach round. Maybe he's buying time while he does that. I can't believe the coach would lie to me. Can you say the same of this New York shyster?'

Shyster? Balthazar was a Jew – of course. And half of Robert was one, too. Is that what she was trying to say – that there had been a conspiracy of *landsmen*? He decided to ignore it. 'Listen, with Balthazar, what you see is what you get. I'm not pretending he's an *attractive* personality. But he's very successful. You can't do that by lying, Dorothy; you get found out. I know. Carlson was either lying to you, or he's changed his mind. Either way, it looks like we've lost the book.'

She didn't reply at first, and stared at her bag. 'Can I go now?' she said flatly, and he wondered what she was thinking.

She seemed shaken, but he couldn't tell if she really cared. 'Sure, go to your lunch. But understand something: I'm going to see Carlson. Don't call him unless he calls you. Is that understood?'

And at least he had the small satisfaction that as Dorothy got up, she nodded.

4

He woke early on Saturday morning to a cooler, overcast sky, and found himself apprehensive about Duval's
arrival. Fortunately, Sophie had a play date with a school
friend – her parents were taking them both to Zion
National Park – and though normally he felt a posses-
sive pang when she wasn't at home during the weekend,
he was glad she would be gone while Duval was there.
Had Anna known that when she asked Duval to come?
He hoped so.

The other parents picked Sophie up at nine, and Duval
showed up half an hour later, driving an old red Impala.
Robert went outside right away.

'You got a car,' he said as Duval got out.

He shook his head. 'It's Jermaine's. He's selling it
because he's got himself a 4x4, but no one's bought it
yet.'

'What's that?' he asked, pointing to a paper bag in
Duval's hand.

'I brought my lunch.'

'Oh, okay,' he said, and realised he was relieved.
'Anna's working upstairs – you'll see her later. Why
don't I show you what the job is?'

He led the way around the side of the house, past
the hose wrapped like a sleeping snake on the ground
and into the back yard. Duval was dressed for heavy
outdoor work – black boots, olive work pants, a long-
sleeved wool shirt that looked ex-army issue. Without
his glasses he looked tougher, lean and muscled rather
than gaunt. Robert felt embarrassed at how little he
was asking him to do.

Their house was at the end of the block. A high privet
hedge separated them from the street; on the other side,

a white picket fence divided them from the Jeffersons, an old retired couple who kept to themselves. The second time Mrs Jefferson had spoken to Anna, it was to complain about the previous owners of the Danziger fence. 'They did *nothing*,' the old lady had hissed. 'They didn't even paint their side of the fence.'

Robert had taken the not-so-subtle hint and was going to paint it himself, until Anna had intervened with her offer. He had bought two five-gallon tins of Dulux, a sponge roller and pans, three brushes of assorted length, and a large bottle of turpentine. He'd put them all on the picnic table in the back yard.

'It really just needs a single coat,' he told Duval, pointing to the fence. 'No need to scrape.'

Duval nodded. 'I'll get started.'

Robert went into the house and upstairs. They had four bedrooms, so both he and Anna had the luxury of their own studies. His was at the front of the house, and if he pushed his chair back he could see Anna at her desk down the hall; she was reading prospectuses for work, but she glanced from time to time out the window at the yard. He pulled his chair back to his desk and tried to concentrate on Dorothy Taylor's draft report on the coming year's programme, but his mind kept wandering – to the yard. He gave up and walked down the hall.

'How's he doing?'

She shrugged and didn't look out the window. 'I'm sure he's being very thorough.'

Robert looked down, where Duval had painted perhaps the first three feet of fence. He wasn't using the roller, but held one of the brushes, and after each stroke he stood back to inspect his handiwork. 'You mean slow, don't you?' he said, and went back to his study.

At eleven they went out to do their weekly shop,

planning to find lunch at one of the bistros and cafés that sprouted in Evanston like alfalfa. 'What's Duval going to eat?' Anna asked, and Robert explained he'd brought his own lunch. When he went out to tell Duval they'd be gone for a while, Anna came with him.

'It looks great, Duval,' she said.

'Good to hear it. Wait 'til I finish and you won't recognise it.'

'We'll be back by two or so, Duval.' Robert pointed to the picnic table. 'Make sure you stop for lunch.'

They bought groceries at the local market, Anna still delighted by the fact that they cost half what she'd have paid in London, and then they ate a mediocre Mexican meal around the corner. When they got home they were putting the groceries away in the kitchen when Robert saw Duval, walking stiffly towards the back door. He went and opened it. 'You okay?'

'Bobby, can I use the bathroom, please? I'm about to burst, man.'

'Of course, Duval. You should have used a bush outside.'

Duval shook his head. 'The old lady next door was keeping watch.'

Robert pointed to the small cloakroom just inside the door. 'Be my guest.'

Anna was by the sink, and she turned towards him angrily. 'Did you lock the back door when we went out?' she hissed.

'Yes. I couldn't see any reason for him to be inside while we were gone.'

'For goodness' sake, Robert.' When she smiled it was at Duval, coming out of the loo.

In the afternoon the cloud cleared and the temperature rose. At three Robert went downstairs and made a pitcher of lemonade out of frozen concentrate, then filled an enormous jelly glass and took it outside. Duval put his brush down at his approach, and Robert handed him the glass and watched as he drank greedily. Sweat streaked both his cheeks like tears, and his forehead was matted with fine bubbles of perspiration. His wool shirt looked soaked through, stained by dark patches of sweat under both underarms and by a blotch the size of a pancake on his chest.

'Duval, why don't you take your shirt off? Nobody's going to mind. It's hotter than hell out here.'

Duval finished drinking and handed the glass back with one hand, while he wiped his lips with the other. 'I don't want to scare anybody.'

What did he mean? Mrs Jefferson again? Did he think the neighbourhood was so lily white that the sight of a half-naked black man would have neighbours calling the police? Maybe he was right. Race reared its unattractive head yet again, and inwardly Robert sighed. It had been gone so long from his life he thought it had disappeared for ever. How wrong I was, he thought wearily, saddened that his old friend and he were not beyond that.

'You're not going to frighten the horses, Duval. You must be boiling.'

Duval's expression suddenly set like plaster. 'Have a look,' he said, and with both hands he lifted the bottom of his sweat-soaked top up to his armpits.

Along Duval's right flank, from his appendix to his collar bone, ran a strip of damaged skin the size of a long skirt steak, marked by crusted bubbles of scar tissue, like a melted cheese sandwich left too long under the grill. It was a revolting sight, and Robert struggled not to look away.

'Jesus Christ, who did that to you?'

Duval gave a bitter laugh. 'Ain't no "who" involved. I didn't get this in Stateville, Bobby. I've had this since I was twelve years old.'

'The fire,' said Robert. Why do I feel guilty? he asked himself. Because he thought I was the hero. Duval had been the brave one.

'That's right. You think this is bad, you ought to see my leg.' He shook his head. 'I know it ain't pretty, Bobby, so that's why I keep my shirt on. Anna or your little girl was to see it, they'd probably faint.'

'I'll be back in a minute.'

He returned to the house and went upstairs to the main bedroom. He found an old striped, short-sleeved shirt in his dresser drawer, and took it outside to Duval.

'Put this on,' he said. 'It's a lot cooler.'

Duval laughed and swapped shirts, placing the sweat-soaked one over the top of the picket fence.

An hour later, upstairs reading in the house, Robert pushed back his chair and saw Anna wasn't sitting in her study. When he went to her window, he saw her in the yard, standing near the fence while Duval crouched down, touching up the bottom of a post with his brush. He looked at her desk and saw a thick document labelled 'Illinois Compiled Statutes', open at the following page:

Sec. 116-Motion for forensic testing not available at trial regarding actual innocence.

(a) A defendant may make a motion before the trial court that entered the judgement of conviction in his or her case for the performance of forensic DNA testing ... on evidence that was secured in relation to the trial which resulted in his or her conviction, and was not subject to the testing which is now requested at the time of trial ...

So: Duval could try and reopen his case because DNA testing had not been available at the time of his trial. But surely it couldn't be that simple – otherwise, everyone convicted by forensic evidence in a pre-DNA age would be filing motions. Maybe they were. Then he saw, further down the page, another paragraph, highlighted by the yellow marker Anna liked to use:

(b) The defendant must present a prima facie case that

(1) Identity was the issue in the trial which resulted in his or her conviction

That fitted Duval all right. Identification had been at the core of his conviction. So these would be the grounds for reopening the case – DNA analysable evidence if it could be found, based on the fact that Peggy Mohan had identified Duval as her attacker in court. He heard Anna coming into the kitchen below, and he went out into the corridor as she came up the stairs, asking, 'How's he getting on?'

'Fine, I think. He was telling me about Vanetta.'

'What about her?'

'Oh, just how she looked after him when he was little. And how he'd met you.'

'That's nice,' he said, but he didn't believe a word of it. When he'd watched from the window, Anna had been doing all the talking.

By five o'clock Duval was only two-thirds of the way along the line of fence. 'I guess he'll have to come back,' said Robert, watching him from Anna's study.

'Not tomorrow – I don't want to ask him to work on a Sunday.'

As if Duval had much else to do. 'I don't want him here when I'm not around.'

'It'll have to be next weekend.'

'I thought we'd go to the dunes.'

'Are you forgetting something?'

She was right; they were having dinner at the president's house.

'All right. I'll see if he can come then.'

And Duval was pleased to be asked back, and more pleased still when Robert handed over $105 in a mixed wad of bills. I could build a new fence for what this is costing me, he thought.

'Same time, same place then?' asked Duval.

'We'll be here,' said Robert, then thanked him and said goodbye. Going back into the house while Duval assembled the paint things, he found the phone ringing in the kitchen. It was the mother of a friend of Sophie's from school, but when he called to Anna he heard her going out the front door. By the time he got off the phone and went out front, Duval's car had gone, and Anna was coming in, with a satisfied look on her face.

'Did you forget to tell him something?'

She looked at him defiantly. 'Yes. I told him not to bring a sandwich next time. He can eat with us.'

5

Emails got ignored, phone calls were not returned – much as Robert didn't want to beard the coach in his den (actually, the university's multimillion-dollar sports complex) Robert knew it was harder for people to give bad news face to face. Though after his conversation with Balthazar he held little hope of changing the coach's mind.

'Virginia Carter.' The voice was pure rural Indiana; it spoke of dairy cows and silos and barn dances.

He explained who he was. 'I wanted to make an appointment to see Coach Carlson.'

'Just a minute.' He heard her paging through a diary. 'Hmm. Well, it's training season now so that's no good. And then the real season starts, of course. Let's see – I could try and slide you in for late October.'

It wasn't even August yet. 'That bad, huh?'

'Yes, sir.'

'It doesn't matter that I'm attached to the university?'

'It's a big university, sir. You should see the ticket requests the coach gets.'

He scratched one side of his chin, finding a patch he hadn't shaved. When Sophie had been little she'd come and watch him lather up, then talking with her he would miss the same spot day in and day out.

'Could you tell the coach I'm seeing President Crullowitch later this week?' Strictly speaking, this was true, since he was having dinner at his house on Saturday. 'I know he wants me to see the coach before then.' Not so strictly true.

There was a momentary silence. 'Hang on a minute. I'm going to put you on hold.' He waited, while a symphonic rendition of the football team fight song played three and a half times. Then she was back.

'Coach Carlson asked if you could come for a drink at his house on Thursday evening? Six o'clock.'

'Sure.'

And she gave him the address, a street of large houses, mansions really, in Kenilworth, a few miles north of his own house. How did a football coach come to live among multimillionaires? Curious, he Googled 'Carlson+football+coach+salary'. There were many entries, but five minutes later he had discovered the

190

coach's annual salary was $650,000. *That's* why he lived in Kenilworth.

He'd need to make sure Anna could stay with Sophie when he went, as otherwise he'd have to line up Mrs Peterson. He thought of ringing his wife, but decided it could wait. Lately she seemed to be working very long hours, and was often coming home late. There was an edge to her talk, and he wondered if she was diverting some personal stress into her work.

But did the extra hours really come from her consulate duties? He couldn't see how, not in the dog days of July. Or was it Duval? More likely, and though worrying, nonetheless more palatable than the third possibility. Philip.

There was a tension now between them, one that had been brewing but only spilled over with her determination to have Duval eat with them inside the house.

He had not felt this strain with her since the very early days of their relationship. When he'd met Anna her flat had been a chaotic mess of dirty dishes, and affidavits on the kitchen table. An unsavoury mix of clients and dodgy suitors had moved in and out of her four-room flat in Kilburn like a pack of undomesticated dogs, sizing up a new place to doss.

He made her get out of the flat and do things – she'd never seen Hampton Court, so they went there; never been to Waddesdon Manor, so he drove her out for lunch and a walk through the Rothschild parkland. Twice she cancelled at the last minute; he didn't know if this was due to the exigencies of her clients or her ropy personal life, and he made it clear he didn't care which – it was unacceptable.

For if at first he had plunged into the centre of her life's counter-centrifugal stew, now he stayed outside the fray, sensing that if he hung around passively waiting for her, he would soon get relegated to the status of these other passers-by, some of whom seemed to have been (he hoped the past tense was accurate) lovers.

There had been a kid named Spado, for example, half-Moroccan, half-Italian, a mix which meant it was unclear whether he could be deported – or where – under the uneasy state of EU laws at the time. He'd done eighteen months in Pentonville for sleeping with an underage girl, and hovered around Anna unattractively. One night when Spado had been allowed to sleep on the sofa in the front living room, he'd opened Anna's bedroom door, unaware that Robert was in there, too. One of the reasons Robert wouldn't stay in her flat any more was that he reckoned fairly soon either he would hurt Spado, or Spado would hurt him.

Anna complained when she came to his Camden Town flat for supper. 'Spado says you were being hostile.'

'Spado's right.'

'Oh,' she said, as if she hadn't considered such a possibility.

He did not hide his impatience. 'Look, if you want to have this circle of creeps floating around you, that's your business. I'm just not going to make it mine.'

'That's a harsh way to describe people who've had their rights violated.'

'But entirely accurate, don't you think?'

It was a critical moment between them. To his everlasting relief she had laughed. Then she caught herself. 'It's my job to look after these "creeps", you know.'

'It's your job to look after their *rights*, and that's all. The rest is a mug's game. If you can't see that, then God help you, Anna. Because I won't.'

'Won't?'

'Can't.'

She thought about this, her face betraying no emotion

until suddenly she crumpled. 'But what should I do?' she said, looking tearful. She added half-accusingly, 'I thought you were different.'

'Why? Because I didn't run off right away? Or stick around and exploit you?'

She contemplated this and he thought she was about to get cross, but she seemed to decide against it. She wiped an angry hand against her nose, which perversely made her even more attractive. Sniffling slightly, she said, 'Something like that. And because you were the only one who liked me more *after* you slept with me.'

'I was just pretending to, so you'd sleep with me again.'

She laughed and reached out for his hand. He said, 'Why don't you stay here from now on? Make your flat your office if you must, but don't sleep there any more.'

He imagined the objections forming in her mind. But to his surprise she said, 'Are you sure?'

'Positive.'

'Last chance,' she said warily, adding, 'You may find I get on your nerves.'

'I'm sure you will. But this way, you can only cheat on me under my nose.'

'I haven't cheated on you at all,' she said, and looked teary-eyed again. 'Big nose.'

So she'd moved in with him, and used her flat as a post collection depot and emergency refuge for her down-and-outs, though the latter usage tailed off once she wasn't there to minister to them. It wasn't that he'd wanted to run her life; it was just that he refused to become one more counter on a board game that had too many pieces and too few rules.

He could see that she was relying on him more than he on her, and did his best not to exploit the advantage, and to accept with gratitude rather than complacency her loyalty to him, which was something he found (though this was his problem, not hers) almost unbelievable. For there remained in him the childhood-bred conviction that it was only a matter of time before she would leave him, a prejudice born in childhood and unshakeable. Women let you down. Men probably did too, but he hadn't ever loved a man that way.

In time this reflexive assumption of his would doubtless have started to damage their relationship, possibly even destroy it, as it had destroyed his relationships before – one marriage, several long-term girlfriends. It was a distrust that would have kept him from the essential closeness that allowed relationships, whatever their ups and downs, disagreements, boredoms, their occasional flurry of agitations, to survive. Yet this time, before the inevitable disintegration could occur, something happened. Sophie.

With Anna pregnant they got married, then sold their respective flats and bought a mortgage-laden house on Ainger Road in Primrose Hill, even then escalating in value with each new rock-star arrival. The smartest investment I ever made, thought Robert now, looking out at the playground from his office window. It had let them come here and make a fresh start, one which Anna seemed to be enjoying even more than him. And now, settled in this brash city, Anna had found her feet and then some.

Until now, it seemed, when the old gallimaufry life seemed to be reasserting itself, all Anna's new calmness deserting her.

He knew he had to talk with Anna about Duval. However much he would prefer to let things lie, Robert was determined to put his foot down: he didn't want Duval in the house, breaking bread at their table. It was starting to look to Robert as if Duval might well have been innocent, and he shared Anna's mixture of excitement and anger over twenty-four wasted years. But helping Duval did not entail bringing him into the house, not as far as Robert was concerned. He didn't want anyone else in his family.

Tonight, he would wait until Sophie had gone to bed, and then he would raise the matter. Maybe Anna and he could compromise on a picnic on Saturday, sit out in the yard while he barbecued chicken and hamburgers, convene at the picnic table after Duval finished the painting job. But not in the house.

6

It was high summer, but already the days were growing shorter. They never seemed that long to begin with; he had grown used to the northern latitude of England, the light fading out as late as ten o'clock. Chicago sat on the eastern edge of its time zone, and it was already dark at eight thirty when Anna came home this evening.

She had called to say she would be late again, and he had given Sophie supper – her new American favourite of sloppy Joes, some leftover minced beef in a barbecue sauce poured over a hamburger bun. He had been tempted to join her out of pique at Anna's delay, but was determined not to sulk and made lamb chops for later, keeping them warm on the stove next to a vast pot of water on the boil for some pasta. He heard the front door open as he sat at the kitchen table, reading a local weekly paper, which was still alien even after almost a year. In the back yard he could just make out the pale penumbra of the fence's new coat of paint.

'I have to go to Washington next Thursday,' she

declared, before she had her coat off. 'I'll only be gone a night.'

'That's sudden,' he said mildly. *Business or pleasure?* That was what he really wanted to ask.

'Philip was supposed to go, but something's come up and he asked if I'd go instead. I don't have to do much, but all the consulates will be there, and we have to have a presence.'

'Where are you staying?'

She seemed to hesitate. 'I think it's the Madison Hotel.'

'How swanky. It's quite a compliment they asked you.'

She shrugged, and taking the open bottle from the fridge, poured herself a glass of white wine. 'I don't know about that. Probably no one else was willing to go. Maggie Trumbull acted like I'd pulled the short straw. Two days in a hot room listening to Foreign Office functionaries boast about how well Atlanta's doing.'

'You've never been to Washington, have you? That will make it interesting.'

'Not much time for fun; I have to have dinner at the embassy the one night I'm there.'

She seemed determined to paint the trip as a grind, so he wasn't going to argue for a rosier picture. He took the chops from the top of the oven, drained the spaghetti, noting that he'd made too much, and put helpings on two of their bone-ware plates, along with a bowl of dressed lettuce. Placing them all on the table, while Anna riffled through the *New York Times*, he said, 'Well, I'm glad it's not this week anyway.'

'Hmm?' she said, eyes still on the paper.

'I'm having drinks with the coach at his house on Thursday. Six o'clock. I should be home by eight. Hope that's okay; it's important I see him.'

'That's fine,' is all she said. She put the paper down and drew her plate towards her. 'This looks delicious.'

This time he did sulk at her lack of interest. She didn't seem to notice his silence, for halfway through her chop she said, 'I think I found out why Duval did so much time.'

Here it was – Duval – and before he'd brought it up himself. Still, he was curious. 'Why?'

'For parole, you need good behaviour and you need remorse. Especially remorse.'

'That was a problem for Duval?'

'Not the behaviour. The remorse. You can't expect it from someone who says he didn't do the crime.' There was no gentleness in her voice.

'Catch-18,' he said.

'What?'

'That was the original title.'

She served herself some salad. 'Spare me the literary allusions, just for once please.'

'I didn't know there were so many of them.'

She seemed about to speak, thought better of it, and shook her head wearily. He didn't see how he could forbid Duval's presence in the house on Saturday without provoking an explosive row. He thought about Anna's discovery. Who would protest their innocence if it meant staying in prison for many more years, unless they were innocent?

'So what's the next step then?' he asked.

'For Duval?'

'Who else?' After all, she didn't want to hear about Coach Carlson.

'I think he needs to talk to professionals. I spoke today with a woman named Donna Kaliski at the Centre for Wrongful Convictions.'

There was a centre for that? It seemed injustice was

big business these days, Robert thought, then felt he was being churlish. He had always admired people like Anna who spent their time helping people who'd been chewed up by a legal system that made its own victims.

Anna said, 'She's happy to meet with Duval, and I think she'll try and overturn the conviction. I'm glad, because there's not much more I can do.' She almost hummed with the patness of this, but he simply didn't believe she intended to walk away from Duval's case.

'Any more pasta?' she asked.

He wanted to say no, since he figured if she could lie to him, he could lie to her. Maybe he was growing up at last, for he forced a smile and said, 'Lots.'

7

The acquisitions meeting was held on Wednesday morning. Robert had chaired it since he'd arrived, taking over from Dorothy who had run it in the hiatus between Robert's arrival and his predecessor's departure. She had been loath to let go, but he had insisted, since he was determined from the start not to isolate himself from the small staff – there were fewer than twenty-five employees, and he let almost all of them attend.

This morning when he came in there was no sign of Dorothy and no one seemed to know where she was. He sensed a slight tension in the room; people weren't joking as they usually did.

It was an even smaller agenda than usual – a couple of history monographs, a coffee-table history of Evanston that was being subsidised by the local historical society. Yes to one of the monographs. Maybe to another (sales wanted to check with a library or two), and a nod-through to the subsidised text.

'Vacation beckons,' he said cheerfully, before turning to progress. 'How many of you are away for part of August?' Half of them raised their hands, but there was something sullen in the way they responded. He resisted the temptation to try and lighten the mood. 'Anything else?' he said, gathering his papers.

Burdick, the production controller, who had been an ally from the start (probably because he clashed continually with Dorothy), raised a hand. 'Someone said there's a problem with the Carlson autobiography. Is that true?'

He turned half-instinctively to Dorothy's usual seat, but of course she wasn't there. Robert realised all eyes were on him, watching intently.

'Hard to say. I'm seeing him soon. We'll know better then.'

He let the meeting end on this inconclusive note, sensing an undercurrent of resentment that he didn't understand. When he got back to his office he looked more carefully at the progress notes for the meeting, and discovered to his surprise that Carlson's book had moved initials.

'Vicky.'

There must have been something steely in his voice, since she was through his door right away. He pointed to the papers on his desk. 'Why did you move the Carlson book to me on the minutes?'

'Dorothy asked me to.' She wouldn't look him in the eye.

'I didn't tell her to do that.'

She shrugged. 'She said it should have happened ages ago.'

'I see,' he said, puzzled. Ages ago? He'd only said last week that he would talk with Carlson, and even then he hadn't said he'd take the book over – if it could be saved, which he doubted. What was going on? Everybody knew she'd signed up the book; everyone knew that she would fight ferociously to keep it under her control.

Then he understood. Dorothy was trying, shamelessly, to shift the blame for losing the book onto him. Not to make him look bad, but to cover her ass – Dorothy was scared of getting fired. What an idiot, he thought. He would never fire someone for losing an author – how could you, in a business where ego, uncontrollable greed, and sheer caprice could overcome in one fell swoop anything more considered? It happened all the time, especially when a bigger cheque book was in sight. What Dorothy didn't seem to realise is that she *would* get fired by playing games. Robert was as disappointed by her cack-handed manoeuvres as he was angry.

Vicky reappeared in the doorway. 'Your wife is on the line,' she said. 'Oh, and Coach Carlson's secretary called to ask if you could see him this evening instead of tomorrow. Same time and place.' Then she disappeared again.

He picked up the phone hesitantly, wondering why Anna was calling.

She said at once, 'I've just had a call from Tim Poindexter.'

'Oh,' he said without enthusiasm, since it was probably an invitation. Tim was a lithe, confident lawyer, who practised at one of Chicago's oldest firms on LaSalle Street. He and his wife Tina were benevolent landlords at the dunes – almost too much so, for they seemed determined to sweep Anna and Robert under their social wing, and hardly a weekend went by without an invitation to their big house up the drive. A mixture of *noblesse oblige* and Anglophilic fascination seemed to be motivating them, which Robert could do without. The whole point of renting the coach house was to get away, not explore an alternative social order.

'He said there were vandals at the dunes last week. They wrecked the hut in their garden and burned down an old boathouse on the beach.'

It must be the same boathouse where Sophie had pretended to disappear. 'That's too bad,' he said insincerely.

'That's not all. They also broke a couple of windows in our garage.'

'Christ. Did they get in the house?'

'No. I don't think they even tried. Tim thought it was probably teenagers from the town.'

'Will he sort it out?' he asked hopefully.

'I don't think so. He didn't actually refer to the lease, but I got the impression he thinks it's up to us to make things right.'

'I bet.' He'd probably argue it was an act of God – some *force majeure* provision. 'Shit. I'm not sure what to do. Tim must have a handyman.' When they'd taken the house, Poindexter had briefed Robert in numbing detail about the water, electricity and oil supply for the coach house. Everything had worked immaculately since then, so this was an inaugural difficulty.

Anna said, 'I didn't ask. I guess I could phone him back.'

He was about to say she should when he had a sudden inspiration, a solution that would solve two problems at once. 'No, that's too complicated. It's better to do it ourselves. I'll go out there Saturday and fix the windows. I'll be back in time for the Crullowitches.'

She said nothing for a moment, then asked, 'What about Duval?'

'That's simple. I'll take him with me. He's always saying he's good with his hands.'

It wasn't that simple at all. He was puzzled when he called Duval with the change of plan to find his old friend reluctant. 'I'll come pick you up,' Robert said. 'Just give me Jermaine's address.'

'It's not that.' He paused, and even over the phone Robert sensed embarrassment. 'I need permission.'

'Whose permission?'

'My officer. I can't leave the city without it. They'd put me right back in Stateville if I got caught.'

'How do you get it?'

'I'd need an invitation from you, Bobby. In writing. Even then they might say no.'

'Fine. I'll write a letter. Get me the number of this guy, and I'll call and find out what I have to do.'

It took him most of the afternoon. He never spoke to the 'officer' himself, just a succession of bored unhelpful people who sometimes answered the phone if he let it ring long enough. Eventually, he secured a fax number, then wrote a formal account of his invitation and printed it out on the press letterhead – he sensed the more official it looked, the better the chances of receiving approval.

At the end of the day, Vicky came into his office, holding a sheet of paper. 'I think this must be for you,' she said, sounding disconcerted. She handed him the paper. It was a faxed copy of his own letter, with a scrawled message and an official stamp. *Authorised/ R B* it read, and he remembered Duval had said the officer's name was Bockbauer. The stamp read *Permission granted from 7/13 8 a.m. until 7/14 6 p.m.* How perverse: he hadn't asked them to let Duval stay overnight, but they'd given him an extra day.

8

Coach Carlson's house was a classic mock-Tudor North Shore pile, nestled in a couple of acres behind a high stone wall. It had been painted recently – against its white stucco the *faux* timbers glistened with a fresh coat of black enamel.

Robert parked in a gravel turnaround, and walked up to a front porch which had roses growing along trelliswork on either side. The door opened before he could ring the bell.

'Mrs Carlson?' he said. She was tall, a handsome woman with a face that didn't smile when he explained who he was.

'Do come in,' she said, but her voice was formal rather than friendly. He followed her into a tiled two-storey hall, and down a corridor towards the back of the house. Paintings lined the wall, and he glanced at a large portrait of a young woman, then realised it was Mrs Carlson twenty years before. She had been strikingly beautiful.

He wished she'd walk by his side so he could break the ice, but she didn't wait for him. He felt half-minded to ask her what he'd done wrong. She was dressed smartly, in a pink skirt, matching cotton jacket, and vanilla heels, and he wondered if she was about to go out – a cocktail party with the neighbours, something like that. Perhaps that was the problem – Robert was delaying her by meeting with her husband.

They passed a dining room and a pantry adjoining a large kitchen, then she stopped and pointed down a short corridor to a closed door. 'You'll find the Great Man in there,' she announced, then turned on her heel and walked away. She's not mad at me, Robert realised; she's mad at the coach.

Carlson seemed about as pleased as his wife to see him. The gangly affable figure Robert remembered from the president's house had been transformed: the coach sat, wearing Bermuda shorts and a T-shirt with the university crest, in a Naugahyde recliner, watching a baseball game on the box, a remote control in his hand. Behind him on the wall were framed photographs of his teams, with the year and their win-and-loss record lettered in at the bottom. Predictable perhaps, though looking at the other walls Robert was surprised to see an array of African art. One painting in particular stood out, of a Nubian woman, a nude, reclining against a background of savannah.

'Have a seat,' Carlson said without looking at Robert.

He sat down on an uncomfortable kitchen chair that had a poor angular view of the TV screen. 'Thanks for seeing me,' Robert said.

Carlson nodded vaguely, then seemed to come to, and with a casual flick of the remote turned off the TV. He sat up in his chair, and Robert realised what a big man he was: 6 foot 2 or 3, maybe 230 pounds – linebacker size. He exuded an authority that women would probably find attractive, men daunting. Robert found himself wishing he had played football at school.

'I told David Balthazar I couldn't really say no,' said Carlson. 'Even if it is a waste of your time.'

Robert had planned a conventional pitch: extolling the advantages of having a local publisher, appealing to Carlson's institutional loyalty. But from his reception he sensed this wouldn't cut any ice, and he decided to forget the usual *spiel*, reckoning he didn't have anything to lose that Dorothy hadn't managed to lose already.

He took a deep breath and plunged in: 'Coach, I don't know your business very well. I'm just your average amateur fan. But if I understand correctly, to do well in your sport you have to have a strong sense of worth – and in your job, you have to inculcate that confidence in your players. Am I right?'

'Of course,' said the coach, sounding bored.

'But that kind of self-esteem isn't enough – otherwise

any puffed-up blowhard could succeed. You've got to be realistic enough to recognise your opponent's strengths, even those areas where he's stronger than you.'

The coach didn't even bother to nod at this. He probably didn't like to be on the receiving end of other people's homilies; Robert most coaches didn't like to be taught themselves. So he got up and handed Carlson one of the catalogues from a major New York publishing house.

'Have a look at that,' he said, sitting down again. 'Those are the titles of one of the houses who want to sign you up. The early pages are their big books for this fall. That's when you sell most books – because of Christmas.' The coach was turning the pages. 'There are some big titles there. *A Life of Sinatra* by Stanley Cullum – Cullum himself is famous, so that will get a lot of publicity. TV talk shows, radio. Then there's *My Time with Lady Di* by one of her ex-boyfriends. And the first stab at fiction by an ex-President, as well as *Kiss and Tell: My Rock 'n' Roll Hell* by a famous groupie.'

The coach laughed. 'Not much like the books you publish, I guess.'

'I'll say. We're fronting with *Trees of Southern Wisconsin*.' When the coach laughed again, Robert pointed at the catalogue. 'The problem you've got with a publishing house like that is that there's competition before the game has even begun. In your own locker room, in fact. I don't care how big the publisher is, there are only so many books they can really promote. Even some big titles are going to be losers.'

'And you're different?' The coach said this challengingly, but he looked unsettled. At least he's listening, thought Robert.

'Of course we are. For two reasons. One, you'll be our biggest title by far. For the autumn, for the year – hell, for the decade. You don't have to worry about competition from *Trees of Southern Wisconsin*, now do you?'

'What's the second reason?'

'The Candy Williams factor.'

'Who is Candy Williams?'

'One of the most successful publicists ever seen in New York publishing. She helped create author tours back when no one had heard of them. She publicised everybody from Toni Morrison to Jimmy Carter.'

'You'd hire her freelance?'

'No,' he said emphatically, thinking a little passion seemed appropriate. 'She works for the press.' As a doubtful look spread across the coach's face, Robert rapidly continued. 'I know what you're thinking: If she's so hot what is she doing working for us? A university press – good reputation, but modest, far from the mainstream. I understand. And the answer is a completely personal one. *Love*.'

'For the press?' He looked bemused.

'Of course not, Coach. For a man, who happened to live in Chicago. So she moved here. Had some kids, did the housework, all that stuff – then she wanted to go to work again. The city's not exactly full of publishers, we were delighted to have someone of her standing, so presto, there she is. And just chafing at the bit to work on your book. You'll get all her attention – and she'll get you national television, all the big papers, radio if you're willing, and she's up to speed with online too. She's a legend in the business. The point is this: we're not going to make you a star, Coach; you already *are* a star. But you'll be the only one in our galaxy. That means you get to shine without worrying about anybody else's light.'

Carlson laughed out loud. 'Buddy, I like that. And I

like you – you sure aren't what Balthazar told me to expect.' He looked at his watch, a big diver's job that looked capable of doing everything except make time stand still. 'But my wife won't like you at all if I let you go on. The Goldfarbs up the road give one hell of a party, and my ass is grass if we're late.'

He started to get up and Robert stood up too, staring at the painting of the Nubian maid. 'Isn't she lovely?' said Carlson, noticing his gaze. *Lovely*. Not a word Robert had been expecting from an American football coach.

Carlson extended a hand that Robert shook tentatively, half-expecting to get crunched. 'You scoot now and I'll do some thinking. I'll be in touch.'

He made his own way out without seeing Mrs Carlson again. Outside, he exhaled loudly, disturbing a marmalade cat that was perched under his car. He felt he'd done what he could, though he was embarrassed by the corny pitch he'd contrived on the spur of the moment.

He hoped the coach wouldn't examine his claims too closely. Candy Williams was a demure woman in her mid-fifties who ran the publicity department of the press with a singular lack of flair. At their one lunch together, shortly after Robert had taken over the press, she had been emboldened by a large glass of Sauvignon to boast that thirty years before she had worked for five months in the publicity department of Farrar, Straus & Giroux. What she would make of his description of her as a 'legend' in the business, Robert could only shudder to think.

9

He left Evanston at eight thirty in the morning and half an hour later found himself on the edges of South Shore, just off Jackson Park, the creation of the World's Fair of 1893 which held the Museum of Science and Industry on its northern border. In his childhood, South Shore had been a middle-class Jewish neighbourhood, already turning black. A trickle became a flood within ten years. For a while the transition had been uncertain: several of the condominium towers that faced the lake had become infested with drug dealers and hookers one step up from the street. But gradually, the neighbourhood had regained its solid middle-class self, and as Robert drove past its well-tended lawns and solid brick houses, he realised that all that had been swapped was black burghers for Jewish ones.

He found the number on South Cornell halfway down the block. This was the western and less prosperous edge of the district, streets of small, tidy bungalows, most with awnings over their front living rooms. The owners of these houses were working people, rather than managers, but the ethos seemed equally aspirant, only on a more modest scale.

Duval must have been looking out for him: he came out of the house at once. Behind him another much younger man emerged from the front door but stayed standing on the front steps, staring at Robert's car. Duval gave a faint wave but the man didn't wave back.

Sensing something had changed, Robert glanced at Duval as he turned onto Stony Island, heading for the Skyway. 'You shaved off your beard,' he exclaimed.

Duval stroked his bare chin, looking simultaneously pleased and embarrassed, like a teenager praised by a parent. 'I thought the ladies might like it.'

Ladies? Robert was momentarily alarmed that Duval was referring to Anna and Sophie. Then he realised what Duval meant – it simply hadn't occurred to Robert before that Duval would want to meet women. He found the idea uncomfortable.

'How's your week been?' he asked.

'Not too good. I thought I had me a date – someone I met, through Jermaine and his wife at their church. We was going to go to a movie.' He paused and shook his head. 'Then she found out where I've been.'

'Maybe you should try another church,' suggested Robert, trying to keep things light.

'I am,' said Duval with a small laugh. 'I been once or twice to the Church of Saints. You remember that one?'

'Where Vanetta used to take us?'

'That's right. Back when she lived on Prairie. It's still rough round there, but the church is going strong. And none of them knows who I am.' He sounded relieved. 'Though people always wants to know what you do for a living, and where you living – it's kind of hard to explain what I'm doing there when I live way south. People are nosy, you know.'

'Yeah.' Robert pointed at the thermos Duval held on his lap. 'What you got there?'

'I brought me some soup.'

'You didn't have to bring that. I'll feed you, Duval. After all, I got to eat too.'

They drove in silence as they moved past Stony Island and onto the thin ascending ramp of the Skyway, climbing slowly at the southernmost tip of the city. He could see the Sky Bridge ahead of them, and found his reflexive tensing begin. He needed to make conversation to take his mind off the impending sharp ascent, the looming feeling of weightless height, the slight panic that worsened when there were no distractions. 'Who was that on Jermaine's porch?'

'That's Lemar. Jermaine's boy.'

'I've seen him before,' he said softly, waiting to see what Duval thought of him.

'Well, then you know he is one bitter young man.'

'What's he bitter about?' Duval was the one with the right to be bitter.

'You tell me. The world. The big wide world.'

'Wide? Or white?'

Duval smiled at the word play. 'Yeah, that too. He's got it into his head that his hands are tied behind his back, all on account of his being black.'

'What do you think, Duval?'

'It ain't no help, Bobby, it ain't no help at all. But no point going on about it. Everybody says it's better than it used to be.' He sounded doubtful himself. 'Jermaine doesn't know how to handle him. He said Vanetta used to chew him out when he went on like that. "Boy, ain't no good blamin' everything on the white man. You got opportunities."'

'Vanetta never liked anyone to feel sorry for themselves.'

But Duval didn't seem to hear him. 'They wouldn't let me go to her funeral.'

'I know.'

'How?' He was suddenly suspicious.

'I was at the funeral, Duval.'

'I thought you was living in England then.'

'I flew back for it.'

Duval nodded, but he was more concerned with his own grievance. 'They said if it had been my mother or father, then they might have considered it. Grandmother, no. I told 'em I'd never had a father, and my mother wasn't worth shit – Vanetta was my mother as far as I was concerned.'

Me too, thought Robert, but it wasn't something he felt entitled to say. He suddenly realised they were past the apex of the Sky Bridge, and saw that Duval was taking in the view. He himself relaxed, contemplating the downward slope of the road, thinking also of the one time he had met Lemar.

X

HE'D FLOWN IN the day before the funeral, through an ice storm over Canada which tossed the 747 like a penny arcade's bucking bronco. They landed in the dark; outside the terminal Robert waited half an hour for a taxi, staring dumbly at the frozen slush and the dirty snow banks – par for the course in February.

He stayed at the Middleton, a small hotel where his grandfather had lived when Robert's grandmother had gone into a nursing home. Then more shabby than genteel, it had been recently renovated, and was also expensive, though the rooms were still little more than large closets. To cheer himself up, Robert gave himself dinner at the Cape Cod Room in the Drake Hotel, catty-corner from his grandparents' old apartment, once Chicago's fanciest restaurant in an era when pork chops were still king of Midwestern cuisine. Suddenly lonely, he thought of people he might call to say he was in town. There was no one.

He'd thought of going to a bar, but felt dissociated in the unrecognisable city of his youth, and knew he didn't want to talk with anyone. So he'd gone back to his room and curled up with the local papers and a bottle of bourbon on the bed, waking in the middle of the night with all his clothes on, the television playing reruns of *Sergeant Bilko*, and the overhead light shining bleakly.

Hotel rooms in the middle of the night filled him with an emotional blankness; they were the scene of an essential solitude which hinted at despair's move towards suicide. The false accoutrements of a home were luxuriously assembled around him – classy soap, *bonnes bouches* of shampoo, body lotion, conditioner; a mini bar, a *luna matrimoniale*-sized bed. None compensated for his sense of aloneness.

He thought of the dead woman he had come all this way to mourn, waiting for eventual exhaustion or, if his anxiety overrode fatigue, the rescuing arrival of the dawn. He was dreading the funeral, he suddenly realised, having deferred any serious contemplation of it as he had hurried to make the arrangements, bought his ticket, cancelled meetings, reassured Sophie he would be home soon. Though Anna had understood at once – to his surprise, perhaps, since his first wife had always mocked his accounts of his closeness to Vanetta.

'Of course you should go,' Anna had said at supper, taking in her stride his announced intention to fly four thousand miles the next day to the funeral of a woman she had never met. The immediacy of her acceptance had touched him; it was not based on any knowledge of the history or circumstances, but simply a statement of faith.

He recognised that the world he would enter the next day would be utterly alien – a service in a church far out on the South Side, where he would be the only white face. He was worried by what might lie in store. Then he drew comfort from his own recent reality – thinking of Anna, now about to leave for work in London after taking Sophie to school. He fell asleep at last, no longer anxious.

In the morning he pondered transport, since he didn't want to rent a car. A cabbie might take him there but then be unwilling to wait around to bring him back. Vanetta's neighbourhood wasn't as bad as when she lived in the ghetto's heart at 58th and Indiana, but a white man wandering around looking for a taxi might be a tempting target.

He ended up being driven by the limousine service from his father's university on the South Side, after agreeing to pay time and a half for the driver to wait until the service had ended. His driver was a Palestinian who had arrived in Chicago only three years before. They left from the near North Side early, but though the church was just five blocks from Vanetta's last house, they managed to get lost just the same.

The church looked like a large unadorned gym, with concrete steps leading to a quadruple series of double doors. Inside there was no one in the outer lobby, and he crept in quietly just as an organ signalled the start of the service. He walked two rows up the centre aisle and sat down in an empty pew, where he surveyed the congregation, ignoring the looks – most just curious, one or two hostile – coming his way.

There must have been two hundred people present, which astonished him until he remembered how large a role Vanetta had always played in the church – regular attendance on Sundays, helping out with the funding suppers, and of course singing in the choir. There was a group of older women, dressed to the nines in colourful pink and blue suits and wearing hats, who must have been Vanetta's choir mates. Family members were presumably in the front rows, and he thought he saw a heavier, older Jermaine sitting next to a tall, lanky teenage boy. For the first time in ages, Robert thought of Duval. There was no sign of him.

The minister came out from a door in the corner and everyone stood. He welcomed them almost exuberantly, as if they were there for a celebration. Perhaps we are, thought Robert, remembering the strong warm woman who had helped raise him.

They sang 'Oh, Happy Days', and then there was a reading by an old woman, immensely fat and wearing a broad-brimmed yellow hat. Then a young girl, probably no more than thirteen or fourteen years, shyly stood and sang an old spiritual.

The minister's sermon was full of a passion that seemed curiously unspecific. 'She came from the heartland of the Mississippi delta,' he began, 'a loving mother, grandmother, and great-grandmother.'

Suddenly someone in a pew shouted, 'She was! Yes, she was!'

The minister was unfazed. 'She was a friend to all, those in need, and those in need of love. A loyal member of the Church, and a dedicated follower of our Lord.'

'Praise be the Lord!' another voice burst out.

The minister continued, with a homiletic eulogy that mixed bible metaphors of a Promised Land with references to this Chicago church. He didn't seem to have known Vanetta very well, and Robert wondered if he was a new appointment. There were occasional interjections from the audience, and gradually Robert realised they were disquieting only to him – everyone else seemed to expect them, nodding and murmuring with each new shout of 'Praise the Lord' or more 'She was, she was'.

Finally the sermon concluded with a hymn, though without a hymn book Robert stood mute, feeling self-conscious, trying to think about Vanetta.

Refreshments had been set out on a table at the back of the room; they reminded Robert of the time Vanetta took him and Duval to her old church off Prairie Avenue. There was a long queue, so he stayed in the middle of the room, trying to pretend he was invisible. He made fleeting eye contact with some of the guests, but no one approached him. Then suddenly, standing in front of him was the tall teenager who'd been sitting next to Jermaine.

'Why are you here, man?' It was said aggressively.

'To pay my respects to your great-grandmother,' he said. The boy must have been Jermaine's son. 'Vanetta worked for my family,' he added softly. 'Your father will remember me.'

'She worked for your family all right.' This was said loudly, rhetorically. There was no immediate audience, but Robert sensed people were watching them, as if they were a couple taking centre stage at a dance. 'She was your people's "help", wasn't she? A modern-day slave.'

Robert suppressed a sigh. He had thought people might be unfriendly, but he hadn't considered a scene to be a possibility. 'I don't think Vanetta would have described it that way,' he said, trying to sound calm, though he didn't feel it.

The boy was warming to some theme. 'How do you know what Vanetta would say?'

'I don't,' said Robert quietly.

'Then maybe you should show some respect.'

What? Robert's fear of a confrontation was suddenly eclipsed by anger, and for a moment he thought he might lose his temper with this pipsqueak. Don't, he told himself, for Vanetta's sake keep your cool.

'Maybe you should do the same,' he said, trying to keep his voice down.

'I didn't exploit Vanetta.'

Oh, so that was it. Robert took a deep breath. 'Look, she was an employee of my family, so I'll stick to the economic history, okay? We'll put aside any emotional displays – the fact I used to say "I love you, Vanetta," when I was a little boy, and as a grown man too. I won't even try to convince you that she meant it when she said "I love you too, Bobby," since from your point of view she didn't have a choice.

'So, we paid the going rate and then some, as I recall, which meant in 1965 Vanetta grossed 60 dollars a week. Not too good, eh? We paid her social security tax and unemployment tax and withholding tax – and every other kind of tax. We didn't pay her cash – she got a cheque each week like many grown-ups do. She had three weeks' vacation a year, all paid, though one year when she went down to Mississippi to see her cousins after Alvin died – do you even know who Alvin was? – she got four. Not a lot perhaps, but more than some people get. We paid sick leave; ask your father what happened when Vanetta was in hospital for kidney stones. And when she couldn't get a mortgage on the Morgan property, my father co-signed it, though when she didn't need his guarantee any more Vanetta got his name removed.'

'Man—' the kid started to say, but Robert held up a warning hand, and continued.

'Since like every story this one hasn't got a happy ending, I admit that my stepmother put your great-grandmother out to seed. Sorry, but she ruled the roost; you know how it is. But Vanetta got three months' wages in a lump sum due to the gratitude of the three spoiled white brats she helped raise. Was it slave labour? The hell if I know, but yes, possibly – she worked hard. Was it appreciated? Well, you tell me. All I can say is that I have flown four thousand miles to be here. Do you have any other questions?'

Suddenly a hefty, older black woman materialised by his side. She was wearing a flowery dress with padded shoulders. And Robert recognised her at once as she snapped, 'Lemar, you talking nice to Mr Danziger?'

'Sure I am, Aunt Trudy,' said the kid.

'It don't look that way to me. Go find your daddy, boy, and ask him when he 'spects to take me home.' The boy dawdled, glaring at Robert. Trudy hissed, 'Go on. Do like I said.' And he moved sulkily away.

'Hello, Trudy,' said Robert. 'I wasn't sure you would remember me.'

'You don't look that much different to me, Bobby,' she said, peering at him through oval glasses looped around her neck with a thin nylon string. She wore an enormous suit of pink chiffon, with bright matching lipstick that highlighted her square thick lips. Older than Vanetta, she was less pretty, less tall, less buxom, and more black. He remembered her testiness, though never with him or the twins. Just with Vanetta – the baby sister, prettier and happier sibling. And with Duval.

He laughed now. 'You still following the White Sox, Trudy?'

'Well,' she said, thinking about it, 'I watch 'em on the TV but I don't go to ball games no more. I hate that new stadium of theirs – that is one cold place, Bobby, and I get dizzy if I got to sit up high. It's so steep, and the place ain't got no character.'

'How about the players, Trudy? Any of them you like?'

She shook her head. 'They just kids to me. Too much money and not enough sense.'

'You remember old Wilhound?' he asked, and a smile broke across her face. Hoyt Wilhelm, a knuckleball relief pitcher of advanced age. Christ, thought Robert, Wilhelm was probably only my age when he came here as a relief pitcher, but he had seemed positively senescent back then.

'That Wilhound,' said Trudy with a half-laughing snort, shaking her head in disbelief.

'They didn't let Duval come, Trudy,' he said, and it was not a question, for he had scanned the room again.

She seemed startled by the name. 'What you know about Duval Morgan?'

'We were friends when I was little, Trudy. Don't you remember?'

She gave a harsh-sounding laugh. 'Then you got the best of him. He turned out bad, that boy. Always told my sister that he would. I ain't surprised he's still locked up.'

'He was a sweet-tempered kid, Trudy. When I knew him he wouldn't have hurt a fly.' He could not imagine what Duval would be like now. It had been twenty years since the trial.

She gazed at him, as if weighing his memory against hers, then decided it was not a contest that interested her. 'Come on,' she said, and he realised it was a command. 'People here who wants to meet you.'

She took him around the room, introducing him to an enormous range of Vanetta's family. He talked politely and drank coffee out of a cup and saucer and even ate half a pecan roll. They introduced the preacher to him, who seemed respected and feared in equal parts by his congregation. He was very friendly to Robert, especially after discovering his profession, suggesting he might send Robert a tranche of his sermons. Robert didn't have the heart to say that there might not be a large audience in the United Kingdom for such a collection.

Then he was alone again. Trudy had done her bit for him, then left with Jermaine and the still angry Lemar and a woman Robert took to be Jermaine's wife. He was looking around the room, feeling isolated and lonely and, for the first time, bereft. He supposed he could get another cup of coffee and hope to find someone else to talk to, but what was the point? He had come here out

219

of obligation to Vanetta; it didn't matter whether he had come forty or four thousand miles; he had done his duty. Anything else now would only be justifying the time and distance taken to come.

He left. Back in the limo he thought fleetingly of his plan to return to the Loop and see the Impressionists in the Art Institute, just as he had so often done as a boy with his grandmother, then eat before catching the bus at the Palmer House for O'Hare and his flight home. But he had no desire now to stir any other memories of his childhood. He felt raw.

For the first time he felt his grief, and put his head in his hands as the driver, baffled by his new instructions to go to the airport, fought his way onto the Ryan. Robert shuddered once, twice, but felt too self-conscious for actual tears. He felt like he had been a neglectful son, separated from his surrogate mother by distance and a painful conversation during Duval's trial. With Vanetta's death he believed the Chicago chapter of his life was finally closed. After all, Duval had not even been allowed at the funeral.

XI

1

HE TRIED TO see the coach house through alien eyes, wondering what Duval made of this small estate, the maple-lined drive off the flat Indiana two-lane highway, and the big twin houses just visible in the distance at the beach-end of the property.

As Robert turned off the drive, Duval gave a low whistle. 'This is pretty,' he said.

'We just rent it.'

'Don't make it less nice.'

Parking the car, Robert could see the broken windows. But there was no sign anyone had come into the garage. Leaving Duval to wait outside, he went and checked the coach house, but it too was undisturbed.

He climbed the garage stairs with Duval behind him, and unlocked the door to its small apartment. All seemed in order: the television sat untouched in a corner, with the CD player beside it – they would have been priorities for any thief.

'Who lives here?' asked Duval.

'It awaits my mother-in-law. She's supposed to come visit this fall.'

'Don't want her in the house?' asked Duval with a sly grin.

'We haven't really got the room,' he said, then laughed in acknowledgement of the truth.

After measuring the broken windows, they drove to a hardware store in the nearest town. It was a small poky place, too near the industrial Indiana belt to be a country town, too poor to be charming. They bought glass panes cut to order, a tin of putty, and a putty knife. Then he bought two steaks at a grocery store. As they drove back Duval started laughing.

'What's so funny?' asked Robert.

'I ain't seen a whiter town than that in a long time. Reminds me of downstate Illinois.'

'You been down there? I mean . . .'

'Yeah. I was six years downstate. Not that I actually saw the town. But I heard about it plenty from the guards. Lordy,' he exclaimed, 'they was a backward bunch of peoples. Illinois 'sposed to be a northern state, but you'd have thought you was in Georgia. *Crackers*.'

'That bad, huh?'

'It was okay if the guards thought you weren't no trouble. They were more scared of us than we were of them – but they got the guns! Some of them had never known any black people 'til they come to work inside.'

Back at the coach house Robert cooked the steaks under the oven's grill, then cut them into thick pink slices onto the buns he warmed in the oven. Taking the plates and two bottles of beer, he and Duval sat out in the small yard, since though the cloud remained it was pale and unthreatening. They ate hungrily, and he went and filled two more buns with the remainder of the steak.

'You like to grill?' asked Duval as he brought them back.

'There's something about the smoky taste.'

Duval nodded knowingly. 'My first meal when I got out was barbecue. I made Jermaine stop the car as soon as we got to Chicago, and bought me a rack of ribs as long as my arm.'

'What was the food like in prison?' He felt able now to ask about life inside.

222

'Some years better than others. That's when you got a choice.' He gave a sour snort. 'Pig slop or beef slop. No ribs, though.'

'Vanetta used to make ribs every week.'

'She did at home, too. Man, she could cook. She told me once her mother taught her when she was just a little-bitty girl.'

'Down in Mississippi?'

'Yeah.'

'You ever go there?'

Duval shook his head. 'Aurelia wouldn't take me. She didn't like it there. She said it was too hot.'

'I can believe that.'

Duval said harshly, 'That wasn't Aurelia's real problem. She wasn't going to like no place where you couldn't get a nickel bag as easy as a Pepsi, and a man with a wallet as big as his dick.'

Robert stood up and collected the empty beer bottles. 'Come on. Time to earn our lunch.'

He decided to cut the strip of grass in their little fenced-in yard while Duval tackled the windows – he didn't feel right reading scripts inside while his friend did manual labour. When he checked an hour later, Duval was almost done, though the putty had been applied unevenly. Next time he'd get the Poindexters' handyman to do it.

He was just handing Duval a beer in the kitchen when he heard a car on the drive. Looking out the window, he was astonished to see the Passat pull into the garage, with Anna at the wheel and Sophie next to her in the front seat.

'I'll be right back,' he said. Outside, he found Sophie rushing out of the garage, and gave her a bewildered hug as Anna emerged more slowly from the car. She was carrying a soft overnight bag. 'What are you doing here?' he demanded.

'We thought we'd see how you're getting on with the DIY. And the Poindexters said there'll be fireworks tonight on the beach.' She avoided his stare.

'Have you forgotten the Crullowitches?'

She looked at him with a studied, defiant air that had recently become commonplace. 'Your president is indisposed. A summer bug, according to Mrs Crullowitch. She sounded quite relieved not to be entertaining us all this evening.'

'We still have to go back,' he said sharply.

'Why? We don't have to go out tonight.'

'Are you forgetting Duval? He's got to be back in Chicago.'

'That's not what his release form says. You left it on the kitchen table. Anyway,' she declared, looking over his shoulder, and her face broke into a grin, 'let's ask the man himself.'

For Duval had come out of the house. He smiled at Anna, then hesitated at the sight of Sophie.

Anna called out. 'Hello, Duval. Sophie, say hello to Mr Morgan.'

Robert waited to see how she would react. An only child, she was easy with adults – too easy, Robert sometimes feared – though occasionally a childlike shyness would assert itself.

Duval bowed down, almost doubled over, and extended a hand, and Sophie extended a limper version. 'How dee do?' he said almost lyrically.

Sophie giggled, and looked at Anna. 'How dee do?' she asked, and giggled again. She pumped Duval's hand in return.

Anna said, 'Is there any reason you can't stay here tonight with us, Duval?'

He didn't look to Robert before answering. 'No, ma'am. I'm good until tomorrow.'

'Well, that's settled then.' She handed the overnight bag to Robert. 'I'll get Sophie's bag out of the car.'

He was glad they had aired the guest flat above the garage, since Robert made sure that's where Duval would be sleeping. He went up with Anna and helped make the bed, leaving Duval to watch baseball on the big television in the coach house living room. He said sharply, 'You should have called and told me what you had in mind.'

'I did. You must have been outside with Duval.'

'What are you playing at?' he asked angrily, but saw nothing but surprise on her face. 'I'm sorry, it's just I think we should be a little careful with this guy.'

'We're only putting him up for the night so Sophie can see the fireworks. You grew up with him – you don't really think he's dangerous, do you?'

Did he? It was the 64,000-dollar question. And the honest answer was no, he didn't. Robert was not naïve about the potential violence in people – he knew he had the potential himself – but he found it hard to see any physical threat coming from Duval. There was something too shy and quiet about him. Doubtless prison had changed him, but not that much.

They ate early, with Sophie, since the fireworks would start as soon as it was dark. They sat at the kitchen table and Anna served them from a big bowl of spaghetti with a Bolognese sauce. Duval hesitated before starting to eat, and Robert suddenly guessed why.

'Do you usually say grace, Duval?'

He nodded. 'Ella is pretty strict that way.' Jermaine's wife.

'Why don't you say it now for us then?'

Sophie looked questioningly at Robert, and Robert put his finger to his lips and gave a little nod. When Duval bowed his head, Sophie imitated him, shutting her eyes as he said, 'For what we are about to receive, may the Lord make us truly thankful.'

'Amen.'

Duval ate quickly, with his fingers wrapped around the fork handle as if it were a hammer. Sophie watched him, open-eyed. 'Gosh, you're hungry, Duval.' He stopped with his fork in mid-air, looking self-conscious.

'Sophie,' said Anna reprovingly.

'The food's real good,' said Duval shyly, as he put his fork down.

'Sophie still eats like a little English girl,' said Robert, trying to put Duval at ease. 'They put their fork in their left hand, their knife in the right.' He demonstrated.

'You eat that way too, Daddy,' Sophie said accusingly.

'Shhh. I don't want Duval to think I went native over there.'

'Daddy says you two knew each other when you were little,' Sophie said to Duval.

'That's right.'

'Did he get in trouble lots of times?' she asked. A recurring motif – when Robert would tuck her in at night, she'd ask for stories about his childhood escapades.

'Oh, not too much,' said Duval, casting a sideways look at Anna. 'I was the rascal.'

'Really? What did you do?'

'Nothing too terrible,' Robert interjected, trying not to think of Lily's panties or the *Playboy* magazine.

After dinner they walked down to the beach, and stood

on the top of the small dunes in the lowering dark, waiting for the firework display to begin down the beach, where the Poindexters and their even wealthier neighbours were gathered in a small group which Robert could just make out. In front of them, the lake stretched like an infinite placid pool in the moonless, windless night.

The first rocket suddenly fizzed into the air, culminating in such a deafening bang that Robert flinched.

'I can't see it very well,' Sophie declared. 'Daddy, can I get on your shoulders?'

'No,' Anna said. 'You know his back's bad.'

Duval said, 'You can go on mine, honey.' Robert watched with mixed emotions as his tall friend reached down and, lifting the little girl up into the air with both hands on her waist, brought Sophie up over his head to sit on his shoulders, her legs dangling on his chest. 'I can see everything now!' she exclaimed.

As the firework display continued, Robert found himself distracted by his daughter's presence on Duval's shoulders. He tried not to let it bother him, but as soon as the fireworks ended, in a crescendo of colourful explosions over the lake, he said, 'Get down, Sophie. Let Duval rest his back.'

'Ain't no problem, Bobby.'

'Come on, Sophie,' he insisted, and eventually she clambered down the tall man's back.

Back at the coach house Duval started to head for the apartment above the garage, but Anna invited him to come into the kitchen for hot chocolate.

'I thought we'd go have lunch at Little Slovakia tomorrow,' Robert said. 'It's a restaurant in Michiana.'

'Michiana?' asked Duval.

'Two states in one,' said Sophie seriously. She remained energised rather than tired.

Anna stood up. 'Come on, Sophie. Time for your bath. It's way past your bedtime.' The little girl said goodnight reluctantly and followed Anna upstairs.

When Anna reappeared, she was yawning. 'Gentlemen, I'm fading, so I think I'll go to bed.'

Duval said, 'I think I'll turn in, too. Could I borrow a radio from you all?'

'Sure,' said Robert. 'Take the one in the kitchen.'

'It helps me sleep. Kind of drowns out the noise.'

What noise? thought Robert.

Robert woke at three, as had been his habit in the days when he drank a bottle of wine a night, which would prompt a middle-of-the-night rising. There was a small stand of poplars that nestled in a semicircle of the back side of the dunes and shimmered now in the breeze that had come up after sundown. Robert lay listening to their thin music, feeling completely awake. He wondered whether to go downstairs and leave Anna undisturbed until he grew tired enough again to sleep.

Then he heard the noise, a faint creak of the outside door, a thump of a footstep. Someone had come into the kitchen. Duval? He waited, suddenly tense, listening carefully, feeling a test was coming. Sure enough, he heard the locked door being tried, between the kitchen and the hallway, the mild shake of its frame as it stayed firmly locked. The noise was unmistakable. Duval had been trying to get in.

He got up at once and grabbed his robe, while Anna stirred. 'What is it?' she whispered.

'Nothing. Just going to the bathroom.'

At the top of the stairs he could see a pencil slant of light from under the kitchen door. Someone was still there.

It had to be Duval. Robert went down the stairs

quickly now, turning the hall light on, making no effort to disguise his footsteps. When he got to the kitchen door he took a deep breath, turned the lock and opened the door.

Duval was sitting at the kitchen table, one hand cupped under his chin in a thinker's pose. He seemed unsurprised to see Robert.

'Did you want something?' Robert asked.

'I couldn't sleep. I was going to read some, but I left my glasses in the living room.' He looked questioningly at Robert. 'Sorry if I woke you up.'

'I couldn't sleep either.' Robert looked over at the kettle. 'You want a hot drink?'

Duval shook his head. 'No, thanks. It would just keep me awake.'

'How about a real drink? I'm going to have some bourbon myself.'

Duval smiled. 'That'd be nice.'

'Come on then. If we keep our voices down, the girls won't hear us.'

They tiptoed down the hallway and into the living room, which had a wall of bookshelves at the near end with a low protruding shelf that served as a bar.

'Have a seat,' Robert said, pointing to the sofa. He poured them each two fingers of Maker's Mark, then handed one of the glasses to Duval. 'Do you mind it straight up?'

'No point diluting the medicine.'

Robert sat down in the leather recliner across from Duval. Each sipped the whiskey in peaceful silence.

Finally Robert broke it. 'How's it going then? Any luck on the job front?'

'Not yet. I got an interview Thursday with a trucking firm. Wants a clerk in their depot to cover the night shift.'

'You mind working nights?'

Duval shrugged. 'I'll work any old time, somebody just give me a job.' He paused and seemed to be listening to something. 'It sure is quiet out here.'

'I know. I'm still not used to it. It's as if I need traffic noise and people talking on the sidewalk before I can go to sleep. The only sound out here is the crickets.'

'Kind of spooky.'

'Yeah, if you're used to people being around you.'

Duval sighed. 'I got used to that all right.'

Of course he did, thought Robert. He must have shared a cell throughout his years inside. He wondered if he would ever have heard crickets there.

'There was always some kind of noise,' said Duval, his voice thoughtful and low. 'Somebody would be crying, or yelling; sometimes there'd be a fight in a cell. Most every night there was something going on – even when there wasn't, the guards would be coming by each hour, shining their flashlights wherever they were disposed to. In your face, on the wall.'

'You get used to it?'

Duval looked at him as if he'd never considered this before. 'I guess you get used to anything, if that means you don't go crazy or kill yourself. It's like fear.'

'Fear?' he said, and just saying the word had the weird effect of chilling him.

'Yeah, fear. You got to understand, in there you're scared all the time. After a while, it's just second nature. It's in your blood. Nothing carefree, everything cautious. You can't even laugh out loud in case somebody thinks you're making fun of them. "*You diss me, man?*"' he said in a high-pitched voice. 'Mocking somebody could get you an unjust reward.'

This explained Duval's covering manoeuvre with his hand each time he started to laugh.

'When the cell door closed at night you could feel safe – ain't that strange? Until you woke up. Then it started all over again.'

'You must have seen some terrible things,' said Robert, wondering if he'd said this only out of curiosity.

Duval looked down at the tumbler he held in his hands. 'I did, though most of them were in my early years. Maybe I just noticed them more then.' He took a sip of whiskey, and Robert noticed his hands were trembling slightly.

'There was a kid my second year that shared my cell. Nice boy, went to service each Sunday, kept his mouth shut, didn't put one foot out of line – not one foot. Then one day some gang dudes got to him in the shower.' He looked up at Robert with disbelief. 'They *strangled* him. There was ten other prisoners in the showers with them and not one of them said a word. I wanted to talk to the assistant warden, tell him what happened, and this other dude says to me, "Man, you do that and you'll be next."

'So I didn't. Everybody knew who did it, but wasn't nothing going to happen from the prison people. Most of them was already in for life, and these days life means life. So what difference did it make?'

They sat in silence again, Duval seemingly lost in his memories. Robert drained the last of his bourbon. 'We'd best be going to bed, Duval. It'll be morning soon if we don't go now.'

'Okay,' said Duval. Robert collected their glasses and they walked to the kitchen, where Robert put the glasses in the sink.

''Night,' said Duval, going out the back door.

'Sleep as late as you like,' Robert called after him, though he doubted Duval would. There would have been too many years of early wake-up calls – Robert's father, after five army years of reveille, could never lie in.

After Duval tramped up the steps to his apartment, Robert heard a tinkling noise, tinny yet reverberating. It was the radio.

2

Robert was up early. He let Anna stay in bed, dozing. He looked in on Sophie and was glad to see her still asleep. There was a soft toy cuddled in her arms. Not for much longer, he thought, since she seemed so intent on growing up fast.

He made coffee and toast, and wondered what Duval would like for breakfast. Pancakes would probably go down well, so he made enough batter for Sophie and Duval, with some extra in case Anna wanted some. Leaving the mix to air, he opened the back door and went out into the yard. The sun was already rising above the birches and warming the air – by late morning it would be thickly hot, and Sophie would want a swim before they left.

When he turned to go back into the house, he saw a police car coming from the Poindexters', cruising gently along the drive. It stopped by the fence and a lone policeman got out. He had an air of small town about him – as if he once had worked for his father's hardware store, or managed a fruit middle-man's depot. His parka was blue and he didn't wear a state cop's wide-brimmed hat. A local cop, Robert decided.

'Morning. Are you Mr Danziger?'

'That's me.' He tried to sound cordial, but all he could think about was Duval. Maybe Robert got the

232

paperwork wrong for his permission to leave the state. Was there a call out now from Duval's officer in Chicago?

'Mr Poindexter reported some damage to his property. I thought I'd better come out and have a look. He said you'd had some too.'

'Just two windows broken in the garage.' With relief, he pointed to the outbuilding. 'I fixed them yesterday.'

'Nothing else?'

'No. I checked the house. There's an apartment upstairs.' He pointed towards Duval's window above the garage. 'But it's fine.'

The policeman nodded. 'You haven't seen anybody hanging around?'

'No, but we're only here at weekends.'

'Mrs Poindexter said there'd been a man on the beach early this morning.' He turned and pointed towards the dunes. 'Just over there.'

'Lots of people walk on the beach. It's public land. By the water anyway.'

'I know, but she saw a man come from this way across the dunes. This was early: Mrs Poindexter says she walks her dog at the crack of dawn. The guy was six feet and a bit, middle-aged.' He paused. 'Gentleman of colour, she says.'

Gentleman of colour? His father had been the last person Robert had known to use the phrase. 'Give me just a second,' he said. He ran up the outside staircase to the apartment. As he neared the top he called out for Duval, then knocking on the door waited. There was no answer, so he went in, crossed the living room and peered through the open door of the bedroom. It was empty, the bed neatly made.

When he came back down Anna was standing in the back door of the coach house, in blue jeans and a

233

plum-coloured T-shirt. Robert said to the cop, 'I think it must be the man who's staying with us.'

The policeman's eyes widened. Robert explained, 'He's helping me with some work here. On the fence and in the yard.'

The cop nodded. 'Okay. Just wanted to make sure. I'll let you know if we find who the vandals were.'

'What was that about?' asked Anna as the patrol car left.

He explained the purpose of the policeman's visit, and Tina Poindexter's sighting of a mysterious black man on 'her' beach. 'It must have been Duval. I don't know where he is – he's not upstairs.'

'Racist bastards.'

'Come on, you can't blame the cop. Not many black people live in this neck of the woods.'

'Bollocks. You're as bad as they are.'

'No, I'm just being realistic. Blacks don't live here, blacks don't come out here – unless it's to—'

'What? Fulfil your stereotype?' She shook her head in disgust. 'Why don't you try thinking about it from a black person's point of view? Say you get invited to a place like this, only to find everybody's suspicious – can you imagine what that feels like? If anything's stolen the first thought is that it has to be you.' She was heading inside, opening the kitchen door, but stopped to deliver a parting shot. 'Come on, Robert, you must be able to see how unfair that is.'

Sure, he thought, it was completely unfair. But also perfectly reasonable. The Poindexters had said there had been a rash of burglaries of the properties along the beach, committed by people who drove out from Gary or Hammond, looking for places to rob during the week when they were empty. 'People', it was clear, given where they were coming from, were black people.

And that was the problem: both sides to the argument thought they were right. No wonder the divide was so great, magnified by white fear and black resentment. Though sometimes the feelings switched sides: he thought of his father and how his early liberalism had receded. Johnny had given large sums when he didn't really have it to give, in the 1950s and '60s, to the United Negro College Fund and the NAACP (how quaint that seemed now), but had grown disillusioned as Black Power and separatism abandoned the integrationism of the early Civil Rights Movement. Blacks moved from being victims to being *angry* victims; his father was puzzled, then infuriated, to discover that he was being blamed too.

Robert had once thought his father's resentment ridiculous, until he went to boarding school. There he had been friends with a black boy, Larry Williamson, also from Chicago. Then all the black students had walked out of morning assembly one day. Robert's fellow white students were mostly the privileged sons of East Coast Wasp wealth, with six-hundred-dollar stereo systems in their rooms, yet they all smoked dope, wore Bass Weejun shoes, and had long hair. For all their hipness, however, they reacted to the black walkout worse than any redneck Robert had known in Michigan. 'I be oppressed by the white motherfuckers so I don't wanna go to school today,' one had mimicked sarcastically, and the others had all laughed. And Robert had thought, These people aren't hip. These people disgust me.

But his own liberalism faltered when Larry Williamson suddenly made it clear he couldn't be pals with a white boy, not even in the rarefied confines of a Yankee prep school. Just as later at college he resented it when black undergraduates almost universally shunned white company. His attitudes were no longer informed by communication across the racial divide other people had struggled for years to bridge.

He realised now that in his adult life, with the exception of Latanya Darling, he had never had a close friend or a lover who was black. Living in England, race had disappeared from his life – it didn't seem to have a role. And somehow he had thought that in his absence it had become a smaller part of American life as well. Had he been kidding himself? It seemed Anna thought so.

Then he saw Duval, heading towards them from the dunes. He waved, and his old friend waved back. When he got back to the coach house, Duval was breathless. 'I had me quite a walk,' he said. 'Must have gone four or five miles down the beach. I still ain't used to so much exercise.'

'See anybody?' asked Robert mildly.

'There was some lady when I started walking, with a big dog that kept barking. She waved at me, but I didn't know her so I didn't wave back. I never did like dogs much.'

3

It was called Little Slovakia, a roomy white pine house converted into a restaurant with a car park where the back yard would have been. It had a small bar with old-fashioned padded leather stools, and one large dining space full of round tables and dark wooden chairs. Locals ate there, and they looked with unfeigned interest as Robert came in with his wife and child and a tall black man.

'This is my shout,' he told Duval when the waitress came with menus, then realised Duval didn't know what he meant. 'It's on me, okay? My treat, to say thanks for coming out all this way.'

When they ordered, Duval looked flustered. So Robert went first, choosing roast duck with cherries, and Duval rapidly said he'd like that, too. While they waited for their food, Sophie coloured in her paper menu.

Watching her, Duval said, 'You're a good artist.'

'Thank you,' said Sophie. She seemed completely at ease with him. 'Hey, Duval,' she said, her eyes on the paper, 'when you were little, did you know Vanetta too?'

'I did.'

'Vanetta was Duval's grandmother,' Robert explained.

'Really?' she asked. She seemed to find it hard to believe that Duval had once been somebody's grandson.

The waitress stopped at their table with a vast aluminium tray. She put it down on a stand and gave Sophie her plate of fried perch, then distributed three duck platters. Duval looked at his with alarm.

Robert said, 'If you don't like it, I'll get you something else.'

Duval gave a friendly shake to his head. 'Your daddy always did look after me,' he said to Sophie.

'Bossed you around more likely,' said Anna.

Duval grinned. 'Yeah, that too.'

But he tucked in promptly and seemed to like the duck – a big half-bird in a cherry-laden sauce, served with mixed white and wild rice, walnut stuffing and green beans. Robert noticed again how ravenously Duval ate. Didn't Jermaine and his family feed the man?

'This is *good*,' said Duval as he ate. 'It's nice eating with you all. Shoot, it's nice to be with such a close family.'

'Are you coming to see us soon in Evanston?' asked Sophie.

237

Duval look wistful. 'That depends if there's more work I can do for you all.'

Sophie said, 'Maybe you can babysit for me when Mom and Dad go out.'

Christ, thought Robert – what will she think of next? Even Anna looked uncomfortable. But Duval batted it back, saying, 'I'm sure you got yourself some nice babysitters already.'

'Mrs Peterson,' said Sophie, and made a face.

'There's plenty of other things to do, Duval.' Anna spoke before Robert could intervene. 'It's a big place – something's always not working right. And there's plenty of gardening jobs. I want to have flower beds dug, and maybe plant some more trees. Once I have a plan, I could use some help.'

She continued talking in this unprecedented horticultural vein until they'd had dessert and Robert paid the bill. Outside the restaurant, when Anna and Sophie said goodbye, the little girl spontaneously hugged Duval. He stooped down awkwardly and put his arms around her in return. Anna shook his hand. 'You make sure you see that Donna lady again at the centre this week,' she said.

That Donna lady? thought Robert. Even Anna's English was turning American.

He stood with Duval as Anna and Sophie drove off, then Robert took three twenty-dollar bills he had folded in his shirt pocket and handed them to Duval.

'What's this for?'

'You did some work, so I owe you some money. Simple as that.'

'I wouldn't call it work. You put me up, you fed me. I had a nice bed.'

'Go on, take it.'

He was glad when Duval did. They got in the car,

staying silent, listening to the radio until they reached the outskirts of Chicago, when Duval suddenly declared, 'You're a lucky man, you know. You got yourself a wonderful family. That little girl – she's a pistol. And Anna, she's as nice as she can be.'

'Thank you,' Robert said, hoping the laudatory gush could now stop. 'Would you like to have a family, Duval?'

'Sure.' His voice was short. 'Not likely though, is it?'

'You're not that old, Duval. Lots of people just get started at our age.'

'I wasn't talking about my age. I'd have to meet somebody who believed me, Bobby. People think if you did the time, you did the crime.'

'Not necessarily. There are all these cases where DNA shows the wrong people have been put in prison. I read about one in the paper just last week.'

'I did too. He done six years.' A mere bagatelle, his voice suggested.

'People aren't so quick to judge now they see that the system can get it wrong. It may take a while but there's no reason you won't meet somebody, settle down, even have kids.'

'It's not just whether I did it that worries them.'

'Oh?' They had come off the Skyway now, and he turned to head for Cornell Avenue, slowing at the corner as an ambulance flashed by with no siren on.

'They have to ignore the missing twenty-four years.' There was a relentless quality to his voice. 'They have to think it didn't twist me up, my being put away so long. They have to trust me.'

'It doesn't seem to me you're twisted up.'

They'd reached Jermaine's house, and Robert pulled over but left the engine running. He reached out a hand and they shook.

'Thank you,' said Duval.

'Thank *you*,' said Robert. 'At least I know the garage window won't fall out tomorrow, which it would if I'd done it.'

Duval gave a weak laugh and opened the door. He got out, then leaned down, his expression suddenly set, and spoke through the open window. 'You should trust me, too, Bobby.'

'I do, Duval.'

'Then why did you lock the door last night?'

4

A front of heavy stratocumulus moved down from Wisconsin and the temperature dropped 20 degrees. Staff were starting to go on summer holiday, but Vicky had deferred hers to coincide with his trip to Frankfurt in October. She seemed determined now to conduct herself at some imagined professional standard – there was no more reading of novels during slow moments. When Balthazar called that afternoon, she put him through right away, and Robert picked up the phone happily, noting that like many friendless people, he was starting to mistake acquaintance for amity.

Balthazar said, 'I *told* him not to talk to you.'

'Excuse me?'

'Coach Carlson. I don't know what you said to him, but it worked.' Balthazar sounded both impressed and irritated. 'Though who the hell is Candy Williams?'

'A legend in her time.'

'What time is that – 1875?'

'I did my best,' said Robert. 'So what's the story?'

'We've had four bids in. Carlson says if you can match the best one, then the book is yours.'

240

'What do I have to pay?' he asked. If silly money was going for the book, he might as well cut and run now – all his showmanship with Carlson wouldn't matter.

'275K.'

'I see,' he said gnomically. There was no point rushing to accept, since it seemed Carlson was calling the shots, not the agent – Balthazar didn't sound happy at all about letting Robert and the press enter the bidding. It was a lot, but the figure was less than he'd feared, and provided the hardback got some decent reviews, he could always sell off the paperback rights.

'That's for North American rights only. You'll have to pay more for World English.'

Robert laughed. Did Balthazar think his brain had turned to mush out in the boondocks? 'I'm happy for you to keep those. Can't see a big sale in Australia for the coach's memoirs.'

'Suit yourself. There's one condition, though.'

He should have known. 'What's that?'

'Carlson wants you to be his editor. Otherwise he'll go with HarperCollins.'

'Me? Why does he want that? I thought he got on with my publishing director. She's a good editor.' If a major pain in the ass who had almost lost the book.

'That's the condition.'

Christ, thought Robert, I don't even like football. Or the coach, for that matter. 'I'm a little surprised by this.'

Balthazar sighed. 'Can we speak frankly?' he said.

'Of course.' It seemed an unnecessary request – he had never known Balthazar to speak in any other way.

'I think the coach got on well with this woman. *Very* well.' He paused to let this sink in. 'But relationships change – as you and I know to our cost.'

A reference to his and Robert's divorces? Probably, but Robert was still trying to digest what the agent had

241

just said – Dorothy had been involved with Coach Carlson. It seemed positively incredible.

'Are you sure about this?'

'I had it from the horse's mouth, as they probably like to say in Chicago.' He added with slight malice, 'It seems my client's fabled interest in African-American athleticism has not been confined to football.'

Cautiously, Robert asked, 'But you say the relationship changed?'

'Apparently. I believe his wife may have had something to do with it.'

'She found out?'

Balthazar grunted a verbal affirmation over the phone. Robert pressed on, intrigued, 'Is that why you went elsewhere with the book?'

'I don't know the precise order of events. And I don't want to,' he said piously, in a rebuke to Robert's probing. 'All I know is, he won't work with that woman. It has to be you.'

Reining in his curiosity, Robert said, 'Okay. Can you give me a day or two?'

'If I must. What's the issue?'

The issue was Dorothy; he would need to talk with her first. But it would alarm Balthazar if he said so – as well as Coach Carlson if Balthazar reported the conversation. 'The money's the issue. It's worth it, no question. I just need clearance at that level of spend.'

'I thought you ran the press.' Balthazar's voice was suddenly less friendly, reminding Robert that if it had been up to the agent, he would not be making this call, but enjoying instead a celebratory lunch at the Four Seasons with the acquiring editor from HarperCollins.

'I need an okay from the university president.' This was pure invention but should sound plausible. 'It's a lot of money for us.'

'That's what's worrying me.'

'Don't let it, or you'll get to hear the *spiel* I gave Carlson on what a great job we'll do on the book.'

And for the first time Balthazar laughed, though Robert didn't join in, since he was pondering with a mix of apprehension and fascination just how he should talk about this to Dorothy Taylor. At least now he understood why Mrs Carlson had been so angry with her husband.

He gave it an hour, then rang and asked Dorothy to come and see him. 'Give me a minute,' she said in her terse way, and it was twenty before she sashayed in and sat down across from him.

He cut to the chase. 'David Balthazar called me.'

If she were surprised, Dorothy didn't show it. 'What did your old pal want?'

He ignored this. 'He's giving us the chance to match the highest offer he's had.'

She nodded, but the way she lowered her head told him she was stunned.

'There's a condition.'

'I'm sure there is,' she said, still not looking at him.

'He wants me to be his editor.' When she kept her head down he added, 'You don't seem surprised.'

When she raised her head it was with the clear-eyed look of a liar. 'Why should I be? You set this up with Balthazar from the beginning.'

He exhaled in disbelief. 'Is that your take on this – that I've been scheming to get this book away from you? Are you serious?'

She shrugged and looked away.

'It's the last thing I need, Dorothy. Can't you see that? This isn't about Balthazar and me – he doesn't even want Carlson to stay with us. But Balthazar's not calling the shots; Carlson is. And the coach doesn't want me – he just doesn't want you.'

'Shit,' she said wearily, putting a hand to her head in what he felt was her first honest reaction since the conversation had started.

'I don't want to know about the coach and you,' he said, and was pleased to see he had her full attention now. 'That's your business. We all have baggage that way – even me, as you know. But I don't want to buy this book if you're not going to be behind it.'

He knew what her dissension could mean: a fatal gnawing away at the book's chances – by marketing, by publicity, even by sales, all orchestrated by a publishing director making it clear that the boss had paid way over the odds for a stinker. With Dorothy's help, the title would become the focus point of any animus he had managed to attract in his brief tenure.

Dorothy sat there thinking for a moment. At last she said softly, 'Buy it.'

'You sure? You're going to have to be behind this, Dorothy, or so help me, I will fire you.'

She laughed out loud. He sensed relief in her that this fear had been forced out into the open. 'You know your problem, Danziger?'

'If I do, I think you want to tell me anyway.'

'You don't know if you want to fuck me, and you don't have the balls to fire me.'

He shook his head wearily. Where had she got this idea?

'Shee-it,' she said, in a parody of a ghetto voice. 'You mean I guessed wrong. You know what they say, "Once you go black you never come back."'

Latanya Darling bites again, he thought. 'You're batting five hundred, Dorothy. Great in baseball but not so good when your job's on the line.'

'I'm not resigning if that's what you're hoping.'

Her lips pursed like a cloth bag as its drawstrings were pulled. He didn't want to reassure her, but felt he had to. 'I don't want you to resign. If I did,' he continued, 'we'd have had this conversation a long time ago. Don't ever think I'd hesitate, balls or no balls.' He looked pointedly at his desk. 'Now if you don't mind, I've got other things to do.'

She didn't rise to go. 'Latanya Darling said you were tough. She was right.'

He turned and looked out the window at the playground in the grey light of the overcast day, empty except for a park employee emptying a litter bin at one corner. Keeping his eyes on the view, he said softly, 'Latanya Darling got me wrong. Just as you have.'

5

'There's not a lot to eat,' he said, peering first into the fridge, then the freezer compartment next to it. 'You can choose, and I'll cook. How's that sound?'

'When's Mom coming back?' Sophie replied.

He laughed. 'Tomorrow. Is my cooking that bad? Tell you what, how about if I get—'

She beat him to the punch. 'Chinese takeaway?'

And sixty-three dollars and a Chinese *grand bouffe* later (Sophie always insisted on Peking duck), he was putting down his chopsticks when the phone rang. 'Why don't you get it?' he said.

He listened as Sophie talked with her mother, promising to go to bed soon, describing their feast.

Then he spoke briefly with her as well. She sounded perfunctory: yes, she had arrived all right; yes, the hotel was very nice; now she was going to bed because she had a breakfast meeting.

He put Sophie to bed, ignoring her complaints that she wanted to stay up since her mother wasn't home. Once she was tucked in (though he suspected she was reading under the covers) he cleaned up in the kitchen.

He felt nervy, uncomposed. He and Anna were rarely apart, since he was able in the new job to keep travel to a minimum. When he was away – usually New York, and just for a night – he felt that Anna, staying at home, functioned as a beacon for him, throwing out light from a hub to give him his bearings. But now that he was the hub, he felt completely in the dark.

He wanted to call Anna back. Was he looking for reassurance, he wondered? Probably. He dialled her cell, but it was switched off. He called information in Washington and got the number of the Madison Hotel. Something was starting to agitate him and he waited impatiently while the switchboard operator searched for Anna's name.

Fruitlessly. He spelled it any number of ways until the operator politely pointed out there was only one resident with a surname starting with 'D' staying at the hotel, and that was a Dr Daniels. He even tried Anna's maiden name, which was Pomfret, but she wasn't there, either. He put down the phone feeling faintly sick, and poured himself three fingers of bourbon, absent-mindedly throwing in a bunch of ice cubes from the freezer's fancy machine. Pacing around the kitchen, he told himself not to jump to any conclusions, though he felt confident that he knew what this meant.

There seemed no point ducking it, for though he thought of trying the cell phone again, that would just provoke another kind of lie. Instead he rang back the hotel, getting the same woman at the switchboard. He thought he heard her sigh when she heard his voice, so he said, 'I don't want to be put through to anyone, miss.

Could you tell me if you've got a guest registered under the name of Masters?'

And she said without hesitation, and without any knowledge of how momentous her words might be to him, 'Philip Masters?'

So now he knew.

6

When he had come to think his ex-wife was going to leave him, it had been a gradual process, moving from intimation to suspicion to certainty. She had taken to going 'on location', a producer's prerogative she had never shown much interest in exercising before. In retrospect he saw that she had gone through a large stage door labelled 'Distrust'. But when he had first had doubts, he had stamped on them. Had he been doing the same with Anna?

A mistake, he thought, as he cleared up the breakfast things, finished making Sophie's packed lunch, then walked his unknowing, happy daughter (Mom would be home that night; Dad was here to spoil her) to the corner just in time for the day camp minivan.

He had been trying to attribute his recent jealousy to his desertion by his ex-wife, telling himself it was natural to be hypersensitive after that had happened. So he had persuaded himself that there was nothing wrong, which made it impossible to voice his suspicions to Anna – not when he doubted them himself.

He didn't have any doubts now, and through the morning at work felt alternately despairing and bewildered. What was he going to do? Would Anna and this man go back to England, taking Sophie with them? Would Robert follow? The only home he felt he had was Anna and Sophie – not Chicago, not Primrose Hill: it didn't matter where he lived if he wasn't living with them. Here in Chicago he had no real friends, but it didn't seem to matter. He felt he could tolerate anything – cuckolding, the loss of Anna's love – if he didn't lose his family.

It came almost as a relief when Duval called him, just before noon. He had just cancelled lunch with Andy Stephens, the accountant, since Robert felt in no condition to talk business for an hour and a half.

'Hi, Duval,' he said, trying to sound cheery.

'Any chance you can meet me in fifteen minutes?'

Why not? It might take his mind off things. 'Sure. Same place?' He was growing attached to the Marchese Building.

'Can you come to the Hancock Building? There's a coffee shop there on the Michigan Avenue side. It's a level down from the street.'

He could see no reason to say no. 'Sure. See you there.'

It was hot enough that he took off his linen jacket on his walk the few blocks north along Michigan Avenue. He remembered the construction of the Hancock Building, how astonished people had been when its bracing angular brackets turned out to be not temporary accompaniments during the build, but an inherent part of the tapering tower itself. It looked elegant now, decades later, a useful meditative point between traditional needle-like skyscrapers, and the post-modernist penchant for Lego-like ins-and-outs or Gehry-like curves.

He spotted Duval standing in the little plaza below street level. Looking down at him, Robert forgot the sheer height of the building above, a blessed minor amnesia for him, height-shy as he was.

'I got us a surprise.' Duval proudly waved two tickets in front of his face.

'What's that?' asked Robert.

'Tickets for the top.'

Robert felt a sudden stab of anxiety. This wasn't part of the plan. He wondered if Duval could get a refund. But before he could say anything, Duval said, 'This time it's my shout.'

He looked so proud of paying for this 'treat' that Robert didn't have the heart to spoil things. He would just have to grit his teeth and get through it.

Inside they waited in a queue of tourists, until a squat man took their tickets and they entered an enormous elevator. Robert headed immediately for the far corner and gripped the rail. The doors closed, and they rose slowly at first, then the elevator accelerated and his stomach struggled to stay on a lower floor. Robert looked up at the LCD floor indicator clicking off the floors – 47, 48 . . .

They stopped with a sudden lurch at the observation deck on the ninety-fourth floor. The doors opened at his end, and he managed to get out, feeling shaky. Then he saw through the windows an apartment block in the far distance, sitting like a child's toy, so far below his line of sight that it made him realise just how high up they were. He began to feel panicked.

He fought the impulse to turn around and run back into the open elevator, and already Duval was striding towards the bank of windows, exclaiming at the view. Robert couldn't desert his friend. He followed cautiously, his legs wobbly as stilts, and when he joined Duval at the window, he grabbed onto the waist-high protective bar, hoping to steady himself.

They were on the south side of the building, with a view of the Loop a mile away, then behind it the neighbourhoods of the South Side, stretching out in an indiscriminate mass of brownstone houses and apartment buildings, dotted with the odd park here and there, the ribbon-like roads of the Ryan and Lake Shore Drive, and on the left edge the bordering blue of Lake Michigan. Robert tried to focus his eyes on individual buildings and places – the Prudential Building, the Millennium Park, in the distance the dome of the Museum of Science and Industry – but coherence seemed unattainable as his agitation increased. So much for 'exposure therapy', he thought bitterly. Faced with his greatest fear he felt swamped by anxiety that showed no sign of subsiding. Inexplicably, he felt the strongest instinct to jump out of the windows.

Duval said, 'Everybody keeps saying how much the city's changed. All these new public places and skyscrapers. But tell you the truth, I never knew it that well before. I hardly ever came downtown – maybe once a year at Christmas. I couldn't tell you if Michigan Avenue's changed. I was just a little ghetto nigger who knew his own neighbourhood. And yours, I 'spose.'

'I had grandparents up here,' Robert said deliberately, trying to picture his words – anything other than the reminders, each time he looked out, of how high up they were. 'But I spent almost all my time in Hyde Park. I thought Chicago *was* Hyde Park.' He dared a quick look down towards the South Side, and regretted it as the world below shuddered vertiginously.

Duval nodded absently, but he didn't seem to be listening. He said, 'When I was young, and white people would see me on the street and look scared, I liked it. But not any more. Now I want to stop and say, "Listen, I'm just like you. And I'm scared, too." Only mine's a different kind of fear. I couldn't even tell you what I was scared of, half the time, and it's the not knowing that makes the fear worse.'

With the mention of fear, an image entered Robert's head. It was from a film he'd seen, a documentary made by a pair of French brothers, about daily life in New York, that had suddenly found itself taken over by an inconceivably larger subject. Municipal workers, laying pipes beneath the surface of a street in downtown Manhattan, turned and watched through a blue sky of autumn clarity – you could feel the crispness of the morning air – as a jet sailed serenely overhead, straight into the North Tower. An eerie normality had preceded the collision – it reminded Robert of the Auden poem in which Icarus fell from the sky, watched by a farmer at his plough on what had been a completely ordinary day.

He knew no one who was not fearful after the Twin Towers had come down, but the public expression of fear was always about Islam's war on the West, breeding a ridiculous paranoia, especially in his native country – rural counties in Michigan getting anti-terrorist subventions from the Federal government, or the coast guard instituting a no-go zone in Lake Michigan to deter incursions by speed boat that might . . . do what? Deposit suicide bombers on Oak Street Beach?

No, for Robert the terror he felt was entirely personal, since the disaster of the Towers represented his own worst nightmare. To be trapped up high with no parachute, no prospect of a helicopter rescue, no way out except the window. Just the certainty of doom, as the smoke and heat rose towards you, imprisoned a thousand feet above *terra firma*, knowing you were going to die.

He shuddered slightly, and scanned the horizon, certain that any minute now he would see an approaching plane.

251

Suddenly he heard Duval say, 'You aren't listening.'

He tried to pull himself together. 'Sorry, Duval. Say it again.'

Duval said, 'I *said* I got a problem, Bobby. Jermaine don't want me in his house no more.'

'Why not?'

'Well, it's probably not Jermaine so much as Ella. She's never been happy about me lodging there.'

'Where are you going to go next?' When he saw Duval's face he wished he had kept his mouth shut.

'I've been thinking. I don't 'spose . . .' began Duval, then paused, while Robert tried to look across the lake at eye level, anything to ignore the sickening, scary effect of looking downward. He sensed what question Duval was asking, but was too seized by anxiety to think of a response, much less make one. He knew he couldn't take being here much longer.

'What's the matter, Bobby?' Duval looked at Robert curiously. 'Don't you feel well?'

'Do you mind if we go down now, Duval?' He didn't want to say anything else.

Duval seemed almost pleased by the request. 'You don't like it up here, do you, Bobby?'

Robert managed to shake his head, trying to control his impatience, verging again on panic. He really wanted to get down right then.

Duval slapped him on the shoulder with an open hand. 'That's all right, we'll go down. Right away.' But he took his time heading for the elevator. 'Man, that's funny. When I was little, I was the one 'fraid of heights. Never could go up that tree.'

The elevator took for ever to come. Robert counted silently to ten, then ten again, only half-listening to Duval. At last the doors opened, and he scooted in as people left from the other side.

As the elevator descended, he gradually regained his equilibrium. Back on the ground, he felt guilty about cutting short this expedition and suggested they go to the coffee shop in the small plaza below street level. Duval agreed but once seated said he didn't want to eat, and this time Robert took him at his word. Duval seemed glum now, and Robert tried to make conversation, talking about the White Sox and a game he'd seen on TV until out of the blue Duval said, 'Do you all need any more work done this weekend?'

Robert shook his head trying to look regretful. 'We're away this weekend, Duval.'

His friend's face fell. Robert added, 'But maybe next weekend. I'll see what needs doing at the house.'

'Don't matter,' Duval said, with resinous depression in his voice.

They got up and Robert paid the bill at the register. Back on street level he said, 'I'm sorry, Duval. I'm not trying to let you down.'

Duval shrugged. 'It don't matter. I'm used to that. Even with you, Bobby.'

Stung, Robert looked at Duval and was struck by his unforgiving eyes. 'I'm sorry if you feel that way.'

Duval was shaking his head. 'Vanetta would always defend you. I don't know why. She said you'd done what you had to do. Didn't make sense to me.'

'I don't know what you mean.' He couldn't tell if Duval was talking about something specific, or if this was a generalised resentment.

'Maybe you don't,' said Duval. His jaw set and he stared rigidly out at the street. 'I best be going.'

He set off, and seemed to float away in the hot, bleary sunshine, like a castaway leaving a mooring he didn't trust.

Robert called out, 'Phone me next week, okay?'

Duval gave a vague acknowledging wave but didn't

turn around. Robert knew Duval was disappointed that Robert wouldn't take him in. But it seemed there was something else Duval resented, something Robert didn't understand.

He had a meeting-less afternoon, and to sit alone in his office seemed unbearable right now, so he turned and walked down the Golden Mile towards the avenue's convergence point with Lake Shore Drive. He passed the Palmolive Building, in his father's day the city's tallest building, a grey stone deco tower of thirty-seven floors with a revolving beacon on its roof to alert night-time aircraft in the old days. How the dimensions of the town had moved skyward: the Palmolive Building looked like a pygmy relic now, hemmed in by taller neighbours.

At Michigan and Lake Shore Drive he stood at the front awning of the Drake Hotel, watching the swimmers across the way in the small crescent of Oak Street beach. He looked up, not very far by present-day standards, and could see his grandparents' former apartment on the twenty-second floor of their old building. He'd slept on a divan in his grandmother's bedroom, waiting for the revolving beacon across the way to flash a pencil of light through the window.

Not all memories were bad, he realised, thinking of his grandparents' warmth, the card games with Gramps, the trips with his grandmother to concerts, movies, lunch in the Art Institute with her own cronies – all in their seventies but still known collectively as 'The Girls'. Even his trip to Hyde Park with Sophie had been a pleasant surprise. The grim snow-bound, shit-filled place he remembered had seemed unexpectedly beautiful – Robie House's sweeping prairie roof, the lush green of the lilac bushes on 58th Street, Botany Pond and the lawns of the Quadrangle.

Yet just as he hoped to grow reconciled to his past, his present life was threatening to unravel. He wondered how things with Anna had suddenly gone so wrong, and sensed a shadow lurking somewhere that had blighted them. And then he saw, not metaphorically but as a clear image in his mind's eye, Duval standing in the background. It was Duval who had driven a wedge between Robert and Anna. Without Duval's re-entry in his life, Robert would have made peace with his own wounds. Instead, he felt he was being forced to bleed for Duval's.

7

He heard the front door open and close, then Anna went upstairs to check on Sophie, who was almost certainly wide awake, waiting for her mother.

'So how was Washington?' he asked when she came down to the kitchen, still wearing her raincoat. He was sitting at the pine table, waiting for their supper to heat up. His voice sounded phoney to himself.

She looked at him sharply, then shrugged. 'Kind of dull.'

'Good meeting?'

'Too long. So much for British reticence.'

'Nice hotel?'

She nodded.

He could not sustain the pretence. He flipped the magazine he was reading onto the table, where it slid, slowed, and finally toppled to the floor. 'After you rang me last night, I tried to call you back. Your mobile was switched off, so I called the hotel. They didn't have anyone registered in your name.'

'You don't say,' she said flatly.

'Though Philip Masters was there, so maybe you were doubling up. Saving the consulate some money.'

She shook her head wearily, then sat down on one of the kitchen chairs, putting her hands in the pockets of the raincoat. 'I spent the night in a Marriott off Route 128.'

'Boston?'

'Quincy, actually.'

'That's near my old school.'

'Don't look alarmed. I wasn't investigating *you*.'

'What were you doing there?'

'Looking for Margaret Tykzinski.' She saw the question on his face. 'That's her married name. She used to be known as Peggy Mohan.'

'Did you find her?' He had known Anna wouldn't give up.

'It wasn't easy,' she said grimly. 'Google was a succession of red herrings – so much for "intelligent search". I tried tracing her through relatives here in Chicago, but the only one I could find was an uncle, and he wouldn't tell me where she was.

'Then I got lucky. Maggie Trumbull has a friend who works at the university hospital. I asked her to check if there was any record of a forwarding address for Mohan – she never went back to work at the hospital. One can hardly blame her. Anyway, this friend had a friend who was friends with someone in personnel – it sounds like a chain in a property deal, but this one held. I got an address.'

'In Boston?'

'No. In Kenosha. I drove up there last week.'

'You might have told me.'

She was unabashed. 'I knew you wouldn't approve. Peggy Mohan lived there for almost ten years, still working as a nurse – in an old people's home. Then she met Mr Tykzinski and moved to Boston. She works in a hospital on the South Shore.'

Never a keen flyer, Anna had found the landing at Logan, coming in over the bay, especially frightening. Renting a car, she had made her way through the new tunnel and joined the Southeast Expressway, getting off fifteen minutes later at the Quincy exit. She decided to check in at a motel first, giving her time to review her approach, and she found a Marriott only a few miles from the address she had in East Milton.

'I had thought I might say I was from the new centre for dispute reconciliation. Part of their thing is to bring together victim and perpetrator to effect "closure" – God, I do hate that term. As if anything ever ends for good. But it seemed too sneaky; besides, the whole point is that they didn't get the right guy. In the end, I went to the house, rang the bell, and told the truth.'

'What was she like?'

'She looked old. I'd have thought she was sixty, though she can't even be fifty yet.'

'I'm not surprised.'

'Other things might have aged her, you know.'

He said nothing, and she kept talking. 'It took her a minute to understand what I was saying – maybe it was my accent. I said I was sorry to stir up the past, but hoped she'd understand why I was there.'

'How did she react?'

Anna laughed sardonically. 'Pretty badly. This meek, middle-aged nurse said she understood all right, then slammed the door in my face. I rang the bell again, but she didn't answer.'

'Is that it?'

She waited for a moment before replying. 'I was tempted to get in my car, drive to Logan and fly back

257

with my tail between my legs. But then I thought of Duval – I couldn't let him down without trying my hardest.'

'Yes, how could you do that?' he asked acidly.

'Piss off,' she said. She seemed determined to finish the story. 'I went back to the car and wrote her a letter. I put it through her mail slot, went back to the motel, and prayed she'd respond. And thank God, she did.'

'What did you say?'

'I said my purpose wasn't to upset her, but to help an innocent man. I said that if she would just talk to me, even for ten minutes, I would never bother her again. But that if she wouldn't, she'd have to understand I couldn't leave it alone.'

'You threatened her?'

'Not at all,' she said with mock innocence. 'Anyway, it must have worked. She rang me an hour later.'

They met that evening at a Brigham's ice-cream parlour on the South Shore. Peggy Mohan sat in silence while Anna made her case – that the identification, through no fault of Peggy Mohan's, might have been questionable, swayed by a zealous cop determined to collar the obvious suspect. That if that had been the case, Peggy Mohan had not been complicit in an injustice, but a victim of one, too.

'That's clever,' said Robert. If you couldn't kindle compassion in the victim for the assailant, then suggest they were both victims of another crime. 'Did she buy it?'

Anna gave another tart laugh. 'Not at all. She listened carefully until I was finished, then thanked me for my interest – those were her exact words – and said she had to leave. She was working the night shift and she couldn't be late.'

'So you didn't get anywhere.' He felt deflated, having

been waiting for some coup. It seemed clear there hadn't been one.

'Not directly, no. I didn't.' Anna didn't seem that let-down herself. Robert kept quiet, and she said, 'But I made some progress in another sense. Last week, I had lunch with Charlie Gehringer, just to go through the trial in case there was anything there. You'd said to me they'd matched Duval's blood type to blood they found on the girl.'

'Yes,' he said. His feeling that she had been busy with all this Duval business was right – Kenosha, lunch with Charlie Gehringer, this disguised trip to Boston. What else had she got up to?

Anna said, 'That never made sense to me – why would Duval have been bleeding? When I asked Charlie about it, he said he thought it was the *girl's* blood they matched – there was blood on Duval's blazer. They found it in his apartment when they arrested him.'

'Oh,' he said. 'I got it wrong. But what difference does it make?'

'It's possible now to match the DNA on the blazer with Peggy Tykzinski's.'

'I see.' And he did: the papers were full of DNA-enhanced discoveries, revisitations to the past that had cleared many a convict, incriminated many an over-zealous posse of policemen and prosecutors. Though you never heard about cases where convictions were simply confirmed by this hi-tech testing.

'But there are two problems. The first is whether they can find the exhibit evidence. In theory, it's stored, but God knows where.'

'I'm surprised they've kept it so long.'

'They may not have. Donna has been looking for a while – with no luck.'

The woman at the centre who worked to overturn

wrongful convictions. It had been smart of Anna to bring her in – on her own, Robert couldn't imagine she'd have got far in the bureaucracy of the State of Illinois.

'But there's another problem, too. Even if we find the blazer we still have to prove the blood belongs to Peggy Tykzinski.'

'That should be easy enough. She just needs to take a blood test.'

'Try telling her that. I did my best to be diplomatic, but you should have seen her hackles rise. I know now what they mean by a blanket refusal.'

'What's it to her?'

Anna drew her arms across her, as if she were cold. Impossible, thought Robert, since it was the now-standard muggy night. He had left the windows open upstairs to let the breeze skim off the top edge of heat in the house, but it was still very warm.

She said, 'It's the past, Robert. She's tried to move on, tried to make a life for herself. Then I show up and stir it all up again. How would you feel? Nobody ever raped you, or tried to kill you. Yet you don't even like going back to Hyde Park.'

He thought of the runt and Mule. She was right: there was no comparison between that and what had happened to Peggy Mohan. 'So she said no?'

'Yes. A big bloody, absolute no.'

'I'm sorry,' said Robert, sensing the frustration this must have caused. Anna had actually persuaded the woman to talk to her, only to run into a brick wall.

She lifted her handbag by its strap from the floor. Reaching into it she took out a zipped plastic bag – a sandwich bag, he realised. It bulged from something bulky inside it. She laid it carefully, almost gently down upon the kitchen table and he stared at what looked like a coffee cup inside the plastic bag. It *was* a coffee cup.

'Is that for me?' he asked, trying to make a joke.

'Not until the lab is done with it.'

'What do you mean?' He stared at the coffee cup in the bag, trying to make the connection. When he looked up at Anna, she seemed impatient.

'We had coffee. That's her cup. She went to the powder room, as you Americans insist on calling it, and I swiped it.' She gave a small laugh in relief. 'The only problem was, the waitress saw me. So I told her I was a private investigator, working a divorce case. I gave her twenty dollars but I don't know if she believed me.'

'Why shouldn't she? Jesus. You *are* a private investigator.' He smiled at her warmly. 'You've done brilliantly. This is a real breakthrough.'

Anna grinned broadly, relaxing for the first time. Robert didn't want her face ever to change, but it did. 'It won't mean anything if we can't find the blazer.'

He nodded.

'You have to trust me, Robert,' she said intently.

'I've heard that before.'

She pursed her lips crossly. 'I'm not your ex-wife.'

'I wasn't thinking of her, actually.'

XII

HE WOULD ALWAYS remember the morning he heard because although the 104 was usually crowded, it was rarely late. But that day he had stood by the bus stop on upper Broadway for forty minutes, half-freezing as the wind whistled in from the East Side, and by the time he got to the office it was almost ten o'clock. Unacceptable to his boss, which alarmed Robert, since three years out of college this was the first job he could truly say he liked – and didn't want to lose.

He was working for a small, good publishing house that was owned and run by a man named Leo Nathan, an old Polish Jew who had escaped from Vichy, France, in 1940 and come to New York via Rio de Janeiro. He spoke stilted old-fashioned English, but read the language like a native. He was tight with money, and Robert was so badly paid that he struggled to afford even the grim room he rented on the Upper West Side, in a neighbourhood yet to be gentrified. But Nathan had a keen eye for a book; Robert suspected he was learning more from the old man than he would ever fully understand.

'You're late and you've had a phone call that is personal,' Nathan said crossly that morning.

'Sorry.'

'Somebody saying he's your brother asks you to call him back.'

He handed Robert a message slip. It was Mike, and Robert was alarmed. Had someone died? His father, or Lily? If it had been Merrill, Mike would have sent a cheerful telegram.

'Where does this brother of yours live?'

'He's stationed in Iowa.'

'Stationed?' said the old man. 'Ah, a soldier boy. Well, do me a favour, and call him back collect. Uncle Sam can afford personal calls better than I can.'

When he got through to his brother, Mike said right away, 'Your friend Duval's been arrested.'

Nobody's died then, Robert thought with relief, and wondered why Mike had rung so urgently. Robert hadn't seen Duval for more than ten years. He knew from Vanetta that he had come back to Chicago six months before, and had been working in Hyde Park, as a security guard at the university hospital.

'What's he done?' he asked now, wondering if it was drugs – Aurelia, Duval's mother, had never managed to stay clean for long.

'They say he raped a nurse at Billings.'

He struggled to adjust his image of Duval to the news. He couldn't. 'When did you find out?'

'Last night. Dad told me.'

'How is Vanetta taking it?'

'Hard, Bobby. You ought to call her.'

He rang that night, unwilling to risk Nathan's wrath with another personal call from the office. He had not spoken to Vanetta for several months and hadn't been to Chicago in two years. When he had last seen her she'd made baked chicken and sat with him in the Cloisters apartment's dining room while he ate. He had asked about her family and noticed she'd said nothing about Aurelia, so her daughter must have been on drugs again. Duval was still living with his mother, she'd said with a sigh, and Robert could tell she was worried about him.

Now on the phone she sounded surprisingly calm,

though insistent that Duval was innocent. Robert himself couldn't imagine the easy-tempered boy he'd known being capable of such violence. Yet later that week when he got clippings sent by Mike from the Chicago papers, he realised things looked bad for Duval.

The nurse had not only been raped, but knifed so badly that it was a miracle she had survived. She'd told the police that her attacker had worn the blue blazer of hospital security, and she'd picked out Duval's photo right away from a pile of mugshots.

The local papers played the story big, drawn no doubt partly by a white girl–black boy angle that touched a racial nerve, clichéd but persisting. Duval was being held without bail in Cook County Jail, which, as Vanetta remarked, was not a picnic for anybody – and certainly not for someone as gentle as Duval. Gentle. That was how he remembered his friend, and what made it difficult to think he'd done the crime.

Several months passed, and Duval remained locked up. Robert thought of visiting Chicago, but there was no suggestion he could do anything helpful by going there. His father told him there was talk of hiring a private attorney, but that in fact the public defenders were very good, and the one assigned to Duval's case seemed especially competent. There was a chance, Johnny added, of what he called a *To Kill a Mockingbird* defence: Duval's chest had been very badly scarred in the fire when he had saved a little girl, yet the rape victim had not mentioned anything unusual about her attacker's physique. This hope proved short-lived, however, for a week later his father reported that according to Gehringer, the public defender, the girl said Duval had never taken his shirt off during her ordeal.

With no date set for trial, Robert put it on a mental

back burner. He was working hard for Nathan, never leaving the office before seven at night, and with limitless reading of submissions to do outside work. He'd also, after two lonely years, met a woman who seemed to like him as much as he liked her. Cathy was from Long Island, yet absolutely mad about New York City, an enthusiasm she was determined Robert should share. In the helter-skelter manner of many young men in Manhattan, he led a frantically busy life, and Duval Morgan did not figure very often in his thoughts.

He was never certain what happened to catalyse him into action, and decide he needed to make an appearance at Duval's trial. Perhaps it was Mike's frequent phone calls, encouraging him in turn to call Vanetta, who though stoic-sounding on the phone was clearly suffering. Or maybe it was Lily's disdain when he mistakenly called her in California one night, thinking she would care. Or – and very potent this – possibly it was Merrill's remark, reported by Mike, that since Duval was facing a sentence of fifty years, then, 'Honestly, wouldn't it be better for him to be executed than spend his whole life in prison?'. Whatever it was (and eventually he decided it was largely his enduring sense of obligation to Vanetta), he decided he had to be there.

Leo Nathan was distinctly unsympathetic. 'Someone you grew up with has got himself in trouble. Do I understand correctly?'

'Yes. You see—'

But Nathan had put up a hand. 'Spare me the details. I had not appreciated you had a law degree.'

'I don't.'

'Then how will your presence be of assistance?'

'I need to show my support. His grandmother was like a mother to me.'

'I see. So he is like a brother then?'

'Sort of,' he said uncertainly.

'You seem to have a lot of brothers. When did you last see this one?'

He started to explain, but Nathan waved it aside. 'Tell this brother of yours you can give him a week. A week, at a busy time of the year. Anything more than that and you can ask your "brother" to give you a job. Because you won't have this one.'

So he felt a clock was ticking when he returned to Chicago on Thursday night, catching a flight after work, a day into the trial. Merrill thought it odd that he had returned at all, and he could tell she hoped he would not be staying for long. She was cross, too, about Vanetta's absence from work, lamenting the inadequacy of the local laundry service that was substituting. His father had voiced no opinion about his son's return, but he let Robert use his car on Friday morning, since otherwise Robert didn't have the faintest idea how to get to the court, at 26th and California.

When he arrived he had to park several streets away, and by the time he found the courtroom on an upper floor, the day's proceedings had begun. As he took a seat in the back row, he was struck by how small the room was, tiny compared to the spacious sets of television drama. He saw Vanetta in the front row, sitting behind a black man at a table. That must be Duval, thought Robert, who could only see the back of his head.

In the witness box, a junior doctor from the hospital's emergency room was describing what he'd found when called, bizarrely, to help someone hurt in the hospital itself. He gave evidence stolidly, consulting notes he had made the morning when Peggy Mohan had been found.

Three times he said the victim had been so badly hurt he thought at first she was dead.

At the recess Robert followed the defence lawyer, Charlie Gehringer, out into the corridor, where he found him smoking a cigarette. Gehringer was young, not much past thirty, a dapper tense-looking man, with the physique of a rake and sharp eyes. Robert introduced himself.

'Ah,' he said and shook hands. 'I was going to call you tonight. Vanetta Simms told me you were in town.'

'How's it going?'

Gehringer dropped his cigarette end and stubbed it out with his foot. 'You want the truth?'

'Of course.'

'Okay, but don't say anything to Mrs Simms. It's not looking good. They found blood on Duval's blazer that matches the victim's blood type. Unless I can shake her ID of Duval, we're in trouble.'

'Is there anything I can do?'

'There might be. If all else fails, I'll have to go on about Duval's unimpeachable character, and hope that will create some doubt about Mohan's testimony. Frankly, if she's any good as a witness, we're on a hiding to nothing, but I don't see what else we can do. I've got a testimonial from the fire department in St Louis – Duval was a real hero down there. But I'd like to call you too if that's okay.'

He felt taken off guard. Although he had come back to show his support for Vanetta, it had never occurred to Robert that he could be of any practical help to Duval.

'I haven't seen Duval in over ten years. I only knew him when I was little.'

Gehringer shrugged. 'According to Mrs Simms, you two were close. And let me be candid – you've got attributes I can use right now. You're white, for one thing, and I hear you went to Yale. I don't get many character witnesses with those kinds of credentials.'

Gehringer watched him carefully. 'Think about it,' said the lawyer. 'You'd be a friendly witness, and it might help a lot. But listen, court's about to start again – why don't you come with me and say hi to Duval?'

There was a policeman standing guard at the defence table, who moved aside as Gehringer approached, and then Robert saw Duval. He wore a dark suit with a white shirt and tie – he looked like one of the earnest young men from the Black Muslims, who stood on street corners selling their newspaper to black passers-by, and ignored the whites.

'Hey, Duval,' said Gehringer cheerfully, 'I brought somebody to see you.'

Duval looked at Robert, trying to figure out who this strange white man was. Then a smile slowly spread across his face, and he stood up. He was tall now – an inch or two over six feet, with sideburns and the shoulders of a grown man. But he still wore glasses, and his front teeth remained slightly protruding.

'Hey, Bobby. What you doin' here? I thought you was in New York.'

'I came to see how you were doing.'

'You seen Vanetta?'

'Not yet.' He'd tried to call Vanetta the night before, but her sister Trudy had said she was at church. 'I will though.'

People were coming back into the courtroom and he knew he should take his seat. Duval said, 'It's been a long time, man. We had fun together, didn't we?'

'We sure did, Duval.' He noticed that Gehringer was looking nervously at his watch. 'Listen, I'll come say hi again, okay?'

'You do that.' As Robert turned away, Duval added, 'Look after the Secret Garden until I get out.'

The trial resumed, and another, more senior doctor described the victim's injuries. The testimony was undramatic and clinical, full of technical medical jargon. He might have been describing the condition of a house plant.

Then Peggy Mohan was called. The gallery stirred a little as a young woman with lank, auburn hair walked down the middle aisle of the courtroom. She had a slight limp that slowed her down, and increased the anticipation in the room. As she took her seat and was sworn in, the spectators seemed to take a long, collective breath. Speaking in a quiet, neutral voice, Peggy Mohan answered the preliminary questions – her name, occupation, address.

Then the DA asked her to tell the jury what had happened on the night of March 13 in the year before. The courtroom was completely quiet.

'My shift ended at ten o'clock. Normally I'd walk out with the other nurses, but that night I stayed a few minutes late, to write up a medication change one of the doctors on call prescribed. By the time I left, everyone else on my shift had gone.

'My car was parked in the garage on Maryland Avenue. The quickest way there was through the west wing they'd been renovating – if I went that way I'd come out right across the street from the garage. Otherwise I'd have to walk all the way around the block. It made me nervous to do that alone.'

She gave a small, sad smile at the irony of the choice she'd made. 'I went through into the renovated wing. I was about halfway down the corridor when suddenly the lights went out. Then I heard someone behind me.

I turned around and asked who was there, and a voice said, "Security." It was a man's voice. He said the temporary exit had been closed. They'd opened another one downstairs, he said. He'd show me the way.' She brought both her hands together, fingers tilted upwards in a steeple, and looked at them. 'I didn't like it – I couldn't see him very well and it seemed weird that the light had gone out just when he showed up. So I said no, I thought I'd go back the way I came and leave by the side entrance. But he insisted. I could see him better now. He was wearing a pink shirt, but the security people's blazer, so I thought he must be okay. So I . . . agreed.

'When we got to the stairwell he wanted me to go first, and I changed my mind again – I just didn't like the way he was acting, especially when he said I shouldn't worry. He said, "Trust me." I tried to go back up, but he grabbed my arm. I yanked it and pushed him to try and get away. That's when he cut me for the first time. He slashed me across the neck.' She stopped and gave out a little choking noise, as if she'd swallowed some gum. Tilting her head down until it rested on her chest, she said in a half-whisper, 'After that I did everything he told me to.'

She explained how he had taken her downstairs, dripping blood, then stopped in what was going to be the new reception area for paediatric neurology. She was precise about the name. Some of the furniture was already in place, and he had pushed her against the reception module, making her lie on its desk surface while he ripped at her blouse until it was off. Then he reached behind her back and cut both straps of her bra.

'He told me to relax. Then he took his hand and reached under my skirt. He grabbed my tights at the waist and started pulling them down . . .'

It took him some time to get them off. He used one

hand to hold the knife against her throat as she lay sprawled on the desktop, while his other hand struggled with the tights, clawing at them, until finally only a bunch of ragged sock-like material remained, balled in a bunch around her ankles. Then he spread her legs apart roughly, and she heard that hand undo his belt and drop his trousers, while the other still pressed the knife against her throat.

The DA said, 'I know this is hard for you, but can you tell us what happened next?'

She nodded silently, and even from the rear of the courtroom Robert could see the tears in her eyes. 'I felt him . . . go inside me. It hurt. I was terrified he was going to cut me again, so I didn't say anything.'

She took a deep breath before continuing. 'When he . . . finished, he put his face right down over mine. Then I did ask, "Why are you doing this?"'

She seemed to choke again, and kept her head bowed down.

'And what did the defendant say?'

Her reply came out in a whisper, her voice so faint that even the judge could not hear her. He looked with bafflement at the DA, who said, 'I'm sorry, Miss Mohan, but can you say that again?'

The courtroom was absolutely silent. Peggy Mohan didn't raise her head, but the words, spoken in a low murmur, were surprisingly clear. 'He said, "Do you like my pink shirt?"'

They broke for a recess. When the trial resumed Peggy Mohan seemed more composed.

She had thought after the first rape that maybe he would let her go, but instead he used some cord to tie her hands together behind her back. She'd whimpered when he twisted it tight around her wrists, and he had

271

suddenly lost his temper, and hit her in the face with his fist. She'd felt a bone crack in her cheek, and cried out despite herself. This time he stabbed her, thrusting the knife into her chest between her breasts. It hurt so much she had to use all of her willpower not to cry out again. She was terrified that if he stabbed her again he might hit an artery or vital organ. She'd worked in the emergency room at Billings, and seen enough knife wounds to know that it was a matter of chance whether you survived a stabbing. The more often you were stabbed, the more likely you would die.

Now he forced her off the desk and made her crawl, naked now, to a corner of the room. Here he had made her kneel on the new carpet, facing the corner. She could smell the fresh paint on the walls – she remembered that.

She'd been on all fours, and suddenly he thrust into her again, this time from behind. Then he had withdrawn, and she thought maybe he was finished, but no – she felt his hand probing her anus, and suddenly he entered her there. In her efforts not to shout at the ripping, horrible pain, she clenched her teeth so hard that she bit halfway through her lower lip.

Throughout this he had the knife near her face; she could see it juddering as he jerked in and out of her. With his other hand, he gripped her around the belly, pinching her hard with his fingers as he moved. He didn't talk at all this time, but as he climaxed she flinched, and he cut her again, drawing the blade against her throat as if he were sharpening the knife against a whetstone.

It was now that Peggy Mohan faltered again. 'For the first time I thought I was going to die. I was bleeding so heavily.'

'Did you manage to say anything?' The DA's voice was extra gentle.

She shook her head. 'I couldn't – my throat was full of blood.'

A woman in the gallery gasped loudly, and the judge looked crossly at the rows of spectators.

'Did he say anything to you?'

Peggy Mohan took a deep breath. 'Yes. He made me lie down, on my stomach. I had my head turned to one side, and he put his face down next to me. He was *this close*.' She held a hand about three inches away from her eyes. 'He said ...' and she shut her eyes as her composure began to break. She managed to get the words out, but her voice sounded half-strangled, like a screechy violin. 'He said he'd let me go after he did it one more time.'

When the DA finished, Gehringer asked to begin his cross-examination on Monday morning – it was by now four o'clock. Robert saw his reasoning: Gehringer wanted the weekend break to distance Peggy Mohan's testimony from his client, sitting less than twenty feet from the jury. If even Robert felt shaken by her testimony, God knows what twelve strangers who'd never known Duval would think.

But the judge denied the request. So Gehringer got up from the table, looking war-weary before the battle had even begun. When he spoke, his voice was subdued.

'Miss Mohan, we all feel absolutely terrible about what happened to you. Nobody admires you more than I do for the bravery you've shown today. But you can understand that a man's freedom is at stake, and we have to make sure justice is done, and that the right person is convicted for this horrific crime. There's nothing that could compensate you for the injuries you've received, but I am sure you would not want another injustice to be done.'

273

The woman looked stonily at Gehringer. He asked, 'Do you remember if before the night of the assault, you ever saw Duval Morgan?'

'It's possible. But I don't remember him.' She spoke tersely, and seemed unwilling to look at Gehringer.

'Did you know any of the security people at Billings?'

'Only to say hello to. Usually when I was coming to work or leaving. You pass by the reception desk.'

'But you don't recall if Duval Morgan was one of them.'

She shrugged. 'No. Like I say, it's possible I said hello.'

'But would it be fair to say that at some point, during the course of your duties at Billings, you would have come across the defendant?'

'I—'

'Objection.' The DA stood up. 'This is pure conjecture, Your Honour. The witness is not here to answer hypothetical questions.'

'Sustained.'

'Okay.' Gehringer moved away from the jury box now until he stood in front of Peggy Mohan. It was casually done, but it forced her to look at him. 'Now, Miss Mohan, when the police came to see you in the hospital, was the first photograph they showed you that of the defendant, Duval Morgan?'

She hesitated. 'I'm not sure.'

Gehringer nodded as if unsurprised, but he looked to Robert like he was thinking hard. 'All right. Let me ask another question then. When you first saw the defendant's photograph, did you identify him immediately as your assailant?'

'Objection.' The DA was on his feet. 'We've already heard testimony from the police officer present that the witness identified Mr Morgan as soon as she saw his photograph.'

Gehringer lifted his hands in mock-disbelief. 'Your Honour, I'd like to hear it from the witness herself. She was the one doing the identifying, not the officer.'

'Objection overruled. Please answer the question, Miss Mohan.'

She looked confused. 'I'm sorry, but can you ask it again?'

'Of course,' said Gehringer, a model of patience. 'When you saw the photograph of the defendant, did you indicate right away that he was your assailant?'

There was a long pause. Then she said, 'I must have.'

The courtroom was suddenly quiet again. Robert could see Vanetta leaning forward, in the row right behind Duval.

Gehringer had been slowly pacing, but now he stood stock still. 'You must have?'

'Yes. He's the one who did it.'

Gehringer ignored this. 'I'm sorry, Miss Mohan, but I asked if, when you saw Duval Morgan's photograph, you identified him right away. And you said you "must have". Not yes or no. I don't understand.'

And for the first time there seemed a glimmer of hope.

'I don't remember,' admitted Peggy Mohan.

'Try hard, please, Miss Mohan. I know it's painful, but it's important – or I wouldn't be asking.'

She didn't answer for several moments. The judge seemed about to prompt her, when suddenly she shook her head, and said, 'I'm sorry but I don't remember anything about my first days in the hospital. They told me later I couldn't even talk – you see, he'd cut my throat so badly that my vocal cords didn't work then.'

There was another gasp at the back of the courtroom. Gehringer started to speak, but Peggy Mohan talked right through him. 'When they took me to the station later, I knew. I said right away who it was.' She looked up past Gehringer towards the defence table. Suddenly she stabbed her finger at Duval. 'It was *him*. He did this to me.'

Now the judge did intervene, ordering a recess until Monday morning. Robert waited for Vanetta outside the courtroom. She looked terribly tired and had her arm around her daughter Aurelia, who had only arrived that afternoon from St Louis for her son's trial. Aurelia was weeping.

'I'll see you Monday,' he said, and Vanetta just nodded.

He drove back to Hyde Park in a mild state of shock, trying to banish the images that flashed through his head like snapshots. Whoever had attacked Peggy Mohan had acted without the smallest mercy. It was the act of someone so filled with misdirected hate that they couldn't see anything human in their victim.

He did not believe it could have been Duval. No one could change that much. Yet as he thought gloomily of Gehringer's failed attempt to shake Peggy Mohan's identification, he had the terrible feeling that his old friend was going to take the rap. For just when it seemed the door had opened a crack, Peggy Mohan had slammed it shut.

It was cold that week in February, and on Saturday morning he stayed inside. Merrill didn't like him there, he knew, so he holed up in his father's small study, reading while his father came in and out in his robust yet abstracted fashion throughout his showering and shaving next door. He'd been home two days now, and what Merrill didn't know was that he might be home for another week. Robert would be speaking with lawyer Gehringer on Monday, and he was going to say he'd be happy to testify. Willing, actually; not happy. The odds now looked so stacked against Duval that Robert didn't feel he had a choice.

The doorbell rang, and he let Merrill answer it, not out of laziness but because she'd made it clear this was her home, not any part of his.

'Why, Vanetta,' he heard Merrill say, 'what are you doing here?'

'I'm just stopping in, Miss Merrill.' Vanetta had always resisted calling her 'Mrs Danziger'. 'I've come to see Bobby.'

He went out to the hall, where Vanetta stood in her coat and boots. 'Won't you come in a minute, V?' Merrill asked.

Vanetta shook her head, and looked at Bobby. 'Come for a walk with me?'

He was puzzled – why couldn't they talk in the apartment, where it was warm? But he got his coat from the hall closet while Merrill retreated to her room.

Outside, it was glaringly bright, and the snow sparkled in the midwinter sun, but it was also near-Siberian with cold. At the corner the wind howled down the narrow tunnel of 58th Street. Ice lay under crusted snow on the sidewalks, where rock salt had uncovered only a thin line of concrete to walk on. Crossing Dorchester Avenue, he took Vanetta's arm, then almost slipped himself on a thin disc of ice.

'Who's holding on to who?' she asked, laughing. They moved along 58th Street until Vanetta stopped to catch her breath. She gazed through the black iron uprights of the fence around Jackman Field, where once Robert had played school games of soccer and softball. Today it lay buried under a frozen blanket of snow.

'You warm enough?' she asked, though it was she who was wearing a thin wool coat, while he had on a ski parka, puffed with goose down. A frayed silk scarf covered her head, a cast-off from Merrill. Without her grey hair showing, she looked years younger – her face was still smooth-skinned.

'It's not exactly Mississippi weather,' he said.

'You tellin' me.' She pointed to the field. 'Hard to believe that in three months kids going to be running around in T-shirts and shorts out there.'

'Do you want to go get warm somewhere?' There was a coffee shop inhabiting the Steinways corner spot now, only two blocks away.

'No. I got to go downtown, see this man Gehringer some more. But I wanted to talk to you first.'

He waited, but she seemed in no hurry. He sensed a terrible sadness in her. She stared out again at Jackman Field. 'You know, when I first came into your life you was a damaged little boy. I was so worried about you – and I thought, If I can show this boy the love he needs maybe he'll be all right. I mean, I knew you would be cared for in all the other respects – your daddy wasn't rich, but he had more money than I'd ever see. You'd always have all the food and clothes you'd ever need, and I knew you'd be going to a good school. What you didn't have was a mama.'

She sighed. 'Duval had a different kind of problem. He had a mama, but his mama was no good.' She looked at Robert dispassionately, though he knew this must hurt to say – Aurelia was her daughter, after all. 'So I needed to help him, too, even if I couldn't provide those other things for him. When you were little and friends with Duval, I used to dream sometimes that maybe he could go to school with you. He'd be with you at your gym time, and over in the classrooms too. He'd get himself educated, that's what I dreamed.' Her voice suddenly lowered. 'I always knew it wasn't going to be a dream come true. He didn't get much schooling, really, nothing that prepared him for a good life. And now it's come to this.'

He didn't know what to say. 'There's still hope, Vanetta.'

She pursed her lips and shook her head; for a moment, he thought she would start crying. He wanted to cheer her up. 'You know, I used to wish you'd kidnap me, Vanetta.' When she gave a laughing snort he added, 'I used to dream you'd stick me and Duval in your car and take us down to Mississippi.'

She looked at him, disbelieving. 'That's not a dream, child, that's a nightmare.'

'But you told me about where you grew up. All the fruit and the corn and the pond at the farm.'

She was shaking her head.

'Don't you remember?' He was almost pleading. 'I used to play a trick on Duval, tell him that over the wall behind the Christian Science church there was a Secret Garden.'

'I know you did. He asked me once if it was true. I said of course it was.'

'Of course it wasn't, you mean. It was just a little patch of dead ground. I shouldn't have fooled him like that. But in my mind there *was* a Secret Garden, and that was your place in Mississippi.'

She sighed again. 'Baby, I told you all the nice things – the watermelons, and the peaches and such – because you were just a little boy who needed something sunny and warm to think about. You wouldn't expect me to say anything else, now would you? I don't want to tell you what life was really like down there. The farm owner, how bad he cheated my daddy each fall, or the white men in town who used to stand around the general store, talking their bullshit to each other. They'd call out to me – I couldn't have been more than ten, eleven years old

– askin' things that make me blush just thinking about them. The white boys, they'd spit on the sidewalk where Alvin was about to step, just to let him know where he belonged.' She stopped and exhaled, her breath hanging like smoke in the cold air. 'Sometimes it seemed if a white person was nice to you, it was either 'cause they wanted something or it was an accident. Chicago ain't been no picnic,' she said. 'But life down there was *hell*.'

He felt as if a picture he had grown up with – his rich great-aunt's Kandinsky, for example, that had sat above her fireplace on Astor Place – had turned out to be counterfeit, composed by some weekend painter in a shed in northern Wisconsin. It didn't seem right.

But Vanetta wasn't done. 'Listen, I wanted to talk to you because I need you to do something for me.'

'Of course,' he said simply. He could not think of anything he would not do for this woman.

'I want you to go back up to the apartment, pack up your clothes, and then go out to the airport and fly back to New York. That's what I want you to do.'

He was stunned. 'Why, Vanetta?'

'Because I'm asking you to.' She was no longer looking at Jackman Field, and he found himself staring into her dark brown eyes.

'But I can help Duval if I stay.'

'No, you can't.'

'What do you mean? His lawyer wants me to testify.'

'That lawyer man doesn't want you on the witness stand. I talked to him last night.'

'What changed his mind?'

'He said he thought about it again and figured that your testifying might just – what's the word? *Boom* something.'

'Boomerang?'

'That's it. Boomerang against Duval.'

280

Robert started to protest, but Vanetta hushed him with a raised hand. 'He said he hadn't realised you'd only known Duval for such a short time, and so long ago. You weren't even ten years old.'

'I told him that,' Robert said crossly.

'That ain't all. He said you could sit up there and say all the nice things in the world 'bout the little boy you used to know, and the prosecutor would ask, "How did you come to know Duval?" And you'd have to say because his grandmother worked for your family.'

'What's wrong with that?' Robert felt confused.

'He says it won't sound to anybody like you and Duval could have been real friends. They'll just think, of course he'd say that.'

'But we *were* friends.'

'I know that, baby. But it's what the jury thinks that counts. That's why the lawyer done changed his mind. You see, you and Duval – it wasn't equal.'

'If Duval goes to prison, Vanetta, I'll never forgive myself if I could have helped. Let me call Gehringer and talk to him.'

'Don't you be bothering him.' She spoke sharply. 'He got enough on his plate without wasting time arguing with you. You understand?'

He felt like she'd slapped him. 'Okay,' he said, feeling hurt.

Her voice softened. 'Listen, don't you think we all want to help him? How do you think I feel? When he came up from St Louis, he wanted to come and live with me. I said no, Bobby.' She looked like she was about to cry, then got hold of herself. 'I told him, "Duval, you a grown man now. You need your own place."' She looked beseechingly at Robert. 'He didn't want to be living with an old lady like me. I thought it would be bad for him.'

He wanted to comfort her, but the moment passed, and she said, lifting her chin up, 'Bobby, there ain't nothing you can do for your friend now, I'm telling you that. All you can do is get on with your own life. At least you got one left; I ain't going to let you waste it by staying here. You go on back to New York today.'

She was being firm rather than hard, but there was no questioning her insistence, or the fact that he found it impossible to defy.

'If I can't help Duval, at least let me stay and try to help you.'

'Baby, if you wants to help me then the best thing you can do is make me proud of you. So go on, get back to your work, and your life.'

He was bewildered but also felt obliged, too, like a grown-up son yielding one last time to a mother's request. 'I love you, Vanetta,' was all he could say.

Her voice was muffled, for her chin was down resting on the tops of her breasts. 'I love you, too, Bobby. Now do what I say, you hear? Go.'

He did, flying back to La Guardia that evening, sitting in the rear of a 727 as it rode a giant tail wind above the clouds, moving him at terrific speed away from Chicago and Duval. And away from Vanetta – he sensed he was crossing another line that put even more distance between them. She had been saying goodbye to him, hadn't she? He knew by now that however much you loved someone, circumstance and brute facts could drive you apart, even someone you loved like the mother you'd never had. In the end, maybe Gehringer was right. *It wasn't equal.*

XIII

1

THEY WENT TO the dunes for the weekend, where he and Anna didn't discuss Duval or Philip or Peggy Mohan, and a fragile peace prevailed. Sometimes you could opt for the unexamined life and get away with it. For two days they did.

He remained worried by his last conversation with Duval. He wished he had done more to help him, even if it had only been encouragement, but he had been too preoccupied with controlling his panic on the ninety-fourth floor to take in the sheer neediness of Duval.

On Sunday morning Anna had a long phone conversation with Donna Kaliski from the centre. From what Robert could overhear of it, as he sat in the living room scanning the annual report of the university trustees, they were working flat out to find the blazer from the trial. Gehringer had been enlisted, motions filed, a formal process initiated – this after Donna's informal efforts had failed to unearth it.

For the first time Robert felt himself rooting for them without reservation. Overturning the conviction was the only tangible hope Duval had to make a new life for himself. Over lunch, Robert wanted to say as much to Anna, but he sensed it was too late to make a show of coming on board.

So he proceeded indirectly. That evening as they drove back to the city he suggested they could use Duval again in Evanston. 'I can think of three or four things he can do.'

283

'Really?' asked Anna. He couldn't tell if she was sceptical that there were actually things to do, or about Robert's show of goodwill.

'Sure,' he said. 'The basement's a mess. He and I could spend a day sorting it out.'

'Okay,' she said. 'I'll call him. I need to talk with him anyway.'

On Wednesday morning he cancelled the acquisitions meeting, since there was nothing on the agenda and so many people were away. Instead he had his postponed meeting with Andy Stephens and was getting ready for his next one, with the 'legendary' Candy Williams, when Anna phoned.

'Have you heard from Duval?'

'No.'

'It's just that I left him a message on Monday, asking him to come on Saturday. But he hasn't called back. I thought he might have called you instead. He was supposed to see Donna Kaliski in Evanston yesterday, but he didn't show.'

'Maybe he changed his mind.'

'I don't see why he would. Donna's taken on his case, and he knows she's very hopeful. But she can't even raise him on his cell phone.'

'I thought he didn't have one.'

'He does now.'

Had Anna bought it? 'Does it matter much?'

'Do you know how many cases this woman has? She hasn't got time to waste.'

Neither do I, he thought, depressed by Anna's snappishness. Yet troubled by the memory of his friend drifting away down Michigan Avenue, he offered to try and reach Duval.

Reluctantly he called Information for Jermaine's

number at the house on South Cornell. Jermaine must be at work, but maybe his wife Ella would know where Duval had gone. When he phoned a man answered.

'Is that Jermaine?'

'No.'

Very helpful. 'Is Duval there?'

'Who wants to know?'

Robert realised it was Jermaine's son Lemar, no friendlier four years on from Vanetta's funeral. 'I'm a friend of his. Do you know how I could reach him?'

'Man, I don't care where he is. All right? Want me to spell it out? I DON'T CARE.'

'When's your father back, Lemar?'

'You talking to me now – is that a problem? Who are you, anyway? You the man who was at Vanetta's funeral?'

'None other.'

'Oh, good. Because let me tell you, white motherfucker, you can go and suck my dick.' He slammed down the phone.

Not your average publishing conversation, Robert thought, and tried to ignore his increased pulse rate while he thought about where Duval could have gone.

He realised how little he knew of Duval's life. He didn't know the name of the church near 58th and Prairie, and if he did, just what would he learn? 'Oh, yeah, that Duval was here on Sunday. What a nice voice he's got.' That wouldn't help him.

Perhaps among the myriad relatives of Vanetta, Duval had struck up a new friendship, but Robert doubted it. After their depressing rendezvous at the Hancock Building, he had a strong feeling Duval might have gone underground. It wouldn't be hard to disappear for a while, as long as he had a little money. He could take a room in a flophouse without anyone having any idea where he was. His picture wouldn't be on TV or in the papers: twenty-four years before, yes, but that was the past. Now no one cared.

Except his parole officer. Robert hesitated before calling him, but there seemed no alternative. If Duval had disappeared, the State was going to hear about it sooner or later.

This time he got through to Bockbauer almost right away. 'I'm trying to contact a former prisoner named Duval Morgan and hoped you could help me. I wanted his address.'

'I can't give that sort of information out,' he said tetchily.

'I'm the guy who invited him out to Indiana. I sent you a form from my office.'

'I still can't talk to you on the phone. Sorry, but you could be anybody.'

He went to see Bockbauer the next day. The parole officer was way down in the black South Side, about a mile from Jermaine. He was a big man in his thirties, and wore dark trousers and black boots and a bullet-proof vest, and a 9mm handgun. Robert had been expecting something softer – a graduate from a social-work school, who would be wearing a tie.

His office was on the second floor of a low modern brick building on the corner of 80th and Cottage Grove Avenue. It had small windows that couldn't be reached from street level, and through one of them Robert could see his car, parked at a meter, in front of a dollar store. It was not a nice neighbourhood.

'Have a seat,' said Bockbauer, sitting down behind his desk. He had blond hair, bleached to white in the sun, cropped short around his ears. Square-faced with a ruddy complexion, he looked like a German-American product of one of the working-class southwest suburbs. Doubtless a former football player.

Bockbauer gestured at his outfit. 'Sorry about this, but I'm going to see a parolee once we're finished.'

'Do you always wear it?'

'Have to. It's not because they'd shoot me – though plenty of them would like to – but there're other people in their neighbourhoods who might.'

'That rough, huh?'

'Yep. Today I'm going to 54th and Prairie.'

'I used to visit someone at 58th and Indiana,' Robert said, realising it sounded like an effort to establish his own street cred.

Bockbauer seemed amused. 'Really? What do you do for a living, Mr Danziger?'

'I'm a book publisher.' He gave a small smile. 'It was a long time ago that I went to 58th and Indiana.'

Bockbauer laughed. 'Must have been. Anyway, you wanted to ask me about Duval Morgan.'

'That's right. He was going to come and do some work at my house. But I haven't heard from him.'

'He didn't tell me about this work, and he's supposed to.' He sounded annoyed. With all the *bratwurst*-and-beer bluffness, there was something unyielding. 'I'm surprised you're tracking me down about a no-show yard man.'

'I've got a personal concern. Duval and I grew up together. Here on the South Side.' He wasn't going to explain.

Bockbauer was surprised. He rubbed the fingertips of one hand back and across the vinyl surface of his desk. He said, 'Duval missed his meeting with me yesterday. I go to him – that's the way it work with parolees – but when I got to his cousin's on Cornell he wasn't there.

'It's the first time it's happened. I left a note, and we've got another meeting scheduled on Saturday. Technically, he's in violation of his release order already, but I've decided to cut him some slack. If he misses the next one, I'll have a warrant issued, and when they find him he'll be back in Stateville.'

'Has he been doing okay?'

'I can't really discuss that with you, Mr Danziger.'

Robert nodded resignedly. 'Understood. It's just that my wife and I have been trying to help him out a bit. I'm worried he's not making it.'

'You're right to worry, but you'd be wrong to think there's much you can do.' He looked at the papers on his desk. 'What can I tell you? I see some of the worst examples of humanity you can find. People who've done things you wouldn't believe, and who have no compunction about doing them again.'

He sat back wearily in his chair. 'If it weren't for what Duval did, I'd have no hesitation in calling him one of the good guys. But it's not my job to judge. It's my job to enforce the rules, nothing more, nothing less. Once I start to say, "So-and-so's okay really, even though he shot a twelve-year-old in the head," then it's time for me to look for another line of work. The only safe way to proceed with ex-cons is to watch them like a hawk.'

'That doesn't make it any easier for them.'

'It's not my job to make it easy for them. I'm paid to protect you. If that means making these guys pay even after they've served their sentence, then that's just the way it's got to be.'

'You must have a few who were innocent.'

Bockbauer looked at him wearily. 'If you listen to these people, *none* of them did the crime. Or they had a good reason that justified it. Even a scumbag doesn't like to admit he's a scumbag.'

'Jesus,' Robert said appreciatively, in the face of his hardness.

Bockbauer gave a snorting laugh. 'Cheer up, Mr Danziger. You don't have to worry about it; that's my job. And believe me, you wouldn't want it any other way. For every Duval there're ten of these guys who'd take your concern and wrap it round your throat if you gave them half a chance.'

'I understand. I just hope I can find him before you put him back in.'

'I just hope he wants to be found.'

Robert got up to go. 'By the way,' said the parole officer, 'are you called Bobby?'

'I was as a kid. That's when I knew Duval.'

'And your wife's named Anna?'

'That's right. Why?'

'You're not exactly African-American, are you?'

'You tell me, officer.'

Bockbauer laughed, and Robert said, 'What's this about?'

Bockbauer shook his head in wonder. 'Duval said you were family. Cousins, I think. He kept talking about Bobby and Anna and your little girl. What's her name?'

'Sophie.' Just saying it in this environment unsettled him.

'Duval told me he wanted to move from Cornell Avenue and come live with you. I told him before I'd even consider it I'd need to meet you first.'

Robert was taken aback. 'You'd know it wasn't true as soon as you saw me. It doesn't make sense.'

Bockbauer looked at him sympathetically. 'You'll find that with a lot of ex-cons there's a strong element of fantasy – you could call it wishful thinking if you wanted to be nice. It serves a purpose – it gives these guys hope that somehow they can live a normal life again.'

He didn't look like he was in the business of being nice, and his eyes made it clear what he thought of their chances. 'The problems start when their balloon gets pricked. That's when a lot of them can't cope. They end up doing something stupid and get sent back to prison.'

He left Bockbauer's office wondering why Duval had lied. He seemed so truthful – were there other things he had lied about?

Thinking hard, he came up with one. In the coffee shop in the Marchese, after Anna had offered him work, Duval had said he didn't need instructions to get to their house, explaining he'd found their address in the phone book. But Robert and Anna weren't in the phone book. And Lily out in California had been emphatic. *Don't worry: I didn't give him your address.*

At the time it had seemed trivial, a mistake rather than a fib. But thinking about it now, Robert suddenly wondered how Duval *had* got their address. Maybe Duval had followed him home one day. Worse, he might have followed Anna.

It bothered Robert, bothered him a lot as he drove through South Shore, and joined the Inner Drive at 67th Street. The gaps in his knowledge of Duval's life were no longer neutral blanks that didn't need to be filled in, but troubling holes. It seemed a terrible irony that just as Robert himself was beginning to accept that Duval was innocent, other reasons cropped up for distrust. Maybe Duval had another agenda.

2

The truce with Anna ended that evening. He was home before her, and found Sophie exhausted from a

290

swimming gala at day camp that afternoon. He gave her early supper, put her in the bath, put her in bed, then read *Tom Sawyer* aloud to her. When Tom duped his friends into whitewashing the fence for him, Sophie started to giggle uncontrollably. Was it that funny? 'It's just like you, Daddy,' she said. 'Getting Duval to paint our fence.' He had to laugh too.

Anna came in late from work looking subdued. He had made supper, but she only picked at her plate, though she drank down the glass of Sauvignon he poured for her.

'Any news of Duval?' he asked.

She shook her head.

'I called his house, but he wasn't there. Neither was Jermaine.' He paused a beat. 'And I talked with his parole officer.'

She looked up, startled. 'Why did you do that? If he thinks Duval has gone AWOL, he'll have him arrested.' She seemed incredulous. 'What were you thinking of?'

He found her tone hard to take. 'I wasn't telling him anything he doesn't know. He said Duval's already missed one appointment. One more and the guy will issue a warrant.'

She poured herself more wine, while he watched uneasily. She was not much of a drinker; it made her sleepy, and sometimes bad-tempered. She said, 'I find it hard to understand what got to him.'

'When I saw him last week he was pretty down. Jermaine told him he couldn't stay there any more.'

'His own cousin wants to throw him out? You didn't tell me that.'

'It's Jermaine's wife apparently.'

'Bitch,' she said sharply. 'Where did Duval think he'd go next?'

'That's what was bothering him.' If he was going to

291

help, he'd better tell Anna everything. 'I think he was hoping to stay with us.'

'That's an idea. I mean, until he can find a place.' Her voice was mellower now, until she saw Robert's face. 'You said no?' she asked, her voice querulous.

'He didn't actually ask so I didn't have to. But I made it clear it wasn't a good idea.'

She was getting agitated. 'Jesus Christ, that's why he's taken off.'

'I hope not.'

'Oh, for fuck's sake. *Of course* it's why he's gone. And just when there may be a breakthrough – Donna's hoping to hear any day about the trial evidence. They've got two people looking for it full-time.'

'They would never have let him stay here. You said yourself they won't let a sex offender near a family.'

'We could have helped him find a place – I bet you didn't offer that. And he's not a sex offender. That's the whole point.'

'Nothing will change until that's actually proven. You're sure of it, but—'

'You're not? Is that what you're telling me?'

He started to speak, but she was talking over him now. 'Sometimes it's as if you *want* Duval to have been guilty.'

He shook his head, but realised there was something in what she'd said. It had been easier all those years ago just to rue the tragedy of a nice little boy who'd turned out rotten, committing a crime of such awfulness that you couldn't do anything but shrug your shoulders at the severity of the sentence and say, *What else can you expect?*

For if Duval had been innocent, then you would be forced to think now of what you might have done to help. Anything rather than contemplate those twenty-four

292

years during which you and everyone else – even Charlie Gehringer – forgot all about Duval. Anna was right: consciously or not, it had been simpler assuming that Duval had done the crime.

'I get the feeling you feel guilty about something.'

This stung. 'Why should I feel guilty?'

'Charlie Gehringer said you wouldn't testify on Duval's behalf.'

She said this so matter-of-factly it took him a moment to understand. Then he felt enveloped by outrage; it was hard to stay calm. 'That's complete bullshit.'

'Keep your voice down – you'll wake Sophie. Are you saying Charlie Gehringer is lying?'

'I didn't testify because Vanetta told me Gehringer had changed his mind – he thought it would do more harm than good. I did what Vanetta asked me to do.'

'That's not what he says.'

'Fuck Charlie Gehringer. Vanetta wouldn't have lied to me. Vanetta didn't tell lies.'

'You're shouting,' she said, but he didn't care. This was too much to take.

And then Anna said, 'There's always a third possibility.'

He saw what that was and exploded. He pushed his chair back, harder than he meant to, and stood up. 'You think *I'm* lying?'

Anna looked shaken by his anger but determined not to show it. 'Robert. Sit down – you're scaring me.'

He looked at her with disbelief, but didn't sit down. 'I don't know what you'd like me to say.'

'And I don't know what to believe,' she said. There was no give in her voice. 'I don't know anything about Vanetta. Sophie knows more about her than I do. Yet you say she was like a mother to you.'

'She was,' he said flatly.

'Then out of the blue, her grandson shows up, after twenty-four years in prison.'

'I wish he never had. Things were okay until he decided to show up.'

'Were they?'

'I thought you liked living here.'

'I do. I like it a lot. There's an energy here unlike anywhere I've ever been. It's naïve, sometimes it's brutal, and the justice system is simply appalling. But it's vibrant, and it's willing to change.'

'And you want to change it?' He was trying not to sound sarcastic.

She looked at him full-on, and spoke without hesitation. 'I certainly want to try. I've talked with Donna about doing things for her.'

'What about the consulate?'

She put down her fork and put her hands together under her chin, as if to pray for forgiveness in selecting such a stupid husband. 'I couldn't give a shit about the consulate. That's the one thing I really don't like. Do you think I care if some cheese manufacturer in Racine, Wisconsin, breaks through in Tesco? And the embassy people in Washington are just the worst. Complacent, superior, patronising about the Yanks – everything about England I was glad to get away from.'

'So you don't want to go back to London?'

'God, no.'

'Or go somewhere else?' He left it ambiguous.

'I don't know,' she said, too promptly for his liking. She picked up her fork, but just held it abstractedly. Then she sighed. 'You know, sometimes I think we wouldn't be sitting here like this if Sophie hadn't arrived.'

How he wished she hadn't said that. He was already feeling assailed: the parole officer, not letting Duval stay, Gehringer's saying that he'd refused to help Duval –

these formed a litany of accusations that angered him. But this was far worse. He wanted to ignore it. Counterfactuals stink, he told himself irritably – when we're not happy about what happened, then we talk about what might have been instead.

'Who knows?' he said dismissively, protecting himself from the implications of what she'd said.

He was surprised to find Anna's eyes brimming with tears. 'I didn't mean it that way,' he protested.

But she shook her head, her upset turning to disdain. 'You've said enough.'

'I'm sorry,' he said forcefully.

But it was too late. Anna said, 'I'm tired.' She got up and took her plate to the sink while he stayed at the table. She turned around from the sink, and she no longer seemed upset.

'I want to be by myself for a while,' she declared. 'I think we need a break from each other.'

He could not mask his alarm. 'Where are you going?'

'Out to the dunes. Tomorrow after work.'

'What about Sophie?'

'You'll manage – I need time by myself. So I'd be grateful if you'd stay here with her this weekend.' She added witheringly, 'Besides, Duval might show up on Saturday after all. I'm sure you wouldn't want to miss that.'

He let Anna go to bed without him, and stayed up late in his study. He knew he should read Dorothy's six-month report – he was seeing her in the morning about it – but it was impossible to concentrate or care. His mind was a slew of allegations and semi-connected conclusions. Why had Gehringer said he refused to testify? It didn't make sense – yet the PD's recall had otherwise been remarkable throughout. And did Duval know this? That would explain his outburst beneath the Hancock Tower that morning, the inexplicable resentment he seemed to nurse. He had said that peculiar thing about being 'let down' – *I'm used to that. Even with you, Bobby*. If Duval held a grudge against Robert, he hadn't shown it. Then Robert remembered the lies Duval had told.

But these were peripheral worries to what kept him thinking at his desk. His conversation with Anna had left him deeply shaken. When he slipped into bed at last Anna was snoring lightly, with the covers off and her nightgown ruffed under her knees. He covered them both with a solitary sheet as he got in. He wanted to wake her up – to hold her, to make love to her, to make up with her. But the clock on the dresser said 02:47 and for once he managed to control his intolerance of ambiguity. Anna had ended the argument by deferring its conclusion; if he pushed her it would only make things worse. He would have to wait for her.

He woke late and found the other side of the bed empty. He could hear Anna and Sophie in the kitchen below. When Anna came into the room he was just sitting up, feeling groggy.

'We're going now,' she said. He noticed she hadn't brought him a cup of coffee. 'I'll pick up Sophie this afternoon and drop her off here. Mrs Peterson will stay until you get home.' Her tone was icily professional; he might have been opposing counsel.

'Will you at least give me some idea when you're coming back?'

She didn't look at him, collecting some change from the dresser and putting it in her purse. 'I'm not sure,' she said, with an indifference that suddenly enraged him.

296

'Should I call Philip Masters to find out?'

She turned to the bed and he saw he'd hit a nerve. 'You *bastard*,' she said through gritted teeth. 'You go on and on about Philip Masters. It's some fantasy that lets you live apart from me in your head.' She gave him such a malicious look that it chilled him. 'But if that's what you'd really like, I'll see what I can do to make your dream come true.'

Then she left the room, calling out to Sophie to get a move on or they'd be late.

3

'You okay?' Dorothy Taylor asked, ten minutes into their meeting.

Robert started to bridle, but the look on her face was concerned rather than challenging. 'I'm a bit preoccupied. Sorry.'

'No problem. Let's do it another time. I'll fix it with Vicky for next week.' She started gathering her papers. 'By the way, I saw that friend of yours the other day.'

What friend? He wanted to say he didn't do friends. It had better not be Latanya Darling saying hi again.

'You know,' she went on, 'the guy who visited you here. African-American.'

Duval. 'Where did you see him?' He realised he sounded aggressive.

'Down the street. He was standing in a doorway. I thought maybe he was waiting for you.'

'When was this?'

'I don't know. A couple of days ago, I guess. Why?'

He was shaking his head. 'I can't get hold of him. He's gone missing, and no one knows where he is.'

'You worried about him?'

'Yeah, I am. He's in trouble.' He hesitated, not sure how much to say. 'His parole officer is looking for him too.'

'Oh,' she said. She seemed surprised. 'How long's he been out?'

'Couple of months.'

'Is he having trouble readjusting?'

'You could say that.' He laughed sourly. 'He was in for twenty-four years.'

'Shit,' she said instinctively, then covered her mouth.

'Let me know if you see him again, will you?'

'Okay. He must have done something real bad, heh?'

'He did the time, Dorothy. He deserves to be treated like anybody else now, doesn't he?'

She looked at him like he was crazy.

He said, 'You think I'm just another soft white liberal?'

'No, I sure don't. That's why you surprise me.'

He didn't respond. Under this kind of stress he was capable of telling her all sorts of things. He'd been too bruised by their encounters not to feel this would be a mistake.

There were no calls from Anna. He had lunch with Burdick, the production controller, at a new Japanese restaurant on Superior, where Burdick ate for two and Robert nibbled at sushi. He was old enough to know he could contain anxiety about his personal life in a professional setting, but it was an effort – he asked Burdick open questions and made sure he listened when the production man was finishing his answers. He drank one bottle of Kirin beer, but wanted twelve.

Back in the office, he struggled yet again to read Dorothy's six-month report, which was long, dense, and detailed. At half-three he gave up and left the office for a breath of fresh air, walking over to Michigan Avenue, where he bought a pack of sugarless gum as self-justification for his exit from the office. When he returned he found Vicky leaving a message on his desk. 'Your wife called.'

'When?'

'About twenty minutes ago. You weren't here,' she said defensively. 'She said, would you please get Sophie from day camp?'

'You're kidding.' He looked at his watch – Anna was supposed to pick their daughter up in ten minutes. He would never get there in time. What was going on? They'd had an arrangement.

'Is that all she said?'

'Yes. She sounded like she was in a hurry.'

Sophie was waiting in the parking lot with the camp director, a butch woman with a whistle on a string around her neck.

'Sorry,' said Robert to the woman. 'Bit of a mix-up.'

'Shit happens,' she said rudely, and left.

'Where's Mom?' asked Sophie as they drove away.

He wondered what to say. 'She's at the dunes,' he said, hoping he was right.

'Are we going there now?'

'No, Mom's got a project she has to finish. So you and I are going to have a bachelor weekend. Lots of treats.'

'I thought a bachelor wasn't married,' Sophie said.

He gave Sophie supper, a short order cook's special of hamburger and French fries, nutritionally redeemed by a side tomato salad, then let her read upstairs while he watched a baseball game on ESPN. He was fixing himself a second large Scotch when the phone rang.

'Is Anna there?' A woman was speaking, with an oddly silky voice.

'No, she's not. Can I help?'

'It's Donna Kaliski from the centre. I'm sorry I didn't get back to her yesterday. I was in Springfield at a meeting. Do you know if by any chance she's heard from someone called Duval Morgan?'

She didn't know he was in the loop. 'Not a word. His case officer doesn't know either. He said Duval missed his last appointment.'

'Oh, no. That's terrible. And just when I've got good news for him.'

'He could use some.'

'We think we've found the evidence from the trial we've been looking for.'

'You mean the blazer?'

'Yes,' she said, surprised. 'I didn't realise you knew that much about it.'

He wanted to say that he'd been at the trial, that he'd known Duval first, and that he was the original link. But this woman wouldn't know that, and it was Anna who was actively helping Duval. Robert's seeing him for coffee every week or so was hardly doing a lot.

Kaliski was talkative. 'It turns out it's been stored downstate – God knows why. We'll be able to get an order from a judge next week. With any luck, we'll have the conviction overturned this autumn.'

'I guess that's good news.'

'Of course it's good news,' she said sharply. 'Are you expecting Anna any time soon?'

'No. She's at our weekend house. Would you like the number?'

'I have it. I tried calling there, but she didn't answer.'

Because she thought it was me, thought Robert, as Kaliski thanked him and said goodbye.

He slept fitfully, waking twice nervously when he heard voices outside which turned out to be couples walking very late towards the lake. Rarely alone at night, he felt childlike in his apprehension. Falling asleep again at four, he had a vivid dream, of Vanetta when he was little in the back yard on Blackstone Avenue. She was boosting him up onto the branch of the tree. He felt both a child's sense of safety and an adult's insecurity, and woke up with a start to discover it was already eight o'clock.

He cooked scrambled eggs for Sophie's breakfast, enough for two, but found he couldn't eat anything himself. She was still in her pyjamas, something Anna never allowed but he couldn't be bothered about right now.

He didn't want to call the dunes this early. If Anna had decided not to pick up the night before, then calling again would just reinforce her decision. *If* she were at the dunes. He tried not to think about where else she might be.

'What would you like to do today, Soph?' he asked, determined to sound cheerful.

'Go see Mom?' she asked.

'She'll be back soon. Probably tomorrow.'

'Isn't Duval coming?' she asked.

'I don't think he's going to make it today.' He'd forgotten all about their original plan. It would be quite wonderful if Duval suddenly arrived, and put their minds at rest. But it wasn't going to happen.

He said to Sophie, 'Maybe we could go to a Cubs game – they're playing at home today.'

'Great,' she said, and he was glad to see her happily

deflected. She hadn't picked up his own uncertainty about Anna's return, since otherwise – like her mother – she wouldn't have left it alone.

At ten he decided Anna should have cooled off by now. Before they were married, their occasional arguments could result in non-speaks and a refusal to pick up the phone, but never for more than a day. But when he rang now, there was still no answer, and this reignited his suspicions. He tried telling himself she might be staying at a friend's; it didn't *have* to be with Philip Masters.

He found Maggie Trumbull's number on the roster they kept pinned by a magnet to the fridge – along with school numbers, doctor, police, etc. Her husband answered; after a minute Maggie came on.

'Hello, Robert.' Her voice was civil rather than friendly. Maybe Anna had been confiding in her.

He explained he was trying to reach Anna at the dunes. 'I can't get through and I'm a little worried. I was wondering if she'd been in touch.'

'Not since yesterday at work. I saw her when she was leaving. She said she had to pick up Sophie from day camp.'

'She did? I got a message from her telling me to do that.'

'Maybe she changed her mind, Robert.'

When he hung up he didn't know whether to be relieved or concerned. Why had Anna changed plans at the last minute? Messing about with Sophie's arrangements was completely out of character. No doubt Robert was now fair game; he couldn't believe Anna felt Sophie was, too.

There was one other call he could make. Philip Masters's number wasn't on the fridge list, so he went upstairs to see if he could find it in Anna's study. But he couldn't find her phone book – she must have it with her. He wasn't about to call Maggie Trumbull again to ask for the number. He didn't know what he was going to say to the man anyway; Masters wasn't going to admit his wife was in his bed at that very moment.

Then he saw the box.

It was a large carton, the cardboard soft from its trip to California and, five years later, back again. Lily had sent it at last; he had forgotten all about it. How long had it been here? he wondered, cross that Mrs Peterson had put it in Anna's study, not his. She must have signed for it the day before.

Lily had not bothered to repackage the contents, but had merely taped the box closed and slapped a Federal Express label on it. He opened it now with a pair of kitchen scissors, and found on the top a square biscuit tin, the kind the family used to receive each Christmas from his mother's few remaining Michigan relatives.

He took the lid off, and found the tin full of buttons, a vast assortment ranging from cuff-sized ivory discs to beetle-sized wedges. Amongst them was a small envelope, with a letter folded inside. Taking it out, he saw that it was addressed in his own hand to Vanetta at the Cloisters address. He stared at its yellowing pages, evidence of his adolescent self:

Dear V

It's getting cold here now and they say there may be snow tomorrow. But people in Boston don't know what snow really is. It's okay because they heat the classrooms really well, and my own room is warm as toast.

I am given lots of schoolwork and doing all right. We were taught about a German named Kant yesterday – I bet you 'can't' believe it!

303

I am playing soccer lots, and there is a chance of playing in the game on Saturday against a school called Belmont Hill. I can't wait for Christmas, and Dad says we will be spending it in Chicago this year, not Michigan, since Gram and Gramps are too old to travel so far. Not that it is that far.

I hope Merrill is behaving! I miss you, V, and can't wait to see you.

Your Bobby

A blanket sat underneath the tin, reeking of old wool and moth balls, folded over to fit in the box. There wasn't much else: two pairs of winter socks, and a paper bag which bore the label of Stop 'N' Shop, once a food emporium in the Loop. Unlikely to have been visited by Vanetta. The bag would have been Merrill's, who had often shopped there when she had her hair done at a fancy salon downtown. Vanetta must have taken it from the apartment when she stored these things downstairs.

There was clothing inside the bag. When Robert reached in and pulled, he found he was holding the collar of a man's shirt – the size tab read 15/35. Mystified, he looked at the shirt, certain he had never seen it before. But then this stuff may have sat in the basement of the Cloisters for twenty years.

The shirt was oddly coloured, alternately dark mocha and light pink. He stood up and held it out in front of him. The dark patches were not some groovy part of the shirt's design, but stains. Bloodstains.

What was it doing here? he wondered. It couldn't have been his father's – Johnny had been a big man, before degenerative arthritis and age had shrunken him to his final shell. And Mike was bull-necked – size 17 at least, with a neck like a wrestler's.

Was it Robert's? No, the 35-inch arms were far too long. As a teenager, moreover, he wouldn't have owned a pink shirt – too faggy, in the delicate words of his peers. And anyway, what would it be doing among Vanetta's personal effects?

Something stirred, some glimmer of memory at once tantalisingly close and elusively distant. Words came to mind – he didn't know why. *Do you like my shirt?* Was that it? And then he heard the voice again, a female voice. *Do you like my* pink *shirt?*

Yes, that was it. And he started to feel numb as he remembered where he had heard these words, more than twenty years before, quiet yet emphatic and distinctly audible in the hushed courtroom.

It was Duval's shirt.

At first Robert was too stunned to believe it. He felt he was in a dream – he wanted to turn back the clock a day, answer the door to the Fed Ex man, shake his head and say, 'Thanks, but no thanks,' then close the door before it was knocked clear off its hinges by the box's explosive contents.

But when he looked at the shirt again, it spoke to him, unavoidably. That is Peggy Mohan's *blood*, he realised – not some metaphor or a memory. There were long smears on both arms, blotches on the front, even a thick dried lump attached to one of its front buttons. All his recollections of Mohan's testimony, painted over by time, were suddenly brought home in the blood-stained cotton he held in his hands. He felt as if ice water had been thrown in his face. Duval was guilty after all. This was the same shirt he'd worn the night . . . the night he'd raped and stabbed Peggy Mohan.

His shock gave way to anger. To think that he had felt sorry for Duval – his pity evaporated in the harsh light of his new knowledge, spattered around him like the blood on the pink shirt. He thought bitterly of how he and Anna had been duped. And to what end? All along Duval knew it could go nowhere.

At least now Robert knew. He put the shirt back in its bag, knowing it might destroy the life he had built with his wife and daughter. He would have to show the shirt to Anna, and pierce for good the bubble of hope she had grown around Duval.

'Dad?' Sophie was standing in the doorway.

'What is it?' he asked, thanking God he had put the shirt back in the bag.

'What are you doing?'

'Just going through some old stuff.'

'Dad, you said Mom's at the dunes.' There was a question in her voice.

'Yes. Why?'

'Is Duval with her?'

'No. What makes you think that?'

'I don't know. It's just I saw him in the parking lot at camp.'

He froze. 'When was this?'

'Yesterday.'

'What time?'

She was starting to look frightened, and he realised he had raised his voice.

'In the afternoon at break time. I shouted but he didn't hear me. What's wrong, Daddy?'

Everything was wrong. What was Duval doing there? He was no longer angry, or anxious, or nervous – he was just plain scared. He tried to speak calmly, 'Did you see Mummy too?'

'Of course not. You picked me up, Dad. Don't you remember?'

'Sure I do,' he said soothingly, doing his best to hide his own mounting fears. They would only stop when he found Anna. He no longer cared where Duval was. Unless he was with Anna.

Poindexter answered on the third ring. Robert could imagine him, standing on the oak floor of his house's airy hallway, in khaki shorts and a Madras shirt.

'Hey. I was about to call you,' Poindexter said.

Another fucking invitation. Robert cut him off. 'Have you seen Anna? I can't reach her – I think the phone in the coach house may be out of order.'

Poindexter's voice lost its bouncy quality. 'You sure she's here? That's why I was about to call you.'

'What do you mean?'

'The delinquents have been back. I'm afraid they've broken your garage windows again. The same two.'

'When was this?'

'Last night just before dark. Tina saw a car come down the drive, and she thought it turned in at the coach house. I went down a few minutes later, and it was just pulling out. I saw it wasn't Anna, so I had a look round. That's when I saw the windows.'

'Was the car an Impala?' he asked impatiently.

'No. It was one of those old boats – a Bonneville. I was surprised it was still on the road.'

So it hadn't been Duval. Then where was Anna?

'Listen, Tim, if you do see Anna will you ask her to call me right away?' There seemed no point hiding anything. 'I'm worried because she's meant to be out there.'

'Of course. I didn't want to go into the house, but the door was locked and no one's broken in.'

'Thanks. I'll be in touch.'

'Let me know when you find her.'

He was getting very scared, so scared that he wanted to know where Anna was, even if the answer was Philip

Masters's flat. How weird, he thought, to wish my wife was having an affair, yet he could tolerate even that if it meant Anna was safe.

He had nothing concrete to go on, which made his urgency agonising – like a hyperactive man forced to sit still. He thought of calling the police, but what could he say? *An ex-con I know is incommunicado; my wife blew up at me and said she wants some space. Ergo, I need your help.* No chance.

There must be clues somewhere in his head, but he found his thoughts whirling too fast to discern them. He had to start looking, but first he needed to do something about Sophie, place her somewhere safe while he tried to find her mother.

Mr Peterson answered the phone. His Christian name was unknown – even his wife, Anne-Marie, spoke of him as Mr Peterson. An old man with a stick, who wore cuffed trousers and a long-sleeved shirt even in summer weather. He handed the phone over to Mrs Peterson without Robert having to ask.

He explained that Anna was away and he had an urgent meeting on the South Side. Please could she help? She was hesitant, reluctant to come on a weekend.

He pressed. 'If it weren't urgent, I wouldn't be bothering you.' He had a small inspiration. 'What if I brought Sophie to you?' Their apartment was on the Evanston–Chicago border, about a mile away.

'That'd be okay. I'm just doing the photo album of my daughter's wedding – Sophie can help me with that.'

When he explained the change of plan, Sophie kicked up. 'I thought we were going to the Cubs game,' she said crossly. It would have been a childish wail not so long ago, but now she spoke like a betrayed adult.

'I'm sorry. Something's come up. I promise we'll go to a game soon.'

'Oh, great, Mom's away, and now you're going away too.'

'It's not like that. I've got my cellphone – you can call me. I'll be back this afternoon.'

'*Afternoon?* I have to spend all day there?'

He felt helpless in the face of her complaint; he couldn't convey his urgency without scaring her. 'I'll be back as soon as I can,' he said, but this did not appease her, and she went off in a sulk.

He hurriedly packed her knapsack with three reading books and a sketchpad, then threw in a Mars bar to give her an unexpected treat. He found Sophie upstairs and hustled her out of the house before she could object some more. When he parked in front of the Petersons' apartment, the second floor of an old wooden three-decker house, she looked at him sceptically. 'Where is Mom really?'

'I told you. She's at the dunes.'

'Why'd she go without us?'

He put both hands on the steering wheel. What to say, what to reveal. He avoided his daughter's gaze. 'Do me a favour, will you? Just put up with this today, and tomorrow we'll spend the day together.'

'With Mom?'

Should he promise this? He couldn't see why not – his fear was multiplying like spawn, but he still wanted to keep it from Sophie. 'Yep.'

'You had a fight, didn't you?'

This he could level about. 'Sure did. A real doozie,' he said with a deliberately lyrical tilt to his voice.

He'd hoped she would laugh, but instead Sophie started crying. Tears first, then long, wracking sobs that seemed to hurt him physically. He thought of their conversation in Hyde Park. Kids knew what was going on; Sophie must be on pins and needles, wondering if

309

her father and mother were about to split up. He leaned over and hugged her. But the sobbing continued.

'Listen, it's not that bad. It was just an argument.'

She didn't answer. He was starting to feel frantic; he could do nothing until he had deposited her safely with Mrs Peterson.

'Come on,' he said, 'you're old enough to understand. Parents fight sometimes – it doesn't mean war has been declared. It was just an argument,' he repeated.

He could tell she wanted to believe him, for she laughed nervously, forcing it. 'Who won?' she asked, then looked at him sagely and said, 'Mom did.'

Her laugh was sincere this time, and he tried his best to join in, then used the opportunity to get her out of the car and up to Mrs Peterson's flat.

A smell of stale cooking and unseasonal central heating greeted him as Mrs Peterson opened the door to their second-floor flat. She looked like a Swedish grandmother, blonde hair now turned white, cheekbones sharp as chicken wings. Sensing his urgency at once, she took Sophie by the hand. Robert saw her husband in the background, sitting in an armchair holding his stick, watching a television Robert couldn't see.

'Thanks so much, Mrs P,' he said. He realised he sounded breathless. He bent down and spontaneously kissed his daughter. 'See you later,' he said.

As he started down the steps Mrs Peterson called out, 'When are you picking her up?'

When I find my wife, he wanted to say. 'I'll call you later this morning,' he shouted up the stairs, and kept going.

He was still transfixed by the shirt as he drove south through light traffic on Lake Shore Drive. A breeze came in off the water, tempering the heat of late July, and already the parks were filling up with ball games and picnicking families. He could smell the charcoal fumes from the barbecues.

What a secret for Vanetta to keep, and he cursed her now for hiding the crucial damning evidence. If the shirt had been turned over all those years ago, there would have been none of this garbage about a wrongful conviction, no crusade by Anna and this Donna Kaliski woman to overturn Duval's conviction. Goddamn them, he thought, wanting to blame someone, and goddamn Vanetta. Yes, especially Vanetta. She should have told the police. There would have been no comeback after that, none of the *I didn't do it* bullshit they had all fallen for.

She had simply loved Duval too much – Robert could see that now, as he drove past the Point, a jutting crop of rocks by the lake where people from Hyde Park liked to swim. She'd loved him far more than Duval's mother ever did. She couldn't bring herself to turn the shirt in.

But then why keep it? And in such a strange place – the basement storage of her employers' apartment block, where it had sat for over twenty years, then been moved entirely by accident to California. She could not possibly have foreseen the circuitous trail which brought it to light, or been confident that it would ever again be recognised.

Then she should have burned it, he thought, still angry with her. But that must have seemed equally impossible to her: the guilt she would have felt must have been massive, enough to keep her from that further irrevocable step. She had been as moral as she was maternal; in this instance, the two qualities had been at war. Part of her must have thought (maybe even hoped, however unconsciously) that one day the truth would come out. What pain her discovery must have caused her.

311

What pain it was causing now, all these years later. Goddamn her, he thought again. Stupid, old, ignorant ... what? Lady? Woman? Mother? Retainer? Servant?

He understood now why she had lied to him that morning outside the Cloisters, when she told him Gehringer had changed his mind. *All you can do is get on with your own life*, she'd said, knowing all the while that Duval had done the crime.

It was incredible to him that while her grandson faced a prison term as long as a piece of string, she had been trying to protect Robert as well. Realising this made him unable to stay angry with her now. However unusual, however much the object of other people's condescension or scorn, their love for each other had been equal after all.

5

Jermaine had grown fat in his forties. Once he had been a lean, narrow-faced boy, with a sweet disposition and a natural singing voice he only reluctantly allowed to be pressed into service by Vanetta's church choir. According to Duval back then, he missed more rehearsals than he attended, since the buffet spreads he loved were only on offer at actual performances. Fat or thin, he had always loved to eat.

Robert found him standing warily, filling the doorway of his bungalow He nodded as Robert came up the front stairs, in acknowledgement rather than welcome. His hair was trimmed like a curly hedge kept in check.

Yes, he said, he remembered Robert, and no, he didn't sing any more. He told Robert that he was working the weekend shift at R.R. Donnelley's, so if Robert could just tell him what it was he wanted, he'd appreciate it, since otherwise he'd be late for work.

'I'm trying to find Duval.'

'The parole officer is looking for him, too. But I don't know where he's at.' He was speaking as if Robert were yet another kind of external authority – not a cop, perhaps, but a case worker.

'I called you and left a message with Lemar. I don't know if you got it.'

'Lemar never mentioned it.' He softened slightly. 'Sorry about that. The boy is kinda upset on account of his car been stolen.' He gave Robert a sideways look and pursed his lips.

'Did Duval take it?'

Reluctantly, Jermaine nodded. 'I ain't told Lemar that, because he'd call the police. I figure Duval's in enough trouble without them looking for him, too.'

'Could he be staying with other relatives?' God knows, there were enough of them.

'I doubt it,' said Jermaine. 'He was only staying here because nobody else would have him.'

'It was good of you to do that,' Robert said, despite knowing Jermaine had been about to turf Duval out.

'I couldn't turn my back on him. He's family.'

'Could I see Duval's room?'

'Why?' For the first time Jermaine sounded defensive.

'I just thought there might be something to indicate where he's gone.'

Jermaine looked at him suspiciously. It was impossible to tell which way the decision would go. Then he turned abruptly with a beckoning hand. 'Come on. It's down here.'

They went along a hallway to the kitchen, where plates stood neatly like old-fashioned LPs in a plastic rack next to the sink. The hallway continued on the far side, terminating abruptly in a bathroom. Just short of it, there was an open door on one side, and Jermaine stood there, waiting impatiently for Robert.

Jermaine hit the switch and an overhead bulb threw out a bleak, oppressive light on a windowless room. It was tiny, sparsely furnished, with a single bed and a low painted chest of drawers. The walls were drab green, and devoid of pictures.

Jermaine looked uncomfortable. 'I know what you're thinking, but it was his choice.'

Robert said nothing. Jermaine went on. 'We got us two spare rooms down the hall. He could have had either one. But no, this is the one he chose. I'm not telling you no lie.'

Robert sensed the awful truth: Duval had picked the room because it was the closest he could come to what he was used to.

'Do you mind if I look around in here?' he asked.

Jermaine shook his head. 'Be my guest, though there ain't much to see. I'm just going to change for work.' And he retreated down the hallway, leaving Robert alone.

He started with the chest of drawers, finding underwear and socks in the top drawer, three or four folded shirts and a pair of work jeans in the bottom drawer. Nothing personal like a ring or some photos, and nothing hidden, like spare cash. In the corner of the room he opened the door of a shallow closet, where a suit jacket hung from a flimsy rail, next to two pairs of trousers and a thin black tie wrapped around the neck of another coat hanger. On the floor, neatly lined up, were two pairs of shoes – cheap slip-ons, one pair black, one yellowish mock-alligator. Robert rummaged through the hanging clothes, but found nothing except a receipt for two packs of Winstons. Duval had never smoked in front of him.

By the bed sat a makeshift table, an oval disk of plywood propped on a small saw horse. It held a lamp with a naked bulb, and a paperback bible, with the corners of many pages turned down. He opened the book to one of them, and found a passage underlined in the Book of Matthew:

Blessed are they that hunger and thirst after justice: for they shall have their fill.

He got down on all fours and looked under the bed, fishing out two magazines. He blew dust off the cover of one and opened its pages, only to find himself staring at a garish colour photo of a naked woman with reddish hair fellating an enormous penis.

He rifled through the magazine, finding a monotonous succession of other pornographic scenes – women licking ejaculate with artificial smiles, or feigning orgasmic pleasure as they were penetrated. It was tawdry stuff: the models were heavily made up and past their prime, the colour of the photos garish. Overall, the effect was of an earlier era – like the furtive skin mags of the 1950s. Which seemed peculiar in the twenty-first century, when mainstream movies showed acts of sexual congress as though they were another form of breakfast. But he supposed pornography must have been a staple of prison life; after so many years inside, Duval was probably addicted to the stuff. Perhaps, too, after an adult life spent in prison, he didn't even want a live woman, such was the power of the fantasy sexual life he'd been forced to build during all the years when he didn't have a real one.

The second magazine was different. He saw right away that it went far beyond standard pornographic terrain into something darker – and violent. The women here were victims rather than colluders, handcuffed to the uprights of beds, tied up with cord, held down by two, even three men. On one page a teenage-looking blonde girl on all fours screamed in pain as a policeman's nightstick was stuck in her anus; another page showed a pudgy woman, opening her mouth to fellate a shaven-headed man while he held a Bowie knife to her throat.

This was about pain, not pleasure, or rather about the pleasure pain gave the perverted. Robert was repelled by the relentless sadism.

He kicked the magazines back under the bed but took the bible, stuffing it into his jacket pocket. Out in the kitchen Jermaine was sitting at a table in the corner, eating cereal and reading the *Sun Times*.

'Find anything?' he asked without looking up.

'Nothing that tells me where he might have gone.' He wasn't going to ask Jermaine's permission to take the bible.

'If you find him, tell him I can't have him back. Not after he took Lemar's car.'

'I wonder if he's gone to Mississippi.'

Jermaine looked startled. 'Why there?'

Robert shrugged. 'I don't know – Vanetta always talked about it. Duval told me he'd never been; he sounded like he wished he had.'

'Ain't no family there no more.' He tipped his bowl and spooned some milk into his mouth. Between swallows he said, 'Can't see it myself.'

'Maybe not.' He stood awkwardly in the doorway. 'If you hear from him could you let me know?' There was a message pad by the wall phone, and he wrote down all his numbers – Evanston, cell phone, work, and the dunes. 'One of these numbers will find me.'

'Sure,' said Jermaine, his eyes on the *Sun Times*.

He felt an urge to get Jermaine to look at him. He asked, 'When did Duval take Lemar's car?'

Jermaine stopped reading and looked annoyed. 'Wednesday. He'd been gone by then, but he must have come back during the day and taken the keys.'

'It's an Impala, right? Maroon colour.'

'That's my car. Lemar's got hisself a golden oldie. A Bonneville.'

'A *Bonneville*?' His voice had risen sharply.

'That's right.' Jermaine stared at him like he was crazy. 'What's it to you?'

But Robert was already moving towards the front door.

Robert's greatest fear was coming true. Duval must be with Anna. Duval *had* been out to the dunes – Poindexter had seen the car. In his mind's eye an image of Anna flared up. On Anna's face pain erupted like sizzling grease, and a knife neared her throat. *Please don't hurt her.*

Outside he ran to his car, then realised he didn't have any idea where to go next. As he jumped in the driver's seat, he tried to harness his racing thoughts. Down the block a car honked, and a girl ran down the front steps of a bungalow, dressed to go out. He hated living now in a parallel universe of trouble – a sealed capsule holding Duval, Anna and himself, separated from the normal lives of the people in this city. He tried to hang on to a sliver of hope that Anna was not with Duval, and that his first instinctive fear was right and she'd gone off with someone. But he knew it wasn't true.

He looked at the bible on the seat next to him, then picked it up and started checking the pages that had their corners turned down.

Genesis with lines underscored in pencil: *The Lord God took the man and put him in the Garden of Eden to work it and take care of it.*

No help at all, and he moved to the next one, ripping a page in his haste. He found Isaiah, similarly marked: *You will be like an oak with fading leaves, like a garden without water*.

A waste of time. Other passages were underlined throughout the book, and Robert forced himself to go through them methodically, turning the pages as fast as his fingers allowed. But the passages all seemed meaningless, and Robert felt increasingly panicked by the clock ticking in his head.

Then he reached the Song of Solomon, where Duval had put a large X in the margin. Robert scanned the lines impatiently, then suddenly stopped:

You are a garden locked up, my sister, my bride; you are a spring enclosed, a sealed fountain.

The garden again. He almost didn't believe it – it was so obvious.

He turned the key so hard the transmission made a harsh grinding sound and almost stalled. 'Calm down,' he shouted aloud at himself, and this time the engine caught. He pulled out so sharply he almost hit a car parked on the other side of the street.

Stony Island was a wide boulevard, divided by a litter-filled middle strip. At 71st Street there were railroad tracks, disused he hoped, and the light went his way in any case. He remembered the cross street as lined by stores, and the location of his paediatrician until he was ten or so – Vanetta had taken him here for shots and check-ups. In the waiting room all the other kids always seemed to have their parents with them. He hadn't cared then – Vanetta was as good as a parent as far as he was concerned.

He let these stray memories flood in – anything to distract him from his near-panic. He was certain he was right about where Duval had gone, but he dreaded what he would find. *You are a garden locked up . . . my bride.*

At 67th the McDonald's where Vanetta had often taken him until his father intervened to limit their forays into the black South Side, was gone. Across the street the park began that stretched down to the Museum of Science and Industry, its golf course touching this corner with the fourth green, where he and Mike, sole white kids on the course, used to get nervous of the junkies gathered across the street in front of one of the neighbourhood's crummy hotels.

He tried to distract himself but images of Anna – writhing, crying out in pain – kept streaking through his head. He glanced leftwards as he crossed 63rd Street, once a byword for the ghetto at its worst, and thunderously noisy from the 'L', the city's elevated train system, long torn down. At 60th he had to stop for a red light, perched on what had been the symbolic frontier between Hyde Park and the black ghetto. He was about to run the light when he saw a patrol car down the block.

When the light changed the car ahead was slow to turn left, and he honked his horn, then accelerated down to the southeast edge of the Midway, turning in front of an advancing bus, being honked at himself for his careless driving.

He was back in Hyde Park, but he felt a surreal estrangement as he sped north along Blackstone Avenue – the English Channel, lined by houses that showed the maddening variety of American architecture a century before. Another image raced before his mind's eye, of Anna naked, bleeding from the throat.

At 57th he failed to break, distracted by how close he was to his intended destination, and was almost hit by a UPS van that swerved, braked, then continued with

319

another telling-off blast of the horn. He parked by a hydrant without second thoughts, forty feet north from the old Christian Science church; he was far beyond precaution now. The blocks of pavement squares as he ran back down the street seemed tilted against him, and he wondered if it was the swelling summer heat or his imagination.

The Church was set back from the street, fronted by grey pillars the height of the adjacent four-storey building where Robert had lived as a boy. It had a centred dome on its roof which was invisible from the front. The dark wooden front doors were disproportionately small, held shut by a locked chain wrapped through their handles. He pulled hard on them, but the chain held firm. When Robert peeked inside through the space between them he could only make out the last row of pews.

Running to the side of the building, he started down the thin alleyway that filled the five-foot gap between the church and its neighbour, first of a row of brick houses stretching north along Blackstone Avenue. Halfway back, a high gate blocked the way, topped by barbed wire that made climbing over it impossible. He pushed against the gate in frustration, and to his surprise it gave way, its padlock falling off as the gate swung open.

He slowed down now, walking cautiously along the side of the church, conscious of the click-click-click sound of his heels on the concrete walk. The light was indirect, but as he reached the back of the building he saw the sun falling onto the ground ahead of him, and turning south had to shield his eyes against the fierce, blinding rays.

He was standing in a small walled yard where he had never been before. But he knew it well. The tree, now cut down, had been just across the far wall, in his own back yard. He remembered climbing it repeatedly to fetch their whiffle ball, then looking down at the little patch of overgrown grass and concrete where he now stood. He was in the Secret Garden.

The rear door to the church was ajar. He peered in, but at first he couldn't see a thing, the contrast too great between the yellow glare outside and the lightless interior of the derelict building. Gradually, large amorphous shapes became distinguishable, like prehistoric mammals emerging out of the mist. He could make out rows of wooden pews facing him, and high up in the back a balcony with a protective railing.

He stepped inside carefully, a wooden board creaking under his foot. To his right he saw two overturned chairs and sheets of music spilled on a dusty floor. The air was thick with damp, swamp-like. To his left, as he turned slowly, there were two other chairs that had not been overturned.

Anna was sitting in one of them.

Was she alive? Her chin sagged, and his first thought was, she's given up, though he could not have said exactly what that meant. Her legs were stretched out before her – he recognised the toffee-coloured slacks and tan sandals. Above her waist she was only wearing a bra.

Only a bra? Oh, Christ, he thought, but then he saw her chest move as she exhaled – she was alive. As he went towards her he saw that Anna's arms were behind her, over the back of the chair. She had been tied up expertly with the kind of white cord they used back in Primrose Hill as a laundry line. Peggy Mohan had been tied up with the same kind of cord.

Anna must have heard him approach, for she lifted her head up and her eyes widened. He was about to speak when she motioned with her eyes towards the back of the church. He nodded, putting his finger to his lips, and looked out towards the lines of empty pews. He could see nothing in the vast arena of unoccupied space. Then he noticed on the other chair a butcher's knife, its blade flat on the seat of the chair like a calculated reminder.

He picked it up, then went behind Anna's chair, where he sawed vigorously until the cord between her wrists gave way and her arms fell loose.

'Where is he?' he said quietly in her ear.

She was rubbing her wrists carefully, trying to drive the blood back into circulation. 'I don't know,' she said in a dull voice. He realised she was in shock.

'Did he hurt you?'

She shook her head.

'Did he—?'

She shook her head again; she knew exactly what he'd meant.

Then she said in a cracked, frightened voice, 'He took me to the dunes – he thought you'd be there for the weekend. He got scared off when Tina Poindexter came by, so he drove me here. He said you'd know where to find us.'

'Is he in there?' He gestured with his head at the pews.

'I heard something moving in the balcony.'

'Here's what I want you to do. Go out that way there—' he pointed to the exit he had come in, where a v-shaped wedge of light slanted through the door – 'and then go round to the street. At the corner there's a restaurant. Get them to call 911 right away.'

'But—'

'No buts. Do what I say. Understand?'

She nodded, and got up slowly from the chair, looking as if her legs might give way. He saw her blouse, crumpled in a heap on the floor, and picked it up and handed it to her.

'What about you?' she said, sounding afraid again. She was putting her shirt on slowly. Too slowly.

'I'll be right behind you. Now get out of here. Quick.'

When he heard her go out the door, he turned towards the pews. He knew he should go, too, but he stood there, stock still. Though he waited, he heard nothing. Maybe Duval had gone, slipped out some other way, or tiptoed out while Anna had her head down. Go to Mississippi, thought Robert. Standing near the former site of the altar, it seemed like a secular benediction. *Take the Bonneville and get out of town. Go anywhere, but for God's sakes, go.*

He should leave, find Anna and wait for the police, then try and rebuild the lives Duval had fractured – their own. He started to walk to the door, when a voice suddenly spoke, out of the darkness behind him.

'I wasn't going to hurt her, Bobby.' There was a pleading note to the words.

Robert stopped and turned around. He peered into the darkness, then said loudly, 'You could have fooled me. You had her tied up. And her shirt was off.'

'I know. But I promise I wasn't going to hurt her.' There was a faint echo to his words. Robert realised he was up on the balcony.

'Is that what you told Peggy Mohan, too?'

'I thought you believed in me, Bobby.' He sounded aggrieved. It was almost convincing. 'Anna does. And Donna.'

'Not for much longer, Duval. Donna Kaliski says they found your blazer.'

Silence hung in the darkness like fog. Robert's voice sliced through it. 'The next step would have been a

DNA test. But you and I know what that would show, now don't we?'

'What you talkin' about?'

'You'd flunk the test. I know that.'

'Then you know something nobody else does, Bobby.'

'Except Vanetta.'

'What's it got to do with Vanetta?' He sounded angry.

'She kept the shirt, Duval. The shirt you wore that night. I've got it now – there's blood all over it. Peggy Mohan's blood.'

Duval said nothing at all. When his silence persisted, Robert peered up through the gloom. He said, 'What I can't understand, is why you put us through such a wild goose chase. What was the point?'

This time Duval replied. 'When I come out of prison I didn't want to bother you, Bobby. I just wanted to know you again. I met your family; that meant a lot to me. I even sent your wife flowers.'

So the mysterious flowers had come from Duval. Robert was dumbfounded. What had been the point? Anna hadn't had the faintest idea who'd sent them to her.

Duval said, 'I was trying to be nice. That's all. I wasn't stalking her, Bobby.'

'But Duval, you hadn't even met Anna when you sent those flowers. You didn't know us at all.'

'But I *wanted* to,' Duval insisted, and the beseeching tone had entered his voice again. 'I already knew Jermaine and his wife didn't want me around. They're family, but it didn't mean anything to them. So I hoped I could find a life with you all instead.' He paused. 'But you let me down.'

'You think *we* let *you* down. How do you figure that?' He realised that through the far wall was the Blackstone apartment where he had grown up. And where he and Duval had played.

'Man, it's always been that way. It started when I was little. I had no father. He wasn't just absent – I didn't even know his name. With Aurelia, it could have been any one of a thousand men. Shit, Bobby, I saw two men fucking my mother when I was five years old. One of 'em caught me watching him and he started to laugh. Then my own mother saw me, and she just looked away.'

'But you had Vanetta, Duval. You know she loved you. She *always* loved you.' He thought of how she had kept Duval's secret.

'I know that, Bobby. You don't have to tell me.' He sounded resentful. 'See, when I first thought I might get out – must be nine or ten years ago – I got really scared, man. Sounds funny, don't it? Here's the one thing I've been waiting for and when it looks like it might happen, my pants filled up.'

'That's not surprising, Duval.' He would have been used to prison; the outside world must have seemed terrifying.

'The one thing I hung on to is that when I got out, Vanetta would be there. This time, she was gonna let me live with her. She said so herself. If she'd only have let me live with her before I wouldn't have got into trouble.'

'What, you think you wouldn't have hurt that girl?'

'Shit, that Mohan girl, she used to be friendly, she used to say hi. Then one night I say "You look mighty fine this evening", and after that she wouldn't even look at me, she wouldn't even acknowledge that I existed. Do you know how that made me feel? She was worse than Lily.'

Lily? Was Duval still nursing his weird complex about Robert's sister? It had been almost *forty* years. He decided to ignore it. 'Is that why you hurt the Mohan woman so bad?'

'I don't know, Bobby.' His voice sobered. 'Something just seemed to give. I can't explain it. Don't think I ain't thought about it.'

There was steel in his voice now, as if he was following an argument he had carved out against the formidable opposition of his conscience and his guilt.

Duval was saying, 'The thing was, I wanted that girl to acknowledge me. No one else did. My momma was sliding down into her hole, and I might as well have never been born as far as she was concerned. Even Vanetta didn't understand – she said I had to stand on my own two feet, just when I felt I had no feet at all.

'I know I was wrong, I know it. But I realise now that it wasn't just me who had to live with what I had done. Nobody else wants to forget about it, either, even after all these years. There're some mistakes a man can make that nobody will forgive him for.'

'You did the time; you paid the price. They forgive you, Duval.'

'No, they don't,' he snapped. Robert thought he could see him now, leaning above the balcony's rail above the centre aisle of the church, a moving square of white. It must be his shirt.

Duval said, 'Think about it, Bobby. 'Spose I'd said to you, "I've done my time, I am a changed man, let's forget about what I did, but yes, sir, I did do it". Would you have been so nice to me? Would you have wanted to know me? Would you have let me meet your wife and daughter?'

There was no point answering. Duval was absolutely right.

'That's why I lied.' He stopped, and Robert heard a rustling noise from the balcony. Then Duval started talking again. 'I didn't lie to fool you or trick you. I lied so you would treat me like a normal man, I lied

326

so you would give me a break. I lied so you wouldn't condemn me before you had a chance to find out what I was like. I lied so you would *know* me.'

Robert said, 'But you must have known you'd be found out, if you insisted on this innocence stuff. Why couldn't you leave it alone?'

'I started something I couldn't stop. Thanks to your wife, and that woman in the centre.' He sounded angry at them now. He suddenly lowered his voice, as if imparting a confidence, but Robert heard him clearly nonetheless. 'Even if I'd thought it through, I would have done the same thing. Because if I said I was guilty, y'all wouldn't want to know.'

Robert was trying to keep Duval talking until the police arrived, but part of him was enthralled. Duval didn't sound crazy at all, even in his distorted rationales. He seemed to recognise the gulf between him and everybody else, though not that he was living in a bubble of his own. What had Bockbauer said? *When their balloon gets pricked ... a lot of them can't cope.* God knows, Duval hadn't coped – or he wouldn't be standing here in the dark on a rotting balcony, having kidnapped Robert's wife.

'You still there, Bobby?'

'Of course I am. Look, Duval, it's not too late. I went to see Bockbauer. He was pissed off, but he said he'd give you another break.'

'Bobby, don't fuck with me now. We both know it's too late.'

Then a siren sounded in the distance, and it was coming closer.

'Duval, I want you to stay right where you are. I'm sorry but that's the cops. You know they had to come.'

'I know.' His voice was flat, but the white square was still there on the balcony; Duval hadn't moved.

'You stay right there, okay? Whatever you do don't come down. They're going to be scared. Just like those guards downstate. I don't want you getting shot, Duval. You hear me?'

Robert couldn't see him on the balcony now. He must have stepped back. 'Duval, I said, did you hear me?'

And then he heard the one word, as if they were boys again and he was telling him to come play ball. 'Okay.'

Robert went out and through the shitty little yard, with its plastic wrappers and a child's toy carelessly thrown over the wall from the Dorchester Avenue side. When he turned the corner to go along the alley to the street, two figures in uniform appeared out of the dark in front of him. One of them started, his hand moving to his sidearm.

Robert shouted, 'Don't shoot!' and put his hands in the air.

The cops came forward carefully. 'Where is the guy?' one of them demanded.

'He's inside.' He sensed his voice was shaky.

'Is he armed?'

He hesitated, thinking fast. 'I don't know.' A *yes* would guarantee Duval didn't leave the church alive. The same officer started to draw his weapon. Robert said sharply, 'Don't go in yet. Please.'

The cop looked at his partner, who shrugged. Robert said, 'He's up in the balcony, but I think he'll come down. Let me talk to him – we grew up together.' And before they could object he turned and went around the corner.

He walked through the rear doorway, calling, '*Duval! Duval!*' as he moved forward into the dark hall, his eyes adjusting to the gloom. 'Come on down. It will be okay. You're safe if you come down *now*.'

The big room was silent, and he felt frightened again, worried that Duval had come down and was hiding, ready to attack him or the police. Looking up towards the empty balcony, he saw something draped over its mahogany rail. He walked quickly down the church's aisle, kicking aside rubbish and hymn books, less afraid now, until he was only about ten feet from the bottom of the balcony.

Duval had done it very neatly. The rope was double hitched around the mahogany rail, and could have held an even greater weight. Height was not a problem, since the top of the rail must have been a good fifteen feet above the ground floor. His eyes were closed, and the look on his face seemed entirely peaceful – save for the odd tilt to his head, as if he'd slept in a funny position and was trying to work out the resulting crick in his neck. He must have broken his neck instantly when he jumped.

He was wearing a white shirt, and the same pressed suit trousers he'd had on that day in the coffee shop when the two old friends had met for the first time in almost twenty-five years. The same trousers he'd had on in court, when Robert said he'd be back to see him again, but never had.

Why had Duval done this? Was it hopelessness, now that his guilt had been exposed? Or was it guilt, both about his lies and his crime, guilt that had been hounding him until he had finally simply given up? Either way, he must have realised he would never be allowed to lead a normal life. Whatever normal meant.

Robert would never know the answer now, or what he could have done that would have kept Duval alive. He held his breath for a moment. He thought of how through coincidence or fate, or both, Duval had emerged from prison after Robert had returned to his home town and their lives had become entwined again, like strands of wool reunited on their original spool.

He remembered the two of them as boys, playing right next door with carefree easiness, too young for disappointments, too young even for hope. It had been an Eden, after all, that small back yard, here on the South Side of Chicago, with its lone big tree, in the days before the runt and Mule had come as harbingers of a crueller life.

Not much of a life for Duval, he thought, as he stared at the pendulous figure of his dead friend. He wondered why, if there were no God, people were placed in their lives so differently, like the diverse tributaries of a river. He wondered whether, if he could have seen his own life ahead of him, he would have lived it just the same. If the dice were thrown ahead of time, would he want them rolled again, or opt to play them as they lay? He didn't know; he only knew that whatever force commanded life, it was blind to the fate of those it consigned. There was no caring master.

'Officer!' he shouted, and within seconds he heard the policemen coming into the church behind him. Robert took a last long look at Duval hanging there in his final effort at peace. Then he walked to the back of the church and collected the knife from the chair. Motioning the cop to come and help, he went to cut his old friend down.

Acknowledgements

I would like to thank Aviva Futorian, a lawyer in Chicago who is renowned for her work on behalf of Death Row and long-term prisoners. Her knowledge of both the mechanisms and the harshness of the State of Illinois's justice system was invaluable to me. She understood from the beginning that my priorities were fiction rather than fact, and she has no responsibility for any errors of fact in my entirely imagined story. I want to thank Elizabeth G Lent for introducing me to her.

I'd like to thank my editors at Random House, Kate Elton and Vanessa Neuling, for their tireless efforts to make this a better book and their unwillingness to let me off the hook. My agent Gillon Aitken and his colleague Clare Alexander were consistently supportive and had useful criticisms, and I want to thank Jon and Ann Conibear for their friendship and generosity.

My brother Dan Rosenheim, who was a reporter in Chicago, read my early drafts with an encouraging but incisive eye; he was never reluctant to let his youngest brother know when he'd gone wrong. James Rosenheim as always proved a thoughtful, careful reader.

My wife Clare cajoled and encouraged me throughout the writing of this novel, and supplied the title; I thank her. I also want to thank my daughters Laura and Sabrina, who put up with their father when he was immersed – perhaps not without complaint, but then they were nine years old when I started.

If you enjoyed *Without Prejudice*,
read on for Chapter One of *Stillriver*,
also by Andrew Rosenheim

One

As he had driven north through the high orchard country he had seen the last sliver of sun slip into Lake Michigan, but here enough light remained for him to make out the birch tree on the corner of the lot, the towering twin maples next to the house, the long expanse of white pine boards and green-shuttered windows that was the house itself. And a patrol car in the drive.

He parked his rental car and got out slowly, stretching after the drive from the little airport in Muskegon and looking around for a minute before going inside. The rough ryegrass (they had never had a silky lawn) was high – why hadn't his brother been round to cut it? He looked across at the Wagners', and was surprised to see four cars parked under the cedar trees there. Then he remembered it was now a bed and breakfast. Tourists up for Memorial Day, hoping that, like a rare restaurant meal served ahead of expectation, summer would come early to dispel this wet, cold weather. There was no sign of the Wagner twins.

He heard the back door groan as it opened, then slammed shut, and he turned round to see Jimmy Olds standing on the porch. He was in blue-grey uniform, and had the crescent moon shades of a motorcycle cop pushed back on his head, covering the top of his balding forehead. He was an improbable policeman – short, skinny, quite the opposite of his predecessor, Jerry Dawson, who had been a bear-like barrel of a man, an ex-marine well over six feet tall and very tough with it.

'Hey Jimmy.' He was trying to sound friendly but could tell his tone was merely resigned.

Jimmy nodded. 'Michael.'

Michael walked to the porch and climbed the steps to shake hands.

'You've had a long trip,' said Jimmy.

'You could say that.'

'Europe, right?' Pronounced *Yurp*. 'How long you been over there?'

'Almost six years.'

'You must like it.'

Michael looked across the street, this time at Bogles. The front yard was surprisingly tidy. He nodded absent¬mindedly. 'It pays the bills,' he said.

'That's what counts,' and they both nodded in mild agreement at the banal correctness of this. They were silent for a minute and Jimmy looked down at his black leather boots. 'Well,' he said, lifting his chin. 'I expect you want to go inside.'

He followed Jimmy in, staring at the walnut grip of his holstered pistol. Jimmy's father had been a local builder, not very successful, one step up really from a handyman. After high school Jimmy had joined him, until the day he announced to his father's chagrin that he had passed the necessary exams and was joining the state police in Fennville. When Jerry Dawson died of cancer Jimmy had become the town's policeman – actually, now one of three of them, since despite a virtual absence of serious crime, Stillriver's governing council, flush with tourist property tax, had decided the community was under-policed. Although Jimmy was the senior officer, there was a morose quality about the man, an air of mild disappoint¬ment, as if he had expected that by stepping into Jerry Dawson's shoes his feet would grow correspondingly. They hadn't.

338

They walked through the kitchen, which had always been the cosiest room in the house, with its wood-burning stove, and the radio tuned to Blue Lake while his mother bustled around and Michael sat after school reading the *Chronicle*. After she'd died, the room assumed a colder, functional air. His father would come in and make supper quickly, Michael and Gary would join him when the meal was ready and the trio would eat methodically – meat, vegetable, and potato; or stew, rice and salad; sometimes just plain stew – seated around the soft-pine kitchen table, talking only occasionally. Gary and he would do the dishes, then quickly go their separate ways, like a pair of cats let out of their carrier basket after a trip to the vet. In the rack by the sink now there was a plate, a glass, knife and fork – the only sign of his father's last supper.

He followed Jimmy into the dining room, a large square with an old-fashioned, heavy-looking mix of dark wainscoting and cream plaster walls, like the interior of an early Frank Lloyd Wright house. An old oak table and matching chairs were grouped in the middle. When his mother was alive they would sit down formally for supper and, at weekends, for lunch as well. But now the table was bare, and dusty from disuse.

On to the living room, again tidy but cold: three soft armchairs, a sofa the colour of groundfall plums, and a maple rocking chair formed a circle around the Mojave rug. Behind the sofa stood the mahogany grand-father clock, ticking with a metronomic resonance. It was an heirloom from Michael's mother's family that his father had wound religiously each Sunday evening. Michael made a mental note to wind it in two days' time – it seemed wrong even to contemplate winding it sooner.

Then to the stairwell, on one side of which was the

small study where his father had taken to sitting, reserving the living room for company. Michael was pretty sure that lately there had not been much of that.

Jimmy stopped at the bottom of the stairs. 'You know he's not here any more, right?'

Yes, of course he'd realized that – it had been almost two days since they'd found his father – but Jimmy's bluntness unnerved him. 'He's in Fennville now,' Jimmy went on. 'At the hospital.'

They climbed the steep stairs and Michael gripped the thin rail of the banister, worn smooth by years of little boys' hands sliding along it. The stairs had been daunting when he was little – one family legend had him pitching down them head first, aged three, only to be caught at the bottom by his father. *Another time he saved my ass*, Michael thought wearily.

On the landing Jimmy turned left but Michael went right. Jimmy called out to him: 'He wasn't in the master bedroom.'

'I know.' His father had moved to the spare room at the back of the house during the last month of his wife's illness, and when she had died he hadn't moved back. *So why am I going here first?* wondered Michael. Maybe to feel some hint of his mother's past presence in the house – there was virtually none in the cold rooms downstairs; maybe somehow to ready himself for the fact that, with his mother long dead, now his father was gone, too.

He opened the door slowly and looked in. The light outside was fading fast, but he could make out the big double bed with its high mahogany headboard, and his mother's oval dressing table, where her set of ivory brushes was lined up carefully. Then he softly closed the door and walked down the hall to Jimmy, who was waiting outside the back bedroom.

'Did Henry usually sleep back here?' Jimmy asked.

'Once my mother died.' Michael sounded formal even to himself.

'The room's been sealed. I'll open it, but don't touch anything. We had the state police in and they've done the forensics – dusting fingerprints mainly – but they may want to come back.' Jimmy peeled back a thick ribbon of yellow adhesive tape. Then he turned the door knob and, reaching in, switched the light on.

There was an armchair of cracked brown leather by the window, with a reading lamp on an adjacent small table. His father's clothes from the day still lay on a wooden kitchen chair near the closet: trousers folded on the seat, his shirt hooked over the uprights of the chair like epaulettes on a store window mannequin. The closet door was open, and Michael could see a few pairs of shoes neatly lined up, some shirts on coat hangers, a fading sports jacket doubtless bought at Vergil's in Fennville. There was an old man's smell in the air – of clean but ageing clothes, of foot powder applied after a bath.

He was avoiding the bed to his right, but eventually forced himself to turn and see what was there. Not his father, he knew, and no longer any bedclothes. 'They've stripped the bed,' he commented flatly.

'They took the sheets away for analysis.'

'Analysis?'

Jimmy sighed. 'Blood. They need to make sure it was just your father's blood.'

'Oh.' He hadn't thought about the blood. 'Was there a lot of it?'

'A fair amount,' Jimmy said quietly.

'Tell me,' he said, keeping his back to Jimmy, 'was there any sign of a struggle?'

'If it's any comfort, Michael, I doubt he knew what hit him.'

'So he was asleep when it happened?'

'Well, he had sat up in the bed. We're pretty sure of that.'

'How do you know?'

'Because he got hit right on top of his head. If he'd been lying down he wouldn't have got hit that way.'

'And that's what killed him?'

Jimmy was silent for a moment. 'He got hit more than once.'

Since he'd first been told, on his mobile phone as he sat in a rowboat inspecting the beam encasing under Anfernachie Bridge, through the hours and hours of travel that got him here, all Michael had been able to imagine was his father's body, inert on the bed. It was the stillness of the image, a snapshot, which held firm in his mind's eye.

But now he could visualize his father startled from sleep, sitting up in surprise, turning towards the door and seeing, seeing exactly what? His killer? Heading towards him, weapon already raised, perhaps already descending – which would leave just enough time for his father to understand that he was about to be hit, about to be killed, in fact. Just enough time to feel the bone-shaking panic of a man about to die. *Christ.*

He had seen enough. He turned around and faced Jimmy. 'What did he get hit with?'

Jimmy shrugged. 'We don't know. So far there's been nothing. No prints, no sign of forced entry—'

'He never locked the back door.'

'The doctor thought it might have been a lead pipe. Something heavy.'

'Doctor Fell?'

Jimmy shook his head. 'He's retired. There's no doctor in town now. This is some guy from Burlington.'

As they left the room Michael switched off the light

and closed the door, then watched as Jimmy patched back the strip of yellow tape. They went down the stairs and walked through the ground floor until they again stood under the covered porch side by side as rain and mist came down in a fine, almost invisible mix. The air felt moist and heavy, and the lights from the Wagners' house seemed to quiver like buoys bobbing at sea.

'Is Gary coming by?' asked Jimmy.

Michael shook his head. 'I told him to come round in the morning.'

'Come here?' Jimmy sounded surprised.

'I'll sleep here tonight. I don't imagine they want to kill me, too.'

Jimmy looked so shocked at this that Michael almost laughed. 'Don't worry, I'll lock the door.' But then suddenly his studied diffidence dissolved. 'Who would have done this, Jimmy?'

Jimmy took a stick of gum from his shirt pocket, unwrapped it and popped it in his mouth. He chewed thoughtfully for a few seconds. 'They told me to ask you, did your dad have any enemies?'

Me, when I was a mixed up kid, he wanted to say, but instead replied with exasperation, 'Jesus Christ, Jimmy, he was a retired schoolteacher.'

'Told 'em that. Taught me three years running. Or tried to anyway.'

'So what do they think – he flunked Oscar Peters twenty years ago and made a lifelong enemy?'

'Oscar's dead.'

Oscar Peters had been the town's closest approximation to a village idiot. 'You know what I mean.'

Jimmy said nothing and when Michael spoke again, his voice was softer. 'All right. I know what they're thinking. Obviously *somebody* didn't like him. But I can't think of anyone obvious. How could I? I haven't been here in six years. Anyway, when was the last murder in this town? I've never even *heard* of one.'

Jimmy looked pensive. 'There was Andy Everitt.'

'That was a mercy killing, as you know perfectly well. He just put her out of her misery. What did he end up serving anyway? Two years?'

Jimmy shrugged. 'Something like that.' He chewed some more on his gum. 'Ronald Duverson *tried* to kill somebody once. That I know for a fact.' He turned and looked blank-eyed at Michael.

Michael heard his heart start to thump like thunder in his ears. He tried to sound calm, almost nonchalant. 'Is that right?'

Jimmy nodded. 'But he's in Texas now. Safe and sound.'

'How do you know?' He tried to keep the urgency out of his voice.

'Because he's sitting in the penitentiary. Down there he *did* manage to kill somebody.'

'Well, that rules him out,' Michael said, his voice pitched high enough for Jimmy to look at him again. 'Seems to me,' he said, his natural deeper tones reasserting themselves, 'that you're looking for a loony.'

'Or fanatic.'

'Meaning what?'

'Hang here a minute.' Jimmy walked down the porch steps and went to his patrol car. When he came back he held a heavy black flashlight in his right hand. 'Come look at this.'

Michael followed him around to the side of the house, where a bough of the peach tree extended almost to the wall. He could smell the incense of the cedars that, mixed with mulberry trees, formed a hedge separating the lot from the Jenkinses next door. Jimmy stopped and swung the flashlight's beam on to the white boards. Michael moved closer to look.

What he saw seemed oddly out of place and time, depicted in black paint strokes on the overlapping edges of five or six of the thin pine boards:

'*What*?' is all he could say.

'Michael.' Jimmy's breath smelled sweet from his chewing gum; his voice was embarrassed and mild. 'Was your father some kind of a Jew?'

Keeping Secrets

Andrew Rosenheim

Thirty years ago, Jack Renoir's idyllic childhood on his uncle's California apple farm was shattered when he witnessed a brutal murder. With a single shot, his life changed forever.

Three decades later, Renoir is a man preoccupied with secrets and lies – a man who's forgotten how to trust. But when Kate Palmer walks into his San Francisco office, his carefully-controlled world is turned upside down. As his defences dissolve, Renoir moves to England with Kate to make a new start. But old habits die hard, and he is soon drawn into a murky world he hoped he had left behind for good. When his efforts to help Kate backfire, Renoir finds his unresolved past threatening to destroy his future . . .

Praise for *Keeping Secrets*:

'Rosenheim delivers some cracking prose and is a writer of discerning intelligence' *Telegraph*

'Gripping' *Daily Mail*

'The pace is fast, the prose lean . . . readers will not find themselves bored for a second' *Guardian*

arrow books